Orson Scott Card is one of the world's most popular science fiction and fantasy writers. In addition to the Ender saga, he is the author of *The Tales of Alvin Maker* and the *Homecoming* series, as well as many other stand-alone novels. He lives in Greensboro, North Carolina.

By Orson Scott Card

Ender
Ender's Game
Speaker for the Dead
Xenocide
Children of the Mind
Ender's Shadow
Shadow of the Hegemon

Homecoming
The Memory of Earth
The Call of Earth
The Ships of Earth
Earthfall
Earthborn

The Tales of Alvin Maker
Seventh Son
Red Prophet
Prentice Alvin
Alvin Journeyman
Heartfire

The Worthing Saga
The Folk of the Fringe
Wyrms
Songmaster
Maps in a Mirror (Volumes 1 and 2)

SHADOW OF THE HEGEMON

Orson Scott Card

orbit

An *Orbit* Book

First published in Great Britain by Orbit 2001
This edition published by Orbit 2001

Copyright © 2000 by Orson Scott Card

The moral right of the author has been asserted.

A CIP catalogue record for this book
is available from the British Library.

ISBN 1 84149 066 0

Printed and bound in Great Britain
by Mackays of Chatham plc, Chatham, Kent

Orbit
A Division of
Little, Brown and Company (UK)
Brettenham House
Lancaster Place
London WC2E 7EN

TO CHARLES BENJAMIN CARD
YOU ARE ALWAYS LIGHT TO US,
YOU SEE THROUGH ALL THE SHADOWS,
AND WE HEAR YOUR STRONG VOICE
SINGING IN OUR DREAMS.

CONTENTS

Part One

VOLUNTEERS

1

PETRA

To:Chamrajnagar%sacredriver@ifcom.gov
From: Locke%espinoza@polnet.gov
Re: What are you doing to protect
the children?

Dear Admiral Chamrajnagar,
I was given your idname by a mutual
friend who once worked for you but
now is a glorified dispatcher—I'm
sure you know whom I mean. I realize
that your primary responsibility
now is not so much military as
logistical, and your thoughts are
turned to space rather than the
political situation on Earth. After
all, you decisively defeated the
nationalist forces led by your
predecessor in the League War, and
that issue seems settled. The I.F.
remains independent and for that we
are all grateful.

What no one seems to understand is that peace on Earth is merely a temporary illusion. Not only is Russia's long-pent expansionism still a driving force, but also many other nations have aggressive designs on their neighbors. The forces of the Strategos are being disbanded, the Hegemony is rapidly losing all authority, and Earth is poised on the edge of cataclysm.

The most powerful resource of any nation in the wars to come will be the children trained in Battle, Tactical, and Command School. While it is perfectly appropriate for these children to serve their native countries in future wars, it is inevitable that at least some nations that lack such I.F.-certified geniuses or who believe that rivals have more-gifted commanders will inevitably take preemptive action, either to secure that enemy resource for their own use or, in any event, to deny the enemy the use of that resource. In short, these children are in grave danger of being kidnapped or killed.

I recognize that you have a hands-off policy toward events on Earth, but it was the I.F. that identified these children and trained them, thus making them targets. Whatever happens to these children, the I.F. has ultimate responsibility. It would go a long way toward protecting them if you were to issue an order placing these children under Fleet protection, warning any nation or group attempting to harm or interfere with them that they would face swift and harsh military retribution. Far from regarding this as interference in Earthside affairs, most nations would welcome this action, and, for whatever it is worth, you would have my complete support in all public forums.

I hope you will act immediately. There is no time to waste.

Respectfully,
Locke

Nothing looked right in Armenia when Petra Arkanian returned home. The mountains were dramatic, of course, but they had not really been part of her childhood experience. It was not until she got to Maralik that she began to see things that should mean something to her. Her father had met her in Yerevan while her mother remained at home with her eleven-year-old brother and the new baby—obviously conceived even before the population restrictions were relaxed when the war ended. They had no doubt watched Petra on television. Now, as the flivver took Petra and her father along the narrow streets, he began apologizing. "It won't seem much to you, Pet, after seeing the world."

"They didn't show us the world much, Papa. There were no windows in Battle School."

"I mean, the spaceport, and the capital, all the important people and wonderful buildings . . ."

"I'm not disappointed, Papa." She had to lie in order to reassure him. It was as if he had given her Maralik as a gift, and now was unsure whether she liked it. She didn't know yet whether she would like it or not. She hadn't liked Battle School, but she got used to it. There was no getting used to Eros, but she had endured it. How could she dislike a place like this, with open sky and people wandering wherever they wanted?

Yet she *was* disappointed. For all her memories of Maralik were the memories of a five-year-old, looking up at tall buildings, across wide streets where large vehicles loomed and fled at alarming speeds. Now she was much older, beginning to come into her womanly height, and the cars were smaller, the streets downright narrow, and the buildings—designed to survive the next earthquake, as the old buildings had not—were squat. Not ugly—there was grace in them, given the eclectic styles that were somehow blended here, Turkish and Russian, Spanish and Riviera, and, most incredibly, Japanese. It was a marvel to see how they were still unified by the choice of colors, the closeness to the street, the almost uniform height as all strained against the legal maximums.

She knew of all this because she had read about it on Eros as she and the other children sat out the League War. She had seen pictures on the nets. But nothing had prepared her for the fact that she had left here as a five-year-old and now was returning at fourteen.

"What?" she said. For Father had spoken and she hadn't understood him.

"I asked if you wanted to stop for a candy before we went home, the way we used to."

Candy. How could she have forgotten the word for candy?

Easily, that's how. The only other Armenian in Battle School had been three years ahead of her and graduated to Tactical School, so they overlapped only for a few months. She had been seven when she got from Ground School to Battle School, and he was ten, leaving without ever having commanded an army. Was it any wonder that he didn't want to jabber in Armenian to a little kid from home? So in effect she had gone without speaking Armenian for nine years. And the Armenian she had spoken then was a five-year-old's language. It was so hard to speak it now, and harder still to understand it.

How could she tell Father that it would help her greatly if he would speak to her in Fleet Common—English, in effect? He spoke it, of course—he and Mother had made a point of speaking English at home when she was little, so she would not be handicapped linguistically if she was taken into Battle School. In fact, as she thought about it, that was part of her problem. How often had Father actually called candy by the Armenian word? Whenever he let her walk with him through town and they stopped for candy, he would make her ask for it in English, and call each piece by its English name. It was absurd, really—why would she need to know, in Battle School, the English names of Armenian candies?

"What are you laughing for?"

"I seem to have lost my taste for candy while I was in

space, Father. Though for old times' sake, I hope you'll have time to walk through town with me again. You won't be as tall as you were the last time."

"No, nor will your hand be as small in mine." He laughed, too. "We've been robbed of years that would be precious now, to have in memory."

"Yes," said Petra. "But I was where I needed to be."

Or was I? I'm the one who broke first. I passed all the tests, until the test that mattered, and there I broke first. Ender comforted me by telling me he relied on me most and pushed me hardest, but he pushed us all and relied upon us all and I'm the one who broke. No one ever spoke of it; perhaps here on Earth not one living soul knew of it. But the others who had fought with her knew it. Until that moment when she fell asleep in the midst of combat, she had been one of the best. After that, though she never broke again, Ender also never trusted her again. The others watched over her, so that if she suddenly stopped commanding her ships, they could step in. She was sure that one of them had been designated, but never asked who. Dink? Bean? Bean, yes—whether Ender assigned him to do it or not, she knew Bean would be watching, ready to take over. She was not reliable. They did not trust her. She did not trust herself.

Yet she would keep that secret from her family, as she kept it in talking to the prime minister and the press, to the Armenian military and the schoolchildren who had been assembled to meet the great Armenian hero of the Formic War. Armenia needed a hero. She was the only candidate out of this war. They had shown her how the online textbooks already listed her among the ten greatest Armenians of all time. Her picture, her biography, and quotations from Colonel Graff, from Major Anderson, from Mazer Rackham.

And from Ender Wiggin. "It was Petra who first stood up

for me at risk to herself. It was Petra who trained me when no one else would. I owe everything I accomplished to her. And in the final campaign, in battle after battle she was the commander I relied upon."

Ender could not have known how those words would hurt. No doubt he meant to reassure her that he did rely upon her. But because she knew the truth, his words sounded like pity to her. They sounded like a kindly lie.

And now she was home. Nowhere on Earth was she so much a stranger as here, because she ought to feel at home here, but she could not, for no one knew her here. They knew a bright little girl who was sent off amid tearful good-byes and brave words of love. They knew a hero who returned with the halo of victory around her every word and gesture. But they did not know and would never know the girl who broke under the strain and in the midst of battle simply . . . fell asleep. While her ships were lost, while real men died, she slept because her body could stay awake no more. That girl would remain hidden from all eyes.

And from all eyes would be hidden also the girl who watched every move of the boys around her, evaluating their abilities, guessing at their intentions, determined to take any advantage she could get, refusing to bow to any of them. Here she was supposed to become a child again—an older one, but a child nonetheless. A dependent.

After nine years of fierce watchfulness, it would be restful to turn over her life to others, wouldn't it?

"Your mother wanted to come. But she was afraid to come." He chuckled as if this were amusing. "Do you understand?"

"No," said Petra.

"Not afraid of you," said Father. "Of her firstborn daughter she could never be afraid. But the cameras. The politicians. The crowds. She is a woman of the kitchen. Not a woman of the market. Do you understand?"

She understood the Armenian easily enough, if that's what he was asking, because he had caught on, he was speaking in simple language and separating his words a little so she would not get lost in the stream of conversation. She was grateful for this, but also embarrassed that it was so obvious she needed such help.

What she did not understand was a fear of crowds that could keep a mother from coming to meet her daughter after nine years.

Petra knew that it was not the crowds or the cameras that Mother was afraid of. It was Petra herself. The lost five-year-old who would never be five again, who had had her first period with the help of a Fleet nurse, whose mother had never bent over her homework with her, or taught her how to cook. No, wait. She had baked pies with her mother. She had helped roll out the dough. Thinking back, she could see that her mother had not actually let her do anything that mattered. But to Petra it had seemed that she was the one baking. That her mother trusted her.

That turned her thoughts to the way Ender had coddled her at the end, pretending to trust her as before but actually keeping control.

And because that was an unbearable thought, Petra looked out the window of the flivver. "Are we in the part of town where I used to play?"

"Not yet," said Father. "But nearly. Maralik is still not such a large town."

"It all seems new to me," said Petra.

"But it isn't. It never changes. Only the architecture. There are Armenians all over the world, but only because they were forced to leave to save their lives. By nature,

Armenians stay at home. The hills are the womb, and we have no desire to be born." He chuckled at his joke.

Had he always chuckled like that? It sounded to Petra less like amusement than like nervousness. Mother was not the only one afraid of her.

At last the flivver reached home. And here at last she recognized where she was. It was small and shabby compared to what she had remembered, but in truth she had not even thought of the place in many years. It stopped haunting her dreams by the time she was ten. But now, coming home again, it all returned to her, the tears she had shed in those first weeks and months in Ground School, and again when she left Earth and went up to Battle School. This was what she had yearned for, and at last she was here again, she had it back . . . and knew that she no longer needed it, no longer really wanted it. The nervous man in the car beside her was not the tall god who had led her through the streets of Maralik so proudly. And the woman waiting inside the house would not be the goddess from whom came warm food and a cool hand on her forehead when she was sick.

But she had nowhere else to go.

Her mother was standing at the window as Petra emerged from the flivver. Father palmed the scanner to accept the charges. Petra raised a hand and gave a small wave to her mother, a shy smile that quickly grew into a grin. Her mother smiled back and gave her own small wave in reply. Petra took her father's hand and walked with him to the house.

The door opened as they approached. It was Stefan, her brother. She would not have known him from her memories of a two-year-old, still creased with baby fat. And he, of course, did not know her at all. He beamed the way the children from the school group had beamed at her, thrilled to meet a celebrity but not really aware of her as a person. He was her brother, though, and so she hugged him and he hugged her back. "You're really Petra!" he said.

"You're really Stefan!" she answered. Then she turned to her mother. She was still standing at the window, looking out.

"Mother?"

The woman turned, tears streaking her cheeks. "I'm so glad to see you, Petra," she said.

But she made no move to come to Petra, or even to reach out to her.

"But you're still looking for the little girl who left nine years ago," said Petra.

Mother burst into tears, and now she reached out her arms and Petra strode to her, to be enfolded in her embrace. "You're a woman now," said Mother. "I don't know you, but I love you."

"I love you too, Mother," said Petra. And was pleased to realize that it was true.

They had about an hour, the four of them—five, once the baby woke up. Petra shunted aside their questions—"Oh, everything about me has already been published or broadcast. It's *you* that I want to hear about"—and learned that her father was still editing textbooks and supervising translations, and her mother was still the shepherd of the neighborhood, watching out for everyone, bringing food when someone was sick, taking care of children while parents ran errands, and providing lunch for any child who showed up. "I remember once that Mother and I had lunch alone, just the two of us," Stefan joked. "We didn't know what to say, and there was so much food left over."

"It was already that way when I was little," Petra said. "I remember being so proud of how the other kids loved my mother. And so jealous of the way she loved them!"

"Never as much as I loved my own girl and boy," said

Mother. "But I do love children, I admit it, every one of them is precious in the sight of God, every one of them is welcome in my house."

"Oh, I've known a few you wouldn't love," said Petra.

"Maybe," said Mother, not wishing to argue, but plainly not believing that there could be such a child.

The baby gurgled and Mother lifted her shirt to tuck the baby to her breast.

"Did I slurp so noisily?" asked Petra.

"Not really," said Mother.

"Oh, tell the truth," said Father. "She woke the neighbors."

"So I was a glutton."

"No, merely a barbarian," said Father. "No table manners."

Petra decided to ask the delicate question boldly and have done with it. "The baby was born only a month after the population restrictions were lifted."

Father and Mother looked at each other, Mother with a beatific expression, Father with a wince. "Yes, well, we missed you. We wanted another little girl."

"You would have lost your job," said Petra.

"Not right away," said Father.

"Armenian officials have always been a little slow about enforcing those laws," said Mother.

"But eventually, you could have lost everything."

"No," said Mother. "When you left, we lost half of everything. Children are everything. The rest is . . . nothing."

Stefan laughed. "Except when I'm hungry. Food is something!"

"You're always hungry," said Father.

"Food is always something," said Stefan.

They laughed, but Petra could see that Stefan had had no illusions about what the birth of this child would have meant. "It's a good thing we won the war."

"Better than losing it," said Stefan.

"It's nice to have the baby and obey the law, too," said Mother.

"But you didn't get your little girl."

"No," said Father. "We got our David."

"We didn't need a little girl after all," said Mother. "We got you back."

Not really, thought Petra. And not for long. Four years, maybe fewer, and I'll be off to university. And you won't miss me by then, because you'll know that I'm not the little girl you love, just this bloody-handed veteran of a nasty military school that turned out to have real battles to fight.

After the first hour, neighbors and cousins and friends from Father's work began dropping by, and it was not until after midnight that Father had to announce that tomorrow was not a national holiday and he needed to have *some* sleep before work. It took yet another hour to shoo everyone out of the house, and by then all Petra wanted was to curl up in bed and hide from the world for at least a week.

But by the end of the next day, she knew she had to get out of the house. She didn't fit into the routines. Mother loved her, yes, but her life centered around the baby and the neighborhood, and while she kept trying to engage Petra in conversation, Petra could see that she was a distraction, that it would be a relief for Mother when Petra went to school during the day as Stefan did, returning only at the scheduled time. Petra understood, and that night announced that she wanted to register for school and begin class the next day.

"Actually," said Father, "the people from the I.F. said that you could probably go right on to university."

"I'm fourteen," said Petra. "And there are serious gaps in my education."

"She never even heard of Dog," said Stefan.

"What?" said Father. "What dog?"

"Dog," said Stefan. "The zip orchestra. You know."

"Very famous group," said Mother. "If you heard them, you'd take the car in for major repairs."

"Oh, *that* Dog," said Father. "I hardly think that's the education Petra was talking about."

"Actually, it is," said Petra.

"It's like she's from another planet," said Stefan. "Last night I realized she never heard of *anybody*."

"I *am* from another planet. Or, properly speaking, asteroid."

"Of course," said Mother. "You need to join your generation."

Petra smiled, but inwardly she winced. Her generation? She had no generation, except the few thousand kids who had once been in Battle School, and now were scattered over the surface of the Earth, trying to find out where they belonged in a world at peace.

School would not be easy, Petra soon discovered. There were no courses in military history and military strategy. The mathematics was pathetic compared to what she had mastered in Battle School, but with literature and grammar she was downright backward: Her knowledge of Armenian was indeed childish, and while she was fluent in the version of English spoken in Battle School—including the slang that the kids used there—she had little knowledge of the rules of grammar and no understanding at all of the mixed Armenian and English slang that the kids used with each other at school.

Everyone was very nice to her, of course—the most popular girls immediately took possession of her, and the teachers treated her like a celebrity. Petra allowed herself to be led around and shown everything, and studied the chatter of her new friends very carefully, so she could learn the slang and hear how school English and Armenian were nuanced. She knew that soon enough the popular girls would tire of her—especially when they realized how bluntly outspoken Petra was, a trait that she had no intention of changing. Petra was quite used to the fact that people who cared about the social hierarchy usually ended up hating her and, if they were wise, fearing her, since pretensions didn't last long in her presence. She would find her real friends over the next few weeks—if, in fact, there were any here who would value her for what she was. It didn't matter. All the friendships here, all the social concerns, seemed so trivial to her. There was nothing at stake here, except each student's own social life and academic future, and what did that matter? Petra's previous schooling had all been conducted in the shadow of war, with the fate of humanity riding on the outcome of her studies and the quality of her skills. Now, what did it matter? She would read Armenian literature because she wanted to learn Armenian, not because she thought it actually mattered what some expatriate like Saroyan thought about the lives of children in a long-lost era of a far-off country.

The only part of school that she truly loved was physical education. To have sky over her head as she ran, to have the track lie flat before her, to be able to run and run for the sheer joy of it and without a clock ticking out her allotted time for aerobic exercise—such a luxury. She could not compete, physically, with most of the other girls. It would take time for her body to reconstruct itself for high gravity, for despite the great pains that the I.F. went to to make sure that soldiers' bodies did not deteriorate too much during long months and years in space, nothing trained you for living on a planet's surface except living there. But Petra didn't care that she was one of the last to complete every race, that she couldn't leap even the lowest hurdle. It felt good simply to run freely, and her weakness gave her goals to meet. She would be competitive soon enough. That was one of the aspects of her innate personality that had taken her to Battle School in the first place—that she had no particular interest in competition because she always started from the assumption that, if it mattered, she would find a way to win.

And so she settled in to her new life. Within weeks she was fluent in Armenian and had mastered the local slang. As she had expected, the popular girls dropped her in about the same amount of time, and a few weeks later, the brainy girls had cooled toward her as well. It was among the rebels and misfits that she found her friends, and soon she had a circle of confidants and co-conspirators that she called her "jeesh," Battle School slang for close friends, a private army. Not that she was the commander or anything, but they were all loyal to each other and amused at the antics of the teachers and the other students, and when a school counselor called her in to tell her that the administration was growing concerned about the fact that Petra seemed to be associating with an antisocial element in school, she knew that she was truly at home in Maralik.

Then one day she came home from school to find the front door locked. She carried no house key—no one did in their neighborhood because no one locked up, or even, in good weather, closed their doors. She could hear the baby crying inside the house, so instead of making her mother come to the front door to let her in, she walked around back and came into the kitchen to find that her mother was tied to a chair, gagged, her eyes wide and frantic with fear.

Before Petra had time to react, a hypostick was slapped against her arm and, without ever seeing who had done it, she slipped into darkness.

2

BEAN

To: Locke%espinoza@polnet.gov
From: Chamrajnagar%%@ifcom.gov
Re: Do not write to me again

Mr. Peter Wiggin,
Did you really think I would not
have the resources to know who you
are? You may be the author of the
"Locke Proposal," giving you a reputation as a peacemaker, but you
are also partly responsible for
the world's present instability by
your jingoist use of your sister's
identity as Demosthenes. I have no
illusions about your motives.

It is outrageous of you to suggest
that I jeopardize the neutrality of
the International Fleet in order to
take control of children who have
completed their military service

with the I.F. If you attempt to
manipulate public opinion to force
me to do so, I will expose your
identity as both Locke and Demosthenes.

I have changed my idname and have
informed our mutual friend that he
is not to attempt to relay communication between you and me again.
The only comfort you are entitled
to take from my letter is this: The
I.F. will not interfere with those
trying to assert hegemony over
other nations and peoples—not even
you.

Chamrajnagar

The disappearance of Petra Arkanian from her home in
Armenia was worldwide news. The headlines were full of
accusations hurled by Armenia against Turkey, Azerbaijan,
and every other Turkish-speaking nation, and the stiff or
fiery denials and counter-accusations that came in reply.
There were the tearful interviews with her mother, the only
witness, who was sure the kidnappers were Azerbaijani. "I
know the language, I know the accent, and that's who took
my little girl!"

Bean was with his family on the second day of their vacation at the beach on the island of Ithaca, but this was Petra, and
he read the nets and watched the vids avidly, along with his
brother, Nikolai. They both reached the same conclusion right

away. "It wasn't any of the Turkish nations," Nikolai announced to their parents. "That's obvious."

Father, who had been working in government for many years, agreed. "Real Turks would have made sure to speak only Russian."

"Or Armenian," said Nikolai.

"No Turk speaks Armenian," said Mother. She was right, of course, since real Turks would never deign to learn it, and those in Turkish countries who did speak Armenian were, by definition, not really Turks and would never be trusted with a delicate assignment like kidnapping a military genius.

"So who was it?" said Father. "Agents provocateurs, trying to start a war?"

"My bet is on the Armenian government," said Nikolai. "Put her in charge of their military."

"Why kidnap her when they could employ her openly?" asked Father.

"Taking her out of school openly," said Nikolai, "would be an announcement of Armenia's military intentions. It might provoke preemptive actions by surrounding Turkey or Azerbaijan."

There was superficial plausibility in what Nikolai was saying, but Bean knew better. He had already foreseen this possibility back when all the militarily gifted children were still in space. At that time the main danger had come from the Polemarch, and Bean wrote an anonymous letter to a couple of opinion leaders on Earth, Locke and Demosthenes, urging them to get all the Battle School children back to Earth so they couldn't be seized or killed by the Polemarch's forces in the League War. The warning had worked, but now that the League War was over, too many governments had begun to think and act complacently, as if the world now had peace instead of a fragile ceasefire. Bean's original analysis still held. It was Russia that was behind the Polemarch's coup attempt in the League War, and it was likely to be Russia that was behind the kidnapping of Petra Arkanian.

Still, he didn't have any hard evidence of this and knew of no way to get it—now that he wasn't inside a Fleet installation, he had no access to military computer systems. So he kept his skepticism to himself, and made a joke out of it. "I don't know, Nikolai," he said. "Since staging this kidnapping is having an even more destabilizing effect, I'd have to say that *if* she was taken by her own government, it proves they really *really* need her, because it was a deeply dumb thing to do."

"If they're *not* dumb," said Father, "who did it?"

"Somebody who's ambitious to fight and win wars and smart enough to know they need a brilliant commander," said Bean. "And either big enough or invisible enough or far enough away from Armenia not to care about the consequences of kidnapping her. In fact, I'll bet that whoever took her would be perfectly delighted if war broke out in the Caucasus."

"So you think it's some large and powerful nation close by?" asked Father. Of course, there was only one large and powerful nation close to Armenia.

"Could be, but there's no telling," said Bean. "Anybody who needs a commander like Petra wants a world in turmoil. Enough turmoil, and anybody might emerge on top. Plenty of sides to play off against each other." And now that Bean had said it, he began to believe it. Just because Russia was the most aggressive nation before the League War didn't mean that other nations weren't going to get into the game.

"In a world in chaos," said Nikolai, "the army with the best commander wins."

"If you want to find the kidnapper, look for the country that talks most about peace and conciliation," said Bean, playing with the idea and saying whatever came to mind.

"You're too cynical," said Nikolai. "Some who talk about peace and conciliation merely want peace and conciliation."

"You watch—the nations that offer to arbitrate are the ones that think they should rule the world, and this is just one more move in the game."

Father laughed. "Don't read too much into *that*," he said. "Most of the nations that are always offering to arbitrate are trying to recover lost status, not gain new power. France. America. Japan. They're always meddling just because they used to have the power to back it up and they haven't caught on yet that they don't anymore."

Bean smiled. "You never know, do you, Papa. The very fact that you dismiss the possibility that they could be the kidnappers makes me regard them as all the more likely candidates."

Nikolai laughed and agreed.

"That's the problem with having two Battle School graduates in the house," said Father. "You think because you understand military thinking that you understand political thinking, too."

"It's all maneuver and avoiding battle until you have overwhelming superiority," said Bean.

"But it's also about the will to power," said Father. "And even if individuals in America and France and Japan have the will to power, the people don't. Their leaders will never get them moving. You have to look at nations on the make. Aggressive peoples who think they have a grievance, who think they're undervalued. Belligerent, snappish."

"A whole nation of belligerent, snappish people?" asked Nikolai.

"Sounds like Athens," said Bean.

"A nation that takes that attitude toward other nations," said Father. "Several self-consciously Islamic nations have the character to make such a play, but they'd never kidnap a Christian girl to lead their armies."

"They might kidnap her to prevent her own nation from using her," said Nikolai. "Which brings us back to Armenia's neighbors."

"It's an interesting puzzle," said Bean, "which we can figure out later, after we get to wherever we're going."

Father and Nikolai looked at him as if he were crazy. "Going?" asked Father.

It was Mother who understood. "They're kidnapping Battle School graduates. Not just that, but a member of Ender's team from the actual battles."

"And one of the best," said Bean.

Father was skeptical. "One incident doesn't make a pattern."

"Let's not wait to see who's next," said Mother. "I'd rather feel silly later for overreacting than grieve because we dismissed the possibility."

"Give it a few days," said Father. "It will all blow over."

"We've already given it six hours," said Bean. "If the kidnappers are patient, they won't strike again for months. But if they're impatient, they're already in motion against all their other targets. For all we know, the only reason Nikolai and I aren't in the bag already is because we threw off their plans by going on vacation."

"Or else," said Nikolai, "our being here on this island gives them the perfect opportunity."

"Father," said Mother, "why don't you call for some protection?"

Father hesitated.

Bean understood why. The political game was a delicate one, and anything Father did right now could have repercussions throughout his career. "You won't be perceived as asking for special privileges for yourself," said Bean. "Nikolai and I are a precious national resource. I believe the prime minister is on record as saying that several times. Letting Athens know where we are and suggesting they protect us and get us out of here is a good idea."

Father got on the cellphone.

He got only a System Busy response.

"That's it," said Bean. "There's no way the phone system can be too busy here on Ithaca. We need a boat."

"An airplane," said Mother.

"A boat," said Nikolai. "And not a rental. They're probably waiting for us to put ourselves in their hands, so there won't be a struggle."

"Several of the nearby houses have boats," said Father. "But we don't know these people."

"They know *us,*" said Nikolai. "Especially Bean. We *are* war heroes, you know."

"But any house around here could be the very one from which they're watching us," said Father. "*If* they're watching us. We can't trust anybody."

"Let's get in our bathing suits," said Bean, "and walk to the beach and then wander as far as we can before we cut inland and find somebody with a boat."

Since no one had a better plan, they put it into action at once. Within two minutes they were out the door, carrying no wallets or purses, though Father and Mother slipped a few identification papers and credit cards into their suits. Bean and Nikolai laughed and teased each other as usual, and Mother and Father held hands and talked quietly, smiling at their sons . . . as usual. No sign of alarm. Nothing to cause anyone watching to spring into action.

They were only about a quarter mile up the beach when they heard an explosion—loud, as if it were close, and the shockwave made them stumble. Mother fell. Father helped her up as Bean and Nikolai looked back.

"Maybe it's not our house," said Nikolai.

"Let's not go back and check," said Bean.

They began to jog up the beach, matching their speed to Mother, who was limping a little from having skinned one knee and twisted the other when she fell. "Go on ahead," she said.

"Mother," said Nikolai, "taking you is the same as taking us, because we'd do whatever they wanted to get you back."

"They don't want to take us," said Bean. "Petra they wanted to use. Me they want dead."

"No," said Mother.

"He's right," said Father. "You don't blow up a house in order to kidnap the occupants."

"But we don't know it was our house!" Mother insisted.

"Mother," said Bean. "It's basic strategy. Any resource you can't get control of, you destroy so your enemy can't have it."

"What enemy?" Mother said. "Greece has no enemies!"

"When somebody wants to rule the world," said Nikolai, "eventually everyone is his enemy."

"I think we should run faster," said Mother.

They did.

As they ran, Bean thought through what Mother had said. Nikolai's answer was right, of course, but Bean couldn't help but wonder: Greece might have no enemies, but *I* have. Somewhere in this world, Achilles is alive. Supposedly he's in custody, a prisoner because he is mentally ill, because he has murdered again and again. Graff promised that he would never be set free. But Graff was court-martialed—exonerated, yes, but retired from the military. He's now Minister of Colonization, no longer in a position to keep his promise about Achilles. And if there's one thing Achilles wants, it's me, dead.

Kidnapping Petra, that's something Achilles would think of. And if he was in a position to cause *that* to happen—if some government or group was listening to him—then it would have been a simple enough matter for him to get the same people to kill Bean.

Or would Achilles insist on being there in person?

Probably not. Achilles was not a sadist. He killed with his own hands when he needed to, but would never put himself at risk. Killing from a distance would actually be preferable. Using other hands to do his work.

Who else would want Bean dead? Any other enemy would seek to capture him. His test scores from Battle School were a matter of public record since Graff's trial. The military in every nation knew that he was the kid who in many ways had topped Ender himself. He would be the one most desired. He would also be the one most feared, if he were on the other side in a war. Any of them might kill him if they knew they couldn't take him. But they would try to take him first. Only Achilles would prefer his death.

But he said nothing of this to his family. His fears about Achilles would sound too paranoid. He wasn't sure whether he believed them himself. And yet, as he ran along the beach with his family, he grew more certain with every step that whoever had kidnapped Petra was in some way under Achilles' influence.

They heard the rotors of helicopters before they saw them, and Nikolai's reaction was instantaneous. "Inland now!" he shouted. They scrambled for the nearest wooden stairway leading up the cliff from the beach.

They were only halfway up before the choppers came into view. There was no point in trying to hide. One of the choppers set down on the beach below them, the other on the bluff above.

"Down is easier than up," said Father. "And the choppers do have Greek military insignia."

What Bean didn't point out, because everyone knew it, was that Greece was part of the New Warsaw Pact, and it was quite possible that Greek military craft might be acting under Russian command.

In silence they walked back down the stairs. Hope and despair and fear tugged at them by turns.

The soldiers who spilled out of the chopper were wearing Greek Army uniforms.

"At least they're not trying to pretend they're Turks," said Nikolai.

"But how would the Greek Army know to come rescue us?" said Mother. "The explosion was only a few minutes ago."

The answer came quickly enough, once they got to the beach. A colonel who Father knew slightly came to meet them, saluting them. No, saluting Bean, with the respect due to a veteran of the Formic War.

"I bring you greetings from General Thrakos," said the colonel. "He would have come himself, but there was no time to waste when the warning came."

"Colonel Dekanos, we think our sons might be in danger," said Father.

"We realized that the moment word came of the kidnapping of Petra Arkanian," said Dekanos. "But you weren't at home and it took a few hours to find out where you were."

"We heard an explosion," said Mother.

"If you had been inside the house," said Dekanos, "you'd be as dead as the people in the surrounding houses. The army is securing the area. Fifteen choppers were sent up to search for you—we hoped—or, if you were dead, the perpetrators. I have already reported to Athens that you are alive and well."

"They were jamming the cellphone," said Father.

"Whoever did this has a very effective organization," said Dekanos. "Nine other children, it turns out, were taken within hours of Petra Arkanian."

"Who?" demanded Bean.

"I don't know the names yet," said Dekanos. "Only the count."

"Were any of the others simply killed?" asked Bean.

"No," said Dekanos. "Not that I've heard, anyway."

"Then why did they blow up our house?" Mother demanded.

"If we knew why," said Dekanos, "we'd know who. And vice-versa."

They were belted into their seats. The chopper rose from the beach—but not very high. By now the other choppers were ranged around them and above them. Flying escort.

"Ground troops are continuing the search for the perpetrators," said Dekanos. "But your survival is our highest priority."

"We appreciate that," said Mother.

But Bean was not all that appreciative. The Greek military would, of course, put them in hiding and protect them carefully. But no matter what they did, the one thing they could not do was conceal the knowledge of his location from the Greek government itself. And the Greek government had been part of the Russia-dominated Warsaw Pact for generations now, since before the Formic War. Therefore

Achilles—if it was Achilles, if it was Russia he worked for, if, if—would be able to find out where they were. Bean knew that it was not enough for him to be in protection. He had to be in true concealment, where no government could find him, where no one but himself would know who he was.

The trouble was, he was not only still a child, he was a famous child. Between his youth and his celebrity, it would be almost impossible for him to move unnoticed through the world. He would have to have help. So for the time being, he had to remain in military custody and simply hope that it would take him less time to get away than it would take Achilles to get to him.

If it was Achilles.

3

MESSAGE IN A BOTTLE

To: Carlotta%agape@vatican.net/
orders/sisters/ind
From: Graff%pilgrimage@colmin.gov
Re: Danger

I have no idea where you are and
that's good, because I believe you
are in grave danger, and the harder
it is to find you, the better.

Since I'm no longer with the I.F.,
I'm not kept abreast of things
there. But the news is full of the
kidnapping of most of the children
who served with Ender in Command
School. That could have been done
by anybody, there is no shortage of
nations or groups that might con-
ceive and carry out such a project.
What you may not know is that there
was no attempt to kidnap one of
them. From a friend of mine I have

learned that the beach house in Ithaca where Bean and his family were vacationing was simply blown up—with so much force that the neighboring houses were also flattened and everyone in them killed. Bean and his family had already escaped and are under the protection of the Greek military. Supposedly this is a secret, in hopes that the assassins will think they succeeded, but in fact, like most governments, Greece leaks like a colander, and the assassins probably already know more than I do about where Bean is.

There is only one person on Earth who would prefer Bean dead.

That means that the people who got Achilles out of that mental hospital are not just using him—he is making, or at least influencing, their decisions to fit his private agenda. The danger to you is grave. The danger to Bean, more so. He must go into deep hiding, and he cannot go alone. To save his life and yours, the only thing I can think of is to get both of you off planet. We are within months of launching our first colony ships.

```
If I am the only one to know your
real identities, we can keep you
safe until launch. But we must get
Bean out of Greece as quickly as
possible. Are you with me?

Do not tell me where you are. We
will work out how to meet.
```

How stupid did they think she was?

It took Petra only about half an hour to realize that these people weren't Turkish. Not that she was some kind of expert on language, but they'd be babbling along and every now and then out would pop a word of Russian. She didn't understand Russian either, except for a few loan words in Armenian, and Azerbaijani had loan words like that, too, but the thing is, when you say a Russian loan word in Armenian, you give it an Armenian pronunciation. These clowns would switch to an easy, native-sounding Russian accent when they hit those words. She would have to have been a gibbon in the slow-learner class not to realize that the Turkish pose was just that, a pose.

So when she decided she'd learned all she could with her eyes closed, listening, she spoke up in Fleet Common. "Aren't we across the Caucasus yet? When do I get to pee?"

Someone said an expletive.

"No, pee," she answered. She opened her eyes and blinked. She was on the floor of some ground vehicle. She started to sit up.

A man pushed her back down with his foot.

"Oh, that's clever. Keep me out of sight as we coast along the tarmac, but how will you get me into the airplane without anyone seeing? You want me to come out walking and acting normal so nobody gets all excited, right?"

"You'll act that way when we tell you to or we'll kill you," said the man with the heavy foot.

"If you had the authority to kill me, I'd be dead back in Maralik." She started to rise again. Again the foot pushed her back down.

"Listen carefully," she said. "I've been kidnapped because somebody wants me to plan a war for them. That means I'm going to be meeting with the top brass. They're not stupid enough to think they'll get anything decent from me without my willing cooperation. That's why they wouldn't let you kill my mother. So when I tell them that I won't do anything for them until I have your balls in a paper bag, how long do you think it will take them to decide what's more important to them? My brain or your balls?"

"We *do* have the authority to kill you."

It took her only moments to decide why such authority might have been given to morons like these. "Only if I'm in imminent danger of being rescued. Then they'd rather have me dead than let somebody else get the use of me. Let's see you make a case for *that* here on the runway at the Gyuniri airport."

A different rude word this time.

Somebody spurted out a sentence of Russian. She caught the gist of it from the intonation and the bitter laughter afterward. "They warned you she was a genius."

Genius, hell. If she was so smart, why hadn't she anticipated the possibility that somebody would make a grab for the kids who won the war? And it had to be kids, not just her, because she was too far down the list for somebody outside Armenia to make her their only choice. When the front door was locked, she should have run for the cops instead of puttering around to the back door. And that was another stupid thing they did, locking the front door. In Russia you had to lock your doors, they probably thought that was normal. They should have done better research. Not that it helped her now, of course. Except that she knew they weren't all that careful and they weren't all that bright. Anybody can kidnap someone who's taking no precautions.

"So Russia makes her play for world domination, is that it?" she asked.

"Shut up," said the man in the seat in front of her.

"I don't speak Russian, you know, and I won't learn."

"You don't have to," said a woman.

"Isn't that ironic?" said Petra. "Russia plans to take over the world, but they have to speak English to do it."

The foot on her belly pressed down harder.

"Remember your balls in a bag," she said.

A moment, and then the foot let up.

She sat up, and this time no one pushed her down.

"Untape me so I can get myself up on the seat. Come on! My arms hurt in this position! Haven't you learned anything since the days of the KGB? Unconscious people don't have to have their circulation cut off. Fourteen-year-old Armenian girls can probably be overpowered quite easily by big strong Russian goons."

By now the tape was off and she was sitting beside Heavy-foot and a guy who never looked at her, just kept watching out the left window, then the right, then the left again. "So this is Gyuniri airport?"

"What, you don't recognize it?"

"I've never been here before. When would I? I've only taken two airplane trips in my life, one out of Yerevan when I was five, and the other coming back, nine years later."

"She knew it was Gyuniri because it's the closest airport

that doesn't fly commercial jets," said the woman. She spoke without any tone in her voice—not contempt, not deference. Just . . . flat.

"Whose bright idea was this? Because captive generals don't strategize all that well."

"First, why in the world do you think anyone would tell us?" said the woman. "Second, why don't you shut up and find things out when they matter?"

"Because I'm a cheerful, talkative extrovert who likes to make friends," said Petra.

"You're a bossy, nosy introvert who likes to piss people off," said the woman.

"Oh, you actually did some research."

"No, just observation." So she did have a sense of humor. Maybe.

"You'd better just pray you can get over the Caucasus before you have to answer to the Armenian Air Force."

Heavy-foot made a derisory noise, proving that he didn't recognize irony when he heard it.

"Of course, you'll probably have only a small plane, and we'll probably fly out over the Black Sea. Which means that I.F. satellites will know exactly where I am."

"You're not I.F. personnel anymore," said the woman.

"Meaning they don't care what happens to you," said Heavy-foot.

By now they had pulled to a stop beside a small plane. "A jet, I'm impressed," said Petra. "Does it have any weaponry? Or is it just wired with explosives so that if the Armenian Air Force does start to force you down, you can blow me up and the whole plane with me?"

"Do we have to tie you again?" asked the woman.

"That would look really good to the people in the control tower."

"Get her out," said the woman.

Stupidly, the men on both sides of her opened their doors and got out, leaving her a choice of exits. So she chose Heavy-foot because she knew he was stupid, whereas the other man was anyone's guess. And, yes, he truly was stupid, because he held her by only one arm as he used his other hand to close the door. So she lurched to one side as if she had stumbled, drawing him off balance, and then, still using his grip to support her weight, she did a double kick, one in the groin and one in the knee. She landed solidly both times, and he let go of her very nicely before falling to the ground, writhing, one hand clutching his crotch and the other trying to slide his kneecap back around to the front of his knee.

Did they think she'd forgotten all her hand-to-hand unarmed combat training? Hadn't she warned him that she'd have his balls in a bag?

She made a good run for it, and she was feeling pretty good about how much speed she had picked up during her months of running at school, until she realized that they weren't following her. And that meant they knew they didn't have to.

No sooner had she noticed this than she felt something sharp pierce the skin over her right shoulder blade. She had time to slow down but not to stop before she collapsed into unconsciousness again.

———

This time they kept her drugged until they reached their destination, and since she never saw any scenery except the walls of what seemed to be an underground bunker, she had no guesses about where they might have taken her. Somewhere in Russia, that's all. And from the soreness of the bruises on her arms and legs and neck and the scrapes on her knees and palms and nose, she guessed that they hadn't been too careful with her. The price she paid for being a bossy, nosy introvert. Or maybe it was the part about pissing people off.

She lay on her bunk until a doctor came in and treated her scrapes with a special no-anesthetic blend of alcohol and acid, or so it seemed. "Was that just in case it didn't hurt enough?" she asked.

The doctor didn't answer. Apparently they had warned the woman what happened to those who spoke to her.

"The guy I kicked in the balls, did they have to amputate them?"

Still no answer. Not even a trace of amusement. Could this possibly be the one educated person in Russia who didn't speak Common?

Meals were brought to her, lights went on and off, but no one came to speak to her and she was not allowed out of her room. She heard nothing through the heavy doors, and it became clear that her punishment for her misbehavior on the trip was going to be solitary confinement for a while.

She resolved not to beg for mercy. Indeed, once it became clear to her that she was in isolation, she accepted it and isolated herself still further, neither speaking nor responding to the people who came and went. They never tried to speak to her, either, so the silence of her world was complete.

They did not understand how self-contained she was. How her mind could show her more than mere reality ever could. She could recall memories by the sheaf, by the bale. Whole conversations. And then new versions of those conversations, in which she was actually able to say the clever things that she only really thought of later.

She could even relive every moment of the battles on Eros. Especially the battle where she fell asleep in the middle. How tired she was. How she struggled frantically to stay awake. How she could feel her mind being so sluggish that she began to forget where she was, and why, and even who she was.

To escape from this endlessly repeating scene, she tried to think of other things. Her parents, her little brother. She could remember everything they had said and done since she returned, but after a while the only memories that mattered to her were the early ones from before Battle School. Memories she had suppressed for nine years, as best she could. All the promises of the family life that was lost to her. The good-bye when her mother wept and let her go. Her father's hand as he led her to the car. That hand had always meant that she was safe, before. But this time that hand led her to a place where she never felt safe again. She knew she had chosen to go— but she was only a child, and she knew that this was what was expected of her. That she should not succumb to the temptation to run to her weeping mother and cling to her and say no, I won't do it, let someone else become a soldier, I want to stay here and bake with Mama and play mother to my own little dolls. Not go off into space where I can learn how to kill strange and terrible creatures—and, by the way, humans as well, who trusted me and then I fell . . . a . . . sleep.

Being alone with her memories was not all that happy for her.

She tried fasting, simply ignoring the food they brought her, the liquids too, nothing by mouth. She expected someone to speak to her then, to cajole. But no. The doctor came in, slapped an injection into her arm, and when she woke up her hand was sore where the IV had been and she realized that there was no point in refusing to eat.

She hadn't thought to keep a calendar at first, but after the

IV she did keep a calendar on her own body, pressing a fingernail into her wrist until it bled. Seven days on the left wrist, then switch to the right, and all she had to remember in her head was the number of weeks.

Except she didn't bother going for three. She realized that they were going to outwait her because, after all, they had the others they had kidnapped, and no doubt some of them were cooperating, so it was perfectly all right with them if she stayed in her cell and got farther and farther behind so that when she finally did emerge, she'd be the worst of them at whatever it was they were doing.

Fine, what did she care? She was never going to help them anyway.

But if she was to have any chance to get free of these people and this place, she had to be out of this room and into a place where she could earn enough trust to be able to get free.

Trust. They'd expect her to lie, they'd expect her to plot. Therefore she had to be as convincing as possible. Her long time in solitary was a help, of course—everyone knew that isolation caused untold mental pressures. Another thing that helped was that it was undoubtedly known to them by now, from the other children, that she was the first one who broke under pressure during the battles on Eros. So they would be predisposed to believe a breakdown now.

She began to cry. It wasn't hard. There were plenty of real tears pent up in her. But she shaped those emotions, made it into a whimpering cry that went on and on and on. Her nose filled with mucus, but she did not blow it. Her eyes streamed with tears but she did not wipe them. Her pillow got soaked with tears and covered with snot but she did not evade the wet place. Instead she rolled her hair right through it as she turned over, did it again and again until her hair was matted with mucus and her face stiff with it. She made sure her crying did not get more desperate—let no one think she was trying to get attention. She toyed with the idea of falling silent when anyone came into the room, but decided against it—she figured it would be more convincing to be oblivious to other people's coming and going.

It worked. Someone came in after a day of this and slapped her with another injection. And this time when she woke up, she was in a hospital bed with a window that showed a cloudless northern sky. And sitting by her bed was Dink Meeker.

"Ho Dink," she said.

"Ho Petra. You pasted these conchos over real good."

"One does what one can for the cause," she said. "Who else?"

"You're the last to come out of solitary. They got the whole team from Eros, Petra. Except Ender, of course. And Bean."

"He's not in solitary?"

"No, they didn't keep it a secret who was still in the box. We thought you made a pretty fine showing."

"Who was second-longest?"

"Nobody cares. We were all out in the first week. You lasted five."

So it had been two and a half weeks before she started her calendar.

"Because I'm the stupid one."

" 'Stubborn' is the right word."

"Know where we are?"

"Russia."

"I meant where in Russia."

"Far from any borders, they assure us."

"What are our resources?"

"Very thick walls. No tools. Constant observation. They weigh our bodily wastes, I'm not kidding."

"What have they got us doing?"

"Like a really dumbed-down Battle School. We put up with it for a long time till Fly Molo finally gave up and when one of the teachers was quoting one of Von Clausewitz's stupider generalizations, Fly continued the quotation, sentence after sentence, paragraph after paragraph, and the rest of us joined in as best we could—I mean, nobody has a memory like Fly, but we do OK—and they finally got the idea that we could teach the stupid classes to them. So now it's just . . . war games."

"Again? You think they're going to spring it on us later that the games are real?"

"No, this is just planning stuff. Strategy for a war between Russia and Turkmenistan. Russia and an alliance between Turkmenistan, Kazakhstan, Azerbaijan, and Turkey. War with the United States and Canada. War with the old NATO alliance except Germany. War with Germany. On and on. China. India. Really stupid stuff, too, like between Brazil and Peru, which makes no sense but maybe they were testing our compliance or something."

"All this in five weeks?"

"Three weeks of kuso classes, and then two weeks of war games. When we finish our plan, see, they run it on the computer to show us how it went. Someday they're going to catch on that the only way to do this that isn't a waste of time is to have one of us making the plan for the opponent as well."

"My guess is you just told them."

"I've told them before but they're hard to persuade. Typical military types. Makes you understand why the whole concept of Battle School was developed in the first place. If the war had been up to adults, there'd be Buggers at every breakfast table in the world by now."

"But they *are* listening?"

"I think they record it all and play it back at slow speeds to see if we're passing messages subvocally."

Petra smiled.

"So why did you finally decide to cooperate?" he asked.

She shrugged. "I don't think I decided."

"Hey, they don't pull you out of the room until you express really sincere interest in being a good, compliant little kid."

She shook her head. "I don't think I did that."

"Yeah, well, whatever you did, you were the last of Ender's jeesh to break, kid."

A short buzzer sounded.

"Time's up," said Dink. He got up, leaned over, kissed her brow, and left the room.

Six weeks later, Petra was actually enjoying the life. By complying with the kids' demands, their captors had finally come up with some decent equipment. Software that allowed them very realistic head-to-head strategic and tactical wargaming. Access to the nets so they could do decent research into terrains and capabilities so their wargaming had some realism—though they knew every message they sent was censored, because of the number of messages that were rejected for one obscure reason or another. They enjoyed each other's company, exercised together, and by all appearances seemed to be completely happy and compliant Russian commanders.

Yet Petra knew, as they all knew, that every one of them was faking. Holding back. Making dumb mistakes which, if they were made in combat, would lead to gaps that a clever enemy could exploit. Maybe their captors realized this, and maybe they didn't. At least it made them all feel better, though they never spoke of it. But since they were all doing it, and cooperating by not exposing those weaknesses by exploiting them in the games, they could only assume that everyone felt the same about it.

They chatted comfortably about a lot of things—their disdain for their captors, memories of Ground School, Battle School, Command School. And, of course, Ender. He was out of the reach of these bastards, so they made sure to mention him a lot, to talk about how the I.F. was bound to use him to counter all these foolish plans the Russians were making. They knew they were blowing smoke, that the I.F. wouldn't do anything, they even said so. But still, Ender was there, the ultimate trump card.

Till the day one of the erstwhile teachers told them that a colony ship had gone, with Ender and his sister Valentine aboard.

"I didn't even know he had a sister," said Hot Soup.

No one said anything, but they all knew that this was impossible. They had all known Ender had a sister. But . . . whatever Hot Soup was doing, they'd play along and see what the game was.

"No matter what they tell us, one thing we know," said Hot Soup. "Wiggin is still with us."

Again, they weren't sure what he meant by this. After the briefest pause, though, Shen clapped his hand to his chest and cried out, "In our hearts forever."

"Yes," said Hot Soup. "Ender is in our hearts."

Just the tiniest extra emphasis on the name "Ender."

But he had said Wiggin before.

And before that, he had called attention to the fact that

they all knew Ender had a sister. They also knew that Ender had a brother. Back on Eros, while Ender was in bed recovering from his breakdown after finding out the battles had been real, Mazer Rackham had told them some things about Ender. And Bean had told them more, as they were trapped together while the League War played itself out. They had listened as Bean expounded on what Ender's brother and sister meant to him, that the reason Ender had been born at all during the days of the two-child law was because his brother and sister were so brilliant, but the brother was too dangerously aggressive and the sister too passively compliant. How Bean knew all this he wouldn't tell, but the information was indelibly planted in their memories, tied as it was with those tense days after their victory over the Formics and before the defeat of the Polemarch in his attempt to take over the I.F.

So when Hot Soup said "Wiggin is still with us," he had not been referring to Ender or Valentine, because they most assuredly were not "with us."

Peter, that was the brother's name. Peter Wiggin. Hot Soup was telling them that he was one whose mind was perhaps as brilliant as Ender's, and he was still on Earth. Maybe, if they could somehow contact him on the outside, he would ally himself with his brother's battle companions. Maybe he could find a way to get them free.

The game now was to find some way to communicate with him.

Sending email would be pointless—the last thing they needed to do was have their captors see a bunch of email addressed to every possible variant of Peter Wiggin's name at every single mailnet that they could think of. And sure enough, by that evening Alai was telling them some tall tale about a genie in a bottle that had washed up on the shore. Everyone listened with feigned interest, but they knew the real story had been stated right at the beginning, when Alai said, "The fisherman thought maybe the bottle had a message from some castaway, but when he popped the cork, a cloud of smoke came out and . . ." and they got it. What they had to do was send a message in a bottle, a message that would go indiscriminately to everyone everywhere, but which could only be understood by Ender's brother, Peter.

But as she thought about it, Petra realized that with all these other brilliant brains working to reach Peter Wiggin, she might as well work on an alternative plan. Peter Wiggin was not the only one outside who might help them. There was Bean. And while Bean was almost certainly in hiding, so that he would have far less freedom of action than Peter Wiggin, that didn't mean they couldn't still find him.

She thought about it for a week in every spare moment, rejecting idea after idea.

Then she thought of one that might get past the censors.

She worked out the text of her message very carefully in her head, making sure that it was phrased and worded exactly right. Then, with that memorized, she figured the binary code of each letter in standard two-byte format, and memorized that. Then she started the really hard stuff. All done in her head, so nothing was ever committed to paper or typed into the computer, where a keystroke monitor could report to their captors whatever she wrote.

In the meantime, she found a complex black-and-white drawing of a dragon on a netsite somewhere in Japan and saved it as a small file. When she finally had the message fully encoded in her mind, it took only a few minutes of fiddling with the drawing and she was done. She added it as part of her signature on every letter she sent. She spent so little time on it that she did not think it would look to her captors like anything more than a harmless whim. If they asked, she could say she added the picture in memory of Ender's Dragon Army in Battle School.

Of course, it wasn't just a picture of a dragon anymore. Now there was a little poem under it.

```
Share this dragon.
If you do,
lucky end for
them and you.
```

She would tell them, if they asked, that the words were just an ironic joke. If they didn't believe her, they would strip off the picture and she'd have to find another way.

She sent it on every letter from then on. Including to the other kids. She got it back from them on messages after that, so they had picked up on what she was doing and were helping. Whether their captors were actually letting it leave the building or not, she had no way of knowing—at first. Finally, though, she started getting it back on messages from outside. A single glance told her that she had succeeded—her coded message was still embedded in the picture. It hadn't been stripped out.

Now it was just a question of whether Bean would see it and look at it closely enough to realize that there was a mystery to solve.

4

CUSTODY

To: Graff%pilgrimage@colmin.gov
From:Chamrajnagar%Jawaharlal@ifcom.
gov
Re: Quandary

You know better than anyone how
vital it is to maintain the independence of the Fleet from the
machinations of politicians. That
was my reason for rejecting
"Locke's" suggestion. But in the
event I was wrong. Nothing jeopard-
izes Fleet independence more than
the prospect of one nation becoming
dominant, especially if, as seems
likely, the particular nation is
one that has already shown a disposition to take over the I.F. and
use it for nationalist purposes.

I'm afraid I was rather harsh with
Locke. I dare not write to him

directly, because, while Locke would be reliable, one can never know what Demosthenes would do with an official letter of apology from the Polemarch. Therefore please arrange for him to be notified that my threat is rescinded and I wish him well.

I do learn from my mistakes. Since one of Wiggin's companions remains outside the control of the aggressor, prudence dictates that young Delphiki be protected. Since you are Earthside and I am not, I give you brevet command over an IFM contingent and any other resources you need, orders forthcoming through level 6 backchannels (of course). I give you specific instructions not to tell me or anyone else of the steps you have taken to protect Delphiki or his family. There is to be no record in the I.F. system or that of any government.

By the way, trust no one in the Hegemony. I always knew they were a nest of careerists, but recent experience shows that the careerist is now being replaced by worse: the ideologue rampant.

> Act swiftly. It appears that we are
> either on the verge of a new war,
> or the League War never quite ended
> after all.

How many days can you stay closed in, surrounded by guards, before you start to feel like a prisoner? Bean never felt claustrophobic in Battle School. Not even on Eros, where the low ceilings of the Buggers' tunnels teetered over them like a car slipping off its jack. Not like this, closed up with his family, pacing the four-room apartment. Well, not actually pacing it. He just *felt* like pacing it, and instead sat still, controlling himself, trying to think of some way to get control of his own life.

Being under someone else's protection was bad enough—he had never liked that, though it had happened before, when Poke protected him on the streets of Rotterdam, and then when Sister Carlotta saved him from certain death by taking him in and sending him to Battle School. But both those times, there were things he could do to make sure everything went right. This was different. He knew something was going to go wrong, and there was nothing he could do about it.

The soldiers guarding this apartment, surrounding the building, they were all good, loyal men, Bean had no reason to doubt that. They weren't going to betray him. Probably. And the bureaucracy that was keeping his location a secret— no doubt it would just be an honest oversight, not a conscious betrayal, that would give his address to his enemies.

And in the meantime, Bean could only wait, pinned down by his protectors. They were the web, holding him in place for the spider. And there wasn't a thing he could say to change this situation. If Greece were fighting a war, they'd set Bean and Nikolai to work, making plans, charting strategies. But when it came to a matter of security, they were just children, to be protected and taken care of. It would do no good for Bean to explain that his best protection was to get out of here, get off completely on his own, make a life for himself on the streets of some city where he could be nameless and faceless and lost and safe. Because they looked at him and saw nothing but a little kid. And who listens to little kids?

Little kids have to be taken care of.

By adults who don't have it in their power to keep those little kids safe.

He wanted to throw something through the window and jump down after it.

Instead he sat still. He read books. He signed on to the nets using one of his many names and cruised around, looking for whatever dribbles of information oozed through the military security systems of every nation, hoping for something to tell him where Petra and Fly Molo and Vlad and Dumper were being held. Some country that was showing signs of a little more cockiness because they thought they had the winning hand now. Or a country that was acting more cautious and methodical because finally somebody with a brain was running their strategy.

But it was pointless, because he knew he wasn't going to find it this way. The real information never got onto the net until it was too late to do anything about it. Somebody knew. The facts he needed to find his way to his friends were available in a dozen sites—he knew that, *knew* it, because that's the way it always was, the historians would find it and wonder for a thousand pages at a time: Why didn't anybody notice? Why didn't anybody put it together? Because the people who had the information were too dim to know what they had, and the people who could have understood it were locked in an apartment in an abandoned resort that even tourists didn't want to come to anymore.

The worst thing was that even Mother and Father were getting on his nerves. After a childhood with no parents, the best thing that had ever happened to him was when Sister Carlotta's research found his biological parents. The war ended, and when all the other kids got to go home to their families, Bean wasn't left over. He got to go home to his family, too. He had no childhood memories of them, of course. But Nikolai had, and Nikolai let Bean borrow them as if they were his own.

They were good people, his mother and his father. They never made him feel as if he were an intruder, a stranger, even a visitor. It was as if he had always belonged with them. They liked him. They loved him. It was a strange, exhilarating feeling to be with people who didn't want anything from you except your happiness, who were glad just to have you around.

But when you're already going crazy from confinement, it doesn't matter how much you like somebody, how much you love them, how grateful you are for their kindness to you. They will make you nuts. Everything they do grates on you like a bad song that won't get out of your head. You just want to scream at them to *shut. Up.* But you don't, because you love them and you know that you're probably driving them crazy too and as long as there's no hope of release you've got to keep things calm . . .

And then finally there comes a knock on the door and you open it up and you realize that something different is finally going to happen.

It was Colonel Graff and Sister Carlotta at the door. Graff in a suit now, and Sister Carlotta in an extravagant auburn wig that made her look really stupid but also kind of pretty. The whole family recognized them at once, except that Nikolai had never met Sister Carlotta. But when Bean and his family got up to greet them, Graff held up a hand to stop them and Carlotta put her finger to her lips. They came inside and closed the door after them and beckoned the family to gather in the bathroom.

It was a tight fit, the six of them in there. Father and Mother ended up standing in the shower while Graff hung a tiny machine from the overhead light. Once it was in place and the red light began blinking, Graff spoke softly.

"Hi," he said. "We came to get you out of this place."

"Why all the precautions in here?" asked Father.

"Because part of the security system here is to listen in on everything said in this apartment."

"To protect us, they spy on us?" asked Mother.

"Of course they do," said Father.

"Since anything we say here might leak into the system," said Graff, "and would most certainly leak right back out of the system, I brought this little machine, which hears every sound we make and produces countersounds that nullify them so we pretty much can't be heard."

"Pretty much?" asked Bean.

"That's why we won't go into any details," said Graff. "I'll tell you only this much. I'm the Minister of Colonization, and we have a ship that leaves in a few months. Just time enough to get you off Earth, up to the ISL, and over to Eros for the launch."

But even as he said it, he was shaking his head, and Sister Carlotta was grinning and shaking *her* head, too, so that they would know that this was all a lie. A cover story.

"Bean and I have been in space before, Mother," said Nikolai, playing along. "It's not so bad."

"It's what we fought the war for," Bean chimed in. "The Formics wanted Earth because it was just like the worlds they already lived on. So now that they're gone, we get *their* worlds, which should be good for us. It's only fair, don't you think?"

Of course their parents both understood what was happening, but Bean knew Mother well enough by now that he wasn't surprised that she had to ask a completely useless and dangerous question just to be sure.

"But we're not really . . ." she began. Then Father's hand gently covered her mouth.

"It's the only way to keep us safe," Father said. "Once we're going at lightspeed, it'll seem like a couple of years to us, while decades pass on Earth. By the time we reach the other planet, everybody who wants us dead will be dead themselves."

"Like Joseph and Mary taking Jesus into Egypt," said Mother.

"Exactly," said Father.

"Except they got to go back to Nazareth."

"If Earth destroys itself in some stupid war," said Father, "it won't matter to us anymore, because we'll be part of a new world. Be happy about this, Elena. It means we can stay together." Then he kissed her.

"Time to go, Mr. and Mrs. Delphiki. Bring the boys, please." Graff reached up and yanked the damper from the ceiling light.

The soldiers who waited for them in the hall wore the uniform of the I.F. Not a Greek uniform was in sight. And these young men were armed to the teeth. As they walked briskly to the stairs—no elevators, no doors that might suddenly open to leave them trapped in a box for an enemy to toss in a grenade or a few thousand projectiles—Bean watched the way the soldier in the lead watched everything, checked every corner, the light under every door in the hall, so that nothing could surprise him. Bean also saw how the man's body moved inside his clothes, with a kind of contained strength that made his clothes seem like Kleenex, he could rip through the fabric just by tugging at it a little, because nothing could hold him in except his own self-control. It was like his sweat was pure testosterone. This was what a man was supposed to be. This was a *soldier.*

I was never a soldier, thought Bean. He tried to imagine himself the way he had been in Battle School, strapping on cut-down flash-suit pieces that never fit him right. He always looked like somebody's pet monkey dressed up as a human for the joke of it. Like a toddler who got clothes out of his big brother's dresser. The man in front of him, that's what Bean wanted to be when he grew up. But try as he might, he could never imagine himself actually being big. No, not even being full size. He would always be looking up at the world. He might be male, he might be human, or at least humanesque, but he would never be manly. No one would ever look at him and say, Now, *that's* a *man.*

Then again, this soldier had never given orders that changed the course of history. Looking great in a uniform wasn't the only way to earn your place in the world.

Down the stairs, three flights, and then a pause for just a moment well back from the emergency exit while two of the soldiers came out and watched for the signal from the men in the I.F. chopper waiting thirty meters away. The signal came. Graff and Sister Carlotta led the way, still at a brisk walk. They looked neither left nor right, just focused on the helicopter. They got in, sat down, buckled up, and the chopper tilted and rose from the grass and flew low out over the water.

Mother was all for demanding to know the real plan, but again Graff cut off all discussion with a cheerful bellow of "Let's wait to discuss this until we can do it without shouting!"

Mother didn't like it. None of them did. But there was Sister Carlotta smiling her best nun smile, like a sort of Virgin-in-training. How could they help but trust her?

Five minutes in the air and then they set down on the deck of a submarine. It was a big one, with the stars and stripes of the United States, and it occurred to Bean that since they didn't know what country had kidnapped the other kids, how could they be sure they weren't just walking into the hands of their enemies?

But once they got down inside the ship, they could see that while the crew was in U.S. uniforms, the only people carrying weapons were the I.F. soldiers who had brought them and a half-dozen more who had been waiting for them with the sub. Since power came from the barrel of a gun, and the only guns on the ship were under Graff's command, Bean's mind was eased a little.

"If you try to tell us that we can't talk *here*," Mother began—but to her consternation Graff again held up a hand, and Sister Carlotta again made a shushing gesture as Graff beckoned them to follow their lead soldier through the narrow corridors of the sub.

Finally the six of them were packed once more into a tiny space—this time the executive officer's cabin—and once again they waited while Graff hung his noise damper and turned it on. When the light started blinking, Mother was the first to speak.

"I'm trying to figure out how we can tell we aren't being

kidnapped just like the others," she said dryly.

"You got it," said Graff. "They were all taken by a group of terrorist nuns, aided by fat old bureaucrats."

"He's joking," said Father, trying to soothe Mother's immediate wrath.

"I know he's joking. I just don't think it's funny. After all we've been through, and then we're supposed to go along without a word, without a question, just . . . *trusting*."

"Sorry," said Graff. "But you were already trusting the Greek government back where you were. You've got to trust somebody, so why not us?"

"At least the Greek Army explained things to us and pretended we had a right to make some decisions," said Mother.

They didn't explain things to me and Nikolai, Bean wanted to say.

"Come, children, no bickering," said Sister Carlotta. "The plan is very simple. The Greek Army continues to guard that apartment building as if you were still inside it, taking meals in and doing laundry. This fools no one, probably, but it makes the Greek government feel like they're part of the program. In the meantime, four passengers answering your description but flying under assumed names are taken to Eros, where they embark on the first colony ship, and only then, when the ship is launched, is an announcement made that for their protection, the Delphiki family have opted for permanent emigration and a new life in a new world."

"And where are we really?" asked Father.

"I don't know," said Graff very simply.

"And neither do I," said Sister Carlotta.

Bean's family looked at them in disbelief.

"I guess that means we won't be staying in the sub," said Nikolai, "because then you'd absolutely know where we are."

"It's a double blind," said Bean. "They're splitting us up. I'll go one way, you'll go another."

"Absolutely not," said Father.

"We've had enough of a divided family," said Mother.

"It's the only way," said Bean. "I knew it already. I . . . want it that way."

"You want to leave us?" said Mother.

"It's me they want to kill," said Bean.

"We don't know that!" said Mother.

"But we're pretty sure," said Bean. "If I'm not with you, then even if you're found, they'll probably leave you alone."

"And if we're divided," said Nikolai, "it changes the profile of what they're looking for. Not a mother and father and two boys. Now it's a mother and father and one boy. And a grandma and her grandchild." Nikolai grinned at Sister Carlotta.

"I was rather hoping to be taken for an aunt," she said.

"You talk as if you already know the plan!" said Mother.

"It was obvious," said Nikolai. "From the moment they told us the cover story in the bathroom. Why else would Colonel Graff bring Sister Carlotta?"

"It wasn't obvious to me," said Mother.

"Or to me," said Father. "But that's what happens when your sons are both brilliant military minds."

"How long?" Mother demanded. "When will it end? When do we get to have Bean back with us?"

"I don't know," said Graff.

"He can't know, Mother," said Bean. "Not until we know who did the kidnappings and why. When we know what the threat actually is, then we can judge when we've taken sufficient countermeasures to make it safe for us to come partway out of hiding."

Mother suddenly burst into tears. "And you *want* this, Julian?"

Bean put his arms around her. Not because he felt any personal need to do it, but because he knew she needed that gesture from him. Living with a family for a year had not given him the full complement of normal human emotional responses, but at least it had made him more aware of what they ought to be. And he did have one normal reaction—he felt a little guilty that he could only fake what Mother needed, instead of having it come from the heart. But such gestures never came from the heart, for Bean. It was a language he had learned too late for it to come naturally to him. He would always speak the language of the heart with an awkward foreign accent.

The truth was that even though he loved his family, he was eager to get to a place where he could get to work making the contacts he needed to get the information that would let him find his friends. Except for Ender, he was the only one from Ender's jeesh who was outside and free. They needed him, and he'd wasted enough time already.

So he held his mother, and she clung to him, and she shed many tears. He also embraced his father, but more briefly; and he and Nikolai only punched each other's arms. All foreign gestures to Bean, but they knew he meant to mean them, and took them as if they were real.

The sub was fast. They weren't very long at sea before they reached a crowded port—Salonika, Bean assumed, though it could have been any other cargo port on the Aegean. The sub never actually entered the harbor. Instead, it surfaced between two ships moving in a parallel track toward the harbor. Mother, Father, Nikolai, and Graff were transferred to a freighter along with two of the soldiers, who were now in civilian clothes, as if that could conceal the soldierly way they acted. Bean and Carlotta stayed behind. Neither group would know where the other was. There would be no effort to contact each other. That had been another hard realization for Mother. "Why can't we write?"

"Nothing is easier to track than email," said Father. "Even if we use disguised online identities, if someone finds us, and we're writing regularly to Julian, then they'll see the pattern and track him down."

Mother understood it then. With her head, if not her heart.

Down inside the sub, Bean and Sister Carlotta sat down at a tiny table in the mess.

"Well?" said Bean.

"Well," said Sister Carlotta.

"Where are *we* going?" asked Bean.

"I have no idea," said Sister Carlotta. "They'll transfer us to another ship at another port, and we'll get off, and I have these false identities that we're supposed to use, but I really have no idea where we should go from there."

"We have to keep moving. No more than a few weeks in any one place," said Bean. "And I have to get on the nets with new identities every time we move, so no one can track the pattern."

"Do you seriously think someone will catalogue all the email in the entire world and follow up on all the ones that move around?" asked Sister Carlotta.

"Yes," said Bean. "They probably already do, so it's just a matter of running a search."

"But that's billions of emails a day."

"That's why it takes so many clerks to check all the email addresses on the file cards in the central switchboard," said Bean. He grinned at Sister Carlotta.

She did not grin back. "You really are a snotty and disrespectful little boy," she said.

"You're really leaving it up to me to decide where we go?"

"Not at all. I'm merely waiting to make a decision until we both agree."

"Oh, now, *that's* a cheap excuse to stay down here in this sub with all these great-looking men."

"Your level of banter has become even more crude than it was when you lived on the streets of Rotterdam," she said, coolly analytical.

"It's the war," said Bean. "It . . . it changes a man."

She couldn't keep a straight face any longer. Even though her laugh was only a single bark, and her smile lasted only a moment longer, it was enough. She still liked him. And he, to his surprise, still liked her, even though it had been years since he lived with her while she educated him to a level where Battle School would take him. He was surprised because, at the time he lived with her, he had never let himself realize that he liked her. After Poke's death, he hadn't been willing to admit to himself that he liked anybody. But now he knew the truth. He liked Sister Carlotta just fine.

Of course, she would probably get on his nerves after a while, too, just like his parents had. But at least when that happened, they could pick up and move. There wouldn't be soldiers keeping them indoors and away from the windows.

And if it ever became truly annoying, Bean could leave and strike out on his own. He'd never say that to Sister Carlotta, because it would only worry her. Besides, she was bound to know it already. She had all the test data. And those tests had been designed to tell everything about a person. Why, she probably knew him better than he knew himself.

Of course, *he* knew that back when he took the tests, there was hardly an honest answer on any of the psychological tests. He had already read enough psychology by the time he took them that he knew exactly what answers were needed to show the profile that would probably get him into Battle School. So in fact she didn't know him from those tests at all.

But then, he didn't have any idea what his real answers would have been, then or now. So it isn't as if he knew himself any better.

And because she had observed him, and she was wise in her own way, she probably *did* know him better than he knew himself.

What a laugh, though. To think that one human being could ever really know another. You could get used to each other, get so habituated that you could speak their words right along with them, but you never knew why other people said what they said or did what they did, because they never even knew themselves. Nobody understands anybody.

And yet somehow we live together, mostly in peace, and get things done with a high enough success rate that people keep trying. Human beings get married and a lot of the marriages work, and they have children and most of them grow up to be decent people, and they have schools and businesses and factories and farms that have results at some level of acceptability—all without having a clue what's going on inside anybody's head.

Muddling through, that's what human beings do.

That was the part of being human that Bean hated the most.

5

AMBITION

To: Locke%espinoza@polnet.gov
From: Graff%%@colmin.gov
Re: Correction

I have been asked to relay a message that a threat of exposure has been rescinded, with apologies. Nor should you be alarmed that your identity is widely known. Your identity was penetrated at my direction several years ago, and while multiple persons then under my command were made aware of who you are, it is a group that has neither reason nor disposition to violate confidentiality. The only exception has now been chastened by circumstance. On a personal level, let me say that I have no doubt of your capacity to achieve your ambition. I can only hope that, in the event of success, you will choose

```
to  emulate  Washington,  MacArthur,
or  Augustus  rather  than  Napoleon,
Alexander,  or  Hitler.

Colmin
```

Now and then Peter was almost overwhelmed by a desire to tell somebody what was actually happening in his life. He never succumbed to the desire, of course, since to tell it would be to undo it. But especially now that Valentine had gone, it was almost unbearable to sit there reading a personal letter from the Minister of Colonization and not shout for the other students in the library to come and see.

When he and Valentine had first broken through and placed essays or, in Valentine's case, diatribes on some of the major political nets, they had done a little hugging and laughing and jumping around. But it never took long for Valentine to remember how much she loathed half the positions she was forced to espouse in her Demosthenes persona, and her resulting gloom would calm him down as well. Peter missed her, of course, but he did not miss the arguments, the whining about having to be the bad guy. She could never see how the Demosthenes persona was the interesting one, the most fun to work with. Well, when he was done with it he'd give it back to her—long before she got to whatever planet it was that she and Ender were heading for. She'd know by then that even at his most outrageous, Demosthenes was a catalyst, making things happen.

Valentine. Stupid to choose Ender and exile over Peter and *life*. Stupid to get so angry over the obvious necessity of keeping Ender off planet. For his own protection, Peter told her, and hadn't events proven it? If he'd come home as

Valentine originally wanted, he'd be a captive somewhere, or dead, depending on whether his captors had been able to get him to cooperate. I was right, Valentine, as I've always been right about everything. But you'd rather be nice than right, you'd rather be liked than powerful, and you'd rather be in exile with the brother who worships you than share power with the brother who made you influential.

Ender was already gone, Valentine. When they took him away to Battle School, he was never coming home—not the precious little Enderpoo that you adored and petted and watched over like a little mommy playing with a doll. They were going to make a soldier out of him, a killer—did you even *look* at the video they showed during Graff's court-martial?—and if something named Andrew Wiggin came home, it would *not* be the Ender you sentimentalized to the point of nausea. He'd be a damaged, broken, useless soldier whose war was finished. Pushing to have him sent off to a colony was the kindest thing I could have done for our erstwhile brother. Nothing would have been sadder than having his biography include the ruin that his life would have become here on Earth, even if nobody bothered to kidnap him. Like Alexander, he'll go out with a flash of brilliant light and live forever in glory, instead of withering away and dying in miserable obscurity, getting trotted out for parades now and then. I was the kind one!

Good riddance to both of you. You would have been drags on my boat, thorns in my side, pains in my ass.

But it would have been fun to show Valentine the letter from Graff—Graff himself! Even though he hid his private access code, even though he was condescending in his urging Peter to emulate the nice guys of history—as if anybody ever *planned* to create an ephemeral empire like Napoleon's or Hitler's—the fact was that even knowing that Locke, far from being some elder statesman speaking anonymously from retirement, was just an underage college student, Graff still thought Peter was worth talking to. Still worth giving advice to, because Graff knew that Peter Wiggin mattered now and would matter in the future. Damn right, Graff!

Damn right, everybody! Ender Wiggin may have saved your asses against the Buggers, but I'm the one who's going to save humanity's collective rectum from its own colostomy. Because human beings have always been more dangerous to the survival of the human race than anything else except the complete destruction of planet Earth, and now we're taking steps to evade even that by spreading our seed—including little Enderseed himself—to other worlds. Does Graff have any idea how hard I worked to make his little Ministry of Colonization come into existence in the first place? Has anybody bothered to track the history of the good ideas that have actually become law to see how many times the trail leads back to Locke?

They actually consulted with me when they were deciding whether to offer you the title of Colmin with which you so affectedly sign your emails. Bet you didn't know *that*, Mr. Minister. Without *me*, you might have been signing your letters with stupid good-luck dragon pictures like half the morons on the net these days.

And for a few minutes it just about killed him that nobody could know about this letter except himself and Graff.

And then . . .

The moment passed. His breathing returned to normal. His wiser self prevailed. It's better not to be distracted by the interference of personal fame. In due course his name would be revealed, he'd take his place in a position of authority instead of mere influence. For now, anonymity would do.

He saved the message from Graff, and then sat there staring at the display.

His hand was trembling.

He looked at it as if it were someone else's hand. What in the world is *that* about, he wondered. Am I such a celebrity hound that getting a letter from a top Hegemony official makes me shake like a teenager at a pop concert?

No. The cool realist took over. He was not trembling out of excitement. That, as always, was transitory, already gone.

He was trembling out of fear.

Because somebody was assembling a team of strategists. The top kids from the Battle School program. The ones they chose to fight the final battle to save humanity. Somebody had them and meant to use them. And sooner or later, that somebody would be Peter's rival, head to head with him, and Peter would have to outthink not only that rival, but also the kids he had managed to bend to his will.

Peter hadn't made it into Battle School. He didn't have what it took. For one reason or another, he was cut from the program without ever leaving home. So *every* kid who went to Battle School was more likely to make a good strategist and tactician than Peter Wiggin, and Peter's principal rival for hegemony had collected around himself the very best of them all.

Except for Ender, of course. Ender, whom I *could* have brought home if I had pulled the right strings and manipulated public opinion the other way. Ender, who was the best of all and might have been standing by my side. But no, I sent him away. For his own damn good. For his own *safety*. And now here I am, facing the struggle that my whole life has been devoted to, and all I've got to face the best of the Battle School is . . . me.

His hand trembled. So what? He'd be crazy *not* to be just a little bit afraid.

But when that moron Chamrajnagar threatened to expose him and bring the whole thing crashing down, just because he was too stupid to see how Demosthenes was necessary in order to bring about results that Locke's persona could never reach for—he had spent weeks in hell over that. Watching as the Battle School kids were kidnapped. Unable to do anything, to say anything pertinent. Oh, he answered letters that some people sent, he did enough investigating to satisfy himself that only Russia had the resources to bring it off. But he dared not use Demosthenes to demand that the I.F. be investigated for its failure to protect these children. Demosthenes could only make some routine suppositions about how it was bound to be the Warsaw Pact that had taken the kids—but of course everyone expected Demosthenes to say that, he was a well-known russophobe, it meant nothing. All because some shortsighted, stupid, self-serving admiral had decided to interfere with the one person on Earth who seemed to care about trying to keep the world from another visit from Attila the Hun. He wanted to scream at Chamrajnagar: I'm the one who writes essays while the other guy kidnaps children, but because you know who I am and you have no clue who *he* is, you reach out to stop *me*? That was about as bright as the pinheads who handed the government of Germany to Hitler because they thought he would be "useful" to them.

Now Chamrajnagar had relented. Sent a cowardly apology through someone else so he could avoid letting Peter have a letter with his signature on it. Too late anyway. The damage was done. Chamrajnagar had not only done nothing, he had kept Peter from doing anything, and now Peter faced a chess game where his side of the board had nothing but pawns, and the other player had a double complement of knights, rooks, and bishops.

So Peter's hand trembled. And he sometimes caught himself wishing that he weren't in this thing so utterly, absolutely alone. Did Napoleon, in his tent alone, wonder what the hell he was doing, betting everything, over and over again, on the ability of his army to do the impossible? Didn't Alexander, once in a while, wish there were someone else he could trust to make a decision or two?

Peter's lip curled in self-contempt. Napoleon? Alexander? It was the other guy who had a stableful of steeds like that to ride. While I have had it certified by the Battle School testing program that I am about as militarily talented as, say, John F. Kennedy, that U.S. President who lost his PT boat through carelessness and got a medal for it because his father had money and political pull, and then became President and made an unbroken string of stupid moves that never hurt him much politically because the press loved him so much.

That's me. I can manipulate the press. I can paint public opinion, nudge and pull and poke and inject things into it, but when it comes to war—and it will come to war—I'm going to look about as clever as the French when the blitzkrieg rolled through.

Peter looked around the reading room. Not much of a library. Not much of a school. But because he entered college early, being a certifiably gifted pupil, and not caring a whit about his formal education, he had gone to the hometown branch of the state university. For the first time he found himself envying the other students who were studying there. All they had to worry about was the next test, or keeping their scholarship, or their dating life.

I could have a life like theirs.

Right. He'd have to kill himself if he ever came to care what some teacher thought of an essay he wrote, or what some girl thought about the clothes he wore, or whether one soccer team could beat another.

He closed his eyes and leaned back in his chair. All this self-doubt was pointless. He knew he would never stop until he was forced to stop. From childhood on, he knew that the world was his to change, if he found the right levers to pull. Other children bought the stupid idea that they had to wait until they grew up to do anything important. Peter knew better from the start. *He* could never have been fooled the way Ender was into thinking he was playing a game. For Peter, the only game worth playing was the real world. The only reason Ender was fooled was because he let other people shape reality for him. That had never been Peter's problem.

Except that all Peter's influence on the real world had been possible only because he could hide behind the anonymity of the net. He had created a persona—two personas—that could change the world because nobody knew they were children and therefore ignorable. But when it came to armies and navies clashing in the real world, the influence of political thinkers receded. Unless, like Winston Churchill, they were recognized as being so wise and so right that when the crisis came, the reins of real power were put in their hands. That was fine for Winston—old, fat, and full of booze as he was, people still took him seriously. But as far as anyone who saw Peter Wiggin could know, he was still a kid.

Still, Winston Churchill had been the inspiration for Peter's plan. Make Locke seem so prescient, so right about everything, that when war began, public fear of the enemy and public trust in Locke would overwhelm their disdain for youth and allow Peter to reveal the face behind the mask and, like Winston, take his place as leader of the good guys.

Well, he had miscalculated. He had not guessed that Chamrajnagar already knew who he was. Peter wrote to him as the first step in a public campaign to get the Battle School children under the protection of the Fleet. Not so that they would actually be removed from their home countries—he never expected any government to allow *that*—but so that, when someone moved against them, it would be widely known that Locke had sounded the warning. But Chamrajnagar had forced Peter to keep Locke silent, so no one knew that Locke had foreseen the kidnappings but Chamrajnagar and Graff. The opportunity had been missed.

Peter wouldn't give up. There was some way to get back on track. And sitting there in the library in Greensboro, North Carolina, leaning back in a chair with his eyes closed like any other weary student, he'd think of it.

They rousted Ender's jeesh out of bed at 0400 and assembled them in the dining room. No one explained anything, and they were forbidden to talk. So they waited for five minutes, ten, twenty. Petra knew that the others were bound to be thinking the same things she was thinking: The Russians had caught on that they were sabotaging their own battle plans. Or maybe somebody had noticed the coded message in the dragon picture. Whatever it was, it wasn't going to be nice.

Thirty minutes after they were rousted, the door opened. Two soldiers came in and stood at attention. And then, to Petra's utter surprise, in walked . . . a kid. No older than they were. Twelve? Thirteen? Yet the soldiers were treating him with respect. And the kid himself moved with the easy confidence of authority. He was in charge here. And he loved it.

Had Petra seen him before? She didn't think so. Yet he looked at them as if he knew them. Well, of course he did— if he had authority here, he had no doubt been observing them for the weeks they'd been in captivity.

A child in charge. Had to be a Battle School kid—why

else would a government give such power to somebody so young? From his age they had to be contemporaries. But she couldn't place him. And her memory was very, very good.

"Don't worry," said the boy. "The reason you don't know me is that I came to Battle School late, and I was only there a little while before you all left for Tactical. But I know *you*." He grinned. "Or is there someone here who *did* know me when I came in? Don't worry, I'll be studying the vid later. Looking for that little shock of recognition. Because if any of you did know me, well, then I'll know something more about you. I'll know that I saw you once before, silhouetted in the dark, walking away from me, leaving me for dead."

With that, Petra knew who he was. Knew because Crazy Tom had told them about it—how Bean had set a trap for this boy that he knew in Rotterdam, and with the help of four other kids had hung him up in an air shaft until he confessed to a dozen murders or so. They left him there, gave the recording to the teachers, and told them where he was. Achilles.

The only member of Ender's jeesh who had been with Bean that day was Crazy Tom. Bean had never talked about it, and no one asked. It made Bean a figure of mystery, that he had come from a life so dark and frightening that it was peopled with monsters like Achilles. What none of them had ever expected was to find Achilles, not in a mental institution or a prison, but here in Russia with soldiers under his command and themselves as his prisoners.

When Achilles studied the vids, it was possible that Crazy Tom would show recognition. And when he told his story, he would no doubt see recognition on all their faces. She had no idea what this meant, but she knew it couldn't be good. One thing was certain—she wasn't going to let Crazy Tom face the consequences alone.

"We all know who you are," said Petra. "You're Achilles. And nobody left you for dead, the way Bean told it. They left you for the teachers. To arrest and send you back to Earth. To a mental institution, no doubt. Bean even showed us your picture. If anybody recognized you, it was from that."

Achilles turned to her and smiled. "Bean would never tell that story. He would never show my picture."

"Then you don't know Bean," said Petra. She hoped the others would realize that admitting they heard it from Crazy Tom would be dangerous to him. Probably fatal, with this oomay in charge of the triggers. Bean wasn't here, so naming him as the source made sense.

"Oh, yes, you're quite the team," said Achilles. "Passing signals to each other, sabotaging the plans you submit, thinking we'll be too stupid to notice. Did you really think we'd set you to work on *real* plans before we turned you?"

As usual, Petra couldn't shut up. But she didn't really want to, either. "Trying to see which of us felt like outsiders, so you could turn them?" she said. "What a joke—there *were* no outsiders in Ender's jeesh. The only outsider here is you."

In fact, though, she knew perfectly well that Carn Carby, Shen, Vlad, and Fly Molo felt like outsiders, for various reasons. She felt like one herself. Her words were designed only to urge them all to maintain solidarity.

"So now you divide us up and start working on us," said Petra. "Achilles, we know your moves before you make them."

"You really can't hurt my pride," said Achilles. "Because I don't have any. All I care about is uniting humanity under one government. Russia is the only nation, the only *people* who have the will to greatness and the power to back it up. You're here because some of you might be useful in that effort. If we think you have what it takes, we'll invite you to join us. The rest of you, we'll just keep on ice till the war is over. The real losers, well, we'll send you home and hope your home government uses you against us." He grinned. "Come on, don't look so grim. You know you were going crazy back home. You didn't even know those people. You left them when you were so little you still got shit on your fingers when you wiped your ass. What did they know about you? What did you know about them? That they let you go. Me, I didn't have any families, Battle School just meant three meals a day. But you, they took away everything from you. You don't owe them anything. What you've got is your mind. Your talent. You've been tagged for greatness. You won their war with the Buggers for them. And they sent you home so your parents could go back to *raising* you?"

Nobody said anything. Petra was sure they all had as much contempt for his spiel as she did. He knew nothing about them. He'd never be able to divide them. He'd never win their loyalty. They knew too much about him. And they didn't like being held against their will.

He knew it, too. Petra saw it in his eyes, the rage dancing there as he realized that they had nothing but contempt for him.

At least he could see *her* contempt, because he zeroed in on her, took a few steps closer, smiling ever more kindly.

"Petra, it's so nice to meet you," he said. "The girl who tested so aggressive they had to check your DNA to make sure you weren't really a boy."

Petra felt the blood drain from her face. Nobody was supposed to know about that. It was a test the psychiatrists in Ground School had ordered when they decided her contempt for them was a symptom of dysfunction instead of what they deserved for asking her such stupid questions. It wasn't even supposed to be in her file. But apparently a record existed somewhere. Which was, of course, the message Achilles intended to get across to them: He knew everything. And, as a side benefit, it would start the others wondering just how piffed up she was.

"Ten of you. Only two missing from the glorious victory. Ender, the great one, the genius, the keeper of the holy grail—he's off founding a colony somewhere. We'll all be in our fifties by the time he gets there, and he'll still be a little kid. We're going to make history. He *is* history." Achilles smirked at his pun.

But Petra knew that mocking Ender wasn't going to play with this group. Achilles no doubt assumed that the ten of them were also-rans, runners-up, the ones who wanted to have Ender's job and had to sit there and watch him do it. He assumed that they were all burning with envy—because he would have been eaten alive with it. But he was wrong. He didn't understand them at all. They *missed* Ender. They were Ender's jeesh. And this yelda actually thought that he could forge them into a team the way Ender had.

"And then there's Bean," Achilles went on. "The youngest of you, the one whose test scores made you all look like halfwits. He could teach the rest of you classes in how to lead armies—except you probably wouldn't understand him, he's such a genius. Where *could* he be? Anybody miss him?"

Nobody answered. This time, though, Petra knew that the silence hid a different set of feelings. There had been some resentment of Bean. Not because of his brilliance, or at least no one admitted resenting him for that. What annoyed them was the way he just assumed he knew better than anyone. And that awkward time before Ender arrived on Eros, when Bean was the acting commander of the jeesh, that was hard on some of them, taking orders from the youngest of them. So maybe Achilles had guessed right about that.

Except that nobody was proud of those feelings, and bringing them out in the open didn't exactly make them love Achilles. Of course, it might be shame he was trying to provoke. Achilles might be smarter than they thought.

Probably not. He was so out of his league in trying to scope this group of military prodigies that he might as well be wearing a clown suit and throwing water balloons for all the respect he was going to get.

"Ah, yes, Bean," said Achilles. "I'm sorry to inform you that he's dead."

This was apparently too much for Crazy Tom, who yawned and said, "No he's not."

Achilles looked amused. "You think you know more about it than I do?"

"We've been on the nets," said Shen. "We'd know."

"You've been away from your desks since 2200. How do you know what's been happening while you slept?" Achilles glanced at his watch. "Oops, you're right. Bean *is* still alive right now. And for another fifteen minutes or so. Then . . . whoosh! A nice little rocket straight to his little bedroom to blow him up right on his little bed. We didn't even have to buy his location from the Greek military. Our friends there gave us the information for free."

Petra's heart sank. If Achilles could arrange for them to be kidnapped, he could certainly arrange for Bean to be killed. Killing was always easier than taking someone alive.

Did Bean already notice the message in the dragon, decode it, and pass along the information? Because if he's dead, there's no one else who'll be able to do it.

Immediately she was ashamed that the news of Bean's death made her think first of herself. But it didn't mean she didn't care about the kid. It meant that she trusted him so much that she had pinned all her hopes on him. If he died, those hopes died with him. It was not indecent of her to think of that.

To say it out loud, *that* would be indecent. But you can't help the thoughts that come to mind.

Maybe Achilles was lying. Or maybe Bean would survive, or get away. And if he died, maybe he'd already decoded the message. Maybe he hadn't. There was nothing Petra could do to change the outcome.

"What, no tears?" said Achilles. "And here I thought you were such close friends. I guess that was all hero-hype." He chuckled. "Well, I'm done with you for now." He turned to a soldier by the door. "Travel time."

The soldier left. They heard a few words of Russian and at once sixteen soldiers came in and divided up, one pair to each of the kids.

"You're being separated now," said Achilles. "Wouldn't want anyone to start thinking of a rescue operation. You can still email each other. We want your creative synergy to continue. After all, you're the finest little military minds that humanity was able to squeeze out in its hour of need. We're all really proud of you, and we look forward to seeing your finest work in the near future."

One of the kids farted loudly.

Achilles only grinned, winked at Petra, and left.

Ten minutes later they were all in separate vehicles, being driven away to points unknown, somewhere in the vast reaches of the largest country on the face of the Earth.

Part Two

ALLIANCES

6

CODE

To: Graff%pilgrimage@colmin.gov
From: Konstan%Briseis@helstrat.gov
Re: Leak

Your Excellency, I write to you
myself because I was most vocifer-
ously opposing to your plan to take
young Julian Delphiki from our protection. I was wrong as we learnt
from the missile assault on former
apartment today leaving two soldiers dead. We are follow your
previous advice by public release
that Julian was killed in attack.
His room was target in late night
and he would die instead of soldiers sleeping there. Penetration
of our system very deep, obviously.
We trust no one now. You were just
in time and I regret my making of
delay. My pride in Hellene military
made me blind. You see I speak

```
Common a little after all, no more
bluffing between me and true friend
to Greece. Because of you and not
me a great national resource is not
destroy.
```

If Bean had to be in hiding, there were worse places he could be than Araraquara. The town, named for a species of parrot, had been kept as something of a museum piece, with cobbled streets and old buildings. They weren't particularly beautiful old buildings or picturesque houses—even the cathedral was rather dull, and not particularly ancient, having been finished in the twentieth century. Still, there was the sense of a quieter way of life that had once been common in Brasil. The growth that had turned nearby Ribeirão Preto into a sprawling metropolis had pretty much passed Araraquara by. And even though the people were modern enough—you heard as much Common on the streets as Portuguese these days—Bean felt at home here in a way that he had never felt in Greece, where the desire to be fully European and fully Greek at the same time distorted public life and public spaces.

"It won't do to feel too much at home," said Sister Carlotta. "We can't stay anywhere for long."

"Achilles is the devil," said Bean. "Not God. He can't reach everywhere. He can't find us without some kind of evidence."

"He doesn't have to reach everywhere," said Sister Carlotta. "Only where we are."

"His hate for us makes him blind," said Bean.

"His fear makes him unnaturally alert."

Bean grinned—it was an old game between them. "It might not be Achilles who took the other kids."

"It might not be gravity that holds us to Earth," said Sister Carlotta, "but rather an unknown force with identical properties."

Then she grinned, too.

Sister Carlotta was a good traveling companion. She had a sense of humor. She understood his jokes and he enjoyed hers. But most of all, she liked to spend hours and hours without saying a thing, doing her work while he did his own. When they did talk, they were evolving a kind of oblique language where they both already knew everything that mattered so they only had to refer to it and the other would understand. Not that this implied they were kindred spirits or deeply attuned. It's just that their lives only touched at a few key points—they were in hiding, they were cut off from friends and family, and the same enemy wanted them dead. There was no one to gossip about because they knew no one. There was no chat because they had no interests beyond the projects at hand: trying to figure out where the other kids were being held, trying to determine what nation Achilles was serving (which would no doubt soon be serving him), and trying to understand the shape the world was taking so they could interfere with it, perhaps bending the course of history to a better end.

That was Sister Carlotta's goal, at least, and Bean was willing to take part in it, given that the same research required for the first two projects was identical to the research required for the last. He wasn't sure that he cared about the shape of history in the future.

He said that to Sister Carlotta once, and she only smiled. "Is it the world outside yourself you don't care about," she said, "or the future as a whole, including your own?"

"Why should I care about narrowing down which things in particular I don't care about?"

"Because if you didn't care about your own future, you wouldn't care whether you were alive to see it, and you wouldn't be going through all this nonsense to stay alive."

"I'm a mammal," said Bean. "I try to live forever whether I actually want to or not."

"You're a child of God, so you care what happens to his children whether you admit it to yourself or not."

It was not her glib response that bothered him, because he expected it—he had provoked it, really, no doubt (he told himself) because he liked the reassurance that *if* there was a God, then Bean mattered to him. No, what bothered him was the momentary darkness that passed across her face. A fleeting expression, barely revealed, which he would not have noticed had he not known her face so well, and had darkness so rarely been expressed on it.

Something that I said made her feel sad. And yet it was a sadness that she wants to conceal from me. What did I say? That I'm a mammal? She's used to my gibes about her religion. That I might not want to live forever? Perhaps she worries that I'm depressed. That I try to live forever, despite my desires? Perhaps she fears that I'll die young. Well, that was why they were in Araraquara—to prevent his early death. And hers, too, for that matter. He had no doubt, though, that if a gun were pointed at him, she would leap in front of him to take the bullet. He did not understand why. He would not do the same for her, or for anyone. He would try to warn her, or pull her out of the way, or interfere with the shooter, whatever he could do that left them both a reasonable chance of survival. But he would not deliberately die to save her.

Maybe it was a thing that women did. Or maybe that grown-ups did for children. To give your life to save someone else. To weigh your own survival and decide that it mattered less to you than the survival of another. Bean could not fathom how anyone could feel that way. Shouldn't the irrational mammal take over, and force them to act for their own survival? Bean had never tried to suppress his own survival instinct, but he doubted that he could even if he tried. But then, maybe older people were more willing to part with their lives, having already spent the bulk of their starting capital. Of course, it made sense for parents to sacrifice themselves for the sake of their children, particularly parents too old to make more babies. But Sister Carlotta had never had children. And Bean was not the only one that she would die for. She would leap out to take a bullet for a stranger. She valued her own life less than anyone's. And that made her utterly alien to him.

Survival, not of the fittest, but of myself—that is the purpose at the core of my being. That is the reason, ultimately, that I do all the things that I've done. There have been moments when I felt compassion—when, alone of Ender's jeesh, I knowingly sent men to their certain deaths, I felt a deep sorrow for them. But I sent them, and they went. Would I, in their place, have gone as they did, obeying an order? Dying to save unknown future generations who would never know their names?

Bean doubted it.

He would gladly serve humanity if it happened also to serve himself. Fighting the Formics alongside Ender and the other kids, that made sense because saving humanity included saving Bean. And if by managing to stay alive somewhere in the world, he was also a thorn in the side of Achilles, making him less cautious, less wise, and therefore easier to defeat—well, it was a pleasant bonus that Bean's pursuit of his own survival happened also to give the human race a chance to defeat the monster. And since the best way to survive would be to find Achilles and kill him first, he might turn out to be one of the great benefactors of human history. Though now that he thought about it, he couldn't remember a single assassin who was remembered as a hero. Brutus, perhaps. His reputation had had its ups and downs. Most assassins, though, were despised by history. Probably because successful assassins tended to be those whose target was not particularly dangerous to anyone. By the time everyone agreed that a particular monster was well worth assassinating, the monster had far too much power and paranoia to leave any possibility of an assassination actually being carried out.

He got nowhere when he tried to discuss it with Sister Carlotta.

"I can't argue with you so I don't know why you bother. I only know that I won't help you plot his assassination."

"You don't consider it self-defense?" said Bean. "What is this, one of those stupid vids where the hero can never actually kill a bad guy who isn't actually pointing a gun at him right that very moment?"

"It's my faith in Christ," said Carlotta. "Love your enemy, do good to those who hate you."

"Well, where does that leave us? The nicest thing we could do for Achilles would be to post our address on the nets and wait for him to send someone to kill us."

"Don't be absurd," said Carlotta. "Christ said be *good* to your enemies. It wouldn't be good for Achilles to find us, because then he'd kill us and have even more murders to answer for before the judgment bar of God. The best thing we can do for Achilles is to keep him from killing us. And if we love him, we'll stop him from ruling the world while we're at it, since power like that would only compound his opportunities to sin."

"Why don't we love the hundreds and thousands and millions of people who'll die in the wars he's planning to launch?"

"We do love them," said Carlotta. "But you're confused the way so many people are, who don't understand the perspective of God. You keep thinking that death is the most terrible thing that can happen to a person, but to God, death just means you're coming home a few moments ahead of schedule. To God, the dreadful outcome of a human life is when that person embraces sin and rejects the joy that God offers. So of all the millions who might die in a war, each individual life is tragic only if it ends in sin."

"So why are you going to such trouble to keep *me* alive?" asked Bean, thinking he knew the answer.

"You want me to say something that will weaken my case," said Carlotta. "Like telling you that I'm human and so I want to prevent your death right now because I love you. And that's true, I have no children but you're as close as I come to having any, and I would be stricken to the soul if you died at the hands of that twisted boy. But in truth, Julian Delphiki, the reason I work so hard to prevent your death is because, if you died today, you would probably go to hell."

To his surprise, Bean was stung by this. He understood enough of what Carlotta believed that he could have predicted this attitude, but the fact that she put it into words still hurt. "I'm not going to repent and get baptized, so I'm bound to go to hell, therefore no matter when I die I'm doomed," he said.

"Nonsense. Our understanding of doctrine is not perfect, and no matter what the popes have said, I don't believe for a moment that God is going to damn for eternity the billions of children he allowed to be born and die without baptism. No, I think you're likely to go to hell because, despite all your brilliance, you are still quite amoral. Sometime before you die, I pray most earnestly that you will learn that there are higher laws that transcend mere survival, and higher causes to serve. When you give yourself to such a great cause, my dear boy, *then* I will not fear your death, because I know that a just God will forgive you for the oversight of not having recognized the truth of Christianity during your lifetime."

"You really are a heretic," said Bean. "None of those doctrines would pass muster with any priest."

"They don't even pass muster with me," said Carlotta. "But I don't know a soul who doesn't maintain two separate lists of doctrines—the ones that they *believe* that they believe; and the ones that they actually try to live by. I'm simply one of the rare ones who knows the difference. You, my boy, are not."

"Because I don't believe in any doctrines."

"That," said Carlotta with exaggerated smugness, "is proof positive of my assertion. You are so convinced that you believe only what you believe that you believe, that you remain utterly blind to what you *really* believe without believing you believe it."

"You were born in the wrong century," said Bean. "You could make Thomas Aquinas tear out his hair. Nietzsche and Derrida would accuse you of obfuscation. Only the Inquisition would know what to do with you—toast you nice and brown."

"Don't tell me you've actually read Nietzsche and Derrida. Or Aquinas, for that matter."

"You don't have to eat the entire turd to know that it's not a crab cake."

"You arrogant impossible boy."

"But Geppetta, I'm *not* a real boy."

"You're certainly not a puppet, or not *my* puppet, anyway. Go outside and play now, I'm busy."

Sending him outside was not a punishment, however. Sister Carlotta knew that. From the moment they got their desks linked to the nets, they had both spent most of every day indoors, gathering information. Carlotta, whose identity was shielded by the firewalls in the Vatican computer system, was able to continue all her old relationships and thus had access to all her best sources, taking care only to avoid saying where she was or even what time zone she was in. Bean, however, had to create a new identity from scratch, hiding behind a double blind of mail servers specializing in anonymity, and even then he kept no identity for longer than a week. He formed no relationships and therefore could develop no sources. When he needed specific information, he had to ask Carlotta to help him find it, and then she had to determine whether it was something she might legitimately ask, or whether it was something that might be a clue that she had Bean with her. Most of the time she decided she dared not ask. So Bean was crippled in his research. Still, they shared what information they could, and despite his disadvantages, there was one advantage that remained to him: The mind looking at his data was his own. The mind that had scored higher than anyone else on the Battle School tests.

Unfortunately, Truth did not care much about such credentials. It refused to give up and reveal itself just because it realized you were bound to find it eventually.

Bean could only take so many hours of frustration before he had to get up and go outside. It wasn't just to get away from his work, however. "The climate agrees with me," he told Sister Carlotta on their second day, when, dripping with sweat, he headed for his third shower since waking. "I was born to live with heat and humidity."

At first she had insisted on going everywhere with him. But after a few days he was able to persuade her of several things. First, he looked old enough not to be accompanied by his grandmother everywhere he went—"Avó Carlotta" was what he called her here, their cover story. Second, she would be no protection for him anyway, since she had no weapons and no defensive skills. Third, he was the one who knew how to live on the streets, and even though Araraquara was hardly the kind of dangerous place that Rotterdam had been when he was younger, he had already mapped in his mind a hundred different escape routes and hiding places, just by reflex. When Carlotta realized that she would need his protection a lot more than he would need hers, she relented and allowed him to go out alone, as long as he did his best to remain inconspicuous.

"I can't stop people from noticing the foreign boy."

"You don't look that foreign," she said. "Mediterranean body types are common here. Just try not to speak a lot. Always look like you have an errand but never like you're in a hurry. But then, it was you who taught *me* that that was how to avoid attracting attention."

And so here he was today, weeks after they arrived in Brasil, wandering the streets of Araraquara and wondering what great cause might make his life worthwhile in Carlotta's eyes. For despite all her faith, it was *her* approval, not God's, that seemed like it might be worth striving for, as long as it didn't interfere with his project of staying alive. Was it enough to be a thorn in Achilles' side? Enough to look for ways to oppose him? Or was there something else he should be doing?

At the crest of one of Araraquara's many hills there was a sorvete shop run by a Japanese-Brazilian family. The family had been in business there for centuries, as their sign proclaimed, and Bean was both amused and moved by this, in light of what Carlotta had said. For this family, making flavored frozen desserts to eat from a cone or cup was the great cause that gave them continuity through the ages. What could be more trivial than that? And yet Bean came here, again and again, because their recipes were, in fact, delicious, and when he thought about how many other people for these past two or three hundred years must have paused and taken a moment's pleasure in the sweet and delicate flavors, in the feel of the smooth sorvete in their mouths, he could not disdain that cause. They offered something that was genuinely good, and people's lives were better because they offered it. It was not a noble cause that would get written up in the histories. But it was not nothing, either. A person could do worse than spend some large percentage of his life in a cause like that.

Bean wasn't even sure what it meant to give himself to a cause. Did that mean turning over his decision-making to someone else? What an absurd idea. In all likelihood there was no one smarter than him on Earth, and though that did not mean he was incapable of error, it certainly meant he'd have to be a fool to turn over his decisions to someone even *more* likely to be wrong.

Why he was wasting time on Carlotta's sentiment-ridden philosophy of life he didn't know. Doubtless that was one of his mistakes—the emotional human aspect of his mentality overriding the inhumanly aloof brilliance that, to his chagrin, only sometimes controlled his thinking.

The sorvete cup was empty. Apparently he had eaten it all without noticing. He hoped his mouth had enjoyed every taste of it, because the eating was done by reflex while he thought his thoughts.

Bean discarded the cup and went his way. A bicyclist

passed him. Bean saw how the cyclist's whole body bounced and rattled and vibrated from the cobblestones. *That* is human life, thought Bean. So bounced around that we can never see anything straight.

Supper was beans and rice and stringy beef in the pensão's public dining room. He and Carlotta ate together in near silence, listening to other people's conversations and the clanking and clinking of dishes and silverware. Any real conversation between them would doubtless leak some memorable bit of information that might raise questions and attract attention. Like, why did a woman who talked like a nun have a grandson? Why did this child who looked to be six talk like a philosophy professor half the time? So they ate in silence except for conversations about the weather.

After supper, as always, they each signed on to the nets to check their mail. Carlotta's mail was interesting and real. All of Bean's correspondents, this week anyway, thought he was a woman named Lettie who was working on her dissertation and needed information, but who had no time for a personal life and so rebuffed with alacrity any attempt at friendly and personal conversation. But so far, there was no way to find Achilles' signature in any nation's behavior. While most countries simply did not have the resources to kidnap Ender's jeesh in such a short time, of those that did have the resources, there was not one that Bean could rule out because they lacked the arrogance or aggressiveness or contempt for law to do it. Why, it could even have been done by Brasil itself—for all he knew, his former companions from the Formic War might be imprisoned somewhere in Araraquara. They might hear in the early morning the rumble of the very garbage truck that picked up the sorvete cup that he threw away today.

"I don't know why people spread these things," said Carlotta.

"What?" asked Bean, grateful for the break from the eye-blearing work he was doing.

"Oh, these stupid superstitious good-luck dragons. There must be a dozen different dragon pictures now."

"Oh, é," said Bean. "They're everywhere, I just don't notice them anymore. Why dragons, anyway?"

"I think this is the oldest of them. At least it's the one I saw first, with the little poem," said Carlotta. "If Dante were writing today, I'm sure there'd be a special place in his hell for people who start these things."

"What poem?"

" 'Share this dragon,' " Carlotta recited. " 'If you do, lucky end for them and you.' "

"Oh, yeah, dragons always bring a lucky end. I mean, what does that poem actually *say*? That you'll die lucky? That it'll be lucky for you to end?"

Carlotta chuckled.

Bored with his correspondence, Bean kept the nonsense going. "Dragons aren't always lucky. They had to discontinue Dragon Army in Battle School, it was so unlucky. Till they revived it for Ender, and no doubt they gave it to him because people thought it was bad luck and they were trying to stack everything against him."

Then a thought passed through his mind, ever so briefly, but it woke him from his lethargy.

"Forward me that picture."

"I bet you already have it on a dozen letters."

"I don't want to search. Send me that one."

"You're still that Lettie person? Haven't you been that one for two weeks now?"

"Five days."

It took a few minutes for the message to be routed to him, but when it finally showed up in his mail, he looked closely at the image.

"Why in the world are you paying attention to this?" asked Carlotta.

He looked up to see her watching him.

"I don't know. Why are you paying attention to the way I'm paying attention to it?" He grinned at her.

"Because you think it matters. I may not be as smart as you are about most things, but I'm very much smarter than you are about you. I know when you're intrigued."

"Just the juxtaposition of the image of a dragon with the word 'end.' Endings really aren't considered all that lucky. Why wouldn't the person write 'luck will come' or 'lucky fate' or something else? Why 'lucky end'?"

"Why not?"

"End. Ender. Ender's army was Dragon."

"Now, that's a little far-fetched."

"Look at the drawing," said Bean. "Right in the middle, where the bitmap is so complicated—there's one line that's damaged. The dots don't line up at all. It's virtually random."

"It just looks like noise to me."

"If you were being held captive but you had computer access, only every bit of mail you sent out was scrutinized, how would you send a message?" asked Bean.

"You don't think this could be a message from—do you?"

"I have no idea. But now that I've thought of it, it's worth looking at, don't you think?"

By now Bean had pasted the dragon image into a graphics program and was studying that line of pixels. "Yes, this is random, the whole line. Doesn't belong here, and it's not just noise because the rest of the image is still completely intact except for this other line that's partly broken. Noise would be randomly distributed."

"See what it is, then," said Carlotta. "You're the genius, I'm the nun."

Soon Bean had the two lines isolated in a separate file and was studying the information as raw code. Viewed as one-byte or two-byte text code, there was nothing that remotely resembled language, but of course it couldn't, could it, or it would never have got out. So *if* it was a message, then it had to be in some kind of code.

For the next few hours Bean wrote programs to help him manipulate the data contained in those lines. He tried mathematical schemes and graphic reinterpretations, but in truth he knew all along that it wouldn't be anything that complex. Because whoever created it would have had to do it without the aid of a computer. It had to be something relatively simple, designed only to keep a cursory examination from revealing what it was.

And so he kept coming back to ways of reinterpreting the binary code as text. Soon enough he came upon a scheme that seemed promising. Two-byte text code, but shifted right by one position for each character, except when the right shift would make it correspond with two actual bytes in memory, in which case double shift. That way a real character would never show up if someone looked at the file with an ordinary view program.

When he used that method on the one line, it came up as text characters only, which was not likely to happen by chance. But the other line came up random-seeming garbage.

So he left-shifted the other line, and it, too, became nothing but text characters.

"I'm in," he said. "And it *is* a message."

"What does it say?"

"I haven't the faintest idea."

Carlotta got up and came to look over his shoulder. "It's not even language. It doesn't divide into words."

"That's deliberate," said Bean. "If it divided into words it would look like a message and invite decoding. The easy way that any amateur can decode language is by checking word lengths and the frequency of appearance of certain letter patterns. In Common, you look for letter groupings that could be 'a' and 'the' and 'and,' that sort of thing."

"And you don't even know what language it's in."

"No, but it's bound to be Common, because they know they're sending it to somebody who doesn't have a key. So it has to be decodable, and that means Common."

"So they're making it easy and hard at the same time?"

"Yes. Easy for me, hard for everyone else."

"Oh, come now. You think this was written to you?"

"Ender. Dragon. I was *in* Dragon Army, unlike most of them. And whom else would they be writing to? I'm outside, they're in. They know that everyone is there but me. And I'm the only person that they'd know they could reach without tipping their hand to everybody else."

"What, did you have some private code?"

"Not really, but what we have is common experience, the slang of Battle School, things like that. You'll see. When I crack it, it'll be because I recognize a word that nobody else would recognize."

"*If* it's from them."

"It is," said Bean. "It's what I'd do. Get word out. This picture is like a virus. It goes everywhere and gets its code into a million places, but nobody knows it's a code because it looks like something that most people think they already understand. It's a fad, not a message. Except to me."

"Almost thou persuadest me," said Carlotta.

"I'll crack it before I go to bed."

"You're too little to drink that much coffee. It'll give you an aneurysm."

She went back to her own mail.

Since the words weren't separated, Bean had to look for other patterns that might give things away. There were no obvious repeated two-letter or three-letter patterns that didn't lead to obvious dead ends. That didn't surprise him. If he had been composing such a message, he would have dropped out all the articles and conjunctions and prepositions and pronouns that he possibly could. Not only that, but most of the words were probably deliberately misspelled to avoid repetitive patterns. But some words would be spelled correctly, and they would be designed to be unrecognizable to most people who weren't from the Battle School culture.

There were only two places where the same character was apparently doubled, one in each line. That might just be the result of one word ending with the same letter that began another, but Bean doubted it. Nothing would be left to chance in this message. So he wrote a little program that would take the doubled letters in one word and, beginning with "aa," show him what the surrounding letters might be to see if anything looked plausible to him. And he started with the doubled letters in the shorter line, because that pair was surrounded by another pair, in a 1221 pattern.

The obvious failures, like "xddx" and "pffp," took no time, but he had to investigate all the variants on "abba" and "adda" and "deed" and "effe" to see what they did to the message. Some were promising and he saved them for later exploration.

"Why is it in Greek now?" asked Carlotta.

She was looking over his shoulder again. He hadn't heard her get up and come over behind him.

"I converted the original message to Greek characters so

that I wouldn't get distracted by trying to read meanings into letters I hadn't decoded yet. The ones I'm actually working on are in Roman letters."

At that moment, his program showed the letters "iggi."

"Piggies," said Sister Carlotta.

"Maybe, but it doesn't flag anything for me." He started cycling through the dictionary matches with "iggi," but none of them did any better than "piggies" had.

"Does it have to be a word?" said Carlotta.

"Well, if it's a number, then this is a dead end," said Bean.

"No, I mean, why not a name?"

Bean saw it at once. "How blind can I be." He plugged the letters *w* and *n* to the positions before and after "iggi" and then spread the results through the whole message, making the program show hyphens for the undeciphered letters. The two lines now read

```
---n--------g---n---n---n---i---n---g
    -n-n-wiggin--
```

"That doesn't look right for Common," said Carlotta. "There should be a lot more *i*'s than that."

"I'm assuming that the message deliberately leaves out letters as much as possible, especially vowels, so it won't look like Common."

"So how will you know when you've decoded it?"

"When it makes sense."

"It's bedtime. I know, you're not sleeping till you've solved it." He barely noticed that she moved away from behind him. He was busy trying the other doubled letter. This time he had a more complicated job, because the letters before and after the double pair were different. It meant far more combinations to try, and being able to eliminate *g, i, n,* and *w* didn't speed up the process all that much.

Again, there were quite a few readings that he saved—more than before—but nothing rang a bell until he got to "jees." The word that Ender's companions in the final battle used for themselves. "Jeesh." Could it be? It was definitely a word that might be used as a flag.

```
h--n--jeesh-g--en--s-ns--n----si---n---s--g
        -n-n-wiggin---
```

If those twenty-seven letters were right, then he had only thirty left to solve. He rubbed his eyes, sighed, and set to work.

It was noon when the smell of oranges woke him. Sister Carlotta was peeling a mexerica orange. "People are eating these things on the street and spitting the pulp on the sidewalk. You can't chew it up enough to swallow it. But the juice is the best orange you'll ever taste in your life."

Bean got out of bed and took the segment she offered him. She was right. She handed him a bowl to spit the pulp into. "Good breakfast," said Bean.

"Lunch," she said. She held up a paper. "I take it you consider this to be a solution?"

It was what he had printed out before going to bed.

```
hlpndrjeeshtgdrenrusbnstun6rmysiz40ntrysbtg
        bnfndwigginptr
```

"Oh," said Bean. "I didn't print out the one with the word breaks." Putting another mexerica segment in his mouth, Bean padded on bare feet to the computer, called up the right file, and printed it. He brought it back, handed it to Carlotta, spat out pulp, and took his own mexerica from her shopping bag and began peeling.

"Bean," she said. "I'm a normal mortal. I get 'help' and is this 'Ender'?"

Bean took the paper from her.

```
hlp ndr jeesh tgdr en rus bns tun 6 rmy siz 40
                   n try sbtg
             bn fnd wiggin ptr
```

"The vowels are left out as much as possible, and there are other misspellings. But what the first line says is, 'Help. Ender's jeesh is together in Russia—' "

"T-g-d-r is 'together'? And 'in' is spelled like French?"

"Exactly," said Bean. "I understood it and it doesn't look like Common." He went on interpreting. "The next part was confusing for a long time, until I realized that the 6 and the 40 were numbers. I got almost all the other letters before I realized that. The thing is, the numbers matter, but there's no way to guess them from context. So the next few words are designed to give a context to the numbers. It says 'Bean's toon was 6'—that's because Ender divided Dragon Army into five toons instead of the normal four, but then he gave me a sort of ad hoc toon, and if you added it to the count, it was number six. Only who would know that except for somebody from Battle School? So only somebody like me would get the number. Same thing with the next one. 'Army size 40.' Everyone in Battle School knew that there were forty soldiers in every army. Unless you counted the commander, in which case it was forty-one, but see, it doesn't matter, because that digit is trivial."

"How do you know that?"

"Because the next letter is *n*. For 'north.' The message is telling their location. They know they're in Russia. And because they can apparently see the sun or at least shadows on the wall, and they know the date, they can calculate their latitude, more or less. Six-four-zero north. Sixty-four north."

"Unless it means something else."

"No, the message is meant to be obvious."

"To you."

"Yes, to me. The rest of that line is 'try sabotage.' I think that means that they're trying to screw up whatever the Russians are trying to make them do. So they're pretending to go along but really gumming up the works. Very smart to get that on record. The fact that Graff was court-martialed after winning the Formic War suggests that they'd better get it on record that they were *not* collaborating with the enemy—in case the other side wins."

"But Russia isn't at war with anybody."

"The Polemarch was Russian, and Warsaw Pact troops were at the heart of his side in the League War. You've got to remember, Russia was the country that was most on the make before the Formics came and started tearing up real estate and forced humanity to unite under the Hegemon and create the International Fleet. They have always felt cheated out of their destiny, and now that the Formics are gone, it makes sense that they'd be eager to get back on the fast track. They don't think of themselves as bad guys, they think of themselves as the only people with the will and the resources to unite the world for real, permanently. They think they're doing a good thing."

"People always do."

"Not always. But yes, to wage war you have to be able to sell your own people on the idea that either you're fighting in self-defense, or you're fighting because you deserve to win, or you're fighting in order to save other people. The Russian people respond to an altruistic sales pitch as easily as anybody else."

"So what about the second line?"

" 'Bean find Wiggin Peter.' They're suggesting that I look for Ender's older brother. He didn't go off on the colony ship with Ender and Valentine. And he's been a player, under the net identity of Locke. And I suppose he's running Demosthenes, too, now that Valentine is gone."

"You knew about that?"

"I knew a lot of things," said Bean. "But the main thing is that they're right. Achilles is hunting for me and he's hunting for you, and he's got all the rest of Ender's jeesh, but he doesn't even know Ender's brother exists and he wouldn't care if he did. But you know and I know that Peter Wiggin would have been in Battle School except for a little character flaw. And for all we know, that character flaw may be exactly what he needs to be a good match against Achilles."

"Or it may be exactly the flaw that makes it so a victory for Peter is no better than a victory for Achilles, in terms of the amount of suffering in the world."

"Well, we won't know until we find him, will we?" said Bean.

"To find him, Bean, you'd have to reveal who you are."

"Yes," said Bean. "Isn't this exciting?" He did an exaggerated wriggle like a little kid being taken to the zoo.

"This is your life you're playing with."

"You're the one who wanted me to find a cause."

"Peter Wiggin isn't a cause, he's dangerous. You haven't heard what Graff had to say about him."

"On the contrary," said Bean. "How do you think I learned about him?"

"But he might be no better than Achilles!"

"I know of several ways already that he's better than Achilles. First, he's not trying to kill us. Second, he's already got a huge network of contacts with people all over the world, some of whom know he's as young as he is but most of whom have no idea. Third, he's ambitious just like Achilles is, only Achilles has already assembled almost all of the children who were tagged as the most brilliant military commanders in the world, while Peter Wiggin will have only one. Me. Do you think he's dumb enough not to use me?"

"*Use* you. That's the operative word here, Bean."

"Well, aren't *you* being used in *your* cause?"

"By God, not by Peter Wiggin."

"I'll bet Peter Wiggin sends a lot clearer messages than God does," said Bean. "And if I don't like what he's doing, I can always quit."

"With someone like Peter, you can't always quit."

"He can't make me think of what I don't want to think about. Unless he's a remarkably stupid genius, he'll know that."

"I wonder if Achilles knows that, as he's trying to squeeze brilliance out of the other children."

"Exactly. Between Peter Wiggin and Achilles, what are the odds that Wiggin could be worse?"

"Oh, it's hard to imagine how that could be."

"So let's start thinking of a way to contact Locke without giving away our identity and our location."

"I'm going to need more mexerica oranges before we leave Brasil," said Carlotta.

Only then did he notice that the two of them had already blown through the whole bagful. "Me too," he said.

As she left, the empty bag in hand, she paused at the door. "You did very well with that message, Julian Delphiki."

"Thanks, Grandma Carlotta."

She left smiling.

Bean held up the message and scanned it again. The only part of the message that he hadn't fully interpreted for her was the last word. He didn't think "ptr" meant Peter. That would have been redundant. "Wiggin" was enough to identify him. No, the "ptr" at the end was a signature. This message was from Petra. She could have tried to write directly to Peter Wiggin. But she had written to Bean, coding it in a way that Peter would never have understood.

She's relying on me.

Bean knew how the others in Ender's jeesh had resented him. Not a lot, but a little. When they were all in Command School on Eros, before Ender arrived, the military had made Bean the acting commander in all their test battles, even though he was the youngest of them all, even younger than Ender. He knew he'd done a good job, and won their respect. But they never liked taking orders from him and were undisguisedly happy when Ender arrived and Bean was dropped back to be one of them. Nobody ever said, "Good job, Bean," or "Hey, you did OK." Except Petra.

She had done for him on Eros the same thing that Nikolai had done for him in Battle School—provided him with a kind word now and then. He was sure that neither Nikolai nor Petra ever realized how important their casual generosity had been to him. But he remembered that when he needed a friend, the two of them had been there for him. Nikolai had turned out, by the workings of not-entirely-coincidental fate, to be his brother. Did that make Petra his sister?

It was Petra who reached out to him now. She trusted him to recognize the message, decode it, and act on it.

There were files in the Battle School record system that said that Bean was not human, and he knew that Graff at least sometimes felt that way because he had overheard those words from his own lips. He knew that Carlotta loved him but she loved Jesus more and anyway, she was old and thought of him as a child. He could rely on her, but she did not rely on him.

In his Earthside life before Battle School, the only friend Bean had ever had was a girl named Poke, and Achilles had murdered her long before. Murdered her only moments after Bean left her, and moments before he realized his mistake and rushed back to warn her and instead found her body floating in the Rhine. She died trying to save Bean, and she died because Bean couldn't be relied upon to take as much care to save her.

Petra's message meant that maybe he had another friend who needed him after all. And this time, he would not turn his back. This time it was his turn to save his friend, or die trying. How's that for a cause, Sister Carlotta?

7

GOING PUBLIC

To:Demosthenes%Tecumseh@freeamer
ica.org, Locke%erasmus@polnet.gov
From: dontbother@firewall.set
Re: Achilles heel

Dear Peter Wiggin,
A message smuggled to me from the
kidnapped children confirms they
are (or were, at the time of sending) together, in Russia near the
sixty-fourth parallel, doing their
best to sabotage those trying to
exploit their military talents.
Since they will doubtless be separated and moved frequently, the
exact location is unimportant, and
I am quite sure you already knew
Russia was the only country with
both the ambition and the means to
acquire all the members of Ender's
jeesh.

I'm sure you recognize the impossibility of releasing these children through military intervention—at the slightest sign of a plausible effort to extract them, they will be killed in order to deprive an enemy of such assets. But it might be possible to persuade either the Russian government or some if not all of those holding the individual children that releasing them is in Russia's best interest. This might be accomplished by exposing the individual who is almost certainly behind this audacious action, and your two identities are uniquely situated to accuse him in a way that will be taken seriously.

Therefore I suggest that you do a bit of research into a break-in at a high-security institution for the criminally insane in Belgium during the League War. Three guards were killed and the inmates were released. All but one were recaptured quickly. The one who got away was once a student at Battle School. He is behind the kidnapping. When it is revealed that this psychopath has control of these children, it will cause grave misgivings inside the Russian command system. It will

```
also give them a scapegoat if they
decide to return the children.

Don't bother trying to trace this
email identity. It already never
existed. If you can't figure out
who I am and how to contact me from
the research you're about to do,
then we don't have much to talk
about anyway.
```

Peter's heart sank when he opened the letter to Demosthenes and saw that it had also been sent to Locke. The salutation "Dear Peter Wiggin" only confirmed it—someone besides the office of the Polemarch had broken his identities. He expected the worst—some kind of blackmail or a demand that he support this or that cause.

To his surprise, the message was nothing of the kind. It came from someone who claimed to have received a message from the kidnapped kids—and gave him a tantalizing path to follow. Of course he immediately searched the news archives and found the break-in at a high-security mental hospital near Genk. Finding the name of the inmate who got away was much harder, requiring that, as Demosthenes, he ask for help from a law enforcement contact in Germany, and then, as Locke, for additional help from a friend in the Anti-Sabotage Committee in the Office of the Hegemon.

It yielded a name that made Peter laugh, since it was in the subject line of the email that prompted this search. Achilles, pronounced "ah-SHEEL" in the French manner. An orphan rescued from the streets of Rotterdam by, of all things, a Catholic nun working for the procurement section of the

Battle School. He was given surgery to correct a crippled leg, then taken up to Battle School, where he lasted only a few days before being exposed as a serial killer by some of the other students, though in fact he had not killed anyone in the Battle School.

The list of his victims was interesting. He had a pattern of killing anyone who had ever made him feel or seem helpless or vulnerable. Including the doctor who had repaired his leg. Apparently he wasn't much for gratitude.

Putting together the information, Peter could see that his unknown correspondent was right. If in fact this sicko was running the operation that was using these kids for military planning, it was almost certain that the Russian officers working with him did not know his criminal record. Whatever agency liberated Achilles from the mental hospital would not have shared that information with the military who were expected to work with him. There would be outrage that would be heard at the highest levels of the Russian government.

And even if the government did not act to get rid of Achilles and release the kids, the Russian Army jealously guarded its independence from the rest of the government, especially the intelligence-and-dirty-jobs agencies. There was a good chance that some of these children might "escape" before the government acted—indeed, such unauthorized actions might force the government to make it official and pretend that the "early releases" had been authorized.

It was always possible, of course, that Achilles would kill one or more of the kids as soon as he was exposed. At least Peter would not have to face those particular children in battle. And now that he knew something about Achilles, Peter was in a much better position to face him in a head-to-head struggle. Achilles killed with his own hands. Since that was a very stupid thing to do, and Achilles did not test stupid, it had to be an irresistible compulsion. People with irresistible compulsions could be terrifying enemies—but they could also be beaten.

For the first time in weeks, Peter felt a glimmer of hope. This was how his work as Locke and Demosthenes paid off—people with certain kinds of secret information that they wanted to make public found ways to hand it to Peter without his even having to ask for it. Much of his power came from this disorganized network of informants. It never bothered his pride that he was being "used" by this anonymous correspondent. As far as Peter was concerned, they were using each other. And besides, Peter had earned the right to get such helpful gifts.

Still, Peter always looked gift horses in the mouth. As either Locke or Demosthenes, he emailed friends and contacts in various government agencies, trying to get confirmation of various aspects of the story he was preparing to write. Could the break-in at the mental institution have been carried out by Russian agents? Did satellite surveillance show any kind of activity near the sixty-fourth parallel that might correspond with the arrival or departure of the ten kidnapped kids? Was anything known about the whereabouts of Achilles that would contradict the idea of his being in control of the whole kidnap operation?

It took a couple of days to get the story right. He tried it first as a column by Demosthenes, but he soon realized that since Demosthenes was constantly putting out warnings about Russian plots, he might not be taken very seriously. It had to be Locke who published this. And that would be dangerous, because up to now Locke had been scrupulous about not seeming to take sides against Russia. That would now make it more likely that his exposure of Achilles would be taken seriously—but it ran a grave risk of costing Locke some of his best contacts in Russia. No matter how much a Russian might despise what his government was doing, the devotion to Mother Russia ran deep. There was a line you couldn't cross. For more than a few of his contacts there, publishing this piece would cross that line.

Until he hit upon the obvious solution. Before submitting the piece to *International Aspects,* he would send copies to his Russian contacts to give a heads-up on what was coming. Of course the exposé would fly through the Russian military. It was possible that the repercussions would begin even before his column officially appeared. And his contacts would know he wasn't trying to hurt Russia—he was giving them a chance to clean house, or at least put a spin on the story before it ran.

It wasn't a long story, but it named names and opened doors that other reporters could follow up on. And they *would* follow up. From the first paragraph, it was dynamite.

> The mastermind behind the kidnapping of Ender's "jeesh" is a serial killer named Achilles. He was taken from a mental institution during the League War in order to bring his dark genius to bear on Russian military strategy. He has repeatedly murdered with his own hands, and now ten brilliant children who once saved the world are completely at his mercy. What were the Russians thinking when they gave power to this psychopath? Or was Achilles' bloody record concealed even from them?

There it was—in the first paragraph, right along with the accusation, Locke was generously providing the spin that would allow the Russian government and military to extricate themselves from this mess.

It took twenty minutes to send the individual messages to all his Russian contacts. In each message, he warned them that they had only about six hours before he had to turn in his column to the editor at *International Aspects*. *IA*'s fact-checkers would add another hour or two to the delay, but they would find complete confirmation of everything.

Peter pushed SEND, SEND, SEND.

Then he settled down to pore over the data to figure out how it revealed to him the identity of his correspondent. Another mental patient? Hardly likely—they were all brought back into confinement. An employee of the mental hospital? Impossible for someone like that to find out who was behind Locke and Demosthenes. Someone in law enforcement? More likely—but few names of investigators were offered in the news stories. Besides, how could he know *which* of the investigators had tipped him off? No, his correspondent had promised, in effect, a unique solution. Something in the data would tell him *exactly* who his inform-ant was, and exactly how to reach him. Emailing investigators indiscriminately would serve only to risk expos-ing Peter with no guarantee that any of the people he contacted would be the right one.

The one thing that did not happen as he searched for his correspondent's identity was any kind of response from any of his Russian friends. If the story had been wrong, or if the Russian military had already known about Achilles' history and wanted to cover it up, he would have been getting con-stant emails urging him not to run the story, then demanding, and finally threatening him. So the fact that no one wrote him at all served as all the confirmation he needed from the Russian end.

As Demosthenes, he was anti-Russian. As Locke, he was reasonable and fair to all nations. As Peter, though, he was

envious of the Russian sense of national identity, the cohe-
siveness of Russians when they felt their country was in
danger. If Americans had ever had such powerful bonds,
they had expired long before Peter was born. To be Russian
was the most powerful part of a person's identity. To be
American was about as important as being a Rotarian—very
important if you were elected to high office, but barely
noticeable in most citizens' sense of who they were. That
was why Peter never planned his future with America in
mind. Americans expected to get their way, but they had no
passion for anything. Demosthenes could stir up anger and
resentment, but it amounted to spitefulness, not purpose.
Peter would have to root himself elsewhere. Too bad Russia
wasn't available to him. It was a nation that had a vast will to
greatness, coupled with the most extraordinary run of stupid
leadership in history, with the possible exception of the kings
of Spain. And Achilles had got there first.

Six hours after sending the article to his Russian contacts,
he pushed SEND once more, submitting it to his editor. As he
expected, three minutes later he got a response.

You're sure?

To which Peter replied, "Check it. My sources confirm."
Then he went to bed.

And woke up almost before he had gone to sleep. He
couldn't have closed his book, and then his eyes, for more
than a couple of minutes before he realized that he had been
looking in the wrong direction for his informant. It wasn't one
of the investigators who tipped him off. It was someone connected to the I.F. at the highest level, someone who knew
that Peter Wiggin was Locke and Demosthenes. But not Graff
or Chamrajnagar—they would not have left hints about who

they really were. Someone else, someone in whom they confided, perhaps.

But no one from the I.F. had turned up in the information about Achilles' escape. Except for the nun who found Achilles in the first place.

He reread the message. Could this have come from a nun? Possibly, but why would she be sending the information so anonymously? And why would the kidnapped children smuggle a message to her?

Had she recruited one of them?

Peter got out of bed and padded to his desk, where he called up the information on all the kidnapped children. Every one of them came to Battle School through the normal testing process; none had been found by the nun, and so none of them would have any reason to smuggle a message to her.

What other connection could there be? Achilles was an orphan on the streets of Rotterdam when Sister Carlotta identified him as having military talent—he couldn't have had any family connections. Unless he was like that Greek kid from Ender's jeesh who was killed in a missile attack a few weeks ago, the supposed orphan whose real family was identified while he was in Battle School.

Orphan. Killed in a missile attack. What was his name? Julian Delphiki. Called Bean. A name he picked up when he was an orphan . . . where?

Rotterdam. Just like Achilles.

It was not a stretch to imagine that Sister Carlotta found both Bean and Achilles. Bean was one of Ender's companions on Eros during the last battle. He was the only one who, instead of being kidnapped, had been killed. Everyone assumed it was because he was so heavily protected by the Greek military that the would-be kidnappers gave up and settled for keeping rival powers from using him. But what if there was never any intention to kidnap him, because Achilles already knew him and, more to the point, Bean knew too much about Achilles?

And what if Bean was not dead at all? What if he was living in hiding, protected by the widespread belief that he was dead? It was absolutely believable that the captive kids would choose him to receive their smuggled message, since he was the only one of their group, besides Ender himself, who wasn't in captivity with them. And who else would have such a powerful motive to work to get them out, along with the proven mental ability to think of a strategy like the one the informant had laid out in his letter?

A house of cards, that's what he was building, one leap after another—but each intuitive jump felt absolutely right. That letter was written by Bean. Julian Delphiki. And how would Peter contact him? Bean could be anywhere, and there was no hope of contacting him since anybody who knew he was alive would be all the more certain to pretend that he was dead and refuse to accept a message for him.

Again, the solution should be obvious from the data, and it was. Sister Carlotta.

Peter had a contact in the Vatican—a sparring partner in the wars of ideas that flared up now and then among those who frequented the discussions of international relations on the nets. It was already morning in Rome, though barely. But if anyone was at his desk early in Italy, it would be a hard-working monk attached to the Vatican foreign-affairs office.

Sure enough, an answer came back within fifteen minutes.

```
Sister  Carlotta's  location  is
protected.  Messages  can be for-
warded.  I will not read what you
send via me. (You can't work here
```

```
if you don't know how to keep your
eyes closed.)
```

Peter composed his message to Bean and sent it—to Sister Carlotta. If anyone knew how to reach Julian Delphiki in hiding, it would be the nun who had first found him. It was the only possible solution to the challenge his informant had given him.

Finally he went back to bed, knowing that he wouldn't sleep long—he'd undoubtedly keep waking through the night and checking the nets to see the reaction to his column.

What if no one cared? What if nothing happened? What if he had fatally compromised the Locke persona, and for no gain?

As he lay in bed, pretending to himself that he might sleep, he could hear his parents snoring in their room across the hall. It was both strange and comforting to hear them. Strange that he could be worrying about whether something he had written might *not* cause an international incident, and yet he was still living in his parents' house, their only child left at home. Comforting because it was a sound he had known since infancy, that comforting assurance that they were alive, they were close by, and the fact that he could hear them meant that when monsters leapt from the dark corners of the room, they would hear him screaming.

The monsters had taken on different faces over the years, and hid in corners of rooms far from his own, but that noise from his parents' bedroom was proof that the world had not ended yet.

Peter wasn't sure why, but he knew that the letter he had just sent to Julian Delphiki, via Sister Carlotta, via his friend in the Vatican, would put an end to his long idyll, playing at world affairs while having his mother do his laundry. He was finally putting himself into play, not as the cool and distant commentator Locke or the hot-blooded demagogue Demosthenes, both of them electronic constructs, but as Peter Wiggin, a young man of flesh and blood, who could be caught, who could be harmed, who could be killed.

If anything should have kept him awake, it was that thought. But instead he felt relieved. Relaxed. The long waiting was almost over. He fell asleep and did not wake until his mother called him to breakfast.

His father was reading a newsprint at breakfast. "What's the headline, Dad?" asked Peter.

"They're saying that the Russians kidnapped those kids. And put them under the control of a known murderer. Hard to believe, but they seem to know all about this Achilles guy. Got busted out of a mental hospital in Belgium. Crazy world we live in. Could have been Ender." He shook his head.

Peter could see how his mother froze for just a moment at the mention of Ender's name. Yes, yes, Mother, I know he's the child of your heart and you grieve every time you hear his name. And you ache for your beloved daughter Valentine who has left Earth and will never return, not in your lifetime. But you still have your firstborn with you, your brilliant and good-looking son Peter, who is bound to produce brilliant and beautiful grandchildren for you someday, along with a few other things like, oh, who knows, maybe bringing peace to Earth by unifying it under one government? Will that console you just a little bit?

Not likely.

"The killer's name is . . . Achilles?"

"No last name. Like some kind of pop singer or something."

Peter cringed inside. Not because of what his father had said, but because Peter had come *this* close to correcting his father's pronunciation of "Achilles." Since Peter couldn't be sure that any of the rags mentioned the French pronunciation of Achilles' name, how would he explain knowing the correct pronunciation to Father?

"Has Russia denied it, of course?" asked Peter.

Father scanned the newsprint again. "Nothing about it in this story," he said.

"Cool," said Peter. "Maybe that means it's true."

"If it was true," said Father, "they *would* deny it. That's the way Russians are."

As if Father knew anything at all about the "way Russians are."

Got to move out, thought Peter, and live on my own. I'm in college. I'm trying to spring ten prisoners from custody a third of the way around the world. Maybe I should use some of the money I've been earning as a columnist to pay rent.

Maybe I should do it right away, so that if Achilles finds out who I am and comes to kill me, I won't bring danger down on my family.

Only Peter knew even as he formed this thought that there was another, darker thought hidden deep inside himself: Maybe if I get out of here, they'll blow up the house when I'm not there, the way they must have done with Julian Delphiki. Then they'll think I'm dead and I'll be safe for a while.

No, I don't wish for my parents to die! What kind of monster would wish for that? I don't want that.

But one thing Peter never did was lie to himself, or at least not for long. He didn't wish for his parents to die, certainly not violently in an attack aimed at him. But he knew that if it did happen, he'd prefer not to be with them at the time. Better, of course, if no one was home. But . . . me first.

Ah yes. *That* was what Valentine hated about him. Peter

had almost forgotten. *That's* why Ender was the son that everyone loved. Sure, Ender wiped out a whole species of aliens, not to mention offing a kid in a bathroom in Battle School. But he wasn't *selfish* like Peter.

"You aren't eating, Peter," said Mother.

"Sorry," said Peter. "I'm getting some test results back today, and I was brooding I guess."

"What subject?" asked Mother.

"World history," said Peter.

"Isn't it strange to realize that when they write history books in the future, your brother's name will always be mentioned?" said Mother.

"Not strange," said Peter. "That's just one of the perks you get when you save the world."

Behind his jocularity, though, he made a much grimmer promise to his mother. Before you die, Mother, you'll see that while Ender's name shows up in a chapter or two, it will be impossible to discuss this century or the next without mentioning my name on almost every page.

"Got to run," said Father. "Good luck with the test."

"Already took the test, Dad. I'm just getting the grade today."

"That's what I meant. Good luck on the grade."

"Thanks," said Peter.

He went back to eating while Mother walked Father to the door so they could kiss good-bye.

I'll have that someday, thought Peter. Someone who'll kiss me good-bye at the door. Or maybe just someone to put a blindfold over my head before they shoot me. Depending on how things turn out.

8

BREAD VAN

To: Demosthenes%Tecumseh@freeamer
ica.org
From: unready%cincinnatus@anon.set
Re: satrep

Satellite reports from date Delphiki
family killed: Nine vehicles simul-
taneous departure from northern
Russia location, 64 latitude. Encrypted destination list attached.
Genuine dispersal? Decoy? What's our
best strategy, my friend? Eliminate
or rescue? Are they children or
weapons of mass destruction? Hard
to know. Why did that bastard Locke
get Ender Wiggin sent away? We
could use that boy now I think. As
for why only nine, not ten vehicles:
Maybe one is dead or sick. Maybe one
has turned. Maybe two have turned
and were sent together. All guess-
work. I only see raw satdat, not

```
intelnetcom reports. If you have
other sources on that, feed some
back to me?

Custer
```

Petra knew that loneliness was the tool they were using against her. Don't let the girl talk to any human at all, then when one shows up she'll be so grateful she'll blurt confessions, she'll believe lies, she'll make friends with her worst enemy.

Weird how you can know exactly what the enemy is doing to you and it still works. Like a play her parents took her to her second week back home after the war. It had a four-year-old girl on the stage asking her mother why her father wasn't home yet. The mother is trying to find a way to tell her that the father was killed by an Azerbaijani terrorist bomb—a secondary bomb that went off to kill people trying to rescue survivors of the first, smaller blast. Her father died as a hero, trying to save a child trapped in the wreckage even after the police shouted at him to stay away, there was probably going to be a second blast. The mother finally tells the child.

The little girl stamps her foot angrily and says, "He's *my* papa! Not that little boy's papa!" And the mother says, "That little boy's mama and papa weren't there to help him. Your father did what he hoped somebody else would do for you, if he couldn't be there for you." And the little girl starts to cry and says, "Now he isn't ever going to be there for me. And I don't want somebody else. I want my papa."

Petra sat there watching this play, knowing exactly how cynical it was. Use a child, play on the yearning for family, tie it to nobility and heroism, make the villains the ancestral enemy, and make the child say childishly innocent things while crying. A computer could have written it. But it still worked. Petra cried like a baby, just like the rest of the audience.

That's what isolation was doing to her and she knew it. Whatever they were hoping for, it would probably work. Because human beings are just machines, Petra knew that, machines that do what you want them to do, if you only know the levers to pull. And no matter how complex people might seem, if you just cut them off from the network of people who give shape to their personality, the communities that form their identity, they'll be reduced to that set of levers. Doesn't matter how hard they resist, or how well they know they're being manipulated. Eventually, if you take the time, you can play them like a piano, every note right where you expect it.

Even me, thought Petra.

All alone, day after day. Working on the computer, getting assignments by mail from people who gave no hint of personality. Sending messages to the others in Ender's jeesh, but knowing that their letters, too, were being censored of all personal references. Just data getting transferred back and forth. No netsearches now. She had to file her request and wait for an answer filtered through the people who controlled her. All alone.

She tried sleeping too much, but apparently they drugged her water—they got her so hopped up she couldn't sleep at all. So she stopped trying to play passive resistance games. Just went along, becoming the machine they wanted her to be, pretending to herself that by only pretending to be a machine, she wouldn't actually become one, but knowing at the same time that whatever people pretend to be, they become.

And then comes the day when the door opens and somebody walks in.

Vlad.

He was from Dragon Army. Younger than Petra, and a good guy, but she didn't know him all that well. The bond between them, though, was a big one: Vlad was the only other kid in Ender's jeesh who broke the way Petra did, had to be pulled out of the battles for a day. Everybody was kind to them but they both knew—it made them the weak ones. Objects of pity. They all got the same medals and commendations, but Petra knew that their medals meant less than the others, their commendations were empty, because they were the ones who hadn't cut it while the others did. Not that Petra had ever talked about it with Vlad. She just knew that he knew the same things she knew, because he had been down the same long dark tunnel.

And here he was.

"Ho, Petra," he said.

"Ho, Vlad," she answered. She liked hearing her own voice. It still worked. Liked hearing his, too.

"I guess I'm the new instrument of torture they're using on you," said Vlad.

He said it with a smile. That told Petra that he wanted it to seem like a joke. Which told her that it wasn't really a joke at all.

"Really?" she said. "Traditionally, you're simply supposed to kiss me and let someone else do the torture."

"It's not really torture. It's the way out."

"Out of what?"

"Out of prison. It's not what you think, Petra. The hegemony is breaking up, there's going to be war. The question is whether it drives the world down into chaos or leads to one nation ruling all the others. And if it's one nation, which nation should it be?"

"Let me guess. Paraguay."

"Close," said Vlad. He grinned. "I know, it's easier for me. I'm from Belarus, we make a big deal about being a separate country, but in our hearts, we don't mind the thought of Russia being the country that comes out on top. Nobody outside of Belarus gives a lobster tit about how we're not really Russians. So sure, I wasn't hard to talk into it. And you're Armenian, and they spent a lot of years being oppressed by Russia in the old Communist days. But Petra, just how Armenian are you? What's really good for Armenia anyway? That's what I'm supposed to say to you, anyway. To get you to see that Armenia benefits if Russia comes out on top. No more sabotage. Really help us get ready for the real war. You cooperate, and Armenia gets a special place in the new order. You get to bring in your whole country. That's not nothing, Petra. And if you don't help, that doesn't do a thing for anybody. Doesn't help you. Doesn't help Armenia. Nobody ever knows what a hero you were."

"Sounds like a death threat."

"Sounds like a threat of loneliness and obscurity. You weren't born to be nobody, Petra. You were born to shine. This is a chance to be a hero again. I know you think you don't care, but come on, admit it—it was great being Ender's jeesh."

"And now we're what's-his-name's jeesh. He'll really share the glory with us," said Petra.

"Why not? He's still the boss, he doesn't mind having heroes serve under him."

"Vlad, he'll make sure nobody knows any of us existed, and he'll kill us when he's done with us." She hadn't meant to speak so honestly. She knew it would get back to Achilles. She knew it would guarantee that her prophecy would come true. But there it was—the lever worked. She was so grateful to have a friend there, even one who had obviously been coopted, that she couldn't help but blurt.

"Well, Petra, what can I say? I told them, you're the tough one. I told you what's on offer. Think about it. There's no hurry. You've got plenty of time to decide."

"You're going?"

"That's the rule," said Vlad. "You say no, I go. Sorry."

He got up.

She watched him go out the door. She wanted to say something clever and brave. She wanted some name to call him to make him feel bad for throwing in his lot with Achilles. But she knew that anything she said would be used against her one way or another. Anything she said would reveal another lever to the lever-pullers. What she'd already said was bad enough.

So she kept her silence and watched the door close and lay there on her bed until her computer beeped and she went to it and there was another assignment and she went to work and solved it and sabotaged it just like usual and thought, This is going rather well after all, I didn't break or anything.

And then she went to bed and cried herself to sleep. For a few minutes, though, just before she slept, she felt that Vlad was her truest, dearest friend and she would have done anything for him, just to have him back in the room with her.

Then that feeling passed and she had one last fleeting thought: If they were really all that smart, they would have known that I'd feel like that, right that moment; and Vlad would have come in and I would have leapt from my bed and thrown my arms around him and told him yes, I'll do it, I'll work with you, thank you for coming to me like that, Vlad, thank you.

Only they missed their chance.

As Ender had once said, most victories came from instantly

exploiting your enemy's stupid mistakes, and not from any particular brilliance in your own plan. Achilles was very clever. But not perfect. Not all-knowing. He may not win. I may even get out of here without dying.

Peaceful at last, she fell asleep.

They woke her in darkness.

"Get up."

No greeting. She couldn't see who it was. She could hear footsteps outside her door. Boots. Soldiers?

She remembered talking to Vlad. Rejecting his offer. He said there was no hurry; she had plenty of time to decide. But here they were, rousting her in the middle of the night. To do what?

Nobody was laying a hand on her. She dressed in darkness—they didn't hurry her. If this was supposed to be some sort of torture session or interrogation they wouldn't wait for her to dress, they'd make sure she was as uncomfortable, as off-balance as possible.

She didn't want to ask questions, because that would seem weak. But then, *not* asking questions was passive.

"Where are we going now?"

No answer. That was a bad sign. Or was it? All she knew about these things was from the few fictional war vids she'd seen in Battle School and a few spy movies in Armenia. None of it ever seemed believable to her, yet here she was in a real spy-movie situation and her only source of information about what to expect was those stupid fictional vids and movies. What happened to her superior reasoning ability? The talents that got her into Battle School in the first place? Apparently those only worked when you thought you were playing games in school. In the real world, fear sets in and you fall back on lame made-up stories written by people who had no idea how things like this really worked.

Except that the people doing these things to her had also seen the same dumb vids and movies, so how did she know they weren't modeling *their* actions and attitudes and even their words on what they'd seen in the movies? It's not like anybody had a training course on how to look tough and mean when you were rousting a pubescent girl in the middle of the night. She tried to imagine the instruction manual. *If she is going to be transported to another location, tell her to hurry, she's keeping everyone waiting. If she's going to be tortured, make snide comments about how you hope she got plenty of rest. If she is going to be drugged, tell her that it won't hurt a bit, but laugh snidely so she'll think you're lying. If she is going to be executed, say nothing.*

Oh, this is good, she told herself. Talk yourself into fearing the absolute worst. Make sure you're as close to a state of panic as possible.

"I've got to pee," she said.

No answer.

"I can do it here. I can do it in my clothes. I can do it naked. I can do it in my clothes or naked wherever we're going. I can dribble it along the way. I can write my name in the snow. It's harder for girls, it requires a lot more athletic activity, but we can do it."

Still no answer.

"Or you can let me go to the bathroom."

"All right," he said.

"Which?"

"Bathroom." He walked out the door.

She followed him. Sure enough, there were soldiers out there. Ten of them. She stopped in front of one burly soldier and looked up at his face. "It's a good thing they brought *you*. If it had just been those other guys, I would have made my stand and fought to the death. But with you here, I had no choice but to give myself up. Good work, soldier."

She turned and walked on toward the bathroom. Wondering if she had seen just the faintest hint of a smile on that soldier's face. *That* wasn't in the movie script, was it? Oh, wait. The hero was supposed to have a smart mouth. She was right in character. Only now she understood that all those clever remarks that heroes made were designed to conceal their raw fear. Insouciant heroes aren't brave or relaxed. They're just trying not to embarrass themselves in the moments before they die.

She got to the bathroom and of course he came right in with her. But she'd been in Battle School and if she'd had a shy bladder she would have died of urea poisoning long ago. She dropped trou, sat on the john, and let go. The guy was out the door long before she was ready to flush.

There was a window. There were ceiling air ducts. But she was in the middle of nowhere and it's not like she had anywhere she could run. How did they do this in the vids? Oh, yeah. A friend would have already placed a weapon in some concealed location and the hero would find it, assemble it, and come out firing. That's what was wrong with this whole situation. No friends.

She flushed, rearranged her clothing, washed her hands, and walked back out to her friendly escorts.

They walked her outside to a convoy, of sorts. There were two black limousines and four escort vehicles. She saw two girls about her size and hair color get into the back of each of the limos. Petra, by contrast, was kept close to the building, under the eaves, until she was at the back of a bakery van. She climbed in. None of her guards came with her. There were two men in the back of the van, but they were in civilian clothes. "What am I, bread?" she asked.

"We understand your need to feel that you're in control of the situation through humor," said one of the men.

"What, a psychiatrist? This is worse than torture. What happened to the Geneva convention?"

The psychiatrist smiled. "You're going home, Petra."

"To God? Or Armenia?"

"At this moment, neither. The situation is still . . . flexible."

"I'd say it's flexible, if I'm going home to a place where I've never been before."

"Loyalties have not yet been sorted out. The branch of government that kidnapped you and the other children was acting without the knowledge of the army or the elected government—"

"Or so they say," said Petra.

"You understand my situation perfectly."

"So who are you loyal to?"

"Russia."

"Isn't that what they'll all say?"

"Not the ones who turned our foreign policy and military strategy over to a homicidal maniac child."

"Are those three equal accusations?" asked Petra. "Because *I'm* guilty of being a child. And homicide, too, in some people's opinion."

"Killing buggers was not homicide."

"I suppose it was insecticide."

The psychiatrist looked baffled. Apparently he didn't know Common well enough to understand a wordplay that nine-year-olds thought was endlessly funny in Battle School.

The van began to move.

"Where are we going, since it's not home?"

"We're going into hiding to keep you out of the hands of this monster child until the breadth of this conspiracy can be discovered and the conspirators arrested."

"Or vice versa," said Petra.

The psychiatrist looked baffled again. But then he understood. "I suppose that's possible. But then, I'm not an important man. How would they know to look for me?"

"You're important enough that you have soldiers who obey you."

"They're not obeying me. We're all obeying someone else."

"And who is that?"

"If, through some misfortune, you were retaken by Achilles and his sponsors, you won't be able to answer that question."

"Besides, you'd all be dead before they could get to me, so your names wouldn't matter anyway, right?"

He looked at her searchingly. "You seem cynical about this. We *are* risking our lives to save you."

"You're risking *my* life, too."

He nodded slowly. "Do you want to return to your prison?"

"I just want you to be aware that being kidnapped a second time isn't exactly the same thing as being set free. You're so sure that you're smart enough and your people are loyal enough to bring this off. But if you're wrong, I could get killed. So yes, you're taking risks—but so am I, and nobody asked me."

"I ask you now."

"Let me out of the van right here," said Petra. "I'll take my chances alone."

"No," said the psychiatrist.

"I see. So I *am* still a prisoner."

"You are in protective custody."

"But I am a certified strategic and tactical genius," said Petra, "and you're not. So why are you in charge of *me*?"

He had no answer.

"I'll tell you why," said Petra. "Because this is not about saving the little children who were stolen away by the evil wicked child. This is about saving Mother Russia a lot of embarrassment. So it isn't enough for me to be safe. You have to return me to Armenia under just the right circumstances, with just the right spin, that the faction of the Russian government that you serve will be exonerated of all guilt."

"We are not guilty."

"My point is not that you're lying about that, but that you regard that as a much higher priority than saving me. Because I assure you, riding along in this van, I fully expect to be retaken by Achilles and his . . . what did you call them? Sponsors."

"And why do you suppose that this will happen?"

"Does it matter why?"

"You're the genius," said the psychiatrist. "Apparently you have already seen some flaw in our plan."

"The flaw is obvious. Far too many people know about it. The decoy limousines, and soldiers, the escorts. You're sure that not one of those people is a plant? Because if *any* of them is reporting to Achilles' sponsors, then they already know which vehicle really has me in it, and where it's going."

"They don't know where it's going."

"They do if the driver is the one who was planted by the other side."

"The driver doesn't know where we're going."

"He's just going around in circles?"

"He knows the first rendezvous point, that's all."

Petra shook her head. "I knew you were stupid, because you became a talk-therapy shrink, which is like being a minister of a religion in which you get to be God."

The psychiatrist turned red. Petra liked that. He was stupid, and he didn't like hearing it, but he definitely needed to hear it because he clearly had built his whole life around the idea that he was smart, and now that he was playing with live ammunition, thinking he was smart was going to get him killed.

"I suppose you're right, that the driver *does* know where we're going *first*, even if he doesn't know where we plan to go from the first rendezvous." The psychiatrist shrugged elaborately. "But that can't be helped. You have to trust *someone*."

"And you decided to trust this driver because . . . ?"

The psychiatrist looked away.

Petra looked at the other man. "You're talkative."

"I am think," said the man in halting Common, "you make Battle School teachers crazy with talk."

"Ah," said Petra. "*You're* the brains of the outfit."

The man looked puzzled, but also offended—he wasn't sure how he had been insulted, since he probably didn't know the word *outfit*, but he knew an insult had been intended.

"Petra Arkanian," said the psychiatrist, "since you're right that I don't know the driver all that well, tell me what I should have done. You have a better plan than trusting him?"

"Of course," said Petra. "You tell him the rendezvous point, plan with him very carefully how he'll drive there."

"I did that," said the psychiatrist.

"I know," said Petra. "Then, at the last minute, just as you're loading me into the van, you take the wheel and make him ride in one of the limousines. And then you drive to a different place entirely. Or better yet, you take me to the nearest town and turn me loose and let me take care of myself."

Again, the psychiatrist looked away. Petra was amused at how transparent his body language was. You'd think a shrink would know how to conceal his own tells.

"These people who kidnapped you," said the psychiatrist, "they are a tiny minority, even within the intelligence organizations they work for. They can't be everywhere."

Petra shook her head. "You're a Russian, you were taught Russian history, and you actually believe that the intelligence service can't be everywhere and hear everything? What, did you spend your entire childhood watching American vids?"

The psychiatrist had had enough. Putting on his finest medical airs, he delivered his ultimate put-down. "And you're a child who never learned decent respect. You may be brilliant in your native abilities, but that doesn't mean you understand a political situation you know nothing about."

"Ah," said Petra. "The you're-just-a-child, you-don't-have-as-much-experience argument."

"Naming it doesn't mean it's untrue."

"I'm sure you understand the nuances of political speeches and maneuvers. But this is a military operation."

"It is a political operation," the psychiatrist corrected her. "No shooting."

Again, Petra was stunned at the man's ignorance. "Shooting is what happens when military operations fail to achieve their purposes through maneuver. *Any* operation that's intended to physically deprive the enemy of a valued asset is military."

"This operation is about freeing an ungrateful little girl and sending her home to her mama and papa," said the psychiatrist.

"You want me to be grateful? Open the door and let me out."

"The discussion is over," said the psychiatrist. "You can shut up now."

"Is that how you end your sessions with your patients?"

"I never said I was a psychiatrist," said the psychiatrist.

"Psychiatry was your education," said Petra. "And I know you had a practice for a while, because *real* people don't talk like shrinks when they're trying to reassure a frightened child. Just because you got involved in politics and changed careers doesn't mean you aren't still the kind of bonehead who goes to witch-doctor school and thinks he's a scientist."

The man's fury was barely contained. Petra enjoyed the momentary thrill of fear that ran through her. Would he slap her? Not likely. As a psychiatrist, he would probably fall back on his one limitless resource—professional arrogance.

"Laymen usually sneer at sciences they don't understand," said the psychiatrist.

"That," said Petra, "is precisely my point. When it comes to military operations, you're a complete novice. A layman. A bonehead. And I'm the expert. And you're too stupid to listen to me even now."

"Everything is going smoothly," said the psychiatrist. "And you'll feel very foolish and apologize as you thank me when you get on the plane to return to Armenia."

Petra only smiled tightly. "You didn't even look in the cab of this delivery van to make sure it was the same driver before we drove off."

"Someone else would have noticed if the driver changed," said the psychiatrist. But Petra could tell she had finally made him uneasy.

"Oh, yes, I forgot, we trust your fellow conspirators to see all and miss nothing, because, after all, *they* aren't psychiatrists."

"I'm a psychologist," he said.

"Ouch," said Petra. "That must have hurt, to admit you're only half-educated."

The psychologist turned away from her. What was the term the shrinks in Ground School used for that behavior—avoidance? Denial? She almost asked him, but decided to leave well enough alone.

And people thought she couldn't control her tongue.

They rode for a while in bristling silence.

But the things she said must have been working on him, nagging at him. Because after a while he got up and walked to the front and opened the door between the cargo area and the cab.

A deafening gunshot rang through the closed interior, and the psychiatrist fell back. Petra felt hot brains and stinging bits of bone spatter her face and arms. The man across from her started reaching for a weapon under his coat, but he was shot twice and slumped over dead without touching it.

The door from the cab opened the rest of the way. It was Achilles standing there, holding the gun in his hand. He said something.

"I can't hear you," said Petra. "I can't even hear my own voice."

Achilles shrugged. Speaking louder and mouthing the words carefully, he tried again. She refused to look at him.

"I'm not going to try to listen to you," she said, "while I still have his blood all over me."

Achilles set down the gun—far out of her reach—and pulled off his shirt. Bare-chested, he handed it to her, and when she refused to take it, he started wiping her face with it until she snatched it out of his hands and did the job herself.

The ringing in her ears was fading, too. "I'm surprised you didn't wait to kill them until you'd had a chance to tell them how smart you are," said Petra.

"I didn't need to," said Achilles. "You already told them how dumb they were."

"Oh, you were listening?"

"Of course the compartment back here was wired for sound," said Achilles. "And video."

"You didn't have to kill them," said Petra.

"That guy was going for his gun," said Achilles.

"Only after his friend was dead."

"Come now," said Achilles. "I thought Ender's whole method was the preemptive use of ultimate force. I only do what I learned from your hero."

"I'm surprised you did this one yourself," said Petra.

"What do you mean, 'this one'?" said Achilles.

"I assumed you were stopping the other rescues, too."

"You forget," said Achilles, "I've already had months to evaluate you. Why keep the others, when I can have the best?"

"Are you flirting with me?" She said it with as much disdain as she could muster. Those words usually worked to shut down a boy who was being smug. But he only laughed.

"I don't flirt," he said.

"I forgot," said Petra. "You shoot first, and then flirting isn't necessary."

That got to him a little—made him pause a moment, brought the slightest hint of a quickening of breath. It occurred to Petra that her mouth was indeed going to get her killed. She had never actually seen someone get shot before, except in movies and vids. Just because she thought of herself as the protagonist of this biographical vid she was trapped in didn't mean she was safe. For all she knew, Achilles meant to kill her, too.

Or did he? Could he have really meant that she was the only one of the team he was keeping? Vlad would be so disappointed.

"How did you happen to choose me?" she asked, changing the subject.

"Like I said, you're the best."

"That is such kuso," said Petra. "The exercises I did for you weren't any better than anyone else's."

"Oh, those battle plans, those were just to keep you busy while the real tests were going on. Or rather, to make you think you were keeping *us* busy."

"What was this real test, then, since I supposedly succeeded at it better than anyone else?"

"Your little dragon drawing," said Achilles.

She could feel the blood drain from her face. He saw it and laughed.

"Don't worry," said Achilles. "You won't be punished. That was the test, to see which of you would succeed in getting a message outside."

"And my prize is staying with you?" She said it with all the disgust she could put in her voice.

"Your prize," said Achilles, "is staying alive."

She felt sick at heart. "Even you wouldn't kill all the others, for no reason."

"If they're killed, there's a reason. If there's a reason, they'll be killed. No, we suspected that your dragon drawing would have *some* meaning to someone. But we couldn't find a code in it."

"There wasn't a code in it," said Petra.

"Oh yes there was," said Achilles. "You somehow encoded it in such a way that someone was able to recognize it and decode it. I know this because the news stories that suddenly appeared, triggering this whole crisis, had some specific information that was more or less correct. One of the messages you guys tried to send must have gotten through. So we went back over every email sent by every one of you, and the only thing that couldn't be accounted for was your dragon clip art."

"If you can read a message in that," said Petra, "then you're smarter than I am."

"On the contrary," said Achilles. "You're smarter than I am, at least about strategy and tactics—like evading the enemy while keeping in close communication with allies. Well, not all *that* close, since it took them so long to publish the information you sent."

"You bet on the wrong horse," said Petra. "It wasn't a message, and therefore however they got the news it must have come from one of the other guys."

Achilles only laughed. "You're a stubborn liar, aren't you?"

"I'm not lying when I tell you that if I have to keep riding with these corpses in this compartment, I'm going to get sick."

He smiled. "Vomit away."

"So your pathology includes a weird need to hang around with the dead," said Petra. "You'd better be careful—you know where that leads. First you'll start dating them, and then one day you'll bring a dead person home to meet your mother and father. Oops. I forgot, you're an orphan."

"So I brought them to show *you*."

"Why did you wait so long to shoot them?" asked Petra.

"I wanted it set up just right. So I could shoot the one while he was standing in the doorway. So his body would block any returning fire from the other guy. And besides, I was also enjoying the way you took them apart. You know, arguing with them like you did. Sounded like you hate shrinks almost as much as I do. And you were never even committed to a mental institution. I would have applauded several of your best bon mots, only I might have been overheard."

"Who's driving this van?" asked Petra, ignoring his flattery.

"Not me," said Achilles. "Are you?"

"How long are you planning to keep me imprisoned?" asked Petra.

"As long as it takes."

"As long as it takes to do what?"

"Conquer the world together, you and I. Isn't that romantic? Or, well, it *will* be romantic, when it happens."

"It will never be romantic," said Petra. "Nor will I help you conquer your dandruff problem, let alone the world."

"Oh, you'll cooperate," said Achilles. "I'll kill the other members of Ender's jeesh, one by one, until you give in."

"You don't have them," said Petra. "And you don't know where they are. They're safe from you."

Achilles grinned mock-sheepishly. "There's just no fooling Genius Girl, is there? But, you see, they're bound to surface somewhere, and when they do, they'll die. I don't forget."

"That's one way to conquer the world," said Petra. "Kill everybody one by one until you're the only one left."

"Your first job," said Achilles, "is to decode that message you sent out."

"What message?"

Achilles picked up his gun and pointed it at her.

"Kill me and you'll always wonder if I really sent out a message at all," said Petra.

"But at least I won't have to listen to your smug voice lying to me," said Achilles. "That would almost be a consolation."

"You seem to be forgetting that I wasn't a volunteer on this expedition. If you don't like listening to me, let me go."

"You're so sure of yourself," said Achilles. "But I know you better than you know yourself."

"And what is it you think you know about me?" asked Petra.

"I know that you'll eventually give in and help me,"

"Well, I know *you* better than you know yourself, too," said Petra.

"Oh, really?"

"I know that eventually you'll kill me. Because you always do. So let's just skip all the boring stuff in between. Kill me now. End the suspense."

"No," said Achilles. "Things like that are much better as a surprise. Don't you think? At least, that's the way God always did it."

"Why am I even talking to you?" asked Petra.

"Because you're so lonely after being in solitary for all these months that you'd do anything for human company. Even talk to *me*."

She hated that he was probably right. "Human company—apparently you're under the delusion that you qualify."

"Oh, you're mean," said Achilles, laughing. "Look, I'm bleeding."

"You've got blood on your hands, all right."

"And you've got it all over your face," said Achilles. "Come on, it'll be fun."

"And here I thought nothing would ever be more tedious than solitary confinement."

"You're the best, Petra," said Achilles. "Except for one."

"Bean," said Petra.

"Ender," said Achilles. "Bean is nothing. Bean is dead."

Petra said nothing.

Achilles looked at her searchingly. "No smart remarks?"

"Bean is dead and you're alive," said Petra. "There's no justice."

The van slowed down and stopped.

"There," said Achilles. "Our lively conversation made the time *fly* by."

Fly. She heard an airplane overhead. Landing or taking off?

"Where are we flying?" she asked.

"Who says we're flying anywhere?"

"I think we're flying out of the country," said Petra, speaking the ideas as they came to her. "I think you realized that you were going to lose your cushy job here in Russia, and you're sneaking out of the country."

"You're really very good. You keep setting a new standard for cleverness," said Achilles.

"And you keep setting a new standard for failure."

He hesitated a moment, then went on as if she hadn't spoken. "They're going to pit the other kids against me," he said. "You already know them. You know their weaknesses. Whoever I'm up against, you're going to advise me."

"Never."

"We're in this together," said Achilles. "I'm a nice guy. You'll like me, eventually."

"Oh, I know," said Petra. "What's not to like?"

"Your message," said Achilles. "You wrote it to Bean, didn't you?"

"What message?" said Petra.

"That's why you don't believe he's dead."

"I believe he's dead," said Petra. But she knew her earlier hesitation had given her away.

"Or else you wonder—if he got your message before I had

him killed, why did it take so long after he died to have it hit the news? And here's the obvious answer, Pet. Somebody else figured it out. Somebody else decoded it. And that really pisses me off. So don't tell me what the message said. I'm going to decode it myself. It can't be that hard."

"Downright easy," said Petra. "After all, I'm dumb enough to end up as your prisoner. So dumb, in fact, that I never sent anybody a message."

"When I do decode it, though, I hope it won't say anything disparaging about me. Because then I'd have to beat the shit out of you."

"You're right," said Petra. "You *are* a charmer."

Fifteen minutes later, they were on a small private jet, flying south by southeast. It was a luxurious vehicle, for its size, and Petra wondered if it belonged to one of the intelligence services or to some faction in the military or maybe to some crime lord. Or maybe all three at once.

She wanted to study Achilles, watch his face, his body language. But she didn't want him to see her showing interest in him. So she looked out the window, wondering as she did so whether she wasn't just doing the same thing the dead psychologist had done—looking away to avoid facing bitter truth.

When the chime announced that they could unbelt themselves, Petra got up and headed for the bathroom. It was small, but compared to commercial airplane toilets it was downright commodious. And it had cloth towels and real soap.

She did her best with a damp towel to wipe blood and body matter from her clothes. She had to keep wearing the dirty clothing but she could at least get rid of the visible chunks. The towel was so foul by the time she finished the job that she tossed it and got a fresh one to start in on her face and hands. She scrubbed until her face was red and raw, but she got it all off. She even soaped her hair and washed it as best she could in the tiny sink. It was hard to rinse, pouring one cup of water at a time over her head.

The whole time, she kept thinking of the fact that the psychiatrist's last minutes were spent listening to her tell him how stupid he was and point out the worthlessness of his life's work. And yes, she was right, as his death proved, but that didn't change the fact that however impure his motives might have been, he *was* trying to save her from Achilles. He had given his life in that effort, however badly planned it might have been. All the other rescues went off smoothly, and they were probably just as badly planned as hers. So much depended on chance. Everybody was stupid about some things. Petra was stupid about the things she said to people who had power over her. Goading them. Daring them to punish her. She did it even though she knew it was stupid. And wasn't it even stupider to do something stupid that you *know* is stupid?

What did he call her? An ungrateful little girl.

He tagged me, all right.

As bad as she felt about his death, as horrified over what she had seen, as frightened as she was to be in Achilles' control, as lonely as she had been for these past weeks, she still couldn't figure out a way to cry about it. Because deeper than all these feelings was something even stronger. Her mind kept thinking of ways to get word to someone about where she was. She had done it once, she could do it again, right? She might feel bad, she might be a miserable specimen of human life, she might be in the midst of a traumatic childhood experience, but she was *not* going to submit to Achilles for one moment longer than she had to.

The plane lurched suddenly, throwing her against the

toilet. She half-fell onto it—there wasn't room to fall down all the way—but she couldn't get up because the plane had gone into a steep dive, and for a few moments she found herself gasping as the oxygen-rich air was replaced by cold upper-level air that left her dizzy.

The hull was breached. They've shot us down.

And for all that she had an indomitable will to live, she couldn't help but think: Good for them. Kill Achilles now, and no matter who else is on the plane, it'll be a great day for humanity.

But the plane soon leveled out, and the air was breathable before she blacked out. They must not have been very high when it happened.

She opened the bathroom door and stepped back into the main cabin.

The side door was partway open. And standing a couple of meters back from it was Achilles, the wind whipping at his hair and clothes. He was posing, as if he knew just how fine a figure he cut, standing there on the brink of death.

She approached him, glancing at the door to make sure she stayed well back from it, and to see how high they were. Not very, compared to cruising altitude, but higher than any building or bridge or dam. Anyone who fell from this plane would die.

Could she get behind him and push?

He smiled broadly when she got near.

"What happened?" she shouted over the noise of the wind.

"It occurred to me," he yelled back, "that I made a mistake bringing you with me."

He opened the door on purpose. He opened it for her.

Just as she began to step back, his hand lashed out and seized her by the wrist.

The intensity of his eyes was startling. He didn't look

crazy. He looked . . . fascinated. Almost as if he found her amazingly beautiful. But of course it wasn't *her*. It was his power over her that fascinated him. It was himself that he loved so intensely.

She didn't try to pull away. Instead, she twisted her wrist so that she also gripped him.

"Come on, let's jump together," she shouted. "That would be the most romantic thing we could do."

He leaned close. "And miss out on all the history we're going to make together?" he said. Then he laughed. "Oh, I see, you thought I was going to throw you out of the plane. No, Pet, I took hold of you so that I could anchor you while you close the door. Wouldn't want the wind to suck you out, would we?"

"I have a better idea," said Petra. "I'll be the anchor, you close the door."

"But the anchor has to be the stronger, heavier one," said Achilles. "And that's me."

"Let's just leave it open, then," said Petra.

"Can't fly all the way to Kabul with the door open."

What did it mean, his telling her their destination? Did it mean that he trusted her a little? Or that it didn't matter what she knew, since he had decided she was going to die?

Then it occurred to her that if he wanted her dead, she would die. It was that simple. So why worry about it? If he wanted to kill her by pushing her out the door, how was that different from a bullet in the brain? Dead was dead. And if he didn't plan to kill her, the door needed to be closed, and having him serve as anchor was the second-best plan.

"Isn't there somebody in the crew who can do this?" she asked.

"There's just the pilot," said Achilles. "Can *you* land a plane?"

She shook her head.

"So he stays in the cockpit, and we close the door."

"I don't mean to be a nag," said Petra, "but opening the door was a really stupid thing to do."

He grinned at her.

Holding tight to his wrist, she slid along the wall toward the door. It was only partially open, the kind of door that worked by sliding up. So she didn't have to reach very far out of the plane. Still, the cold wind snatched at her arm and made it very hard to get a grip on the door handle to pull it down into place. And even when she got it down into position, she simply didn't have the strength to overcome the wind resistance and pull it snug.

Achilles saw this, and now that the door wasn't open enough for anyone to fall out and the wind could no longer suck anybody out, he let go of her and of the bulkhead and joined her in pulling at the handle.

If I push instead of pulling, thought Petra, the wind will help me, and maybe we'll both get sucked right out.

Do it, she told herself. Do it. Kill him. Even if you die doing it, it's worth it. This is Hitler, Stalin, Genghis, Attila all rolled into one.

But it might not work. He might not get sucked out. She might die alone, pointlessly. No, she would have to find a way to destroy him later, when she could be sure it would work.

At another level, she knew that she simply wasn't ready to die. No matter how convenient it might be for the rest of humanity, no matter how richly Achilles deserved to die, she would not be his executioner, not now, not if she had to give her own life to kill him. If that made her a selfish coward, so be it.

They pulled and pulled and finally, with a whoosh, the

door passed the threshold of wind resistance and locked nicely into place. Achilles pulled the lever that locked it.

"Traveling with you is always such an adventure," said Petra.

"No need to shout," said Achilles. "I can hear you just fine."

"Why can't you just run with the bulls at Pamplona, like any normal self-destructive person?" asked Petra.

He ignored her gibe. "I must value you more than I thought." He said it as if it took him rather by surprise.

"You mean you still have a spark of humility? You might actually need someone else?"

Again he ignored her words. "You look better without blood all over your face."

"But I'll never be as pretty as you."

"Here's my rule about guns," said Achilles. "When people are getting shot, always stand behind the shooter. It's a lot less messy there."

"Unless people are shooting back."

Achilles laughed. "Pet, I *never* use a gun when someone might shoot back."

"And you're so well-mannered, you always open a door for a lady."

His smile faded. "Sometimes I get these impulses," he said. "But they're not irresistible."

"Too bad. And here you had such a good insanity defense going."

His eyes blazed for a moment. Then he went back to his seat.

She cursed herself. Goading him like this, how is it different from jumping out of the airplane?

Then again, maybe it was the fact that she spoke to him without cringing that made him value her.

Fool, she said to herself. You are not equipped to understand this boy—you're not insane enough. Don't try to guess why he does what he does, or how he feels about you or anybody or anything. Study him so you can learn how he makes his plans, what he's likely to do, so that someday you can defeat him. But don't ever try to understand. If you can't even understand yourself, what hope do you have of comprehending somebody as deformed as Achilles?

They did not land in Kabul. They landed in Tashkent, refueled, and then went over the Himalayas to New Delhi.

So he lied to her about their destination. He hadn't trusted her after all. But as long as he refrained from killing her, she could endure a little mistrust.

9

COMMUNING WITH
THE DEAD

To: Carlotta%agape@vatican.net/or
ders/sisters/ind
From: Locke%erasmus@polnet.gov
Re: An answer for your dead friend

If you know who I really am, and
you have contact with a certain
person purported to be dead, please
inform that person that I have done
my best to fulfill expectations. I
believe further collaboration is
possible, but not through intermediaries. If you have no idea what
I'm talking about, then please inform me of that, as well, so I can
begin my search again.

Bean came home to find that Sister Carlotta had packed their
bags.

"Moving day?" he asked.

They had agreed that either one of them could decide that it was time to move on, without having to defend the decision. It was the only way to be sure of acting on any unconscious cues that someone was closing in on them. They didn't want to spend their last moments of life listening to each other say, "I knew we should have left three days ago!" "Well why didn't you say so?" "Because I didn't have a *reason*."

"We have two hours till the flight."

"Wait a minute," said Bean. "You decide we're going, I decide the destination." That was how they'd decided to keep their movements random.

She handed him the printout of an email. It was from Locke. "Greensboro, North Carolina, in the U.S.," she said.

"Perhaps I'm not decoding this right," said Bean, "but I don't see an invitation to visit him."

"He doesn't want intermediaries," said Carlotta. "We can't trust his email to be untraced."

Bean took a match and burned the email in the sink. Then he crumbled the ashes and washed them down the drain. "What about Petra?"

"Still no word. Seven of Ender's jeesh released. The Russians are simply saying that Petra's place of captivity has not yet been discovered."

"Kuso," said Bean.

"I know," said Carlotta, "but what can we do if they won't tell us? I'm afraid she's dead, Bean. You've got to realize that's the likeliest reason for them to stonewall."

Bean knew it, but didn't believe it. "You don't know Petra," he said.

"You don't know Russia," said Carlotta.

"Most people are decent in every country," said Bean.

"Achilles is enough to tip the balance wherever he goes."

Bean nodded. "Rationally, I have to agree with you. Irrationally, I expect to see her again someday."

"If I didn't know you so well, I might interpret that as a sign of your faith in the resurrection."

Bean picked up his suitcase. "Am I bigger, or is this smaller?"

"The case is the same size," said Carlotta.

"I think I'm growing."

"Of course you're growing. Look at your pants."

"I'm still wearing them," said Bean.

"More to the point, look at your ankles."

"Oh." There was more ankle showing than when he bought them.

Bean had never seen a child grow up, but it bothered him that in the weeks they had been in Araraquara, he had grown at least five centimeters. If this was puberty, where were the other changes that were supposed to go along with it?

"We'll buy you new clothes in Greensboro," said Sister Carlotta.

Greensboro. "The place where Ender grew up."

"And where he killed for the first time," said Sister Carlotta.

"You just won't let go of that, will you?" said Bean.

"When you had Achilles in your power, *you* didn't kill him."

Bean didn't like hearing himself compared to Ender that way. Not when it showed Ender at a disadvantage. "Sister Carlotta, we'd have a whole lot less difficulty right now if I *had* killed him."

"You showed mercy. You turned the other cheek. You gave him a chance to make something worthwhile out of his life."

"I made sure he'd get committed to a mental institution."

"Are you so determined to believe in your own lack of virtue?"

"Yes," said Bean. "I prefer truth to lies."

"There," said Carlotta. "Yet another virtue to add to my list."

Bean laughed in spite of himself. "I'm glad you like me," he said.

"Are you afraid to meet him?"

"Who?"

"Ender's brother."

"Not afraid," said Bean.

"How *do* you feel, then?"

"Skeptical," said Bean.

"He showed humility in that email," said Sister Carlotta. "He wasn't sure that he'd figured things out exactly right."

"Oh, there's a thought. The humble Hegemon."

"He's not Hegemon yet," said Carlotta.

"He got seven of Ender's jeesh released, just by publishing a column. He has influence. He has ambition. And now to learn he has humility—well, it's just too much for me."

"Laugh all you want. Let's go out and find a cab."

There was no last-minute business to take care of. They had paid cash for everything, owed nothing. They could walk away.

They lived on money drawn from accounts Graff had set up for them. There was nothing about the account Bean was using now to tag it as belonging to Julian Delphiki. It held his military salary, including his combat and retirement bonuses. The I.F. had given all of Ender's jeesh very large trust funds that they couldn't touch till they came of age. The saved-up pay and bonuses were just to tide them over during their childhood. Graff had assured him that he would not run out of money while he was in hiding.

Sister Carlotta's money came from the Vatican. One person there knew what she was doing. She, too, would have money enough for her needs. Neither of them had the temperament to exploit the situation. They spent little, Sister Carlotta because she wanted nothing more, Bean because he knew that any kind of flamboyance or excess would mark him in people's memories. He always had to seem to be a child running errands for his grandmother, not an undersized war hero cashing in on his back pay.

Their passports caused them no problems, either. Again, Graff had been able to pull strings for them. Given the way they looked—both of Mediterranean ancestry—they carried passports from Catalonia. Carlotta knew Barcelona well, and Catalan was her childhood language. She barely spoke it now, but no matter—hardly anyone did. And no one would be surprised that her grandson couldn't speak the language at all. Besides, how many Catalans would they meet in their travels? Who would try to test their story? If someone got too nosy, they'd simply move on to some other city, some other country.

They landed in Miami, then Atlanta, then Greensboro. They were exhausted and slept the night at an airport hotel. The next day, they logged in and printed out guides to the county bus system. It was a fairly modern system, enclosed and electric, but the map made no sense to Bean.

"Why don't any of the buses go through here?" he asked.

"That's where the rich people live," said Sister Carlotta.

"They make them all live together in one place?"

"They feel safer," said Carlotta. "And by living close together, they have a better chance of their children marrying into other rich families."

"But why don't they want buses?"

"They ride in individual vehicles. They can afford the

fees. It gives them more freedom to choose their own schedule. And it shows everyone just how rich they are."

"It's still stupid," said Bean. "Look how far the buses have to go out of their way."

"The rich people didn't want their streets to be enclosed in order to hold a bus system."

"So what?" asked Bean.

Sister Carlotta laughed. "Bean, isn't there plenty of stupidity in the military, too?"

"But in the long run, the guy who wins battles gets to make the decisions."

"Well, these rich people won the economic battles. Or their grandparents did. So now they get their way most of the time."

"Sometimes I feel like I don't know anything."

"You've lived half your life in a tube in space, and before that you lived on the streets of Rotterdam."

"I've lived in Greece with my family and in Araraquara, too. I should have figured this out."

"That was Greece. And Brazil. This is America."

"So money rules in America, but not those other places?"

"No, Bean. Money rules almost everywhere. But different cultures have different ways of displaying it. In Araraquara, for instance, they made sure that the tram lines ran out to the rich neighborhoods. Why? So the servants could come to work. In America, they're more afraid of criminals coming to steal, so the sign of wealth is to make sure that the only way to reach them is by private car or on foot."

"Sometimes I miss Battle School."

"That's because in Battle School, you were one of the very richest in the only coin that mattered there."

Bean thought about that. As soon as the other kids realized that, young and small as he was, he could outperform them in every class, it gave him a kind of power. Everyone knew who he was. Even those who mocked him had to give him a grudging respect. But . . . "I didn't always get my way."

"Graff told me some of the outrageous things you did," said Carlotta. "Climbing through the air ducts to eavesdrop. Breaking into the computer system."

"But they caught me."

"Not as soon as they'd like to have caught you. And were you punished? No. Why? Because you were rich."

"Money and talent aren't the same thing."

"That's because you can inherit money that was earned by your ancestors," said Sister Carlotta. "And everybody recognizes the value of money, while only select groups recognize the value of talent."

"So where does Peter live?"

She had the addresses of all the Wiggin families. There weren't many—the more common spelling had an *s* at the end. "But I don't think this will help us," said Carlotta. "We don't want to meet him at home."

"Why not?"

"Because we don't know whether his parents are aware of what he's doing or not. Graff was pretty sure they don't know. If two foreigners come calling, they're going to start to wonder what their son is doing on the nets."

"Where, then?"

"He could be in secondary school. But given his intelligence, I'd bet on his being in college." She was accessing more information as she spoke. "Colleges colleges colleges. Lots of them in town. The biggest first, the better for him to disappear in . . ."

"Why would he need to disappear? Nobody knows who he is."

"But he doesn't want anyone to realize that he spends no

time on his schoolwork. He has to look like an ordinary kid his age. He should be spending all his free time with friends. Or with girls. Or with friends looking for girls. Or with friends trying to distract themselves from the fact that they can't find any girls."

"For a nun, you seem to know a lot about this."

"I wasn't born a nun."

"But you were born a girl."

"And no one is a better observer of the folkways of the adolescent male than the adolescent female."

"What makes you think he doesn't do all those things?"

"Being Locke and Demosthenes is a fulltime job."

"So why do you think he's in college at all?"

"Because his parents would be upset if he stayed home all day, reading and writing email."

Bean wouldn't know about what might make parents upset. He'd only known his parents since the end of the war, and they'd never found anything serious to criticize about him. Or maybe they never felt like he was really theirs. They didn't criticize Nikolai much, either. But . . . more than they did Bean. There simply hadn't been enough time together for them to feel as comfortable, as parental, with their new son Julian.

"I wonder how my parents are doing."

"If anything was wrong, we would have heard," said Carlotta.

"I know," said Bean. "That doesn't mean I can't wonder."

She didn't answer, just kept working her desk, bringing new pages into the display. "Here he is," she said. "A non-resident student. No address. Just email and a campus box."

"What about his class schedule?" asked Bean.

"They don't post that."

Bean laughed. "And that's supposed to be a problem?"

"No, Bean, you aren't going to crack their system. I can't think of a better way for you to attract attention than to trip some trap and get a mole to follow you home."

"I don't get followed by moles."

"You never see the ones that follow you."

"It's just a college, not some intelligence service."

"Sometimes people with the least that is worth stealing are the most concerned with giving the appearance of having great treasures hidden away."

"Is that from the Bible?"

"No, it's from observation."

"So what do we do?"

"Your voice is too young," said Sister Carlotta. "I'll work the phone."

She talked her way to the head registrar of the university. "He was a very nice boy to carry all my things after the wheel broke on my cart, and if these keys are his I want to get them back to him right away, before he worries. . . . No I will not drop them in the mail, how would that be 'right away'? Nor will I leave them with you, they might not be his, and *then* what would I do? If they *are* his keys, he will be very glad you told me where his classes are, and if they aren't his keys, then what harm will it cause? . . . All right, I'll wait."

Sister Carlotta lay back on the bed. Bean laughed at her. "How did a nun get so good at lying?"

She held down the MUTE button. "It isn't lying to tell a bureaucrat whatever story it takes to get him to do his job properly."

"But if he does his job properly, he won't give you any information about Peter."

"If he does his job properly, he'll understand the purpose of the rules and therefore know when it is appropriate to make exceptions."

"People who understand the purpose of the rules don't become bureaucrats," said Bean. "That's something we learned really fast in Battle School."

"Exactly," said Carlotta. "So I have to tell him the story that will help him overcome his handicap." Abruptly she refocused her attention on the phone. "Oh, how very nice. Well, that's fine. I'll see him there."

She hung up the phone and laughed. "Well, after all that, the registrar emailed him. His desk was connected, he admitted that he *had* lost his keys, and he wants to meet the nice old lady at Yum-Yum."

"What is *that*?" asked Bean.

"I haven't the slightest idea, but the way she said it, I figured that if I were an old lady living near campus, I'd already know." She was already deep in the city directory. "Oh, it's a restaurant near campus. Well, this is it. Let's go meet the boy who would be king."

"Wait a minute," said Bean. "We can't go straight there."

"Why not?"

"We have to get some keys."

Sister Carlotta looked at him like he was crazy. "I made up the bit about the keys, Bean."

"The registrar knows that you're meeting Peter Wiggin to give him back his keys. What if he happens to be going to Yum-Yum right now for lunch? And he sees us meet Peter, and nobody gives anybody any keys?"

"We don't have a lot of time."

"OK, I have a better idea. Just act flustered and tell him that in your hurry to get there to meet him, you forgot to *bring* the keys, so he should come back to the house with you."

"You have a talent for this, Bean."

"Deception is second nature to me."

The bus was on time and moved briskly, this being an off-peak time, and soon they were on campus. Bean was better at translating maps into real terrain, so he led the way to Yum-Yum.

The place looked like a dive. Or rather, it was trying to look like a dive from an earlier era. Only it really *was* run-down and under-maintained, so it was a dive trying to look like a nice restaurant decorated to look like a dive. Very complicated and ironic, Bean decided, remembering what Father used to say about a neighborhood restaurant near their house on Crete: Abandon lunch, all ye who enter here.

The food looked like common-people's restaurant food everywhere—more about delivering fats and sweets than about flavor or nutrition. Bean wasn't picky, though. There were foods he liked better than others, and he knew something of the difference between fine cuisine and plain fare, but after the streets of Rotterdam and years of dried and processed food in space, anything that delivered the calories and nutrients was fine with him. But he made the mistake of going for the ice cream. He had just come from Araraquara, where the sorvete was memorable, and the American stuff was too fatty, the flavors too syrupy. "Mmmm, deliciosa," said Bean.

"Fecha a boquinha, menino," she answered. "E não fala português aqui."

"I didn't want to critique the ice cream in a language they'd understand."

"Doesn't the memory of starvation make you more patient?"

"Does everything have to be a moral question?"

"I wrote my dissertation on Aquinas and Tillich," said Sister Carlotta. "All questions are philosophical."

"In which case, all answers are unintelligible."

"And you're not even in grad school yet."

A tall young man slid onto the bench beside Bean. "Sorry I'm late," he said. "You got my keys?"

"I feel so foolish," said Sister Carlotta. "I came all the way here and then I realized I left them back home. Let me buy you some ice cream and then you can walk home with me and get them."

Bean looked up at Peter's face in profile. The resemblance to Ender was plain, but not close enough that anyone could ever mistake one for the other.

So this is the kid who brokered the ceasefire that ended the League War. The kid who wants to be Hegemon. Good looking, but not movie-star handsome—people would like him, but still trust him. Bean had studied the vids of Hitler and Stalin. The difference was palpable—Stalin never had to get elected; Hitler did. Even with that stupid mustache, you could see it in Hitler's eyes, that ability to see into you, that sense that whatever he said, wherever he looked, he was speaking to you, looking at you, that he cared about you. But Stalin, he looked like the liar that he was. Peter was definitely in the charismatic category. Like Hitler.

Perhaps an unfair comparison, but those who coveted power invited such thoughts. And the worst was seeing the way Sister Carlotta played to him. True, she was acting a part, but when she spoke to him, when that gaze was fixed on her, she preened a little, she warmed to him. Not so much that she'd behave foolishly, but she was aware of him with a heightened intensity that Bean didn't like. Peter had the seducer's gift. Dangerous.

"I'll walk home with you," said Peter. "I'm not hungry. Have you already paid?"

"Of course," said Sister Carlotta. "This is my grandson, by the way. Delfino."

Peter turned to notice Bean for the first time—though Bean was quite sure Peter had sized him up thoroughly before he sat down. "Cute kid," he said. "How old is he? Does he go to school yet?"

"I'm little," said Bean cheerfully, "but at least I'm not a yelda."

"All those vids of Battle School life," said Peter. "Even little kids are picking up that stupid polyglot slang."

"Now, children, you must get along, I insist on it." Sister Carlotta led the way to the door. "My grandson is visiting this country for the first time, young man, so he doesn't understand American banter."

"Yes I do," said Bean, trying to sound like a petulant child and finding it quite easy, since he really was annoyed.

"He speaks English pretty well. But you better hold his hand crossing this street, the campus trams zoom through here like Daytona."

Bean rolled his eyes and submitted to having Carlotta hold his hand across the street. Peter was obviously trying to provoke him, but why? Surely he wasn't so shallow as to think humiliating Bean would give him some advantage. Maybe he took pleasure in making other people feel small.

Finally, though, they were away from campus and had taken enough twists and turns to make sure they weren't being followed.

"So you're the great Julian Delphiki," said Peter.

"And you're Locke. They're touting you for Hegemon when Sakata's term is over. Too bad you're only virtual."

"I'm thinking of going public soon," said Peter.

"Ah, that's why you got the plastic surgery to make you so pretty," said Bean.

"This old face?" said Peter. "I only wear it when I don't care how I look."

"Boys," said Sister Carlotta. "*Must* you display like baby chimps?"

Peter laughed easily. "Come on, Mom, we was just playin'. Can't we still go to the movies?"

"Off to bed without supper, the lot of you," said Sister Carlotta.

Bean had had enough of this. "Where's Petra?" he demanded.

Peter looked at him as if he were insane. "*I* don't have her."

"You have sources," said Bean. "You know more than you're telling me."

"You know more than you're telling me, too," said Peter. "I thought we were working on trusting each other, and *then* we open the floodgates of wisdom."

"Is she dead?" said Bean, not willing to be deflected.

Peter looked at his watch. "At this moment. I don't know."

Bean stopped walking. Disgusted, he turned to Sister Carlotta. "We wasted a trip," he said. "And risked our lives for nothing."

"Are you sure?" said Sister Carlotta.

Bean looked back at Peter, who seemed genuinely bemused. "He wants to be Hegemon," said Bean, "but he's nothing." Bean walked away. He had memorized the route, of course, and knew how to get to the bus station without Sister Carlotta's help. Ender had ridden these buses as a child younger than Bean. It was the only consolation for the bitter disappointment of finding out that Peter was a game-playing fool.

No one called after him, and he did not look back.

———

Bean took, not the bus to the hotel, but the one that passed nearest the school Ender had attended just before being taken into Battle School. The whole story of Ender's life had come out in the inquiry into Graff's conduct: Ender's first killing had taken place here, a boy named Stilson who had set on Ender with his gang. Bean had been there for Ender's second killing, which was pretty much the same situation as the first. Ender—alone, outnumbered, surrounded—talked his way into single combat and then fought to destroy his enemy so no will to fight would remain. But he had known it here, at the age of six.

I knew things at that age, thought Bean. And younger, too. Not how to kill—that was beyond me, I was too small. But how to live, that was hard.

For me it was hard, but not for Ender. Bean walked through the neighborhoods of modest old houses and even more modest new ones—but to him they were all miracles. Not that he hadn't had plenty of chances, living with his family in Greece after the war, to see how most children grew up. But this was different. This was the place that had spawned Ender Wiggin.

I had more native talent for war than Ender had. But he was still the better commander. Was this the difference? He grew up where he never worried about finding another meal, where people praised him and protected him. I grew up where if I found a scrap of food I had to worry that another street kid might kill me for it. Shouldn't that have made *me* the one who fought desperately, and Ender the one who held back?

It wasn't the place. Two people in identical situations would never make exactly the same choices. Ender is who he is, and I am who I am. It was in him to destroy the Formics. It was in me to stay alive.

So what's in me now? I'm a commander without an army.

I have a mission to perform, but no knowledge of how to perform it. Petra, if she's still alive, is in desperate peril, and she counts on me to free her. The others are all free. She alone remains hidden. What has Achilles done to her? I will not have Petra end like Poke.

There it was. The difference between Ender and Bean. Ender came out of his bitterest battle of childhood undefeated. He had done what was required. But Bean had not even realized the danger his friend Poke was in until too late. If he had seen in time how immediate her peril was, he could have warned her, helped her. Saved her. Instead, her body was tossed into the Rhine, to be found bobbing like so much garbage among the wharves.

And it was happening again.

Bean stood in front of the Wiggin house. Ender had never spoken of it, nor had pictures of it been shown at the court of inquiry. But it was exactly what Bean had expected. A tree in the front yard, with wooden slats nailed into the trunk to form a ladder to the platform in a high crotch of the tree. A tidy, well-tended garden. A place of peace and refuge. What did Ender ever know of fear?

Where is Petra's garden? For that matter, where is mine?

Bean knew he was being unreasonable. If Ender had come back to Earth, he too would no doubt be in hiding, if Achilles hadn't simply killed him straight off. And even as things stood, he couldn't help but wonder if Ender might not prefer to be living as Bean was, on Earth, in hiding, than where he was now, in space, bound for another world and a life of permanent exile from the world of his birth.

A woman came out of the front door of the house. Mrs. Wiggin?

"Are you lost?" she asked.

Bean realized that in his disappointment—no, call it

despair—he had forgotten his vigilance. This house might be watched. Even if it was not, Mrs. Wiggin herself might remember him, this young boy who appeared in front of her house during school hours.

"Is this where Ender Wiggin grew up?"

A cloud passed across her face, just momentarily, but Bean saw how her expression saddened before her smile could be put back. "Yes, it is," she said. "But we don't give tours."

For reasons Bean could not understand, on impulse he said, "I was with him. In the last battle. I fought under him."

Her smile changed again, away from mere courtesy and kindness, toward something like warmth and pain. "Ah," she said. "A veteran." And then the warmth faded and was replaced by worry. "I know all the faces of Ender's companions in that last battle. You're the one who's dead. Julian Delphiki."

Just like that, his cover was blown—and he had done it to himself, by telling her that he was in Ender's jeesh. What was he thinking? There were only eleven of them. "Obviously, there's someone who wants to kill me," he said. "If you tell anyone I came here, it will help him do it."

"I won't tell. But it was careless of you to come here."

"I had to see," said Bean, wondering if that was anything like a true explanation.

She didn't wonder. "That's absurd," she said. "You wouldn't risk your life to come here without a reason." And then it came together in her mind. "Peter's not home right now."

"I know," Bean said. "I was just with him at the university." And then he realized—there was no reason for her to think he was coming to see Peter, unless she had some idea of what Peter was doing. "You know," he said.

She closed her eyes, realizing now what she had

confessed. "Either we are both very great fools," she said, "or we must have trusted each other at once, to let our guard down so readily."

"We're only fools if the other can't be trusted," said Bean.

"We'll find out, won't we?" Then she smiled. "No use leaving you standing out here on the street, for people to wonder why a child your size is not in school."

He followed her up the walkway to the front door. When Ender left home, did he walk down this path? Bean tried to imagine the scene. Ender never came home. Like Bonzo, the other casualty of the war. Bonzo, killed; Ender, missing in action; and now Bean coming up the walk to Ender's home. Only this was no sentimental visit with a grieving family. It was a different war now, but war it was, and she had another son at risk these days.

She was not supposed to know what he was doing. Wasn't that the whole point of Peter's having to camouflage his activities by pretending to be a student?

She made him a sandwich without even asking, as if she simply assumed that a child would be hungry. It was, of all things, that plain American cliché, peanut butter on white bread. Had she made such sandwiches for Ender?

"I miss him," said Bean, because he knew that would make her like him.

"If he had been here," said Mrs. Wiggin, "he probably would have been killed. When I read what . . . *Locke* . . . wrote about that boy from Rotterdam, I couldn't imagine he would have let Ender live. You knew him, too, didn't you. What's his name?"

"Achilles," said Bean.

"You're in hiding," she said. "But you seem so young."

"I travel with a nun named Sister Carlotta," said Bean. "We claim we're grandmother and grandson."

"I'm glad you're not alone."

"Neither is Ender."

Tears came to her eyes. "I suppose he needed Valentine more than we did."

On impulse—again, an impulsive act instead of a calculated decision—Bean reached out and set his hand in hers. She smiled at him.

The moment passed. Bean realized again how dangerous it was to be here. What if this house was under surveillance? The I.F. knew about Peter—what if they were observing the house?

"I should go," said Bean.

"I'm glad you came by," she said. "I must have wanted very much to talk to someone who knew Ender without being envious of him."

"We were all envious," said Bean. "But we also knew he was the best of us."

"Why else would you envy him, if you didn't think he was better?"

Bean laughed. "Well, when you envy somebody, you tell yourself he isn't really better after all."

"So . . . did the other children envy his abilities?" asked Mrs. Wiggin. "Or only the recognition he received?"

Bean didn't like the question, but then remembered who it was that was asking. "I should turn that question back on you. Did Peter envy his abilities? Or only the recognition?"

She stood there, considering whether to answer or not. Bean knew that family loyalty worked against her saying anything. "I'm not just idly asking," Bean said. "I don't know how much you know about what Peter's doing . . ."

"We read everything he publishes," said Mrs. Wiggin. "And then we're very careful to act as if we hadn't a clue what's going on in the world."

"I'm trying to decide whether to throw in with Peter," said Bean. "And I have no way of knowing what to make of him. How much to trust him."

"I wish I could help you," said Mrs. Wiggin. "Peter marches to a different drummer. I've never really caught the rhythm."

"Don't you like him?" asked Bean, knowing he was too blunt, but knowing also that he wasn't going to get many chances like this, to talk to the mother of a potential ally—or rival.

"I love him," said Mrs. Wiggin. "He doesn't show us much of himself. But that's only fair—we never showed our children much of ourselves, either."

"Why not?" asked Bean. He was thinking of the openness of his mother and father, the way they knew Nikolai, and Nikolai knew them. It had left him almost gasping, the unguardedness of their conversations with each other. Clearly the Wiggin household did not have that custom.

"It's very complicated," said Mrs. Wiggin.

"Meaning that you think it's none of my business."

"On the contrary, I know it's very much your business." She sighed and sat back down. "Come on, let's not pretend this is only a doorstep conversation. You came here to find out about Peter. The easy answer is simply to tell you that we don't know a thing. He never tells anyone anything they want to know, unless it would be useful to him for them to know it."

"But the hard answer?"

"We've been hiding from our children, almost from the start," said Mrs. Wiggin. "We can hardly be surprised or resentful when they learned at a very early age to be secretive."

"What were you hiding?"

"We don't tell our children, and I should tell you?" But she answered her own question at once. "If Valentine and Ender were here, I think we *would* talk to them. I even tried to explain some of this to Valentine before she left to join Ender in . . . space. I did a very bad job, because I had never put it in words before. Let me just . . . let me start by saying . . . we were going to have a third child anyway, even if the I.F. hadn't asked us to."

Where Bean had grown up, the population laws hadn't meant much—the street children of Rotterdam were all extra people and knew perfectly well that by law not one of them should have been born, but when you're starving, it's hard to care much about whether you're going to get into the finest schools. Still, when the laws were repealed, he read about them and knew the significance of their decision to have a third child. "Why would you do that?" asked Bean. "It would hurt all your children. It would end your careers."

"We were very careful not to *have* careers," said Mrs. Wiggin. "Not careers that we'd hate to give up. What we had was only jobs. You see, we're religious people."

"There are lots of religious people in the world."

"But not in America," said Mrs. Wiggin. "Not the kind of fanatic that does something so selfish and antisocial as to have more than two children, just because of some misguided religious ideas. And when Peter tested so high as a toddler, and they started monitoring him—well, that was a disaster for us. We had hoped to be . . . unobtrusive. To disappear. We're very bright people, you know."

"I wondered why the parents of such geniuses didn't have noted careers of their own," said Bean. "Or at least some kind of standing in the intellectual community."

"Intellectual community," said Mrs. Wiggin scornfully. "America's intellectual community has never been very bright. Or honest. They're all sheep, following whatever the intellectual fashion of the decade happens to be. Demanding that everyone follow their dicta in lockstep. Everyone has to be open-minded and tolerant of the things they believe, but God forbid they should ever concede, even for a moment, that someone who disagrees with them might have some fingerhold on truth."

She sounded bitter.

"I sound bitter," she said.

"You've lived your life," said Bean. "So you think you're smarter than the smart people."

She recoiled a bit. "Well, that's the kind of comment that explains why we never discuss our faith with anyone."

"I didn't mean it as an attack," said Bean. "I think I'm smarter than anybody I've ever met, because I am. I'd have to be dumber than I am not to know it. You really believe in your religion, and you resent the fact that you had to hide it from others. That's all I was saying."

"Not religion, reli*gions*," she said. "My husband and I don't even share the same doctrine. Having a large family in obedience to God, that was about the only thing we agreed on. And even at that, we both had elaborate intellectual justifications for our decision to defy the law. For one thing, we didn't think it would hurt our children at all. We meant to raise them in faith, as believers."

"So why didn't you?"

"Because we're cowards after all," said Mrs. Wiggin. "With the I.F. watching, we would have had constant interference. They would have intervened to make sure we didn't teach our children anything that would prevent them from fulfilling the role that Ender and you ended up fulfilling. That's when we started hiding our faith. Not really from our children, just from the Battle School people. We were so relieved when Peter's monitor was taken away. And then Valentine's. We thought we were done. We were going to move to a place where we wouldn't be so badly treated, and have a third child, and a fourth, as many as we could have before they arrested us. But then they came to us and requisitioned a third child. So we didn't have to move. You see? We were lazy and frightened. If the Battle School was going to give us a cover to allow us to have one more child, then why not?"

"But then they took Ender."

"And by the time they took him, it was too late. To raise Peter and Valentine in our faith. If you don't teach children when they're little, it's never really inside them. You have to hope they'll come to it later, on their own. It can't come from the parents, if you don't begin when they're little."

"Indoctrinating them."

"That's what parenting is," said Mrs. Wiggin. "Indoctrinating your children in the social patterns that you want them to live by. The intellectuals have no qualms about using the schools to indoctrinate our children in *their* foolishness."

"I wasn't trying to provoke you," said Bean.

"And yet you use words that imply criticism."

"Sorry," said Bean.

"You're still a child," said Mrs. Wiggin. "No matter how bright you are, you still absorb a lot of the attitudes of the ruling class. I don't like it, but there you are. When they took Ender away, and we finally could live without constant scrutiny of every word that we said to our children, we realized that Peter was already completely indoctrinated in the foolishness of the schools. He would never have gone along with our earlier plan. He would have denounced us. We would have lost him. So do you cast off your firstborn child in order to give birth to a fourth or fifth or sixth? Peter seemed sometimes not to have any conscience at all. If ever anyone needed to believe in God, it was Peter, and he didn't."

"He probably wouldn't have anyway," said Bean.

"You don't know him," said Mrs. Wiggin. "He lives by pride. If we had made him proud of being a secret believer, he would have been valiant in that struggle. Instead he's . . . not."

"So you never even tried to convert him to your beliefs?" asked Bean.

"Which ones?" asked Mrs. Wiggin. "*We* had always thought that the big struggle in our family would be over which religion to teach them, his or mine. Instead we had to watch over Peter and find ways to help him find . . . decency. No, something much more important than that. Integrity. Honor. We monitored him the way that the Battle School had monitored all three of them. It took all our patience to keep our hands off when he forced Valentine to become Demosthenes. It was so contrary to her spirit. But we soon saw that it was not changing her—that her nobility of heart was, if anything, stronger through resistance to Peter's control."

"You didn't try to simply block him from what he was doing?"

She laughed harshly. "Oh, now, you're supposed to be the smart one. Could someone have blocked *you*? And Peter failed to get into Battle School because he was *too* ambitious, too rebellious, too unlikely to fulfill assignments and follow orders. *We* were supposed to influence him by forbidding him or blocking him?"

"No, I can see you couldn't," said Bean. "But you did nothing at all?"

"We taught him as best we could," said Mrs. Wiggin.

"Comments at meals. We could see how he tuned us out, how he despised our opinions. It didn't help that we were trying so hard to conceal that we knew everything he'd written as Locke; our conversations really were . . . abstract. Boring, I suppose. And we didn't have those intellectual credentials. Why should he respect us? But he *heard* our ideas. Of what nobility is. Goodness and honor. And whether he believed us at some level or simply found such things within himself, we've seen him grow. So . . . you ask me if you can trust him, and I can't answer, because . . . trust him to do what? To act as you want him to? Never. To act according to some predictable pattern? I should laugh. But we've seen signs of honor. We've seen him do things that were very hard, but that seemed to be not just for show, but because he really believed in what he was doing. Of course, he might have simply been doing things that would make Locke seem virtuous and admirable. How can we know, when we can't ask him?"

"So you can't talk to him about what matters to you, because you know he'll despise you, and he can't talk to you about what matters to him, because you've never shown him that you actually have the understanding to grasp what he's thinking."

Tears sprang to her eyes and glistened there. "Sometimes I miss Valentine so much. She was so breathtakingly honest and good."

"So she told you she was Demosthenes?"

"No," said Mrs. Wiggin. "She was wise enough to know that if she didn't keep Peter's secret, it would split the family apart forever. No, she kept that hidden from us. But she made sure we knew just what kind of person Peter was. And about everything else in her life, everything Peter left for her to decide for herself, she told us that, and she listened to us, too, she cared what we thought."

"So you told her what you believe?"

"We didn't tell her about our faith," said Mrs. Wiggin. "But we taught her the results of that faith. We did the best we could."

"I'm sure you did," said Bean.

"I'm not stupid," said Mrs. Wiggin. "I know you despise us, just as we know Peter despises us."

"I don't," said Bean.

"I've been lied to enough to recognize it when you do it."

"I don't despise you for . . . I don't despise you at all," said Bean. "But you have to see that the way you all hide from each other, Peter growing up in a family where nobody tells anybody anything that matters—that doesn't make me really optimistic about ever being able to trust him. I'm about to put my life in his hands. And now I find out that in his whole life, he's never had an honest relationship with anybody."

Her eyes grew cold and distant then. "I see that I've provided you with useful information. Perhaps you should go now."

"I'm not judging you," said Bean.

"Don't be absurd, of course you are," said Mrs. Wiggin.

"I'm not condemning you, then."

"Don't make me laugh. You condemn us, and you know what? I agree with you. I condemn us too. We set out to do God's will, and we've ended up damaging the one child we have left to us. He's grimly determined to make his mark in the world. But what sort of mark will it be?"

"An indelible one," said Bean. "If Achilles doesn't destroy him first."

"We did some things right," said Mrs. Wiggin. "We gave him the freedom to test his own abilities. We could have stopped him from publishing, you know. He thinks he outsmarted us, but only because we played incredibly dumb. How many parents would have let their teenage son meddle in world affairs? When he wrote against . . . against letting Ender come home—you don't know how hard it was for me not to claw his arrogant little eyes out. . . ."

For the first time, he saw something of the rage and frustration she must have been going through. He thought: This is how Peter's mother feels about him. Maybe orphanhood wasn't such a drawback.

"But I didn't, did I?" said Mrs. Wiggin.

"Didn't what?"

"Didn't stop him. And he turned out to be right. Because if Ender were here on Earth, he'd either be dead, or he would have been one of the kidnapped children, or he'd be in hiding like you. But I still . . . Ender is his brother, and he exiled him from Earth forever. And I couldn't help but remember the terrible threats he made when Ender was still little, and lived with us. He told Ender and Valentine then that someday he would kill Ender, and pretend that it was an accident."

"Ender's not dead."

"My husband and I have wondered, in the dark nights when we try to make sense of what has happened to our family, to all our dreams, we've wondered if Peter got Ender exiled because he loved him and knew the dangers he'd face if he returned to Earth. Or if he exiled him because he feared that if Ender came home Peter would kill him, just as he threatened to—so then, exiling Ender could be viewed as a sort of, I don't know, an elementary kind of self-control. Still, a very selfish thing, but still showing a sort of vague respect for decency. That would be progress."

"Or maybe none of the above."

"Or maybe we're all guided by God in this, and God has brought you here."

"So Sister Carlotta says."

"She might be right."

"I don't much care either way," said Bean. "If there is a God, I think he's pretty lousy at his job."

"Or you don't understand what his job is."

"Believe me, Sister Carlotta is the nunnish equivalent of a Jesuit. Let's not even get into trading sophistries, I've been trained by an expert and, as you say, you're not in practice."

"Julian Delphiki," said Mrs. Wiggin, "I knew when I saw you out on the front sidewalk that I not only could, I *must* tell you things that I have spoken of to no one but my husband, and I've even said things that I've never said to him. I've told you things that Peter never imagined that I knew or thought or saw or felt. If you have a low opinion of my mothering, please keep in mind that whatever you know, you know because I told you, and I told you because I think that someday Peter's future may depend on your knowing what he's going to do, or how to help him. Or—Peter's future as a decent human being might depend on his helping *you*. So I bared my heart to you. For Peter's sake. And I face your scorn, Julian Delphiki, for Peter's sake as well. So don't fault my love for my son. Whether he thinks he cares or not, he grew up with parents who love him and have done everything we could for him. Including lie to him about what we believe, what we know, so that he can move through his world like Alexander, boldly reaching for the ends of the earth, with the complete freedom that comes from having parents who are too stupid to stop you. Until you've had a child of your own and sacrificed for that child and twisted your life into a pretzel, into a knot for him, don't you dare to judge me and what I've done."

"I'm not judging you," said Bean. "Truly I'm not. As you said, I'm just trying to understand Peter."

"Well, do you know what I think?" said Mrs. Wiggin. "I think you've been asking all the wrong questions. 'Can I trust him?' " She mimicked him scornfully. "Whether you trust somebody or distrust him has a lot more to do with the kind of person *you* are than the kind of person he is. The real question you ought to be asking is, Do you really want Peter Wiggin to rule the world? Because if you help him, and he somehow lives through all this, that's where it will lead. He won't stop until he achieves that. And he'll burn up your future along with anybody else's, if it will help him reach that goal. So ask yourself, will the world be a better place with Peter Wiggin as Hegemon? And not some benign ceremonial figurehead like the ineffectual toad who holds that office now. I mean Peter Wiggin as the Hegemon who reshapes this world into whatever form he wants it to have."

"But you're assuming that I care whether the world is a better place," said Bean. "What if all I care about is my own survival or advancement? Then the only question that would matter is, Can I use Peter to advance my own plans?"

She laughed and shook her head. "Do *you* believe that about yourself? Well, you *are* a child."

"Pardon me, but did I ever pretend to be anything else?"

"You pretend," said Mrs. Wiggin, "to be a person of such enormous value that you can speak of 'allying' with Peter Wiggin as if you brought armies with you."

"I don't bring armies," said Bean, "but I bring victory for whatever army he gives me."

"Would Ender have been like you, if he had come home? Arrogant? Aloof?"

"Not at all," said Bean. "But I never killed anybody."

"Except buggers," said Mrs. Wiggin.

"Why are we at war with each other?" said Bean.

"I've told you everything about my son, about my family, and you've given me nothing back. Except your . . . sneer."

"I'm not sneering," said Bean. "I like you."

"Oh, thank you very much."

"I can see in you the mother of Ender Wiggin," said Bean. "You understand Peter the way Ender understood his soldiers. The way Ender understood his enemies. And you're bold enough to act instantly when the opportunity presents itself. I show up on your doorstep, and you give me all this. No, ma'am, I don't despise you at all. And you know what I think? I think that, perhaps without even realizing it yourself, you believe in Peter completely. You want him to succeed. You think he should rule the world. And you've told me all this, not because I'm such a nice little boy, but because you think that by telling me, you'll help Peter move that much closer toward ultimate victory."

She shook her head. "Not everybody thinks like a soldier."

"Hardly anyone does," said Bean. "Precious few soldiers, for that matter."

"Let me tell you something, Julian Delphiki. You didn't have a mother and father, so you need to be told. You know what I dread most? That Peter will pursue these ambitions of his so relentlessly that he'll never have a life."

"Conquering the world isn't a life?" asked Bean.

"Alexander the Great," said Mrs. Wiggin. "He haunts my nightmares for Peter. All his conquests, his victories, his grand achievements—they were the acts of an adolescent boy. By the time he got around to marrying, to having a child, it was too late. He died in the midst of it. And he probably wouldn't have done a very good job of it either. He was already too powerful before he even tried to find love. That's what I fear for Peter."

"Love? That's what this all comes down to?"

"No, not just love. I'm talking about the cycle of life. I'm talking about finding some alien creature and deciding to marry her and stay with her forever, no matter whether you even like each other or not a few years down the road. And why will you do this? So you can make babies together, and try to keep them alive and teach them what they need to know so that someday *they'll* have babies, and keep the whole thing going. And you'll never draw a secure breath until you have grandchildren, a double handful of them, because then you know that your line won't die out, your influence will continue. Selfish, isn't it? Only it's not selfish, it's what life is for. It's the only thing that brings happiness, ever, to anyone. All the other things—victories, achievements, honors, causes—they bring only momentary flashes of pleasure. But binding yourself to another person and to the children you make together, that's life. And you can't do it if your life is centered on your ambitions. You'll never be happy. It will never be enough, even if you rule the world."

"Are you telling me? Or telling Peter?" asked Bean.

"I'm telling you what I truly want for Peter," said Mrs. Wiggin. "But if you're a tenth as smart as you think you are, you'll get that for yourself. Or you'll never have real joy in this life."

"Excuse me if I'm missing something here," said Bean, "but as far as I can tell, marrying and having children has brought you nothing but grief. You've lost Ender, you've lost Valentine, and you spent your life pissed off at Peter or fretting about him."

"Yes," she said. "Now you're getting it."

"Where's the joy? That's what I'm not getting."

"The grief *is* the joy," said Mrs. Wiggin. "I have someone to grieve for. Whom do you have?"

Such was the intensity of their conversation that Bean

had no barrier in place to block what she said. It stirred something inside him. All the memories of people that he'd loved—despite the fact that he refused to love anyone. Poke. Nikolai. Sister Carlotta. Ender. His parents, when he finally met them. "I have someone to grieve for," said Bean.

"You think you do," said Mrs. Wiggin. "Everyone thinks they do, until they take a child into their heart. Only then do you know what it is to be a hostage to love. To have someone else's life matter more than your own."

"Maybe I know more than you think," said Bean.

"Maybe you know nothing at all," said Mrs. Wiggin.

They faced each other across the table, a loud silence between them. Bean wasn't even sure they'd been quarreling. Despite the heat of their exchange, he couldn't help but feel that he'd just been given a strong dose of the faith that she and her husband shared with each other.

Or maybe it really was objective truth, and he simply couldn't grasp it because he wasn't married.

And never would be. If there was ever anyone whose life virtually guaranteed that he'd be a terrible father, it was Bean. Without ever exactly saying it aloud, he'd always known that he would never marry, never have children.

But her words had this much effect: For the first time in his life, he found himself almost wishing that it were not so.

In that silence, Bean heard the front door open, and Peter's and Sister Carlotta's voices. At once Bean and Mrs. Wiggin rose to their feet, feeling and looking guilty, as if they had been caught in some kind of clandestine rendezvous. Which, in a way, they had.

"Mother, I've met a traveler," said Peter when he came into the room.

Bean heard the beginning of Peter's lie like a blow to the face—for Bean knew that the person Peter was lying to knew his story was false, and yet would lie in return by pretending to believe.

This time, though, the lie could be nipped in the bud.

"Sister Carlotta," said Mrs. Wiggin. "I've heard so much about you from young Julian here. He says you are the world's only Jesuit nun."

Peter and Sister Carlotta looked at Bean in bafflement. What was he doing there? He almost laughed at their consternation, in part because he couldn't have answered that question himself.

"He came here like a pilgrim to a shrine," said Mrs. Wiggin. "And he very bravely told me who he really is. Peter, you must be very careful not to tell anyone that this is one of Ender's companions. Julian Delphiki. He wasn't killed in that explosion, after all. Isn't that wonderful? We must make him welcome here, for Ender's sake, but he's still in danger, so it has to be our secret who he is."

"Of course, Mother," said Peter. He looked at Bean, but his eyes betrayed nothing of what he was feeling. Like the cold eyes of a rhinoceros, unreadable, yet with enormous danger behind them all the same.

Sister Carlotta, though, was obviously appalled. "After all our security precautions," she said, "and you just blurt it out? And this house is bound to be watched."

"We had a good conversation," said Bean. "That's not possible in the midst of lies."

"It's my life you were risking here, too, you know," said Carlotta.

Mrs. Wiggin touched her arm. "Do stay here with us, won't you? We have room in our house for visitors."

"We can't," said Bean. "She's right. Coming here at all has compromised us both. We'll probably want to fly out of Greensboro first thing in the morning."

He glanced at Sister Carlotta, knowing that she would understand that he was really saying they should leave by train that night. Or by bus the day after tomorrow. Or rent an apartment under assumed names and stay here for a week. The lying had begun again, for safety's sake.

"At least stay for dinner?" asked Mrs. Wiggin. "And meet my husband? I think he'll be just as intrigued as I was to meet a boy who is so famously dead."

Bean saw Peter's eyes glaze over. He understood why—to Peter, a dinner with his parents would be an excruciating social exercise during which nothing important could be said. Wouldn't all your lives be simpler if you could all just tell each other the truth? But Mrs. Wiggin had said that Peter needed to feel that he was on his own. If he knew that his parents knew of his secret activities, that would infantilize him, apparently. Though if he were really the sort of man that could rule the world, surely he could deal with knowing that his parents were in on his secrets.

Not my decision. I gave my word.

"We'd be glad to," said Bean. "Though there's a danger of having your house blown up because we're in it."

"Then we'll eat out," said Mrs. Wiggin. "See how simple things can be? If something's going to be blown up, let it be a restaurant. They carry insurance for that sort of thing."

Bean laughed. But Peter didn't. Because, Bean realized, Peter doesn't know how much she knows, and therefore he thinks her comment was idiocy instead of irony.

"Not Italian food," said Sister Carlotta.

"Oh, of course not," said Mrs. Wiggin. "There's never been a decent Italian restaurant in Greensboro."

With that, the conversation turned to safe and meaningless topics. Bean took a certain relish in watching how Peter squirmed at the utter waste of time that such chitchat represented. I know more about your mother than you do, thought Bean. I have more respect for her.

But you're the one she loves.

Bean was annoyed to notice the envy in his own heart. Nobody's immune from those petty human emotions, he knew that. But somehow he had to learn how to distinguish between true observations and what his envy told him. Peter had to learn the same. The trust that Bean had given so easily to Mrs. Wiggin would have to be earned step by step between him and Peter. Why?

Because he and Peter were so alike. Because he and Peter were natural rivals. Because he and Peter could so easily be deadly enemies.

As I am a second Ender in his eyes, is he a second Achilles in mine? If there were no Achilles in the world, would I think of Peter as the evil I must destroy?

And if we do defeat Achilles together, will we then have to turn and fight each other, undoing all our triumphs, destroying everything we've built?

10

BROTHERS IN ARMS

To: RusFriend%BabaYaga@MosPub.net
From: VladDragon%slavnet.com
Re: allegiance

Let's make one thing clear. I never
"joined" with Achilles. From all I
could see, Achilles was speaking for
Mother Russia. It was Mother Russia
that I agreed to serve, and that is
a decision I did not and do not regret. I believe the artificial di-
visions among the peoples of
Greater Slavia serve only to keep
any of us from achieving our potential in the world. In the chaos
that has resulted from the exposure
of Achilles' true nature, I would
be glad of any opportunity to
serve. The things I learned in Battle School could well make a difference to the future of our
people. If my link with Achilles

makes it impossible for me to be of
service, so be it. But it would be
a shame if we all suffered from
that last act of sabotage by a psychopath. It is precisely now that I
am most needed. Mother Russia will
find no more loyal son than this
one.

For Peter, the dinner at Leblon with his parents and Bean and Carlotta consisted of long periods of excruciating boredom interrupted by short passages of sheer panic. Nothing that anyone was saying mattered in the slightest. Because Bean was passing himself off as little more than a tourist visiting Ender's shrine, all anyone could talk about was Ender Ender Ender. But inevitably the conversation would skirt topics that were highly sensitive, things that might give away what Peter was really doing and the role that Bean might end up playing.

The worst was when Sister Carlotta—who, nun or not, clearly knew how to be a malicious bitch when she wanted to—began probing Peter about his studies at UNCG, even though she knew perfectly well that his schoolwork there was merely a cover for far more important matters. "I'm just surprised, I suppose, that you spend your time on a regular course of study when clearly you have abilities that should be used on a broader stage," she said.

"I need the degree, just like anyone else," said Peter, writhing inside.

"But why not study things that will prepare you to play a role on the great stage of world affairs?"

Ironically, it was Bean who rescued him. "Come now,

Grandmother," he said. "A man of Peter Wiggin's ability is ready to do anything he wants, whenever he wants. Formal study is just busywork to him anyway. He's only doing it to prove to other people that he's able to live by the rules when he needs to. Right, Peter?"

"Close enough," Peter said. "I'm even less interested in my studies than you all are, and you shouldn't be interested in them at all."

"Well, if you hate it so much, why are we paying for tuition?" asked Father.

"We're not," Mother reminded him. "Peter has such a nice scholarship that they're paying *him* to attend there."

"Not getting their money's worth, though, are they?" said Father.

"They're getting what they want," said Bean. "For the rest of his life, whatever Peter here accomplishes, it will be mentioned that he studied at UNCG. He'll be a walking advertisement for them. I'd call that a pretty good return on investment, wouldn't you?"

The kid had mastered the kind of language Father understood—Peter had to credit Bean with knowing his audience when he spoke. Still, it annoyed Peter that Bean had so easily sussed what kind of idiots his parents were, and how easily they could be pandered to. It was as if, by pulling Peter's conversational irons out of the fire, Bean was rubbing it in about Peter's still being a child living at home, while Bean was out dealing with life more directly. It made Peter chafe all the more.

Only at the end of the dinner, as they left the Brazilian restaurant and headed for the Market/Holden station, did Bean drop his bombshell. "You know that since we've compromised ourselves here, we have to go back into hiding at once." Peter's parents made little noises of sympathy, and then Bean said, "What I was wondering was, why doesn't Peter go with us? Get out of Greensboro for a while? Would you like to, Peter? Do you have a passport?"

"No, he doesn't," said Mother, at exactly the same moment that Peter said, "Of course I do."

"You do?" asked Mother.

"Just in case," said Peter. He didn't add: I have six passports from four countries, as a matter of fact, and ten different bank identities with funds from my writing gigs socked away.

"But you're in the middle of a semester," said Father.

"I can take a leave whenever I want," said Peter. "It sounds interesting. Where are you going?"

"We don't know," said Bean. "We don't decide until the last minute. But we can email you and tell you where we are."

"Campus email addresses aren't secure," said Father helpfully.

"No email is really secure, is it?" asked Mother.

"It will be a coded message," said Bean. "Of course."

"It doesn't sound very sensible to me," said Father. "Peter may think his studies are just busywork, but in fact you have to have that degree just to get started in life. You need to stick to something long term and finish it, Peter. If your transcript shows that you did your education in fits and starts, that won't look good to the best companies."

"What career do you think I'm going to pursue?" Peter asked, annoyed. "Some kind of corporate dull bob?"

"I really hate it when you use that ersatz Battle School slang," said Father. "You didn't go there, and it makes you sound like some kind of teenage wannabe."

"I don't know about that," said Bean, before Peter could blow up. "I *was* there, and I think that stuff is just part of the language. I mean, the word 'wannabe' was once slang, wasn't it? It can grow into the language just by people using it."

"It makes him sound like a kid," said Father, but it was just a parting shot, Father's pathetic need to have the last word.

Peter said nothing. But he wasn't grateful to Bean for taking his side. On the contrary, the kid really pissed him off. It's like Bean thought he could come into Peter's life and intervene between him and his parents like some kind of savior. It diminished Peter in his own eyes. None of the people who wrote to him or read his work as Locke or Demosthenes ever condescended to him, because they didn't know he was a kid. But the way Bean was acting was a warning of things to come. If Peter did come out under his real name, he would immediately have to start dealing with condescension. People who had once trembled at the idea of coming under Demosthenes' scrutiny, people who had once eagerly sought Locke's imprimatur, would now poo-poo anything Peter wrote, saying, Of course a child would think that way, or, more kindly but no less devastatingly, When he has more experience, he'll come to see that. . . . Adults were always saying things like that. As if experience actually had some correlation with increased wisdom; as if most of the stupidity in the world were not propounded by adults.

Besides, Peter couldn't help but feel that Bean was enjoying it, that he loved having Peter at such a disadvantage. Why *had* the little weasel gone to his house? Oh, pardon, to *Ender's* house, naturally. But he knew it was Peter's house, and to come home and find Bean sitting there talking to his mother, that was like catching a burglar in the act. He hadn't liked Bean from the beginning—especially not after the petulant way he walked off just because Peter didn't immediately answer the question he was asking. Admittedly, Peter *had* been teasing him a little, and there was an element of condescension about it—toying with the little kid before telling him what he wanted to know. But Bean's retaliation had gone way overboard. Especially this miserable dinner.

And yet . . .

Bean was the real thing. The best that Battle School had produced. Peter could use him. Peter might actually even need him, precisely because he could not yet afford to come out publicly as himself. Bean had the credibility despite his size and age, because he'd fought the fight. He could actually do things instead of having to pull strings in the background or try to manipulate government decisions by influencing public opinion. If Peter could secure some kind of working alliance with him, it might go a long way toward compensating for his impotence. If only Bean weren't so insufferably smug.

Can't let my personal feelings interfere with the work at hand.

"Tell you what," Peter said. "Mom and Dad, you've got stuff to do tomorrow, but my first class isn't till noon. Why don't I go with these two wherever they're spending the night and talk through the possibility of maybe taking a field trip with them."

"I don't want you just taking off and leaving your mother to worry about what's happening to you," said Father. "I think it's very clear to all of us that young Mr. Delphiki here is a trouble magnet, and I think your mother has lost enough children without having to worry about something even worse happening to you."

It made Peter cringe the way Father always talked as if it were only Mother who would be worried, only Mother who cared what happened to him. And if it was true—who could tell, with Father?—that was even worse. Either Father didn't care what happened to Peter, or he did care but was such a git that he couldn't admit it.

"I won't leave town without checking in with Mommy," said Peter.

"You don't need to be sarcastic," said Father.

"Dear," said Mother, "Peter isn't five, to be rebuked in front of company." Which, of course, made him seem to be maybe six years old. Thanks so much for helping, Mom.

"Aren't families complicated?" said Sister Carlotta.

Oh, thanks, thou holy bitch, said Peter silently. You and Bean are the ones who complicated the situation, and now you make smug little comments about how much better it is for unconnected people like you. Well, these parents are my *cover*. I didn't pick them, but I have to use them. And for you to mock my situation only shows your ignorance. And, probably, your envy, seeing how you are never going to have children or even get laid in your whole life, Mrs. Jesus.

"Poor Peter has the worst of both worlds," said Mother. "He's the oldest, so he was always held to a higher standard, and yet he's the last of our children left at home, which means he also gets babied more than he can bear. It's so awful, the fact that parents are mere human beings and constantly make mistakes. I think sometimes Peter wishes he had been raised by robots."

Which made Peter want to slide right down into the sidewalk and spend the rest of his life as an invisible patch of concrete. I converse with spies and military officers, with political leaders and power brokers—and my mother still has the power to humiliate me at will!

"Do what you want," said Father. "It's not like you're a minor. We can't stop you."

"We could never stop him from doing what he wanted even when he *was* a minor," said Mother.

Damn right, thought Peter.

"The curse of having children who are smarter than you," said Father, "is that they think their superior rational process is enough to compensate for their lack of experience."

If I were a little brat like Bean, that comment would have been the last straw. I would have walked away and not come home for a week, if ever. But I'm not a child and I can control my personal resentments and do what's expedient. I'm not going to throw off my camouflage out of pique.

At the same time, I can't be faulted, can I, for wondering if there's any chance that my father might have a stroke and go permanently mute.

They were at the station. With a round of good-byes, Father and Mother took the bus north toward home, and Peter got on an eastbound bus with Bean and Carlotta.

And, as Peter expected, they got off at the first stop and crossed over to catch the westbound bus. They really made a religion out of paranoia.

Even when they got back to the airport hotel, they did not enter the building. Instead they walked through the shopping mall that had once been a parking garage back when people drove cars to the airport. "Even if they bug the mall," said Bean, "I doubt they can afford the manpower to listen to everything people say."

"If they're bugging your room," said Peter, "that means they're already on to you."

"Hotels routinely bug their rooms," said Bean. "To catch vandals and criminals in the act. It's a computer scan, but nothing stops the employees from listening in."

"This is America," said Peter.

"You spend way too much time thinking about global

affairs," said Bean. "If you ever do have to go underground, you won't have a clue how to survive."

"You're the one who invited me to join you in hiding," said Peter. "What was that nonsense about? I'm not going anywhere. I have too much work to do."

"Ah, yes," said Bean. "Pulling the world's strings from behind a curtain. The trouble is, the world is about to move from politics to war, and your strings are going to be snipped."

"It's still politics."

"But the decisions are made on the battlefield, not in the conference rooms."

"I know," said Peter. "That's why we should work together."

"I can't think why," said Bean. "The one thing I asked you for—information about where Petra is—you tried to sell me instead of just giving it to me. Doesn't sound like you want an ally. Sounds like you want a customer."

"Boys," said Sister Carlotta. "Bickering isn't how this is going to work."

"If it's going to work," said Peter, "it's going to work however Bean and I make it work. Between us."

Sister Carlotta stopped cold, grabbed Peter's shoulder, and drew him close. "Get this straight right now, you arrogant twit. You're not the only brilliant person in the world, and you're far from being the only one who thinks he pulls all the strings. Until you have the courage to come out from behind the veil of these ersatz personalities, you don't have much to offer those of us who are working in the real world."

"Don't ever touch me like that again," said Peter.

"Oh, the personage is sacred?" said Sister Carlotta. "You really do live on Planet Peter, don't you?"

Bean interrupted before Peter could answer the bitch. "Look, we gave you everything we had on Ender's jeesh, no strings attached."

"And I used it. I got most of them out, and pretty damn fast, too."

"But not the one who sent the message," said Bean. "I want Petra."

"And I want world peace," said Peter. "You think too small."

"I may think too small for you," said Bean, "but you think too small for me. Playing your little computer games, juggling stories back and forth—well, my friend trusted me and asked me for help. She was trapped with a psychopathic killer and she doesn't have anyone but me who cares a rat's ass what happens to her."

"She has her family," murmured Sister Carlotta. Peter was pleased to learn that she corrected Bean, too. An all-purpose bitch.

"You want to save the world, but you're going to have to do it one battle at a time, one country at a time. And you need people like me, who get our hands dirty," said Bean.

"Oh, spare me your delusions," said Peter. "You're a little boy in hiding."

"I'm a general who's between armies," said Bean. "If I weren't, you wouldn't be talking to me."

"And you want an army so you can go rescue Petra," said Peter.

"So she's alive?"

"How would I know?"

"I don't know how you'd know. But you know more than you're telling me, and if you don't give me what you have, right now, you arrogant oomay, I'm done with you, I'll leave you here playing your little net games, and go find somebody who's not afraid to come out of Mama's house and take some risks."

Peter was almost blind with rage.

For a moment.

And then he calmed himself, forced himself to stand outside the situation. What was Bean showing him? That he cared more for personal loyalty than for longterm strategy. That was dangerous, but not fatal. And it gave Peter leverage, knowing what Bean cared about more than personal advancement.

"What I know about Petra," said Peter, "is that when Achilles disappeared, so did she. My sources inside Russia tell me that the only liberation team that was interfered with was the one rescuing her. The driver, a bodyguard, and the team leader were shot dead. There was no evidence that Petra was injured, though they know she was present for one of the killings."

"How do they know?" asked Bean.

"The spatter pattern from a head shot had been blocked in a silhouette about her size on the inside wall of the van. She was covered with the man's blood. But there was no blood from her body."

"They know more than that."

"A small private jet, which once belonged to a crimelord but was confiscated and used by the intelligence service that sponsored Achilles, took off from a nearby airfield and flew, after a refueling stop, to India. One of the airport maintenance personnel said that it looked to him like a honeymoon trip. Just the pilot and the young couple. But no luggage."

"So he has her with him," said Bean.

"In India," said Sister Carlotta.

"And my sources in India have gone silent," said Peter.

"Dead?" asked Bean.

"No, just careful," said Peter. "The most populous country on Earth. Ancient enmities. A chip on the national shoulder from being treated like a second-class country by everyone."

"The Polemarch is an Indian," said Bean.

"And there's reason to believe he's been passing I.F. data to the Indian military," said Peter. "Nothing that can be proved, but Chamrajnagar is not as disinterested as he pretends to be."

"So you think Achilles may be just what India wants to help them launch a war."

"No," said Peter. "I think India may be just what Achilles wants to help him launch an empire. Petra is what *they* want to help them launch a war."

"So Petra is the passport Achilles used to get into a position of power in India."

"That would be my guess," said Peter. "That's all I know, and all I guess. But I can also tell you that your chance of getting in and rescuing her is nil."

"Pardon me," said Bean, "but you don't know what I'm capable of doing."

"When it comes to intelligence-gathering," said Peter, "the Indians aren't in the same league as the Russians. I don't think your paranoia is needed anymore. Achilles isn't in a position to do anything to you right now."

"Just because Achilles is in India," said Bean, "doesn't mean that he's limited to knowing only what the Indian intelligence service can find out for him."

"The agency that's been helping him in Russia is being taken over and probably will be shut down," said Peter.

"I know Achilles," said Bean, "and I can promise you—if he really is in India, working for them, then it is absolutely certain that he has already betrayed them and has connections and fallback positions in at least three other places. And at least one of them will have an intelligence service with excellent worldwide reach. If you make the mistake of thinking Achilles is limited by borders and loyalties, he'll destroy you."

Peter looked down at Bean. He wanted to say, I already knew all that. But it would be a lie if he said that. He hadn't known that about Achilles, except in the abstract sense that he tried never to underestimate an opponent. Bean's knowledge of Achilles was better than his. "Thank you," said Peter. "I wasn't taking that into account."

"I know," said Bean ungraciously. "It's one of the reasons I think you're headed for failure. You think you know more than you actually know."

"But I listen," said Peter. "And I learn. Do you?"

Sister Carlotta laughed. "I do believe that the two most arrogant boys in the world have finally met, and they don't much like what they see."

Peter did not even glance at her, and neither did Bean. "Actually," said Peter, "I *do* like what I see."

"I wish I could say the same," said Bean.

"Let's keep walking," said Peter. "We've been standing in one place too long."

"At least he's picking up on our paranoia," said Sister Carlotta.

"Where will India make its move?" asked Peter. "The obvious thing would be war with Pakistan."

"Again?" said Bean. "Pakistan would be an indigestible lump. It would block India from further expansion, just trying to get the Muslims under control. A terrorist war that would make the old struggle with the Sikhs look like a child's birthday party."

"But they can't move anywhere else as long as they have

Pakistan poised to plunge a dagger in their back," said Peter.

Bean grinned. "Burma? But is it worth taking?"

"It's on the way to more valuable prizes, if China doesn't object," said Peter. "But are you just ignoring the Pakistan problem?"

"Molotov and Ribbentrop," said Bean.

The men who negotiated the nonaggression pact between Russia and Germany in the 1930s that divided Poland between them and freed Germany to launch World War II. "I think it will have to be deeper than that," said Peter. "I think, at some level, an alliance."

"What if India offers Pakistan a free hand against Iran? It can go for the oil. India is free to move east. To scoop up the countries that have long been under her cultural influence. Burma. Thailand. Not Muslim countries, so Pakistan's conscience is clear."

"Is China going to sit and watch?" asked Peter.

"They might if India tosses them Vietnam," said Bean. "The world is ripe to be divided up among the great powers. India wants to be one. With Achilles directing their strategy, with Chamrajnagar feeding them information, with Petra to command their armies, they can play on the big stage. And then, when Pakistan has exhausted itself fighting Iran . . ."

The inevitable betrayal. If Pakistan didn't strike first. "That's too far down the line to predict now," said Peter.

"But it's the way Achilles thinks," said Bean. "Two betrayals ahead. He was using Russia, but maybe he already had this deal with India in place. Why not? In the long run, the whole world is the tail, and India is the dog."

More important than Bean's particular conclusions was the fact that Bean had a good eye. He lacked detailed intelligence, of course—how would he get that?—but he saw the big picture. He thought the way a global strategist had to think.

He was worth talking to.

"Well, Bean," said Peter, "here's my problem. I think I can get you in position to help block Achilles. But I can't trust you not to do something stupid."

"I won't mount a rescue operation for Petra until I know it will succeed."

"That's a foolish thing to say. You never *know* a military operation will succeed. And that's not what worries me. I'm sure if you mounted a rescue, it would be a well-planned and well-executed one."

"So what worries you about me?" asked Bean.

"That you're making the assumption that Petra wants to be rescued."

"She does," said Bean.

"Achilles seduces people," said Peter. "I've read his files, his history. This kid has a golden voice, apparently. He makes people trust him—even people who know he's a snake. They think, He won't betray *me,* because we have such a special closeness."

"And then he kills them. I know that," said Bean.

"But does Petra? *She* hasn't read his file. *She* didn't know him on the streets of Rotterdam. She didn't even know him in the brief time he was in Battle School."

"She knows him now," said Bean.

"You're sure of that?" asked Peter.

"But I'll promise you—I won't try to rescue her until I've been in communication with her."

Peter mulled this over for a moment. "She might betray you."

"No," said Bean.

"Trusting people will get you killed," said Peter. "I don't want you to bring me down with you."

"You have it backward," said Bean. "I don't trust anybody,

except to do what they think is necessary. What they think they have to do. But I know Petra, and I know the kind of thing she'll think she has to do. It's *me* I'm trusting, not her."

"And he can't bring you down," said Sister Carlotta, "because you're not up."

Peter looked at her, making little effort to conceal his contempt. "I am where I am," he said. "And it's not down."

"Locke is where Locke is," said Carlotta. "And Demosthenes. But Peter Wiggin is nowhere. Peter Wiggin is nothing."

"What's your problem?" Peter demanded. "Is it bothering you that your little puppet here might actually be cutting a few of the strings you pull?"

"There are no strings," said Carlotta. "And you're too stupid, apparently, to realize that *I'm* the one who believes in what you're doing, not Bean. He couldn't care less who rules the world. But I do. Arrogant and condescending as you are, I've already made up my mind that if anybody's going to stop Achilles, it's you. But you're fatally weakened by the fact that you are ripe to be blackmailed by the threat of exposure. Chamrajnagar knows who you are. He's feeding information to India. Do you really think for one moment that Achilles won't find out—and soon, if not already—exactly who is behind Locke? The one who got him booted out of Russia? Do you really think he isn't already working on plans to kill you?"

Peter blushed with shame. To have this nun tell him what he should have realized by himself was humiliating. But she was right—he wasn't used to thinking of physical danger.

"That's why we wanted you to come with us," said Bean.

"Your cover is already blown," said Sister Carlotta.

"The moment I go public as a kid," said Peter Wiggin, "most of my sources will dry up."

"No," said Sister Carlotta. "It all depends on *how* you come out."

"Do you think I haven't thought this through a thousand times?" said Peter. "Until I'm old enough . . ."

"No," said Sister Carlotta. "Think for a minute, Peter. National governments have just gone through a nasty little scuffle over ten *children* that they want to have command their armies. You're the older brother of the greatest of them all. Your youth is an asset. And if you control the way the information comes out, instead of having somebody else expose you . . ."

"It will be a momentary scandal," said Peter. "No matter how my identity comes out, there'll be a flurry of commentary on it, and then I'll be old news—only I'll have been fired from most of my writing gigs. People won't return my calls or answer my mail. I really *will* be a college student then."

"That sounds like something you decided years ago," said Sister Carlotta, "and haven't looked at with fresh eyes since then."

"Since this seems to be tell-Peter-he's-stupid day, let's hear *your* plan."

Sister Carlotta grinned at Bean. "Well, I was wrong. He actually *can* listen to other people."

"I told you," said Bean.

Peter suspected that this little exchange was designed merely to make him think Bean was on his side. "Just tell me your plan and skip the sucking-up phase."

"The term of the current Hegemon will end in about eight months," said Sister Carlotta. "Let's get several influential people to start floating the name of Locke as the replacement."

"That's your plan? The office of Hegemon is worthless."

"Wrong," said Sister Carlotta, "and wrong. The office is not worthless—eventually you'll have to have it in order to make you the legitimate leader of the world against the threat posed by Achilles. But that's later. Right now, we float the name of Locke, not so you'll get the office, but so that you can have an excuse to publically announce, as Locke, that you can't be considered for such an office because you are, after all, merely a teenager. *You* tell people that you're Ender Wiggin's older brother, that you and Valentine worked for years to try to hold the League together and to prepare for the League War so that your little brother's victory didn't lead to the self-destruction of humanity. But you are still too young to take an actual office of public trust. See how it works? Now your announcement won't be a confession or a scandal. It will be one more example of how nobly you place the interest of world peace and good order ahead of your own personal ambition."

"I'll still lose some of my contacts," said Peter.

"But not many. The news will be positive. It will have the right spin. All these years, Locke has been the brother of the genius Ender Wiggin. A prodigy."

"And there's no time to waste," said Bean. "You have to do it before Achilles can strike. Because you *will* be exposed within a few months."

"Weeks," said Sister Carlotta.

Peter was furious with himself. "Why didn't I see this? It's obvious."

"You've been doing this for years," said Bean. "You had a pattern that worked. But Achilles has changed everything. You've never had anybody gunning for you before. What matters to me is not that you failed to see it on your own. What matters is that when we pointed it out to you, you were willing to hear it."

"So I've passed your little test?" said Peter nastily.

"Just as I hope I'll pass yours," said Bean. "If we're going to work together, we have to be able to tell each other the truth. Now I know you'll listen to me. You just have to take my word for it that I'll listen to you. But I listen to *her*, don't I?"

Peter was churning with dread. They were right, the time had come, the old pattern was over. And it was frightening. Because now he had to put everything on the line, and he might fail.

But if he didn't act now, if he didn't risk everything, he would certainly fail. Achilles' presence in the equation made it inevitable.

"So how," said Peter, "will we get this groundswell started so I can decline the honor of being a candidate for the Hegemony?"

"Oh, that's easy," said Carlotta. "If you give the OK, then by tomorrow there can be news stories about how a highly placed source at the Vatican confirms that Locke's name is being floated as a possible successor when the current Hegemon's term expires."

"And then," said Bean, "a highly placed officer in the Hegemony—the Minister of Colonization, to be exact, though no one will say that—will be quoted as saying that Locke is not just a good candidate, he's the best candidate, and may be the only candidate, and with the support of the Vatican he thinks Locke is the frontrunner."

"You've planned this all out," said Peter.

"No," said Sister Carlotta. "It's just that the only two people we know are my highly placed friend in the Vatican and our good friend ex-Colonel Graff."

"We're committing all our assets," said Bean, "but they'll be enough. The moment those stories run—tomorrow—you be ready to reply for the next morning's nets. At the same time that everybody's giving their first reactions to your brand-new frontrunner status, the world will be reading your announcement that you refuse to be considered for such an office because your youth would make it too difficult for you to wield the authority that the office of Hegemon requires."

"And that," said Sister Carlotta, "is the very thing that gives you the moral authority to be accepted as Hegemon when the time comes."

"By declining the office," said Peter, "I make it more likely that I'll get it."

"Not in peacetime," said Carlotta. "Declining an office in peacetime takes you out of the running. But there's going to be war. And then the fellow who sacrificed his own ambition for the good of the world will look better and better. Especially when his last name is Wiggin."

Do they have to keep bringing up the fact that my relationship to Ender is more important than my years of work?

"You aren't against using that family connection, are you?" asked Bean.

"I'll do what it takes," said Peter, "and I'll use whatever works. But . . . tomorrow?"

"Achilles got to India yesterday, right?" said Bean. "Every day we delay this is a day that he has a chance to expose you. Do you think he'll wait? You exposed *him*—he'll crave the turnabout, and Chamrajnagar won't be shy about telling him, will he?"

"No," said Peter. "Chamrajnagar has already shown me how he feels about me. He'll do nothing to protect me."

"So here we are once again," said Bean. "We're giving you something, and you're going to use it. Are you going to help me? How can I get into a position where I have troops to train and command? Besides going back to Greece, I mean."

"No, not Greece," said Peter. "They're useless to you, and they'll end up doing only what Russia permits. No freedom of action."

"Where, then?" said Sister Carlotta. "Where do you have influence?"

"In all modesty," said Peter, "at this moment, I have influence everywhere. Day after tomorrow, I may have influence nowhere."

"So let's act now," said Bean. "Where?"

"Thailand," said Peter. "Burma has no hope of resisting an Indian attack, or of putting together an alliance that might have a chance. But Thailand is historically the leader of southeast Asia. The one nation that was never colonized. The natural leader of the Tai-speaking peoples in the surrounding nations. And they have a strong military."

"But I don't speak the language," said Bean.

"Not a problem," said Peter. "The Thai have been multilingual for centuries, and they have a long history of allowing foreigners to take positions of power and influence in their government, as long as they're loyal to Thailand's interests. You have to throw in your lot with them. They have to trust you. But it seems plain enough that you know how to be loyal."

"Not at all," said Bean. "I'm completely selfish. I survive. That's all I do."

"But you survive," said Peter, "by being absolutely loyal to the few people you depend on. I read just as much about you as I did about Achilles."

"What was written about me reflects the fantasies of the newspeople," said Bean.

"I'm not talking about the news," said Peter. "I read Carlotta's memos to the I.F. about your childhood in Rotterdam."

They both stopped walking. Ah, have I surprised you? Peter couldn't help but take pleasure in knowing that he had shown that he, too, knew some things about *them*.

"Those memos were eyes only," said Carlotta. "There should have been no copies."

"Ah, but whose eyes?" said Peter. "There are no secrets to people with the right friends."

"*I* haven't read those memos," said Bean.

Carlotta looked searchingly at Peter. "Some information is worthless except to destroy," she said.

And now Peter wondered what secrets she had about Bean. Because when he spoke of "memos," he in fact was thinking of a report that had been in Achilles' file, which had drawn on a couple of those memos as a source about life on the streets of Rotterdam. The comments about Bean had been merely ancillary matters. He really hadn't read the actual memos. But now he wanted to, because there was clearly something that she didn't want Bean to know.

And Bean knew it, too.

"What's in those memos that you don't want Peter to tell me?" Bean demanded.

"I had to convince the Battle School people that I was being impartial about you," said Sister Carlotta. "So I had to make negative statements about you in order to get them to believe the positive ones."

"Do you think that would hurt my feelings?" said Bean.

"Yes, I do," said Carlotta. "Because even if you understand the reason why I said some of those things, you'll never forget that I said them."

"They can't be worse than what I imagine," said Bean.

"It's not a matter of being bad or worse. They can't be *too* bad or you wouldn't have got into Battle School, would you? You were too young and they didn't believe your test scores and they knew there wouldn't be time to train you unless you really were . . . what I said. I just don't want you to have my words in your memory. And if you have any sense, Bean, you'll never read them."

"Toguro," said Bean. "I've been gossiped about by the person I trust most, and it's so bad she begs me not to try to find out."

"Enough of this nonsense," said Peter. "We've all faced some nasty blows today. But we've got an alliance started here, haven't we? You're acting in my interest tonight, getting that groundswell started so I can reveal myself on the world's stage. And I've got to get you into Thailand, in a position of trust and influence, before I expose myself as a teenager. Which of us gets to sleep first, do you think?"

"Me," said Sister Carlotta. "Because I don't have any sins on my conscience."

"Kuso," said Bean. "You have all the sins of the world on your mind."

"You're confusing me with somebody else," said Sister Carlotta.

To Peter their banter sounded like family chatter—old jokes, repeated because they're comfortable.

Why didn't his own family have any of that? Peter had bantered with Valentine, but she had never really opened up to him and played that way. She always resented him, even feared him. And their parents were hopeless. There was no clever banter there, there were no shared jokes and memories.

Maybe I really was raised by robots, Peter thought.

"Tell your parents we really appreciated the dinner," said Bean.

"Home to bed," said Sister Carlotta.

"You won't be sleeping in your hotel tonight, will you?" said Peter. "You'll be leaving."

"We'll email you how to contact us," said Bean.

"You'll have to leave Greensboro yourself, you know," said Sister Carlotta. "Once you reveal your identity, Achilles will know where you are. And even though India has no reason to kill you, Achilles does. He kills anyone who has even *seen* him in a position of helplessness. You actually *put* him in that position. You're a dead man, as soon as he can reach you."

Peter thought of the attempt that had been made on Bean's life. "He was perfectly happy to kill your parents right along with you, wasn't he?" Peter asked.

"Maybe," said Bean, "you should tell your mom and dad who you are before they read about it on the nets. And then help them get out of town."

"At some point we have to stop hiding from Achilles and face him openly."

"Not until you have a government committed to keeping you alive," said Bean. "Until then, you stay in hiding. And your parents, too."

"I don't think they'll even believe me," said Peter. "My parents, I mean. When I tell them that I'm really Locke. What parents would? They'll probably try to commit me as delusional."

"Trust them," said Bean. "I think you think they're stupid. But I can assure you that they're not. Or at least your mother isn't. You got your brains from somebody. They'll deal with this."

So it was that when Peter got home at ten o'clock, he went to his parents' room and knocked on their door.

"What is it?" asked Father.

"Are you awake?" Peter asked.

"Come in," said Mother.

They chatted mindlessly for a few minutes about dinner

and Sister Carlotta and that delightful little Julian Delphiki, so hard to believe that a child that young could possibly have done all that he had done in his short life. And on and on, until Peter interrupted them.

"I have something to tell you," said Peter. "Tomorrow, some friends of Bean's and Carlotta's will be starting a phony movement to get Locke nominated as Hegemon. You know who Locke is? The political commentator?"

They nodded.

"And the next morning," Peter went on, "Locke is going to come out with a statement that he has to decline such an honor because he's just a teenage boy living in Greensboro, North Carolina."

"Yes?" said Father.

Did they really not get it? "It's me, Dad," said Peter. "I'm Locke."

They looked at each other. Peter waited for them to say something stupid.

"Are you going to tell them that Valentine was Demosthenes, too?" asked Mother.

For a moment he thought she was saying that as a joke, that she thought that the only thing more absurd than Peter being Locke would be Valentine being Demosthenes.

Then he realized that there was no irony in her question at all. It was an important point, and one he needed to address— the contradiction between Locke and Demosthenes had to be resolved, or there *would* still be something for Chamrajnagar and Achilles to expose. And blaming Valentine for Demosthenes right from the start was an important thing to do.

But not as important to him as the fact that Mother knew it. "How long have you known?" he asked.

"We've been very proud of what you've accomplished," said Father.

"As proud as we've ever been of Ender," Mother added.

Peter almost staggered under the emotional blow. They had just told him the thing that he had wanted most to hear his entire life, without ever quite admitting it to himself. Tears sprang to his eyes.

"Thanks," he murmured. Then he closed the door and fled to his room. Somehow, fifteen minutes later, he got enough control of his emotions that he could write the letters he had to write to Thailand, and begin writing his self-exposure essay.

They knew. And far from thinking him a second-rater, a disappointment, they were as proud of him as they had ever been of Ender.

His whole world was about to change, his life would be transformed, he might lose everything, he might win everything. But all he could feel that night, as he finally went to bed and drifted off to sleep, was utter, foolish happiness.

Part Three

MANEUVERS

11

BANGKOK

Posted on Military History Forum by
HectorVictorious@firewall.net
Topic: Who Remembers Briseis?

When I read the Iliad, I see the
same things everyone else does—the
poetry, of course, and the information about heroic bronze-age
warfare. But I see something else,
too. It might have been Helen whose
face launched a thousand ships, but
it was Briseis who almost wrecked
them. She was a powerless captive,
a slave, and yet Achilles almost
tore the Greek alliance apart because he wanted her.

The mystery that intrigues me is:
Was she extraordinarily beautiful?
Or was it her mind that Achilles
coveted? No, seriously: Would she

have been happy for long as Achilles' captive? Would she, perhaps, have gone to him willingly? Or remained a surly, resistant slave?

Not that it would have mattered to Achilles—he would have used his captive the same way, regardless of her feelings. But one imagines Briseis taking note of the tale about Achilles' heel and slipping that information to someone within the walls of Troy . . .

Briseis, if only I could have heard from you!

—Hector Victorious

Bean amused himself by leaving messages for Petra scattered all over the forums that she might visit—if she was alive, if Achilles allowed her to browse the nets, if she realized that a topic heading like "Who Remembers Briseis?" was a reference to her, and if she was free to reply as his message covertly begged her to do. He wooed her under other names of women loved by military leaders: Guinevere, Josephine, Roxane—even Barsine, the Persian wife of Alexander that Roxane murdered soon after his death. And he signed himself with the name of a nemesis or chief rival or successor: Mordred, Hector, Wellington, Cassander.

He took the dangerous step of allowing these identities to continue to exist, each consisting only of a forwarding order to another anonymous net identity that held all mail it received as encrypted postings on an open board with no-tracks protocols. He could visit and read the postings without leaving a trace. But firewalls could be pierced, protocols broken.

He could afford to be a little more careless now about his online identities, if only because his real-world location was now known to people whose trustworthiness he could not assess. Do you worry about the fifth lock on the back door, when the front door is open?

They had welcomed him generously in Bangkok. General Naresuan promised him that no one would know his real identity, that he would be given soldiers to train and intelligence to analyze and his advice would be sought constantly as the Thai military prepared for all kinds of future contingencies. "We are taking seriously Locke's assessment that India will soon pose a threat to Thai security, and we will of course want your help in preparing contingency plans." All so warm and courteous. Bean and Carlotta were installed in a general-officer-level apartment on a military base, given unlimited privileges concerning meals and purchases, and then . . . ignored.

No one called. No one consulted. The promised intelligence did not flow. The promised soldiers were never assigned.

Bean knew better than to even inquire. The promises were not forgotten. If he asked about them, Naresuan would be embarrassed, would feel challenged. That would never do. Something had happened. Bean could only imagine what.

At first, of course, he feared that Achilles had gotten to the

Thai government somehow, that his agents now knew exactly where Bean was, that his death was imminent.

That was when he sent Carlotta away.

It was not a pleasant scene. "You should come with me," she said. "They won't stop you. Walk away."

"I'm not leaving," said Bean. "Whatever has gone wrong is probably local politics. Somebody here doesn't like having me around—maybe Naresuan himself, maybe someone else."

"If you feel safe enough to stay," said Sister Carlotta, "then there's no reason for me to go."

"You can't pass yourself off as my grandmother here," said Bean. "The fact that I have a guardian weakens me."

"Spare me the scene you're trying to play," said Carlotta. "I know there are reasons why you'd be better off without me, and I know there are ways that I could help you greatly."

"If Achilles knows where I am already, then his penetration of Bangkok is deep enough that I'll never get away," said Bean. "You might. The information that an older woman is with me might not have reached him yet. But it will soon, and he wants you dead as much as he wants to kill me. I don't want to have to worry about you here."

"I'll go," said Carlotta. "But how do I write to you, since you never keep the same address?"

He gave her the name of his folder on the no-tracks board he was using, and the encryption key. She memorized it.

"One more thing," said Bean. "In Greensboro, Peter said something about reading your memos."

"I think he was lying," said Carlotta.

"I think the way you reacted proved that whether he read them or not, there *were* memos, and you don't want me to read them."

"There were, and I don't," said Carlotta.

"And that's the other reason I want you to leave," said Bean.

The expression on her face turned fierce. "You can't trust me when I tell you that there is nothing in those memos that you need to know right now?"

"I need to know everything about myself. My strengths, my weaknesses. You know things about me that you told Graff and you didn't tell me. You're still not telling me. You think of yourself as my master, able to decide things for me. That means we're not partners after all."

"Very well," said Carlotta. "I am acting in your best interest, but I understand that you don't see it that way." Her manner was cold, but Bean knew her well enough to recognize that it was not anger she was controlling, but grief and frustration. It was a cold thing to do, but for her own sake he had to send her away and keep her from being in close contact with him until he understood what was going on here in Bangkok. The contretemps about the memos made her willing to go. And he really was annoyed.

She was out the door in fifteen minutes and on her way to the airport. Nine hours later he found a posting from her on his encrypted board: She was in Manila, where she could disappear within the Catholic establishment there. Not a word about their quarrel, if that's what it had been. Only a brief reference to "Locke's confession," as the newspeople were calling it. "Poor Peter," wrote Carlotta. "He's been hiding for so long, it's going to be hard for him to get used to having to face the consequences of his words."

To her secure address at the Vatican, Bean replied, "I just hope Peter has the brains to get out of Greensboro. What he needs right now is a small country to run, so he can get some administrative and political experience. Or at least a city water department."

And what I need, thought Bean, is soldiers to command. That's why I came here.

For weeks after Carlotta left, the silence continued. It became obvious, soon enough, that whatever was going on had nothing to do with Achilles, or Bean would be dead by now. Nor could it have had anything to do with Locke being revealed as Peter Wiggin—the freeze-out had already begun before Peter published his declaration.

Bean busied himself with whatever tasks seemed meaningful. Though he had no access to military-level maps, he could still access the publicly available satellite maps of the terrain between India and the heart of Thailand—the rough mountain country of northern and eastern Burma, the Indian Ocean coastal approaches. India had a substantial fleet, by Indian Ocean standards—might they attempt to run the Strait of Malacca and strike at the heart of Thailand from the gulf? All possibilities had to be prepared for.

Some basic intelligence about the makeup of the Indian and Thai military was available on the nets. Thailand had a powerful air force—there was a chance of achieving air dominance, if they could protect their bases. Therefore it would be essential to have the capability of laying down emergency airstrips in a thousand different places, an engineering feat well within the reach of the Thai military—if they trained for it now and dispersed crews and fuel and spare parts throughout the country. That, along with mines, would be the best protection against a coastal landing.

The other Indian vulnerability would be supply lines and lanes of advance. Since India's military strategy would inevitably depend on throwing vast, irresistible armies against the enemy, the defense was to keep those vast armies hungry and harry them constantly from the air and from raiding parties. And if, as was likely, the Indian Army reached the fertile plain of the Chao Phraya or the Aoray Plateau, they had to find the land utterly stripped, the food supplies dispersed and hidden—those that weren't destroyed.

It was a brutal strategy, because the Thai people would suffer along with the Indian Army—indeed, they would suffer more. So the destruction had to be set up so it would only take place at the last minute. And, as much as possible, they had to be able to evacuate women and children to remote areas or even to camps in Laos and Cambodia. Not that borders would stop the Indian army, but terrain might. Having many isolated targets for the Indians would force them to divide their forces. Then—and only then—would it make sense for the Thai military to take on smaller portions of the Indian army in hit-and-run engagements or, where possible, in pitched battles where the Thai side would have temporary numerical parity and superior air support.

Of course, for all Bean knew this was already the long-standing Thai military doctrine and if he made these suggestions he would only annoy them—or make them feel that he had contempt for them.

So he worded his memo very carefully. Lots of phrases like, "No doubt you already have this in place," and "as I'm sure you have long expected." Of course, even those phrases could backfire, if they *hadn't* thought of these things—it would sound patronizing. But he had to do something to break this stalemate of silence.

He read the memo over and over, revising each time. He waited days to send it, so he could see it in new perspectives. Finally, certain that it was as rhetorically inoffensive as he could make it, he put it into an email and sent it to the Office of the Chakri—the supreme military commander. It was the most public and potentially embarrassing way he could deliver the memo, since mail to that address was inevitably sorted and read by aides. Even printing it out and carrying it by hand would have been more subtle. But the idea was to stir things up; if Naresuan wanted him to be subtle, he would have given him a private email address to write to.

Fifteen minutes after he sent the memo, his door unceremoniously opened and four military police came in. "Come with us, sir," said the sergeant in charge.

Bean knew better than to delay or to ask questions. These men knew nothing but the instructions they had been given, and Bean would find out what those were by waiting to see what they did.

They did not take him to the office of the Chakri. Instead he was taken to one of the temporary buildings that had been set up on the old parade grounds—the Thai military had only recently given up marching as part of the training of soldiers and the display of military might. Only three hundred years after the American Civil War had proven that the days of marching in formation into battle were over. For military organizations, that was about the normal time lag. Sometimes Bean half-expected to find some army somewhere that was still training its soldiers to fight with sabers from horseback.

There was no label, not even a number, on the door they led him to. And when he came inside, none of the soldier-clerks even looked up at him. His arrival was both expected and unimportant, their attitude said. Which meant, of course, that it was *very* important, or they would not be so studiously perfect about not noticing him.

He was led to an office door, which the sergeant opened for him. He went in; the military police did not. The door closed behind him.

Seated at the desk was a major. This was an awfully high

rank to have manning a reception desk, but today, at least, that seemed to be the man's duty. He depressed the button on an intercom. "The package is here," he said.

"Send it in." The voice that came back sounded young. So young that Bean understood the situation at once.

Of course. Thailand had contributed its share of military geniuses to Battle School. And even though none of Ender's jeesh had been of Thai parentage, Thailand, like many east and south Asian countries, was overrepresented in the population of Battle School as a whole.

There had even been three Thai soldiers who served with Bean in Dragon Army. Bean remembered every kid in that army very well, along with his complete dossier, since he was the one who had drawn up the list of soldiers who should make up Ender's army. Since most countries seemed to value their returning Battle School graduates in proportion to their closeness to Ender Wiggin, it was most likely one of those three who had been given a position of such influence here that he would be able to intercept a memo to the Chakri so quickly. And of the three, the one Bean would expect to see in the most prominent position, taking the most aggressive role, was . . .

Surrey. Suriyawong. "Surly," as they called him behind his back, since he always seemed to be pissed off about something.

And there he was, standing behind a table covered with maps.

Bean saw, to his surprise, that he was actually almost as tall as Suriyawong. Surrey had not been very big, but everyone towered over Bean in Battle School. Bean was catching up. He might not spend his whole life hopelessly undersized. It was a promising thought.

There was nothing promising about Surrey's attitude,

though. "So the colonial powers have decided to use India and Thailand to fight their surrogate wars," he said.

Bean knew at once what had gotten under Suriyawong's skin. Achilles was a Belgian Walloon by birth, and Bean, of course, was Greek. "Yes, of course," said Bean. "Belgium and Greece are bound to fight out their ancient differences on bloody battlefields in Burma."

"Just because you were in Ender's jeesh," said Suriyawong, "does not mean that you have any understanding of the military situation of Thailand."

"My memo was designed to show how limited my knowledge was, because Chakri Naresuan has not provided me with the access to intelligence that he indicated I would receive when I arrived."

"If we ever need your advice, we'll provide you with intelligence."

"If you only provide me with the intelligence you think I need," said Bean, "then my advice will only consist of telling you what you already know, and I might as well go home now."

"Yes," said Suriyawong. "That would be best."

"Suriyawong," said Bean, "you don't really know me."

"I know you were always an emossin' little showoff who always had to be smarter than everybody else."

"I *was* smarter than everybody else," said Bean. "I've got the test scores to prove it. So what? That didn't mean they made me commander of Dragon Army. It didn't mean Ender made me a toon leader. I know just how worthless being smart is, compared with being good at command. I also know just how ignorant I am here in Thailand. I didn't come here because I thought Thailand would be prostrate without my brilliant mind to lead you into battle. I came here because the most dangerous human on this planet is running the show in India and by my best calculations, Thailand is going to be his primary target. I came here because if Achilles is going to be stopped from setting up his tyranny over the world, this is where it has to be done. And I thought, like George Washington in the American revolution, you might actually welcome a Lafayette or a Steuben to help in the cause."

"If your foolish memo was an example of your 'help,' you can leave now."

"So you already have the capability of making temporary airstrips within the amount of time that a fighter is in the air? So they can land at an airstrip that didn't exist when they took off?"

"That *is* an interesting idea and we're having the engineers look at it and evaluate the feasibility."

Bean nodded. "Good. That tells me all I needed to know. I'll stay."

"No, you will not!"

"I'll stay because, despite the fact that you're pissed off that I'm here, you still recognized a good idea when you heard it and put it into play. You're not an idiot, and therefore you're worth working with."

Suriyawong slapped the table and leaned over it, furious. "You condescending little oomay, I'm not your moose."

Bean answered him calmly. "Suriyawong, I don't want your job. I don't want to run things here. I just want to be useful. Why not use me the way Ender did? Give me a few soldiers to train. Let me think of weird things to do and figure out how to do them. Let me be ready so that when the war comes, and there's some impossible thing you need done, you can call me in and say, Bean, I need you to do something to slow down this army for a day, and I've got no troops anywhere near there. And I'll say, Are they drawing water from a river? Good, then let's give their whole army dysentery for a week. That should slow them down. And I'll get in there, get a bioagent into the water, bypass their water purification system, and get out. Or do you already have a water-drugging diarrhea team?"

Suriyawong held his expression of cold anger for a few moments, and then it broke. He laughed. "Come on, Bean, did you make that up on the spot, or have you really planned an operation like that?"

"Made it up just now," said Bean. "But it's kind of a fun idea, don't you think? Dysentery has changed the course of history more than once."

"Everybody immunizes their soldiers against the known bioagents. And there's no way of stopping downstream collateral damage."

"But Thailand is bound to have some pretty hot and heavy bioresearch, right?"

"Purely defensive," said Suriyawong. Then he smiled and sat down. "Sit, sit. You really are content to take a background position?"

"Not only content, but eager," said Bean. "If Achilles knew I was here, he'd find a way to kill me. The last thing I need is to be prominent—until we actually get into combat, at which time it might be a nice psychological blow to give Achilles the idea that I'm running things. It won't be true, but it might make him even crazier to think it's me he's facing. I've outmaneuvered him before. He's afraid of me."

"It's not my own position I was trying to protect," said Suriyawong. Bean understood this to mean that of course it *was* his position he was protecting. "But Thailand kept its independence when every other country in this area was ruled by Europeans. We're very proud of keeping foreigners out."

"And yet," said Bean, "Thailand also has a history of letting foreigners in—and using them effectively."

"As long as they know their place," said Suriyawong.

"Give me a place, and I'll remember to stay in it," said Bean.

"What kind of contingent do you want to work with?"

What Bean asked for wasn't a large number of men, but he wanted to draw them from every branch of service. Only two fighter-bombers, two patrol boats, a handful of engineers, a couple of light armored vehicles to go along with a couple of hundred soldiers and enough choppers to carry everything but the boats and planes. "And the power to requisition odd things that we think of. Rowboats, for instance. High explosives so we can train in making cliffs fall and bridges collapse. Whatever I think of."

"But you don't actually commit to combat without permission."

"Permission," said Bean, "from whom?"

"Me," said Suriyawong.

"But you're not Chakri," said Bean.

"The Chakri," said Suriyawong, "exists to provide me with everything I ask for. The planning is entirely in my hands."

"Glad to know who's aboon here." Bean stood up. "For what it's worth, I was most help to Ender when I had access to everything he knew."

"In your dreams," said Suriyawong.

Bean grinned. "I'm dreaming of good maps," said Bean. "And an accurate assessment of the current situation of the Thai military."

Suriyawong thought about that for a long moment.

"How many of your soldiers are you sending into battle blindfolded?" asked Bean. "I hope I'm the only one."

"Until I'm sure you really are my soldier," said Suriyawong, "the blindfold stays on. But . . . you can have the maps."

"Thank you," said Bean.

He knew what Suriyawong feared: that Bean would use any information he got to come up with alternate strategies and persuade the Chakri that he would do a better job as chief strategist than Suriyawong. For it was patently untrue that Suriyawong was the aboon here. Chakri Naresuan might trust him and had obviously delegated great responsibility to him. But the authority remained in Naresuan's hands, and Suriyawong served at his pleasure. That's why Suriyawong feared Bean—he could be replaced.

He'd find out soon enough that Bean was not interested in pal-ace politics. If he remembered correctly, Suriyawong was of the royal family—though the last few polygynist kings of Siam had had so many children that it was hard to imagine that there were many Thais who were not royal to one degree or another. Chulalongkorn had established the principle, centuries ago, that princes had a duty to serve, but not a right to high office. Suriyawong's life belonged to Thailand as a matter of honor, but he would hold his position in the military only as long as his superiors considered him the best for the job.

Now that Bean knew who it was who had been keeping him down, it would be easy enough to destroy Surrey and take his place. After all, Suriyawong had been given the responsibility to carry out Naresuan's promises to Bean. He had deliberately disobeyed the Chakri's orders. All Bean really needed to do was use a back door—some connection of Peter's, probably—to get word to Naresuan that Suriyawong had blocked Bean from getting what he needed, and there would be an inquiry and the first seeds of doubt about Suriyawong would be planted.

But Bean did not want Suriyawong's job.

He wanted a fighting force that he could train to work together so smoothly, so resourcefully, so brilliantly that when he made contact with Petra and found out where she was, he could go in and get her out alive. With or without Surly's permission. He'd help the Thai military as best he could, but Bean had his own objectives, and they had nothing to do with building a career in Bangkok.

"One last thing," said Bean. "I have to have a name here, something that won't alert anyone outside Thailand that I'm a child and a foreigner—that might be enough to tip off Achilles about who I am."

"What name do you have in mind? How about Süa—it means tiger."

"I have a better name," said Bean. "Borommakot."

Suriyawong looked puzzled for a moment, till he remembered the name from the history of Ayudhya, the ancient Tai city-state of which Siam was the successor. "That was the nickname of the uparat who stole the throne from Aphai, the rightful successor."

"I was just thinking of what the name means," said Bean. " 'In the urn. Awaiting cremation.' " He grinned. "As far as Achilles is concerned, I'm just a walking dead man."

Suriyawong relaxed. "Whatever. I thought as a foreigner you might appreciate having a shorter name."

"Why? I don't have to say it."

"You have to sign it."

"I'm not issuing written orders, and the only person I'll be reporting to is you. Besides, Borommakot is fun to say."

"You know your Thai history," said Suriyawong.

"Back in Battle School," said Bean. "I got fascinated with Thailand. A nation of survivors. The ancient Tai people managed to take over vast reaches of the Cambodian Empire and spread throughout southeast Asia, all without anybody noticing. They were conquered by Burma and emerged stronger than ever. When other countries were falling under European domination, Thailand managed to expand its borders for a surprisingly long time, and even when it lost Cambodia and Laos, it held its core. I think Achilles is going to find what everybody else has found—the Thai are not easily conquered, and, once conquered, not easily ruled."

"Then you have some idea of the soul of the Thai," said Suriyawong. "But no matter now long you study us, you will never be one of us."

"You're mistaken," said Bean. "I already am one of you. A survivor, a free man, no matter what."

Suriyawong took this seriously. "Then as one free man to another, welcome to the service of Thailand."

They parted amicably, and by the end of the day, Bean saw that Suriyawong intended to keep his word. He was provided with a list of soldiers—four preexisting fifty-man companies with fair records, so they weren't giving him the dregs. And he would have his helicopters, his jets, his patrol boats to train with.

He should have been nervous, preparing to face soldiers who were bound to be skeptical about having him as their commander. But he had been in that situation before, in Battle School. He would win over these soldiers by the simplest expedient of all. Not flattery, not favors, not folksy friendliness. He would win their loyalty by showing them that he knew what to do with an army, so they would have the confidence that when they went into battle, their lives would not be wasted in some doomed enterprise. He would tell them, from the start, "I will never lead you into an action unless I know we can win it. Your job is to become such a brilliant fighting force that there is no action I can't lead you into. We're not in this for glory. We're in this to destroy the enemies of Thailand any way we can."

They'd get used to being led by a little Greek boy soon enough.

12

ISLAMABAD

To:GuillaumeLeBon%Egalite@Haiti.gov
From: Locke%erasmus@polnet.gov
Re: Terms for Consultation

M. LeBon, I appreciate how difficult it was for you to approach me. I believe that I could offer you worthwhile views and suggestions, and, more to the point, I believe you are committed to acting courageously on behalf of the people you govern and therefore any suggestions I made would have an excellent chance of being put into effect.

But the terms you suggest are unacceptable to me. I will not come to Haiti by dark of night or masked as a tourist or student, lest anyone find out that you are consulting a teenage boy from America. I am still the author of every word written by Locke, and it is as that widely known figure, whose name is on the proposals that ended the League War, that I will come openly to consult with you. If my previous reputation were not reason enough for you to be able to invite me openly, then the fact that I am the brother of Ender Wiggin, on whose shoulders the fate of all humanity so recently was placed, should set a precedent you can follow without embarrassment. Not to mention the presence of children from Battle School in almost every military headquarters on Earth. The sum you offered is a princely one. But it will never be paid, for under the terms you suggested, I will not come, and if you invite me openly, I will certainly come but will accept no payment—not even for my expenses while I am in your country. As a foreigner, I could not possibly match your deep and abiding love for the people of Haiti, but I care very much that every nation and people on Earth share in the prosperity and freedom that are their birthright, and I will accept no fee for helping in that cause.

By bringing me openly, you decrease your personal risk, for if my suggestions are unpopular, you can lay the blame on me. And the personal risk I take by coming openly is far greater, for if the world judges my proposals to be unsound or if, in implementing them, you discover them to be unworkable, I will publicly bear the discredit. I speak candidly, because these are realities we both must face: Such is my confidence that my suggestions will be excellent and that you will be able to implement them effectively. When we have finished our work, you can play Cincinnatus and retire to your farm, while I will play Solon and leave the shores of Haiti, both of us confident that we have given your people a fair chance to take their proper place in the world.

Sincerely,
Peter Wiggin

Petra never forgot for an instant that she was a captive and a slave. But, like most captives, like most slaves, as she lived from day to day she became accustomed to her captivity and found ways to be herself within the tight boundaries around her.

She was guarded every moment, and her desk was

crippled so she could send no outgoing messages. There would be no repetition of her message to Bean. And even when she saw that someone—could it be Bean, not killed after all?—was trying to speak to her, leaving messages on every military, historical, and geographic forum that spoke about women held in bondage to some warrior or other, she did not let it fret her. She could not answer, so she would waste no time trying.

Eventually the work that was forced on her became a challenge that she found interesting for its own sake. How to mount a campaign against Burma and Thailand and, eventually, Vietnam that would sweep all resistance before it, yet never provoke China to intervene. She saw at once that the vast size of the Indian Army was its greatest weakness, for the supply lines would be impossible to defend. So, unlike the other strategists Achilles was using—mostly Indian Battle School graduates—Petra did not bother with the logistics of a sledgehammer campaign. Eventually the Indian forces would have to divide anyway, unless the Burmese and Thai armies simply lined up to be slaughtered. So she planned an unpredictable campaign—dazzling thrusts by small, mobile forces that could live off the land. The few pieces of mobile armor would race forward, supplied with petrol by air tankers.

She knew her plan was the only one that made sense, and not just because of the intrinsic problems it solved. Any plan that involved putting ten million soldiers so near to the border with China would provoke Chinese intervention. Her plan would never put enough soldiers near China to constitute a threat. Nor would her plan lead to a war of attrition that would leave both sides exhausted and weak. Most of India's strength would remain in reserve, ready to strike wherever the enemy showed weakness.

Achilles gave copies of her plan to the others, of course—he called it "cooperation," but it functioned as an exercise in one-upmanship. All the others had quickly climbed into Achilles' pocket, and now were eager to please him. They sensed, of course, that Achilles wanted Petra humiliated, and duly gave him what he wanted. They mocked her plan as if any fool could see it was hopeless, even though their criticisms were specious and her main points were never even addressed. She bore it, because she was a slave, and because she knew that eventually, some of them were bound to catch on to the way Achilles manipulated them and used them. But she knew that she had done a brilliant job, and it would be a delicious irony if the Indian Army—no, be honest, if Achilles—did not use her plan, and marched head-on to destruction.

It did not bother her conscience to have come up with an effective strategy for Indian expansion in southeast Asia. She knew it would never be used. Even her strategy of small, quick strike forces did not change the fact that India could not afford a two-front war. Pakistan would not let the opportunity pass if India committed itself to an eastern war.

Achilles had simply chosen the wrong country to try to lead into war. Tikal Chapekar, the Indian prime minister, was an ambitious man with delusions of the nobility of his cause. He might very well believe in Achilles' persuasions and long to begin an attempt to "unify" southeast Asia. A war might even begin. But it would founder quickly as Pakistan prepared to attack in the west. Indian adventurism would evaporate as it always had.

She even said as much to Achilles when he visited her one morning after her plans had been so resoundingly rejected by her fellow strategists. "Follow whatever plan you like, nothing will ever work as you think it will."

Achilles simply changed the subject—when he visited her, he preferred to reminisce with her as if they were a couple of old people remembering their childhoods together. Remember this about Battle School? Remember that? She wanted to scream in his face that he had only been there for a few days before Bean had him chained up in an air shaft, confessing to his crimes. He had no right to be nostalgic for Battle School. All he was accomplishing was to poison her own memories of the place, for now when Battle School came up, she just wanted to change the subject, to forget it completely.

Who would have imagined that she would ever think of Battle School as her era of freedom and happiness? It certainly hadn't seemed that way at the time.

To be fair, her captivity was not painful. As long as Achilles was in Hyderabad, she had the run of the base, though she was never unobserved. She could go to the library and do research—though one of her guards had to thumb the ID pad, verifying that she had logged on as herself, with all the restrictions that implied, before she could access the nets. She could run through the dusty countryside that was used for military maneuvers—and sometimes could almost forget the other footfalls keeping syncopated rhythm with her own. She could eat what she wanted, sleep when she wanted. There were times when she almost forgot she wasn't free. There were far more times when, knowing she was not free, she almost decided to stop hoping that her captivity would ever end.

It was Bean's messages that kept her hope alive. She could not answer him, and therefore stopped thinking of his messages as actual communications. Instead they were something deeper than mere attempts at making contact. They were proof that she had not been forgotten. They were proof that Petra Arkanian, Battle School brat, still had a friend who respected her and cared for her enough to refuse to give up. Each message was a cool kiss to her fevered brow.

And then one day Achilles came to her and told her he was going on a trip.

She assumed at once that this meant she would be confined to her room, locked down and under guard, until Achilles returned.

"No locks this time," said Achilles. "You're coming with me."

"So it's someplace inside India?"

"In one sense yes," said Achilles. "In another, no."

"I'm not interested in your games," she said, yawning. "I'm not going."

"Oh, you won't want to miss this," said Achilles. "And even if you did, it wouldn't matter, because I need you, so you'll be there."

"What can you possibly need me for?"

"Oh, well, when you put it that way, I suppose I should be more precise. I need you to see what takes place at the meeting."

"Why? Unless there's a successful assassination attempt, there's nothing I want to see you do."

"The meeting," said Achilles, "is in Islamabad."

Petra had no smart reply to that. The capital of Pakistan. It was unthinkable. What possible business could Achilles have there? And why would he bring her?

They flew—which of course reminded her of the eventful flight that had brought her to India as Achilles' prisoner. The open door—should I have pulled him out with me and brought him brutally down to earth?

During the flight Achilles showed her the letter he had sent to Ghaffar Wahabi, the "prime minister" of Pakistan—

actually, of course, the military dictator . . . or Sword of Islam, if you preferred it that way. The letter was a marvel of deft manipulation. It would never have attracted any attention in Islamabad, however, if it had not come from Hyderabad, the headquarters of the Indian Army. Even though Achilles' letter never actually said so, it would be assumed in Pakistan that Achilles came as an unofficial envoy of the Indian government.

How many times had an Indian military plane landed at this military airbase near Islamabad? How many times had Indian soldiers in uniform been allowed to set foot on Pakistani soil—bearing their sidearms, no less? And all to carry a Belgian boy and an Armenian girl to talk to whatever lower-level official the Pakistanis decided to fob off on them.

A bevy of stone-faced Pakistani officials led them to a building a short distance from where their plane was being refueled. Inside, on the second floor, the leading official said, "Your escort must remain outside."

"Of course," said Achilles. "But my assistant comes in with me. I must have a witness to remind me in case my memory flags."

The Indian soldiers stood near the wall at full attention. Achilles and Petra walked through the open door.

There were only two people in the room, and she recognized one of them immediately from his pictures. With a gesture, he indicated where they should sit.

Petra walked to her chair in silence, never taking her eyes off Ghaffar Wahabi, the prime minister of Pakistan. She sat beside and slightly behind Achilles, as a lone Pakistani aide sat just at Wahabi's right hand. This was no lower-level official. Somehow, Achilles' letter had opened all the doors, right to the very top.

They needed no interpreter, for Common was, though not their birth language, a childhood acquisition for both of them, and they spoke without accent. Wahabi seemed skeptical and distant, but at least he did not play any humiliation games—he did not keep them waiting, he ushered them into the room himself, and he did not challenge Achilles in any way.

"I have invited you because I wish to hear what you have to say," said Wahabi. "So please begin."

Petra wanted so badly for Achilles to do something horribly wrong—to simper and beam, or to try to strut and show off his intelligence.

"Sir, I'm afraid that it may sound at first as if I am trying to teach Indian history to you, a scholar in that field. It is from your book that I learned everything I'm about to say."

"It is easy to read my book," said Wahabi. "What did you learn from it that I do not already know?"

"The next step," said Achilles. "The step so obvious that I was stunned when you did not take it."

"So this is a book review?" asked Wahabi. But with those words he smiled faintly, to take away the edge of hostility.

"Over and over again, you show the great achievements of the Indian people, and how they are overshadowed, swallowed up, ignored, despised. The civilization of the Indus is treated as a poor also-ran to Mesopotamia and Egypt and even that latecomer China. The Aryan invaders brought their language and religion and imposed it on the people of India. The Moguls, the British, each with their overlay of beliefs and institutions. I must tell you that your book is regarded with great respect in the highest circles of the Indian government, because of the impartial way you treated the religions brought to India by invaders."

Petra knew that this was not idle flattery. For a Pakistani scholar, especially one with political ambitions, to write a history of the subcontinent without praising the Muslim influence and condemning the Hindu religion as primitive and destructive was brave indeed.

Wahabi raised a hand. "I wrote then as a scholar. Now I am the voice of the people. I hope my book has not led you into a quixotic quest for reunification of India. Pakistan is determined to remain pure."

"Please do not leap to conclusions," said Achilles. "I agree with you that reunification is impossible. Indeed, it is a meaningless term. Hindu and Muslim were never united except under an oppressor, so how could they be reunited?"

Wahabi nodded, and waited for Achilles to go on.

"What I saw throughout your account," said Achilles, "was a profound sense of the greatness inherent in the Indian people. Great religions have been born here. Great thinkers have arisen who have changed the world. And yet for two hundred years, when people think of the great powers, India and Pakistan are never on the list. And they never have been. And this makes you angry, and it makes you sad."

"More sad than angry," said Wahabi, "but then, I'm an old man, and my temper has abated."

"China rattles its swords, and the world shivers, but India is barely glanced at. The Islamic world trembles when Iraq or Turkey or Iran or Egypt swings one way or another, and yet Pakistan, stalwart for its entire history, is never treated as a leader. Why?"

"If I knew the answer," said Wahabi, "I would have written a different book."

"There are many reasons in the distant past," said Achilles, "but they all come down to one thing. The Indian people could never act together."

"Again, the language of unity," said Wahabi.

"Not at all," said Achilles. "Pakistan cannot take his

rightful place of leadership in the Muslim world, because whenever he looks to the west, Pakistan hears the heavy steps of India behind him. And India cannot take her rightful place as the leader of the east, because the threat of Pakistan looms behind her."

Petra admired the deft way Achilles made his choice of pronouns seem casual, uncalculated—India the woman, Pakistan the man.

"The spirit of God is more at home in India and Pakistan than any other place. It is no accident that great religions have been born here, or have found their purest form. But Pakistan keeps India from being great in the east, and India keeps Pakistan from being great in the west."

"True, but insoluble," said Wahabi.

"Not so," said Achilles. "Let me remind you of another bit of history, from only a few years before Pakistan's creation as a state. In Europe, two great nations faced each other— Stalin's Russia and Hitler's Germany. These two leaders were great monsters. But they saw that their enmity had chained them to each other. Neither could accomplish anything as long as the other threatened to take advantage of the slightest opening."

"You compare India and Pakistan to Hitler and Stalin?"

"Not at all," said Peter, "because so far, India and Pakistan have shown less sense and less self-control than either of those monsters."

Wahabi turned to his aide. "As usual, India has found a new way to insult us." The aide arose to help him to his feet.

"Sir, I thought you were a wise man," said Achilles. "There is no one here to see you posture. No one to quote what I have said. You have nothing to lose by hearing me out, and everything to lose by leaving."

Petra was stunned to hear Achilles speak so sharply.

Wasn't this taking his non-flatterer approach a little far? Any normal person would have apologized for the unfortunate comparison with Hitler and Stalin. But not Achilles. Well, this time he had surely gone too far. If this meeting failed, his whole strategy would come to nothing, and the tension he was under had led to this misstep.

Wahabi did not sit back down. "Say what you have to say, and be quick," he said.

"Hitler and Stalin sent their foreign ministers, Ribbentrop and Molotov, and despite the hideous denunciations that each had made against the other, they signed a nonaggression pact and divided Poland between them. It's true that a couple of years later, Hitler abrogated this pact, which led to millions of deaths and Hitler's eventual downfall, but that is irrelevant to your situation, because unlike Hitler and Stalin, you and Chapekar are men of honor—you are of India, and you both serve God faithfully."

"To say that Chapekar and I both serve God is blasphemy to one or the other of us, or both," said Wahabi.

"God loves this land and has given the Indian people greatness," said Achilles—so passionately that if Petra had not known better, she might have believed he had some kind of faith. "Do you really believe it is the will of God that both Pakistan and India remain in obscurity and weakness, solely because the people of India have not yet awakened to the will of Allah?"

"I do not care what atheists and madmen say about the will of Allah."

Good for you, thought Petra.

"Nor do I," said Achilles. "But I can tell you this. If you and Chapekar signed an agreement, not of unity, but of nonaggression, you could divide Asia between you. And if the decades pass and there is peace between these two great

Indian nations, then will the Hindu not be proud of the Muslim, and the Muslim proud of the Hindu? Will it not be possible then for Hindus to hear the teachings of the Quran, not as the book of their deadly enemy, but rather as the book of their fellow Indians, who share with India the leadership of Asia? If you don't like the example of Hitler and Stalin, then look at Portugal and Spain, ambitious colonizers who shared the Iberian Peninsula. Portugal, to the west, was smaller and weaker—but it was also the bold explorer that opened up the seas. Spain sent one explorer, and he was Italian—but he discovered a new world."

Petra again saw the subtle flattery at work. Without saying so directly, Achilles had linked Portugal—the weaker but braver nation—to Pakistan, and the nation that prevailed through dumb luck to India.

"They might have gone to war and destroyed each other, or weakened each other hopelessly. Instead they listened to the Pope, who drew a line on the earth and gave everything east of it to Portugal and everything west of it to Spain. Draw your line across the Earth, Ghaffar Wahabi. Declare that you will not make war against the great Indian people who have not yet heard the word of Allah, but will instead show to all the world the shining example of the purity of Pakistan. While in the meantime, Tikal Chapekar will unite eastern Asia under Indian leadership, which they have long hungered for. Then, in the happy day when the Hindu people heed the Book, Islam will spread in one breath from New Delhi to Hanoi."

Wahabi slowly sat back down.

Achilles said nothing.

Petra knew then that his boldness had succeeded.

"Hanoi," said Wahabi. "Why not Beijing?"

"On the day that the Indian Muslims of Pakistan are made

guardians of the sacred city, on that day the Hindus may imagine entering the forbidden city."

Wahabi laughed. "You are outrageous."

"I am," said Achilles. "But I'm right. About everything. About the fact that this is what your book was pointing to. That this is the obvious conclusion, if only India and Pakistan are blessed to have, at the same time, leaders with such vision and courage."

"And why does this matter to you?" said Wahabi.

"I dream of peace on Earth," said Achilles.

"And so you encourage Pakistan and India to go to war?"

"I encourage you to agree *not* to go to war with each other."

"Do you think Iran will peacefully accept Pakistan's leadership? Do you think the Turks will embrace us? It will have to be by conquest that we create this unity."

"But you *will* create it," said Achilles. "And when Islam is united under Indian leadership, it will no longer be humiliated by other nations. One great Muslim nation, one great Hindu nation, at peace with each other and too powerful for any other nation to dare to attack. That is how peace comes to Earth. God willing."

"Inshallah," echoed Wahabi. "But now it is time for me to know by what authority you say these things. You hold no office in India. How do I know you have not been sent to lull me while Indian armies amass for yet another unprovoked assault?"

Petra wondered if Achilles had planned to get Wahabi to say something so precisely calculated to give him the perfect dramatic moment, or if it was just chance. For Achilles' only answer to Wahabi was to draw from his portfolio a single sheet of paper, bearing a small signature at the bottom in blue ink.

"What is that?" said Wahabi.

"My authority," said Achilles. He handed the paper to Petra. She arose and carried it to the middle of the room, where Wahabi's aide took it from her hand.

Wahabi perused it, shaking his head. "And this is what he signed?"

"He more than signed it," said Achilles. "Ask your satellite team to tell you what the Indian Army is doing even as we speak."

"They are withdrawing from the border?"

"Someone has to be the first to offer trust. It's the opportunity you've been waiting for, you and all your predecessors. The Indian Army is withdrawing. You could send your troops forward. You could turn this gesture of peace into a bloodbath. Or you could give the orders to move your troops west and north. Iran is waiting for you to show them the purity of Islam. The Caliphate of Istanbul is waiting for you to unshackle it from the chains of the secular government of Turkey. Behind you, you will have only your brother Indians, wishing you well as you show the greatness of this land that God has chosen, and that finally is ready to rise."

"Save the speech," said Wahabi. "You understand that I have to verify that this signature is genuine, and that the Indian troops are moving in the direction that you say."

"You will do what you have to do," said Achilles. "I will return to India now."

"Without waiting for my answer?"

"I haven't asked you a question," said Achilles. "Tikal Chapekar has asked that question, and it is to him you must give your answer. I am only the messenger."

With that, Achilles rose to his feet. Petra did, too. Achilles strode boldly to Wahabi and offered his hand. "I hope you will forgive me, but I could not bear to return to India without being able to say that the hand of Ghaffar Wahabi touched mine."

Wahabi reached out and took Achilles' hand. "Foreign meddler," said Wahabi, but his eyes twinkled, and Achilles smiled in reply.

Could this possibly have *worked*? Petra wondered. Molotov and Ribbentrop had to negotiate for weeks, didn't they? Achilles did this in a single meeting.

What were the magic words?

But as they walked out of the room, escorted again by the four Indian soldiers who had come with them—her guards—Petra realized there had been no magic words. Achilles had simply studied both men and recognized their ambitions, their yearning for greatness. He had told them what they most wanted to hear. He gave them the peace that they had secretly longed for.

She had not been there for the meeting with Chapekar that led to Achilles' getting that signed nonaggression pact and the promise to withdraw, but she could imagine it. "You must make the first gesture," Achilles must have said. "It's true that the Muslims might take advantage of it, might attack. But you have the largest army in the world, and govern the greatest people. Let them attack, and you will absorb the blow and then return to roll over them like water bursting from a dam. And no one will criticize you for taking a chance on peace."

And now it finally struck home. The plans she had been drawing up for the invasion of Burma and Thailand were not mere foolery. They would be used. Hers or someone else's. The blood would begin to flow. Achilles would get his war.

I didn't sabotage my plans, she realized. I was so sure

they could not be used that I didn't bother to build weaknesses into them. They might actually work.

What have I done?

And now she understood why Achilles had brought her along. He wanted to strut in front of her, of course—for some reason, he felt the need to have someone witness his triumphs. But it was more than that. He also wanted to rub her face in the fact that he was actually going to do what she had so often said could not be done.

Worst of all, she found herself hoping that her plan would be used, not because she wanted Achilles to win his war, but because she wanted to stick it to the other Battle School brats who had mocked her plan so mercilessly.

I have to get word to Bean somehow. I have to warn him, so he can get word to the governments of Burma and Thailand. I have to do something to subvert my own plan of attack, or their destruction will be on my shoulders.

She looked at Achilles, who was dozing in his seat, oblivious to the miles racing by beneath him, returning him to the place where his wars of conquest would begin. If she could only remove his murders from the equation, on balance he would be quite a remarkable boy. He was a Battle School discard with the label "psychopath" attached to him, and yet somehow he had gotten not one but three major world governments to do his bidding.

I was a witness to this most recent triumph, and I'm still not sure how he brought it off.

She remembered the story from her childhood, about Adam and Eve in the garden, and the talking snake. Even as a little girl she had said—to the consternation of her family—What kind of idiot was Eve, to believe a snake? But now she understood, for she had heard the voice of the snake and had watched as a wise and powerful man had fallen under its spell.

Eat the fruit and you can have the desires of your heart. It's not evil, it's noble and good. You'll be praised for it.

And it's delicious.

13

WARNINGS

To: Carlotta%agape@vatican.net/or
ders/sisters/ind
From: Graff%bonpassage@colmin.gov
Re: Found?

I think we've found Petra. A good
friend in Islamabad who is aware of
my interest in finding her tells me
that a strange envoy from New Delhi
came for a brief meeting with Wahabi yesterday—a teenage boy who
could only be Achilles; and a
teenage girl of the right description who said nothing. Petra? I
think it likely.

Bean needs to know what I've
learned. First, my friend tells me
that this meeting was almost immediately followed by orders to the
Pakistani military to move back
from the border with India. Couple

that with the already-noted Indian removal from that frontier, and I think we're witnessing the impossible—after two centuries of intermittent but chronic warfare, a real attempt at peace. And it seems to have been done by or with the help of Achilles. (Since so many of our colonists are Indian, there are those in my ministry who fear that an outbreak of peace on the subcontinent might jeopardize our work!)

Second, for Achilles to bring Petra along on this sensitive mission implies that she is not an unwilling participant in his projects. Given that in Russia Vlad also was seduced into working with Achilles, however briefly, it is not unthinkable that even as confirmed a skeptic as Petra might have become a true believer while in captivity. Bean must be made aware of this possibility, for he may be hoping to rescue someone who does not wish to be rescued.

Third, tell Bean that I can make contacts in Hyderabad, among former Battle School students working in the Indian high command. I will not ask them to compromise their

loyalty to their country, but I
will ask about Petra and find out
what, if anything, they have seen
or heard. I think old school loyalty may trump patriotic secrecy on
this point.

Bean's little strike force was all that he could have hoped for.
These were not elite soldiers the way Battle School students
had been—they were not selected for the ability to command. But in some ways this made them easier to train. They
weren't constantly analyzing and second-guessing. In Battle
School, too, many soldiers kept trying to show off to everyone, so they could enhance their reputation in the
school—commanders constantly had to struggle to keep their
soldiers focused on the overall goal of the army.

Bean knew from his studies that in real-world armies, the
opposite was more usually the problem—that soldiers tried
not to do brilliantly at anything, or learn too quickly, for fear
of being thought a suckup or show-off by their fellow soldiers. But the cure for both problems was the same. Bean
worked hard to earn a reputation for tough, fair judgment.

He played no favorites, made no friends, but always
noticed excellence and commented on it. His praise, however, was not effusive. Usually he would simply make a note
about it in front of others. "Sergeant, your team made no
mistakes." Only when an accomplishment was exceptional
did he praise it explicitly, and then only with a terse "Good."

As he expected, the rarity of his praise as well as its fair-
ness soon made it the most valued coin in his strike force.
Soldiers who did good work did not have special privileges
and were given no special authority, so they were not

resented by the others. The praise was not effusive, so it never embarrassed them. Instead, they were admired by the others, and emulated. And the focus of the soldiers became the earning of Bean's recognition.

That was true power. Frederick the Great's dictum that soldiers had to fear their officers more than they feared the enemy was stupid. Soldiers needed to believe they had the respect of their officers, and to value that respect more than they valued life itself. Moreover, they had to know that their officers' respect was justified—that they really were the good soldiers their officers believed them to be.

In Battle School, Bean had used his brief time in command of an army to teach himself—he led his men to defeat every time, because he was more interested in learning what he could learn than in racking up points. This was demoralizing to his soldiers, but he didn't care—he knew that he would not be with them long, and that the time of the Battle School was nearly over. Here in Thailand, though, he knew that the battles coming up were real, the stakes high, and his soldiers' lives would be on the line. Victory, not information, was the goal.

And, behind that obvious motive, there lay an even deeper one. Sometime in the coming war—or even before, if he was lucky—he would be using a portion of this strike force to make a daring rescue attempt, probably deep inside India. There would be zero tolerance for error. He *would* bring Petra out. He *would* succeed.

He drove himself as hard as he drove any of his men. He made it a point to train alongside them—a child going through all the exercises the men went through. He ran with them, and if his pack was lighter it was only because he needed to carry fewer calories in order to survive. He had to carry smaller, lighter weapons, but no one begrudged him that—besides, they saw that his bullets went to the mark as often as theirs. There was nothing he asked them to do that he did not do himself. And when he was not as good as his men, he had no qualms about going to one of the best of them and asking him for criticism and advice—which he then followed.

This was unheard of, for a commander to risk allowing himself to appear unskilled or weak in front of his men. And Bean would not have done it, either, because the benefits did not usually outweigh the risks. However, he was planning to go along with them on difficult maneuvers, and his training had been theoretical and game-centered. He had to become a soldier, so he could be there to deal with problems and emergencies during operations, so he could keep up with them, and so that, in a pinch, he could join effectively in a fight.

At first, because of his youth and small stature, some of the soldiers had tried to make things easier for him. His refusal had been quiet but firm. "I have to learn this too," he would say, and that was the end of the discussion. Naturally, the soldiers watched him all the more intensely, to see how he measured up to the high standard he set for them. They saw him tax his body to the utmost. They saw that he shrank from nothing, that he came out of mudwork slimier than anyone, that he went over obstacles just as high as anyone's, that he ate no better food and slept on no better a patch of ground on maneuvers.

They did not see how much he modeled this strike force on the Battle School armies. With two hundred men, he divided them into five companies of forty. Each company, like Ender's Battle School army, was divided into five toons of eight men each. Every toon was expected to be able to carry out operations entirely on its own; every company was expected to be able to deal with complete independence. At the same time, he made sure that they became skilled observers, and trained them to see the kinds of things he needed them to see.

"You are my eyes," he said. "You need to see what I would look for *and* what you would see. I will always tell you what I am planning and why, so you will know if you see a problem I didn't anticipate, which might change my plan. Then you will make sure I know. My best chance of keeping you all alive is to know everything that is in your heads during battle, just as your best chance of staying alive is to know everything that is in my head."

Of course, he knew that he could not tell them everything. No doubt they understood this as well. But he spent an inordinate amount of time, by standard military doctrine, telling his men the reasoning behind his orders, and he expected his company and toon commanders to do the same with their men. "That way, when we give you an order without any reasons, you will know that it's because there's no time for explanation, that you must act now—but that there *is* a good reason, which we *would* tell you if we could."

Once when Suriyawong came to observe his training of his troops, he asked Bean if this was how he recommended training soldiers throughout the whole army.

"Not a chance," said Bean.

"If it works for you, why wouldn't it work everywhere?"

"Usually you don't need it and can't afford the time," said Bean.

"But you can?"

"These soldiers are going to be called on to do the impossible. They aren't going to be sent to hold a position or advance against an enemy posting. They're going to be sent to do difficult, complicated things right under the eyes of the enemy, under circumstances where they can't go back for new instructions but have to adapt and succeed. That is impossible if they don't understand the purpose behind all their orders. And they have to know exactly how their commanders think so that trust is perfect—and so they can compensate for their commanders' inevitable weaknesses."

"*Your* weaknesses?" asked Suriyawong.

"Hard to believe, Suriyawong, but yes, I have weaknesses."

That earned a faint smile from Surly—a rare prize. "Growing pains?" asked Suriyawong.

Bean looked down at his ankles. He had already had new uniforms made twice, and it was time for a third go. He was almost as tall now as Suriyawong had been when Bean first arrived in Bangkok half a year before. Growing caused him no pain. But it worried him, since it seemed unconnected with any other sign of puberty. Why, after all these years of being undersized, was his body now so determined to catch up?

He experienced none of the problems of adolescence—not the clumsiness that comes from having limbs that swing farther than they used to, not the rush of hormones that clouded judgment and distracted attention. So if he grew enough to carry better weapons, that could only be a plus.

"Someday I hope to be as fine a man as you," said Bean.

Suriyawong grunted. He knew that Surly would take it as a joke. He also knew that, somewhere deeper than consciousness, Suriyawong would also take it at face value, for people always did. And it was important for Suriyawong to have the constant reassurance that Bean respected his position and would do nothing to undermine him.

That had been months ago, and Bean was able to report to Suriyawong a long list of possible missions that his men had been trained for and could perform at any time. It was his declaration of readiness.

Then came the letter from Graff. Carlotta forwarded it to him as soon as she got it. Petra was alive. She was probably with Achilles in Hyderabad.

Bean immediately notified Suriyawong that an intelligence source of a friend of his verified an apparent nonaggression pact between India and Pakistan, and a movement of troops away from the shared border—along with his opinion that this guaranteed an invasion of Burma within three weeks.

As to the other matters in the letter, Graff's assertion that Petra might have gone over to Achilles' cause was, of course, absurd—if Graff believed that, he didn't know Petra. What alarmed Bean was that she had been so thoroughly neutralized that she could *seem* to be on Achilles' side. This was the girl who always spoke her mind no matter how much abuse it caused to come down on her head. If she had fallen silent, it meant she was in despair.

Isn't she getting my messages? Has Achilles cut her off from information so thoroughly that she doesn't even roam the nets? That would explain her failure to answer. But still, Petra was used to standing alone. That wouldn't explain her silence.

It had to be her own strategy for mastery. Silence, so that Achilles would forget how much she hated him. Though surely she knew him well enough by now to know that he never forgot anything. Silence, so that she could avoid even deeper isolation—that was possible. Even Petra could keep her mouth shut if every time she spoke up it cut her off from more and more information and opportunities.

Finally, though, Bean had to entertain the possibility that Graff was right. Petra was human. She feared death like anyone else. And if she had, in fact, witnessed the death of her two guardians in Russia, and if Achilles had committed the killings with his own hands—which Bean believed likely—then Petra was facing something she had never faced before. She could speak up to idiotic commanders and teachers in Battle School because the worst that could happen was reprimands. With Achilles, what she had to fear was death.

And the fear of death changed the way a person saw the world, Bean knew that. He had lived his first years of life under the constant pressure of that fear. Moreover, he had spent a considerable time specifically under Achilles' power. Even though he never forgot the danger Achilles posed, even Bean had come to think Achilles wasn't such a bad guy, that in fact he was a good leader, doing brave and bold things for his "family" of street urchins. Bean had admired him and learned from him—right up to the moment when Achilles murdered Poke.

Petra, fearing Achilles, submitting to his power, had to watch him closely just to stay alive. And, watching him, she would come to admire him. It's a common trait of primates to become submissive and even worshipful toward one who has the power to kill them. Even if she fought off those feelings, they would still be there.

But she'll awaken from it, when she's out from under that power. I did. She will. So even if Graff is right, and Petra has become something of a disciple to Achilles, she will turn heretic once I get her out.

Still, the fact remained—he had to be prepared to bring her out even if she resisted rescue or tried to betray them.

He added dartguns and will-bending drugs to his army's arsenal and training.

Naturally, he would need more hard data than he had if he was to mount an operation to rescue her. He wrote to Peter, asking him to use some of his old Demosthenes contacts in the U.S. to get what intelligence data they had on Hyderabad.

Beyond that, Bean really had no resources to tap without giving away his location. Because it was a sure thing that he couldn't ask Suriyawong for information about Hyderabad. Even if Suriyawong was feeling favorably disposed—and he *had* been sharing more information with Bean lately—there was no way to explain why he could possibly need information about the Indian high command base at Hyderabad.

Only after days of waiting for Peter, while training his men and himself in the use of darts and drugs, did Bean realize another important implication of discovering that Petra might actually be cooperating with Achilles. Because none of their strategy was geared to the kind of campaign Petra might design.

He requested a meeting with both Suriyawong and the Chakri. After all these months of never seeing the Chakri's face, he was surprised that the meeting was granted—and without delay. He sent his request when he got up at five in the morning. At seven, he was in the Chakri's office, with Suriyawong beside him.

Suriyawong only had time to mouth, with annoyance, the words "What is this?" before the Chakri started the meeting.

"What is this?" said the Chakri. He smiled at Suriyawong; he knew he was echoing Suriyawong's question. But Bean also knew that it was a smile of mockery. You couldn't control this Greek boy after all.

"I just found out information that you both need to know," said Bean. Of course, this implied that Suriyawong might not have recognized the importance of the information, so that Bean had to bring it to Chakri Naresuan directly. "I meant no lack of respect. Only that you must be aware of this immediately."

"What possible information can you have," said Chakri Naresuan, "that we don't already know?"

"Something that I learned from a well-connected friend," said Bean. "All our assumptions were based on the idea of the Indian Army using the obvious strategy—to overwhelm Burmese and Thai defenses with huge armies. But I just learned that Petra Arkanian, one of Ender Wiggin's jeesh, may be working with the Indian Army. I never thought she would collaborate with Achilles, but the possibility exists. And if she's directing the campaign, it won't be a flood of soldiers at all."

"Interesting," said the Chakri. "What strategy would she use?"

"She would still overwhelm you with numbers, but not with massed armies. Instead there would be probing raids, incursions by smaller forces, each one designed to strike, draw your attention, and then fade. They don't even have to retreat. They just live off the land until they can re-form later. Each one is easily beaten, except that there's nothing to beat. By the time we get there, they're gone. No supply lines. No vulnerabilities, just probe after probe until we can't respond to them all. Then the probes start getting bigger. When we get there, with our thinly stretched forces, the enemy is waiting. One of our groups destroyed, then another."

The Chakri looked at Suriyawong. "What Borommakot says is possible," said Suriyawong. "They can keep up such a strategy forever. We never damage them, because they have an infinite supply of troops, and they risk little on each attack. But every loss we suffer is irreplaceable, and every retreat gives them ground."

"So why wouldn't this Achilles think of such a strategy on his own?" asked the Chakri. "He's a very bright boy, they say."

"It's a cautious strategy," said Bean. "One that is very frugal with the lives of the soldiers. And it's slow."

"And Achilles is never careful with the lives of his soldiers?"

Bean thought back to his days in Achilles' "family" on the streets of Rotterdam. Achilles was, in fact, careful of the lives of the other children. He took great pains to make sure they were not exposed to risk. But that was because his power base absolutely depended on losing none of them. If any of the children had been hurt, the others would have melted away. That would not be the case with the Indian Army. Achilles would spend them like autumn leaves.

Except that Achilles' goal was not to rule India. It was to rule the world. So it did matter that he earn a reputation as a beneficent leader. That he seem to value the lives of his people.

"Sometimes he is, when it suits him," said Bean. "That's why he would follow such a plan if Petra outlined it for him."

"So what would it mean," said the Chakri, "if I told you that the attack on Burma has just been launched, and it is a massive frontal assault by huge Indian forces, just as you originally outlined in your first memo to us?"

Bean was stunned. Already? The apparent nonaggression pact between India and Pakistan was only a few days old. They could not possibly have amassed troops that quickly.

Bean was surprised to see that Suriyawong also had been unaware that war had begun.

"It was an extremely well-planned campaign," said the Chakri. "The Burmese only had a day's warning. The Indian troops moved like smoke. Whether it is your evil friend Achilles or your brilliant friend Petra or the mere simpletons of the Indian high command, they managed it superbly."

"What it means," said Bean, "is that Petra is not being listened to. Or that she is deliberately sabotaging the Indian Army's strategy. I'm relieved to know this, and I apologize for raising a warning that was not needed. May I ask, sir, if Thailand is coming into the war now?"

"Burma has not asked for help," said the Chakri.

"By the time Burma asks Thailand for help," said Bean, "the Indian Army will be at our borders."

"At that point," said the Chakri, "we will not wait for them to ask."

"What about China?" asked Bean.

The Chakri blinked twice before answering. "What about China?"

"Have they warned India? Have they responded in any way?"

"Matters with China are handled by a different branch of government," said the Chakri.

"India may have twice the population of China," said Bean, "but the Chinese Army is better equipped. India would think twice before provoking Chinese intervention."

"Better equipped," said the Chakri. "But is it deployed in a usable way? Their troops are kept along the Russian border. It would take weeks to bring them down here. If India plans a lightning strike, they have nothing to fear from China."

"As long as the I.F. keeps missiles from flying," said Suriyawong. "And with Chamrajnagar as Polemarch, you can be sure no missiles will attack India."

"Oh, that's another new development," said the Chakri. "Chamrajnagar submitted his resignation from the I.F. ten minutes after the attack on Burma was launched. He will return to Earth—to India—to accept his new appointment as leader of a coalition government that will guide the newly enlarged Indian empire. For of course, by the time a ship can bring him back to Earth, the war will be over, one way or another."

"Who is the new Polemarch?" asked Bean.

"That is the dilemma," said the Chakri. "There are those

who wonder whom the Hegemon can nominate, considering that no one can quite trust anyone now. Some are wondering why the Hegemon should name a Polemarch at all. We've done without a Strategos since the League War. Why do we need the I.F. at all?"

"To keep the missiles from flying," said Suriyawong.

"That is the only serious argument in favor of keeping the I.F.," said the Chakri. "But many governments believe that the I.F. should be reduced to the role of policing above the atmosphere. There is no reason for any but a tiny fraction of the I.F.'s strength to be retained. And as for the colonization program, many are saying it is a waste of money, when war is erupting here on Earth. Well, enough of this little school class. There is grown-up work to be done. You will be consulted if we find that you are needed."

The Chakri's dismissive air was surprising. It revealed a high level of hostility to both of these Battle School graduates, not just the foreign one.

It was Suriyawong who challenged the Chakri on this. "Under what circumstances would we be called upon?" he asked. "Either the plans I drew up will work or they won't. If they work, you won't call on me. If they don't, you'll regard that as proof that I didn't know what I was doing, and you still won't call on me."

The Chakri pondered this for a few moments. "Why, I'd never thought of it that way. I believe you're right."

"No, you're wrong," said Suriyawong. "Nothing ever goes as planned during a war. We have to be able to adapt. I and the other Battle School graduates are trained for that. We should be kept informed of every development. Instead, you have cut me off from the intelligence that is flowing in. I should have seen this information the moment I woke up and looked at my desk. Why are you cutting me off?"

For the same reason you cut *me* off, Bean thought. So that when victory comes, all the credit can flow to the Chakri. "The Battle School children advised in the planning stages, but of course during the actual war, we did not leave it up to the children." And if things went badly, "We faithfully executed the plans drawn up by the Battle School children, but apparently schoolwork did not prepare them for the real world." The Chakri was covering his ass.

Suriyawong seemed to understand this also, for he gave no more argument. He arose. "Permission to leave, sir," he said.

"Granted. To you, too, Borommakot. Oh, and we'll probably be taking back the soldiers Suriyawong gave you to play with. Restoring them to their original units. Please prepare them to leave at once."

Bean also rose to his feet. "So Thailand is entering the war?"

"You will be informed of anything you need to know, when you need to know it."

As soon as they were outside the Chakri's office, Suriyawong sped up his pace. Bean had to run to catch up.

"I don't want to talk to you," said Suriyawong.

"Don't be a big baby about it," said Bean scornfully. "He's only doing to you what you already did to me. Did I run off and pout?"

Suriyawong stopped and whirled on Bean. "You and your stupid meeting!"

"He already cut you off," said Bean. "Already. Before I even asked to meet."

Suriyawong knew that Bean was right. "So I'm stripped of influence."

"And I never had any," said Bean. "What are we going to do about it?"

"Do?" said Suriyawong. "If the Chakri forbids it, no one

will obey my orders. Without authority, I'm just a boy, still too young to enlist in the army."

"What we'll do first," said Bean, "is figure out what this all means."

"It means the Chakri is an oomay careerist," said Suriyawong.

"Come, let's walk out of the building."

"They can draw our words out of the open air, too, if they want," said Suriyawong.

"They have to *try* to do that. Here, anything we say is automatically recorded."

So Suriyawong walked with Bean out of the building that housed the highest of the Thai high command, and together they wandered toward the married officers' housing, to a park with playground equipment for the children of junior officers. When they sat on the swings, Bean realized that he was actually getting a little too big for them.

"Your strike force," said Suriyawong. "Just when it might have been most needed, it'll be dispersed."

"No it won't," said Bean.

"And why not?"

"Because you drew it from the garrison protecting the capital. Those troops won't be sent away. So they'll remain in Bangkok. The important thing is to keep all our matériel together and within easy reach. Do you think you still have authority for that?"

"As long as I call it routine cycling into storage," said Suriyawong, "I suppose so."

"And you'll know where these men are assigned, so when we need to, we can call them back to us."

"If I try that, I'll be cut off from the net," said Suriyawong.

"If we try that," said Bean, "it will be because the net doesn't matter."

"Because the war is lost."

"Think about it," said Bean. "Only a stupid careerist would openly disdain you like this. He *wanted* to shame and discourage you. Have you given him some offense?"

"I always give offense," said Suriyawong. "That's why everyone called me Surly behind my back in Battle School. The only person I know who *is* more arrogant than I *seem* is you."

"Is Naresuan a fool?" asked Bean.

"I had not thought so," said Suriyawong.

"So this is a day for people who are not fools to act like fools."

"Are you saying I am also a fool?"

"I was saying that Achilles is apparently a fool."

"Because he is attacking with massed forces? You told us that was what we should expect. Apparently Petra did not give him the better plan."

"Or he's not using it."

"But he'd have to be a fool not to use it," said Suriyawong.

"So *if* Petra gave him the better plan, and he declined to use it, then he *and* the Chakri are both fools today. As when the Chakri pretended that he has no influence over foreign policy."

"About China, you mean?" Suriyawong thought about this for a moment. "You're right, of course he has influence. But perhaps he simply didn't want us to know what the Chinese were doing. Perhaps that was why he was so sure he didn't need us, that he didn't need to enter Burma. Because he *knows* the Chinese are coming in."

"So," said Bean. "While we sit here, watching the war, we will learn much from the plain events as they unfold. If China intervenes to stop the Indians before Achilles ever gets to

Thailand, then we know Chakri Naresuan is a smart careerist, not a stupid one. But if China does not intervene, then we have to wonder why Naresuan, who is not a foolish man, has chosen to act like one."

"What do you suspect him of?" asked Suriyawong.

"As for Achilles," said Bean, "no matter how we construe these events, he has been a fool."

"No, he's only a fool if Petra actually gave him the better plan and he's ignoring it."

"On the contrary," said Bean. "He's a fool no matter what. To enter into this war with even the possibility that China will intervene, that is foolish in the extreme."

"So perhaps he knows that China will not intervene, and then the Chakri would be the only fool," said Suriyawong.

"Let's watch and see."

"I'll watch and grind my teeth," said Suriyawong.

"Watch with me," said Bean. "Let's drop this stupid competition between us. You care about Thailand. I care about figuring out what Achilles is doing and stopping him. At this moment, those two concerns coincide almost perfectly. Let's share everything we know."

"But you know nothing."

"I know nothing that *you* know," said Bean. "And you know nothing that I know."

"What can you possibly know?" said Suriyawong. "I'm the eemo who cut you off from the intelligence net."

"I knew about the deal between India and Pakistan."

"So did we."

"But you didn't tell me," said Bean. "And yet I knew."

Suriyawong nodded. "Even if the sharing is mostly one way, from me to you, it's long overdue, don't you think?"

"I'm not interested in what's early or late," said Bean. "Only what happens next."

They went to the officers' mess and had lunch, then walked back to Suriyawong's building, dismissed his staff for the rest of the day, and, with the building to themselves, sat in Suriyawong's office and watched the progress of the war on Worldnet. Burmese resistance was brave but futile.

"Poland in 1939," said Bean.

"And here in Thailand," said Suriyawong, "we're being as timid as France and England."

"At least China isn't invading Burma from the north, the way Russia invaded Poland from the east," said Bean.

"Small mercies," said Suriyawong.

But Bean wondered. Why *doesn't* China step in? Beijing wasn't saying anything to the press. No comment, about a war on their doorstep? What does China have up its sleeve?

"Maybe Pakistan wasn't the only country to sign a nonaggression pact with India," said Bean.

"Why? What would China gain?" asked Suriyawong.

"Vietnam?" said Bean.

"Worthless, compared to the menace of having India poised with a vast army at the underbelly of China."

Soon, to distract themselves from the news—and from their loss of any kind of influence—they stopped paying attention to the vids and reminisced about Battle School. Neither of them brought up the really bad experiences, only the funny things, the ridiculous things, and they laughed their way into the evening, until it was dark outside.

This afternoon with Suriyawong, now that they were friends, reminded Bean of home—in Crete, with his parents, with Nikolai. He tried to keep from thinking about them most of the time, but now, laughing with Suriyawong, he was filled with a bittersweet longing. He had that one year of something like a normal life, and now it was over. Blown to bits like the house they had been vacationing in. Like the government-protected apartment Graff and Sister Carlotta had taken them away from in the nick of time.

Suddenly a thrill of fear ran through Bean. He knew something, though he could not say how. His mind had made some connection and he didn't understand how, but he had no doubt that he was right.

"Is there any way out of this building that can't be seen from the outside?" asked Bean, in a whisper so faint he could hardly hear himself.

Suriyawong, who had been in the middle of a story about Major Anderson's penchant for nose-picking when he thought nobody was watching, looked at him like he was crazy. "What, you want to play hide-and-seek?"

Bean continued to whisper. "A way out."

Suriyawong took the hint and whispered back. "I don't know. I always use the doors. Like most doors, they're visible from both sides."

"A sewer line? A heating duct?"

"This is Bangkok. We don't have heating ducts."

"*Any* way out."

Suriyawong's whisper changed back to voice. "I'll look at the blueprints. But tomorrow, man, tomorrow. It's getting late and we talked right through dinner."

Bean grabbed his shoulder, forced him to look into his eyes. "Suriyawong," he whispered, even more softly, "I'm not joking. Right now, out of this building unobserved."

Finally Suriyawong got it: Bean was genuinely afraid. His whisper was quiet again. "Why, what's happening?"

"Just tell me how."

Suriyawong closed his eyes. "Flood drainage," he whispered. "Old ditches. They just laid these temporary buildings down on top of the old parade ground. There's a shallow ditch that runs right under the building. You can hardly tell it's there, but there's a gap."

"Where can we get under the building from inside?"

Suriyawang rolled his eyes. "These temporary buildings are made of lint." To prove his point, he pulled away the corner of the large rug in the middle of the room, rolled it back, and then, quite easily, pried up a floor section.

Underneath it was sod that had died from lack of sunlight. There were no gaps between floor and sod.

"Where's the ditch?" asked Bean.

Suriyawong thought again. "I think it crosses the hall. But the carpet is tacked down there."

Bean turned up the volume of the vid and went out the door of Suriyawong's office and through the anteroom to the hall. He pried up a corner of the carpet and ripped. Carpet fluff flew, and Bean kept pulling until Suriyawong stopped him. "I think about here," he said.

They pulled up another floor section. This time there was a depression in the yellowed sod.

"Can you get through that?" asked Bean.

"Hey, you're the one with the big head," said Suriyawong.

Bean threw himself down. The ground was damp—this *was* Bangkok—and he was clammy and filthy in moments as he wriggled along. Every floor joist was a challenge, and a couple of times he had to dig with his army-issue knife to make way for his head. But he made good progress anyway, and wriggled out into the darkness only a few minutes later. He stayed down, though, and saw that Suriyawong, despite not knowing what was going on, did not raise his head when he emerged from under the building, but continued to creep along just as Bean was doing.

They kept going until they reached the next point where the old eroded ditch went under another temporary building.

"Please tell me we're not going under another building."

Bean looked at the pattern of lights from the moon, from nearby porches and area lights. He had to count on his enemies being at least a little careless. If they were using infrared, this escape was meaningless. But if they were just eyeballing the place, watching the doors, he and Surly were already where slow, easy movement wouldn't be seen.

Bean started to roll himself up the incline.

Suriyawong grabbed him by the boot. Bean looked at him. Suriyawong pantomimed rubbing his cheeks, his forehead, his ears.

Bean had forgotten. His Greek skin was lighter than Suriyawong's. He would catch more light.

He rubbed his face, his ears, his hands with damp soil from under the grass. Suriyawong nodded.

They rolled—at a deliberate pace—up out of the ditch and wriggled slowly along the base of the building until they were around the corner. Here there were bushes to offer some shelter. They stood in the shadows for a moment, then walked, casually, away from the building as if they had just emerged from the door. Bean hoped not to be visible to anyone watching Suriyawong's building, but even if they could be seen, they shouldn't attract any attention, as long as no one noticed that they seemed to be just a little undersized.

Not until they were a quarter mile away did Suriyawong finally speak. "Do you mind telling me the name of this game?"

"Staying alive," said Bean.

"I never knew paranoid schizophrenia could strike so fast."

"They've tried twice," said Bean. "And they had no qualms about killing my family along with me."

"But we were just talking," said Suriyawong. "What did you see?"

"Nothing."

"Or hear?"

"Nothing," said Bean. "I had a feeling."

"Please don't tell me that you're a psychic."

"No, I'm not. But something about the events of the past few hours must have made some unconscious connection. I listen to my fears. I act on them."

"And this works?"

"I'm still alive," said Bean. "I need a public computer. Can we get off the base?"

"It depends on how all-pervasive this plot against you is," said Suriyawong. "You need a bath, by the way."

"What about some place with ordinary public computer access?"

"Sure, there are visitor facilities near the tram station entrance. But would it be ironic if your assassins were using it?"

"My assassins aren't visitors," said Bean.

This bothered Suriyawong. "You don't even know if anybody's really out to kill you, but you're sure it's somebody in the Thai Army?"

"It's Achilles," said Bean. "And Achilles isn't in Russia. India doesn't have any intelligence service that could carry out an operation like this inside the high command. So it has to be somebody that Achilles has corrupted."

"Nobody here is in the pay of India," said Suriyawong.

"Probably not," said Bean. "But India isn't the only place Achilles has friends by now. He was in Russia for a while. He has to have made other connections."

"It's so hard to take this seriously, Bean," said Suriyawong. "If you suddenly start laughing and say Gotcha that time, I *will* kill you."

"I might be wrong," said Bean, "but I'm not joking."

They got to the visitor facility and found no one using any of the computers. Bean logged on using one of his many false identities and wrote a message to Graff and Sister Carlotta.

> You know who this is. I believe
> an attempt is about to be made on
> my life. Would you send immediate
> messages to contacts within the
> Thai government, warning them
> that such an attempt is coming
> and tell them that it involves
> conspirators inside the Chakri's
> inner circle. No one else could
> have the access. And I believe
> the Chakri had prior knowledge.
> Any Indians supposedly involved
> are fall guys.

"You can't write that," said Suriyawong. "You have no evidence to accuse Naresuan. I'm annoyed with him, but he's a loyal Thai."

"He's a loyal Thai," said Bean, "but you can be loyal and still want me dead."

"But not *me*," said Suriyawong.

"If you want it to look like the evil action of outsiders," said Bean, "then a brave Thai has to die along with me. What if they make our deaths look as if an Indian strike force did it? That would be provocation for a declaration of war, wouldn't it?"

"The Chakri doesn't need a provocation."

"He does if he wants the Burmese to believe that Thailand

isn't just grabbing for a piece of Burma." Bean went back to his note.

```
Please tell them that Suriyawong
and I are alive. We will come out
of hiding when we see Sister
Carlotta with at least one high
government official who Suriya-
wong would recognize on sight.
Please act immediately. If I am
wrong, you will be embarrassed.
If I am right, you will have saved
my life.
```

"I'm sick to my stomach thinking of how humiliated I'm going to be. Who are these people you're writing to?"

"People I trust. Like you."

Then, before sending the message, he added Peter's "Locke" address to the destination box.

"You know Ender Wiggin's brother?" asked Suriyawong.

"We've met."

Bean logged off.

"What now?" asked Suriyawong.

"We hide somewhere, I guess," said Bean.

Then they heard an explosion. Windows rattled. The floor trembled. The power flickered. The computers began to reboot.

"Got that done just in time," said Bean.

"Was that it?" asked Suriyawong.

"É," said Bean. "I think we're dead."

"Where do we hide?"

"If they did the deed, it's because they think we were still in there. So they won't be watching for us now. We can go to my barracks. My men will hide me."

"You're willing to bet my life on that?" asked Suriyawong.

"Yes," said Bean. "My track record of keeping you alive is pretty good so far."

As they walked out of the building, they saw military vehicles rushing toward where gray smoke was billowing up into the moonlit night. Others were heading for the entrances to the base. No one would be getting in or out.

By the time they reached the barracks where Bean's strike force was quartered, they could hear bursts of gunfire. "Now they're killing all the fake Indian spies this will be blamed on," said Bean. "The Chakri will regretfully inform the government that they all resisted capture and none were taken alive."

"Again you accuse him," said Suriyawong. "Why? How did you know this would happen?"

"I think I knew because there were too many smart people acting stupidly," said Bean. "Achilles *and* the Chakri. And he treated us angrily. Why? Because killing us bothered him. So he had to convince himself that we were disloyal children who had been corrupted by the I.F. We were a danger to Thailand. Once he hated us and feared us, killing us was justified."

"That's a long stretch from there to knowing they were about to kill us."

"They were probably set to do it at my quarters. But I stayed with you. It was quite possible they were planning for another opportunity—the Chakri would summon us to meet him somewhere, and we'd be killed instead. But when we stayed for hours and hours in your quarters, they realized *this* was the perfect opportunity. They had to check with the Chakri and get his consent to do it ahead of schedule. They probably had to rush to get the Indian stooges into place—they might even be genuine captured spies. Or they might be drugged Thai criminals who will have incriminating documents found on them."

"I don't care who they are," said Suriyawong. "I still don't understand how you knew."

"Neither do I," said Bean. "Most of the time, I analyze things very quickly and understand exactly why I know what I know. But sometimes my unconscious mind runs ahead of my conscious mind. It happened that way in the last battle, with Ender. We were doomed to defeat. I couldn't see a solution. And yet I said something, an ironic statement, a bitter joke—and it contained within it exactly the solution Ender needed. From then on, I've been trying to heed those unconscious processes that give me answers. I've thought back over my life and seen other times when I said things that were not really justified by my conscious analysis. Like the time when we stood over Achilles as he lay on the ground, and I told Poke to kill him. She wouldn't do it, and I couldn't persuade her, because I truly didn't understand why. Yet I understood what he was. I knew he had to die, or he would kill her."

"You know what I think?" said Suriyawong. "I think you heard something outside. Or noticed something subliminally on the way in. Somebody watching. And that's what triggered you."

Bean could only shrug. "You may well be right. As I said, I don't know."

It was after hours, but Bean could still palm his way through the locks to get in without setting off alarms. They hadn't bothered to deauthorize him. His entry into the building would show up on a computer somewhere, but it was a drone program and by the time any human looked at it, Bean's friends should have things well in motion.

Bean was glad to see that even though his men were in their home barracks on the grounds of the Thai high command base, they had not slacked in their discipline. No sooner were they inside the door than both Bean and Suriyawong were seized and pressed against the wall while they were checked for weapons.

"Good work," said Bean.

"Sir!" said the surprised soldier.

"And Suriyawong," said Bean.

"Sir!" said both the sentries.

A few others had been wakened by the scuffle.

"No lights," Bean said quickly. "And no loud talking. Weapons loaded. Prepare to move out on a moment's notice."

"Move out?" said Suriyawong.

"If they realize we're in here and decide to finish the job," said Bean, "this place is indefensible."

While some soldiers quietly woke the sleepers and all were busy dressing and loading their weapons, Bean had one of the sentries lead them to a computer. "You sign on," he said to the soldier.

As soon as he had logged on, Bean took his place and wrote, using the soldier's identity, to Graff, Carlotta, and Peter.

```
Both packages safe and awaiting
pickup. Please come right away
before packages are returned to
sender.
```

Bean sent out one toon, divided into four pairs, to reconnoiter. When each pair returned another pair from another toon replaced them. Bean wanted to have enough warning to get these men out of the barracks before any kind of assault could be mounted.

In the meanwhile, they turned on a vid and watched the news. Sure enough, here came the first report. Indian agents had apparently penetrated the Thai command base and blown up a temporary building, killing Suriyawong, Thailand's most distinguished Battle School graduate, who had headed military doctrine and strategic planning for the past year and a half, since returning from space. It was a great national tragedy. There was no confirmation yet, but preliminary reports indicated that some of the Indian agents had been killed by the heroic soldiers defending Suriyawong. A visiting Battle School graduate had also been killed.

Some of Bean's soldiers chuckled, but soon enough they were all grim-faced. The fact that the reporters had been told Bean and Suriyawong were dead meant that whoever made the report believed they were both inside the offices at an hour when the only way anyone could know that was if the bodies had been found, or the building had been under observation. Since the bodies had obviously not been found, whoever was writing the official reports from the Chakri's office must have been part of the plot.

"I can understand someone wanting to kill Borommakot," said Suriyawong. "But why would anyone want to kill *me*?"

The soldiers laughed. Bean smiled.

Patrols returned and went out, again, again. No movement toward the barracks. The news carried the initial response from various commentators. India apparently wanted to cripple the Thai military by eliminating the nation's finest military mind. This was intolerable. The government would have no choice now but to declare war and join Burma in the struggle against Indian aggression.

Then new information came. The Prime Minister had declared that he would take personal control of this disaster.

Someone in the military had obviously slipped badly to allow a foreign penetration of the high command's own base. Therefore, to protect the Chakri's reputation and make sure there was no hint of a cover-up of military errors, Bangkok city police would be supervising the investigation, and Bangkok city fire officials would investigate the wreckage of the exploded building.

"Good job," said Suriyawong. "The Prime Minister's cover story is strong and the Chakri won't resist letting police onto the base."

"If the fire investigators arrive soon enough," said Bean, "they might even prevent the Chakri's men from entering the building as soon as it cools enough from the fire. So they won't even know we weren't there."

Sirens moving through the base announced the arrival of the police and fire department. Bean kept waiting for the sound of gunfire. But it never came.

Instead, two of the patrols came rushing back.

"Someone is coming, but not soldiers. Bangkok police, sixteen of them, with a civilian."

"Just one?" asked Bean. "Is one of them a woman?"

"Not a woman, and just one. I believe, sir, that it is the Prime Minister himself."

Bean sent out more patrols to see if any military forces were within range.

"How did they know we were here?" asked Suriyawong.

"Once they took control of the Chakri's office," said Bean, "they could use the military personnel files to find out that the soldier who sent that last email was in this barracks when he sent it."

"So it's safe to come out?"

"Not yet," said Bean.

A patrol returned. "The Prime Minister wishes to enter

this barracks alone, sir."

"Please," said Bean. "Invite him in."

"So you're sure he's not wired up with explosives to kill us all?" asked Suriyawong. "I mean, your paranoia has kept us alive so far."

As if in answer, the vid showed Chakri driving away from the main entrance to the base, under police escort. The reporter was explaining that Naresuan had resigned as Chakri, but the Prime Minister insisted that he merely take a leave of absence. In the meantime, the Minister of Defense was taking direct personal control of the Chakri's office, and generals from the field were being brought in to staff other positions of trust. Until then, the police had control of the command system. "Until we know how these Indian agents penetrated our most sensitive base," the Minister of Defense said, "we cannot be sure of our security."

The Prime Minister entered the barracks.

"Suriyawong," he said. He bowed deeply.

"Mr. Prime Minister," said Suriyawong, bowing noticeably less deeply. Ah, the vanity of a Battle School graduate, thought Bean.

"A certain nun is flying here as quickly as she can," said the Prime Minister, "but we hoped that you might trust me enough to come out without waiting for her arrival. She was on the opposite side of the world, you see."

Bean strode forward and spoke in his not-bad Thai. "Sir," he said, "I believe Suriyawong and I are safer here with these loyal troops than we would be anywhere else in Bangkok."

The Prime Minister looked at the soldiers standing, fully armed, at attention. "So someone has a private army right in the middle of this base," he said.

"I did not make my meaning clear," said Bean. "These soldiers are absolutely loyal to *you*. They are yours to command, because you are Thailand at this moment, sir."

The Prime Minister bowed, very slightly, and turned to the soldiers. "Then I order you to arrest this foreigner."

Immediately Bean's arms were gripped by the soldiers nearest to him, as another soldier patted him down for weapons.

Suriyawong's eyes widened, but he gave no other sign of surprise.

The Prime Minister smiled. "You may release him now," he said. "The Chakri warned me, before he took his voluntary leave of absence, that these soldiers had been corrupted and were no longer loyal to Thailand. I see now that he was misinformed. And since that is the case, I believe you are right. You are safer here, under their protection, until we explore the limits of the conspiracy. In fact, I would appreciate it if I could deputize a hundred of your men to serve with my police force as it takes control of this base."

"I urge you to take all but eight of them," said Bean.

"Which eight?" asked the Prime Minister.

"Any of these toons of eight, sir, could stand for a day against the Indian Army."

This was, of course, absurd, but it had a fine ring to it, and the men loved hearing him say it.

"Then, Suriyawong," said the Prime Minister, "I would appreciate your taking command of all but eight of these men and leading them in taking control of this base in my name. I will assign one policeman to each group, so that they can clearly be identified as acting under my authority. And one group of eight will, of course, remain with you for your protection at all times."

"Yes sir," said Suriyawong.

"I remember saying in my last campaign," said the Prime Minister, "that the children of Thailand held the keys to our national survival. I had no idea at the time how literally and how quickly that would be fulfilled."

"When Sister Carlotta arrives," said Bean, "you can tell her that she is no longer needed, but I would be glad to see her if she has the time."

"I'll tell her that," said the Prime Minister. "Now let's get to work. We have a long night ahead of us."

Everyone was quite solemn as Suriyawong called out the toon leaders. Bean was impressed that he knew who they were by name and face. Suriyawong might not have sought out Bean's company very much, but he had done an excellent job of keeping track of what Bean was doing. Only when everyone had moved out on their assignments, each toon with its own cop like a battle flag, did Suriyawong and the Prime Minister allow themselves to smile. "Good work," said the Prime Minister.

"Thank you for believing our message," said Bean.

"I wasn't sure I could believe Locke," said the Prime Minister, "and the Hegemon's Minister of Colonization is, after all, just a politician now. But when the Pope telephoned me personally, I had no choice but to believe. Now I must go out and tell the people the absolute truth about what happened here."

"That Indian agents did indeed attempt to kill me and an unnamed foreign visitor," asked Suriyawong, "but we survived because of quick action by heroic soldiers of the Thai Army? Or did the unnamed foreign visitor die?"

"I fear that he died," Bean suggested. "Blown to bits in the explosion."

"In any event," said Suriyawong, "you will assure the people, the enemies of Thailand have learned tonight that the Thai military may be challenged, but we cannot be defeated."

"I'm glad you were trained for the military, Suriyawong," said the Prime Minister. "I would not want to face you as an opponent in a political campaign."

"It is unthinkable that we would be opponents," said Suriyawong, "since we could not possibly disagree on any subject."

Everyone got the irony, but no one laughed. Suriyawong left with the Prime Minister and eight soldiers. Bean remained in the barracks with the last toon, and together they watched as the lies unfolded on the vid.

And as the news droned on, Bean thought of Achilles. Somehow he had found out Bean was alive—but that would be the Chakri, of course. But if the Chakri had turned to Achilles' side, why was he spinning the story of Suriyawong's death as a pretext for war with India? It made no sense. Having Thailand in the war from the beginning could only work against India. Add that to India's use of the clunky, obvious, life-wasting strategy of mass attack, and it began to look as though Achilles were some kind of idiot.

He was not an idiot. Therefore he was playing some sort of deeper game, and despite the much-vaunted cleverness of his unconscious mind, Bean did not yet know what it was. And Achilles would know soon enough, if he did not know already, that Bean was not dead.

He's in a killing mood, thought Bean.

Petra, thought Bean. Help me find a way to save you.

14

HYDERABAD

Posted on the International Politics
Forum by EnsiRaknor@TurkMilNet.gov
Topic: Where is Locke when we need
him?

Am I the only one who wishes we had
Locke's take on the recent develop-
ments in India? With India across
the Burmese border and Pakistani
troops massing in Baluchistan,
threatening Iran and the gulf, we
need a new way of looking at south
Asia. The old models clearly don't
work.

What I want to know is, did IntPol-
For drop Locke's column when Peter
Wiggin came forward as the author,
or did Wiggin resign? Because if it
was IPF's decision, it was, to put
it bluntly, a stupid one. We never

knew who Locke was—we listened to him because he made sense, and time after time he was the only one who made sense out of problematical situations, or at least was the first to see clearly what was going on. What does it matter if he's a teenager, an embryo, or a talking pig?

For that matter, as the Hegemon's term is near expiration, I am more and more uneasy with the current Hegemon-designate. Whoever suggested Locke almost a year ago had the right idea. Only now let's put him in office under his own name. What Ender Wiggin did in the Formic War, Peter Wiggin might be able to do in the conflagration that looms—put an end to it.

Reply 14, by Talleyrandophile@pol-net.gov

I don't mean to be suspicious, but how do we know you're not Peter Wiggin, trying to put his name into play again?

Reply 14.1, by EnsiRaknor@TurkMi Net.gov

I don't mean to get personal, but Turkish Military Network IDs aren't given out to American teenagers doing consultation work in Haiti. I realize that international politics can make paranoids seem sane, but if Peter Wiggin could write under this ID, he must already run the world. But perhaps who I am does make a difference. I'm in my twenties now, but I'm a Battle School grad. So maybe that's why the idea of putting a kid in charge of things doesn't sound so crazy to me.

Virlomi knew who Petra was the moment she first showed up in Hyderabad—they had met before. Even though she was considerably older, so her time in Battle School overlapped Petra's by only a year, in those days Virlomi took notice of every girl in the place. An easy task, since Petra's arrival brought the total number of girls to nine—five of whom graduated at the same time as Virlomi. It seemed as though having girls in the school were regarded as an experiment that had failed.

Back in Battle School, Petra had been a tough launchy with a smart mouth, who proudly refused all offers of advice. She seemed determined to make it as a girl among boys, meeting the same standards, taking their guff without help. Virlomi understood. She had had the same attitude herself, at first. She just hoped that Petra would not have to have such painful experiences as those Virlomi had had before finally realizing that the hostility of boys was, in most cases, insuperable, and a girl needed all the friends she could get.

Petra was memorable enough that of course Virlomi recognized her name when the stories of Ender's jeesh came out after the war. The one girl among them, the Armenian Joan of Arc. Virlomi read the articles and smiled. So Petra had been as tough as she thought she'd be. Good for her.

Then Ender's jeesh was kidnapped or killed, and when the kidnapped ones were returned from Russia, Virlomi was heartsick to see that the only one whose fate remained unknown was Petra Arkanian.

Only she didn't have long to grieve. For suddenly the team of Indian Battle School graduates had a new commander, whom they immediately recognized as the same Achilles that Locke had accused of being a psychopathic killer. And soon they found that he was frequently shadowed by a silent, tired-looking girl whose name was never spoken.

But Virlomi knew her. Petra Arkanian.

Whatever Achilles' motive in keeping her name to himself, Virlomi didn't like it and so she made sure that everyone on the strategy team knew that this was the missing member of Ender's jeesh. They said nothing about Petra to Achilles, of course—merely responded to his instructions and reported to him as required. And soon enough Petra's silent presence was treated as if it were ordinary. The others hadn't known her.

But Virlomi knew that if Petra was silent, it meant something quite dreadful. It meant Achilles had some hold over her. A hostage—some kidnapped family member? Threats? Or something else? Had Achilles somehow overmastered Petra's will, which had once seemed so indomitable?

Virlomi took great pains to make sure that Achilles did not notice her paying special attention to Petra. But she watched the younger girl, learning all she could. Petra used her desk as the others did, and took part in reading intelligence reports and everything else that was sent to all of them. But something was wrong, and it took a while for Virlomi to realize what it was—Petra never typed anything at all while she was logged on to the system. There were a lot of netsites that required passwords or at least registration to sign on. But after typing her password to simply log on in the morning, Petra never typed again.

She's been blocked, Virlomi realized. That's why she never emails any of us. She's a prisoner here. She can't pass messages outside. And she doesn't talk to any of us because she's been forbidden to.

When she wasn't logged on, though, she must have been working furiously, because now and then Achilles would send a message to all of them, detailing new directions their planning should go. The language in these messages was not Achilles'—it was easy to spot the shift in style. He was getting these strategic insights—and they were good ones—from Petra, who was one of the nine who were chosen to save humanity from the Formics. One of the finest minds on Earth. And she was enslaved by this psychopathic Belgian.

So, while the others admired the brilliant strategies they were developing for aggressive war against Burma and Thailand, as Achilles' memos whipped up their enthusiasm for "India finally rising to take her rightful place among the nations," Virlomi grew more and more skeptical. Achilles cared nothing for India, no matter how good his rhetoric sounded. And when she found herself tempted to believe in him, she had only to look at Petra to remember what he was.

Because the others all seemed to buy into Achilles' version of India's future, Virlomi kept her opinions to herself.

And she watched and waited for Petra to look at her, so she could give her a wink or a smile.

The day came. Petra looked. Virlomi smiled.

Petra looked away as casually as if Virlomi had been a chair and not a person trying to make contact.

Virlomi was not discouraged. She kept trying for eye contact until finally one day Petra passed near her on the way to a water fountain and slipped and caught herself on Virlomi's chair. In the midst of the noise of Petra's scuffling feet, Virlomi clearly heard her words: "Stop it. He's watching."

And that was it. Confirmation of what Virlomi had suspected about Achilles, proof that Petra had noticed her, and a warning that her help was not needed.

Well, that was nothing new. Petra never needed help, did she?

Then came the day, only a month ago, when Achilles sent a memo around ordering that they needed to update the old plans—the original strategy of mass assault, throwing huge armies with their huge supply lines against the Burmese. They were all stunned. Achilles gave no explanation, but he seemed unusually taciturn, and they all got the message. The brilliant strategy had been set aside by the adults. Some of the finest military minds in the world had come up with the strategy, and the adults were going to ignore them.

Everyone was outraged, but they soon settled back into the routine of work, trying to get the old plans into shape for the coming war. Troops had moved, supplies had been replenished in one area or fallen short in another. But they worked out the logistics. And when they received Achilles'—or, as Virlomi assumed, Petra's—plan for moving the bulk of the army from the Pakistani border to face the Burmese, they admired the brilliance of it, fitting the needs of the army into the existing rail and air traffic so that from satellites, no unusual movements would be visible until suddenly the armies were on the border, forming up. At most the enemy would have two days' notice; if they were careless, only a single day before it became obvious.

Achilles left on one of his frequent trips, only this time Petra disappeared too. Virlomi feared for her. Had she served her purpose, and now that he was done with her, would he kill her?

But no. She came back the same night, when Achilles did.

And the next morning, word came to begin the movement of troops. Following Petra's deft plan to get them to the Burmese border. And then, ignoring Petra's equally deft plan, they would launch their clumsy mass attack.

It makes no sense, thought Virlomi.

Then she got the email from the Hegemony Minister of Colonization—Colonel Graff, that old sabeek.

```
I'm sure you're aware that one of
our  Battle  School  graduates,
Petra Arkanian, was not returned
with  the  others  who  took  part
with  Ender  Wiggin  in  the  final
battle. I am very interested in
locating her, and believe she may
have been transported against her
will to a place within the bor-
ders of India. If you know any-
thing about her whereabouts and
present condition, could you let
someone know? I'm sure you'd want
someone to do the same for you.
```

Almost immediately there came an email from Achilles.

```
I'm sure you understand that be-
cause this is wartime, any at-
tempt to convey information to
someone outside the Indian mili-
tary will be regarded as espi-
onage and treason, and you will
be killed forthwith.
```

So Achilles was definitely keeping Petra incommunicado, and cared very much that she remain hidden to outsiders.

Virlomi did not even have to think about what she would do. This had nothing to do with Indian military security. So, while she took his death threat seriously, she did not believe there was anything morally wrong with attempting to circumvent it.

She could not write directly to Colonel Graff. Nor could she send any kind of message containing any reference, however oblique, to Petra. Any email going out from Hyderabad was going to be scrutinized. And, now that Virlomi thought about it, she and the other Battle School graduates ensconced here in the Planning and Doctrine Division were only slightly more free than Petra. She could not leave the grounds. She could not have contact with anyone who was not military with a high-level security clearance.

Spies have radio equipment or dead drops, thought Virlomi. But how do you go about becoming a spy when you have no way to reach outside but writing letters, yet there's no one you can write a letter to and no way to say what you need to say without getting caught?

She might have thought of a solution on her own. But Petra simplified the process for her by coming up behind her at the drinking fountain. As Virlomi straightened up from drinking and Petra slipped in to take her place, Petra said, "I am Briseis."

And that was all.

The reference was obvious—everyone in Battle School knew the Iliad. And with Achilles being their overseer at the moment, the Briseis references was obvious. And yet it was not. Briseis had been held by someone else, and Achilles— the original one—had been furious because he felt slighted that he didn't have her. So what could she mean by saying she was Briseis?

It had to do with the letter from Graff and Achilles' warning. So it must be a key, a way to get word out about Petra. And to get word out required the net. So *Briseis* must mean something to someone out on the net. Perhaps there was some kind of coded electronic dead drop, keyed on the name Briseis. Perhaps Petra had already found someone to contact, but could not do it because she was cut off from the nets.

Virlomi didn't bother doing a general search. If someone out there was looking for Petra, the message would have to be at a site that Petra would be able to find without deviating from legitimate military research. Which meant that Virlomi probably already knew the site where the message was waiting.

The problem she was officially working on at the moment was to determine the most efficient way to minimize risk to supply helicopters while not consuming too much fuel. The problem was so technical that there was no way she could explain doing historical or theoretical research.

But Sayagi, a Battle School graduate five years her senior, was working on problems of pacifying and winning the allegiance of local populations in occupied countries. So Virlomi went to him. "I've gone greeyaz on my algorithms."

"You want my help?" he asked.

"No, no, I just need to set it aside for a couple of hours so I can come back to it fresh. Anything I can help you look for?"

Of course Sayagi had received the same messages as Virlomi, and he was sharp enough not to take Virlomi's offer at face value.

"I don't know, what kind of thing could you do?"

"Any historical research? Or theoretical? On the nets?" She was tipping him to what she needed. And he understood.

"Toguro. I hate that stuff. I need data on failed approaches to pacification and conciliation. Besides killing or deporting everybody and moving in a new population."

"What do you already have?"

"You're wide open, I've been avoiding it."

"Thanks. You want a report or just links?"

"Paste-ups are enough. No links, though. That's too much like doing the work myself."

A perfectly innocent exchange. Virlomi had her cover now.

She went back to her desk and began browsing the historical and theoretical sites. She never actually ran a search on the name "Briseis"—that would be too obvious, the monitoring software would pick that right up and Achilles, if he saw it, would make the connection. Instead, Virlomi browsed through the sites, looking at subject headings.

Briseis showed up on the second site she tried.

It was a posting from someone calling himself HectorVictorious. Hector was not exactly an auspicious name—he was a hero, and the only person who was any kind of match for Achilles, but in the end Hector was killed and Achilles dragged his corpse around the walls of Troy.

Still, the message was clear, if you knew to think of Briseis as a codename for Petra.

Virlomi worked her way through several other postings, pretending to read them while actually composing her reply to HectorVictorious. When she was ready, she went back and typed it in, knowing as she did it that it might well be the cause of her own immediate execution.

```
I vote for her remaining a re-
sistant slave. Even if she was
forced into silence, she would
find a way to hold on to her
soul. As for slipping a message
to someone inside Troy, how do
you know she didn't? And what
good would it have done? It was-
n't that long afterward that
everyone in Troy was dead. Or
didn't you ever hear of the Tro-
jan horse? I know—Briseis should
have warned the Trojans to beware
of Greeks bearing gifts. Or found
a friendly native to do it for
her.
```

She signed it with her own name and email address. After all, this was supposed to be a perfectly innocent posting. Indeed, she worried that it might be *too* innocent. What if the person who was looking for Petra didn't realize that her references to Briseis resisting and being forced into silence were actually eyewitness reports? Or that the "friendly native" reference was to Virlomi herself?

But her address inside the Indian military network should alert whoever this was to pay special attention.

Now, of course, with the message posted, Virlomi had to

continue going through the motions of doing the useless research that Sayagi had "asked" her to do. It would be a couple of tedious hours—wasted time, if no one got the message.

Petra tried not to be obvious about watching what Virlomi was doing. After all, if Virlomi was as smart as she needed to be in order to bring this off, she wouldn't do anything that was worth watching. But Petra saw when Virlomi went over to Sayagi and talked for a while. And Petra noticed that Virlomi seemed to be browsing when she got back to her desk, mousing through online pages instead of writing or calculating. Was she going to spot those HectorVictorious postings?

Either she would or she wouldn't. Petra couldn't allow herself to think about it any more. Because in a way it would be better for everyone if Virlomi simply didn't get it. Who knew how subtle Achilles was? For all Petra knew, those postings might be traps designed to catch her getting someone else to help her. That could be fatal all the way around.

But Achilles couldn't be everywhere. He was bright, he was suspicious, he played a deep game. But he was only one person and he couldn't think of everything. Besides, how important was Petra to him, really? He hadn't even used her campaign strategy. Surely he kept her around as a vanity, nothing more.

The reports coming back from the front were just what one might expect—Burmese resistance was only token, since they were massing their main forces in places where the terrain favored them. Canyons. River crossings.

All futile, of course. No matter where the Burmese made their stand, the Indian Army would simply flow around them.

There weren't enough Burmese soldiers to make serious efforts at more than a handful of places, while there were so many Indians that they could press forward at every point, leaving only enough men at the Burmese strong points to keep them pinned down while the bulk of the Indian Army completed the takeover of Burma and moved on toward the mountain passes into Thailand.

That's where the challenge would begin, of course. For Indian supply lines would stretch all the way across Burma by then, and the Thai Air Force was formidable, especially since they had been observed testing a new temporary airfield system that could be built in many cases during the time a bomber was airborne. Not really worth it, bombing airfields when they could be replaced in two or three hours.

So even though the intelligence reports from inside Thailand were very good—detailed, accurate, and recent—on the most important points they didn't matter. There were few meaningful targets, given the strategy the Thai were using.

Petra knew Suriyawong, the Battle School grad who was running strategy and doctrine in Bangkok. He was good. But to Petra it looked a little suspicious that the new Thai strategy began, abruptly, only a few weeks after Petra and Achilles arrived in India from Russia. Suriyawong had already been in place in Bangkok for a year. Why the sudden change? It might be that someone had tipped them off about Achilles' presence in Hyderabad and what that might mean. Or it might be that someone else had joined Suriyawong and influenced his thinking.

Bean.

Petra refused to believe that he was dead. Those messages had to be from him. And even though Suriyawong was perfectly capable of thinking of the new Thai strategy himself, it was such a comprehensive set of changes, without any sign of gradual development, that it cried out for the obvious explanation—it came from a fresh set of eyes. Who else but Bean?

The trouble was, if it *was* Bean, Achilles' intelligence sources inside Thailand were so good that it was quite possible Bean would be spotted. And if Achilles' earlier attempt to kill Bean had failed, there was no chance that Achilles would refrain from trying again.

She couldn't think about that. If he had saved himself once, he could do it again. After all, maybe someone had excellent intelligence sources inside India, too.

And it might not be Bean leaving those Briseis messages. It might be Dink Meeker, for instance. Only that really wasn't Dink's style. Bean had always been something of a sneak. Dink was confrontational. He would go on the nets proclaiming that he knew Petra was in Hyderabad and demanding that she be released at once. Bean was the one who had figured out that the Battle School kept track of where students were by monitoring transmitters in their clothing. Take off all your clothes and go around buck naked, and the Battle School administrators wouldn't have a clue where you were. Not only had Bean thought of it, he had done it, climbing around in airshafts in the middle of the night. When he told her about it, as they waited around on Eros for the League War to settle down so they could go home, Petra hadn't really believed him at first. Not until he looked her coldly in the eye and said, "I don't joke, and if I did, this isn't particularly funny."

"I didn't think you were joking," said Petra. "I thought you were bragging."

"I was," said Bean. "But I wouldn't waste my time bragging about things I hadn't actually done."

That was Bean—admitting his faults right along with his virtues. No false modesty, and no vanity, either. If he bothered to talk to you at all, he never shaped his words to make himself look better or worse than he was.

She hadn't really known him in Battle School. How could she? She was older, and even though she noticed him and spoke to him a few times—she always made a point of speaking to new kids who were getting the pariah treatment, since she knew they needed friends, even if it was only a girl—she simply hadn't had much reason to talk to him.

And then there was the disastrous time when Petra had been suckered into trying to give Ender a warning—which turned out to be bogus, and in fact Ender's enemies were using Petra's attempt to warn Ender as the opportunity to jump him and beat him up. Bean was the one who saw through it and broke it up. And, quite naturally, he leapt to the conclusion that Petra was part of the conspiracy against Ender. He had continued to suspect her for quite a while. Petra wasn't really sure when he finally believed in her innocence. But it had been a barrier between them for a long time on Eros. So it wasn't until after the war ended that they even had a chance to get to know each other.

That was when Petra realized what Bean really was. It was hard to see past his small size and think of him as anything other than a preschooler or launchy or something. Even though everyone knew that he was the one that would have been chosen to take Ender's place, if Ender had broken under the strain of battle. A lot of them resented the fact. But Petra didn't. She knew Bean was the best of Ender's jeesh. It didn't bother her.

What was Bean, really? A dwarf. That's what she had to realize. With adult dwarfs, you could see in their faces that they were older than their size would indicate. But because

Bean was still a child, and had none of the short-limbed deformations of dwarfism, he looked like the age his size implied. If you talked to him like a child, though, he tuned you out. Petra never had done that, so except when he thought she was a traitor to Ender, Bean always treated her with respect.

The funny thing was, it was all based on a misunderstanding. Bean thought Petra talked to him like a regular human being because she was so mature and wise that she didn't treat him like a little kid. But the truth was, she *did* treat him exactly the way she treated little kids. It's just that she always treated little kids like adults. So she got credit for being understanding, when in fact she was just lucky.

By the time the war was over, though, it didn't matter. They knew they were going home—all of them, it turned out, but Ender—and once they got back to Earth, they expected they wouldn't see each other again. So there was a kind of freedom, caution tossed to the wind. You could say what you wanted. You didn't have to take offense at anything because it wouldn't matter in a few months. It was the first time they could actually have fun.

And the person Petra enjoyed the most was Bean.

Dink, who had been close to Petra for a while in Battle School, was a little miffed by the way Petra was always with Bean. He even accused her—obliquely, because he didn't want to get frozen out completely—of having something romantic going on with Bean. Well, of course he thought that way—puberty had already struck Dink Meeker, and like all boys that age, he thought everybody's mental processes were infused with testosterone.

It was something else, though, between Petra and Bean. Not brother and sister, either. Not mother-son or any other weird psychofake analogy she could think of. She just . . .

liked him. She had spent so long having to prove to prickly, envious, and frightened boys that she was, in fact, smarter and better at everything than they were, that it took her quite by surprise to be with someone so arrogant, so absolutely sure of his own brilliance, that he didn't feel at all threatened by her. If she knew something that he didn't know, he listened, he watched, he learned. The only other person she'd known who was like that with her was Ender.

Ender. She missed him terribly sometimes. She had tutored him—and taken a lot of heat from Bonzo Madrid, their commander at the time, for doing it. And as it became clear what Ender was, and she joined gladly with those who followed him, obeyed him, gave themselves to him, she nevertheless had a secret place in her memory where she kept the knowledge that she had been Ender's friend at a time when no one else had the courage. She had made a difference in his life, and even when others thought she had betrayed him, Ender never thought that.

She loved Ender with a helpless mixture of worship and longing that led to foolish dreams of impossible futures, tying her life with his until they died. She fantasized about raising children together, the most brilliant children in the world. About being able to stand beside the greatest human being in the world—for so she thought he was—and having everybody recognize that he had chosen her to stand with him forever.

Dreams. After the war, Ender was beaten down. Broken. Finding out that he had actually caused the extermination of the Formics was more than he could bear. And because she, too, had broken during the war, her shame kept her away from him until it was too late, until they had divided Ender from the rest of them.

Which is why she knew that her feelings toward Bean

were completely different. No such dreams and fantasies. Just a sense of complete acceptance. She belonged with Bean, not the way a wife belonged with a husband or, God forbid, a girlfriend with a boyfriend, but rather the way a left hand belonged with the right. They simply fit. Nothing exciting about it, nothing to write home about. But it could be counted on. She imagined that, of all the Battle School kids, of all the members of Ender's jeesh, it would be Bean that she would remain close to.

Then they got off the shuttle and were dispersed throughout the world. And even though Armenia and Greece were relatively close together—compared to, say, Shen in Japan or Hot Soup in China—they never saw each other, they never even wrote. She knew that Bean was going home to meet a family that he had never known, and she was busy trying to get involved with her own family again. She didn't exactly pine for him, or he for her. And besides, they didn't need to hang out together or chat all the time for her to know that, left hand with right hand, they were still friends, still belonged together. That when she needed someone, the first person she should call on was Bean.

In a world that didn't have Ender Wiggin in it, that meant he was the person she loved most. That she would miss most if anything happened to him.

Which is why she could pretend that she wasn't going to worry about Bean getting folded by Achilles, but it wasn't true. She worried all the time. Of course, she worried about herself, too—and maybe a little more about herself than about him. But she'd already lost one love in her life, and even though she told herself that these childhood friendships wouldn't matter in twenty years, she didn't want to lose the other.

Her desk beeped at her.

There was a message in the display.

```
When did I designate this as nap-
time? Come see me.
```

Only Achilles wrote with such peremptory rudeness. She hadn't been napping. She had been thinking. But it wasn't worth arguing with him about it.

She logged off and got up from her desk.

It was evening, getting dark outside. Her mind really had wandered. Most of the others on the day shift in Planning and Doctrine had already left, and the night response team was coming in. A couple of the day shift were still at their desks, though.

She caught a glance from Virlomi, one of the late ones. The girl looked worried. That meant she probably *had* done something in response to the Briseis posting, and now feared repercussions. Well, she was right to worry. Who knew how Achilles would speak or write or act if he was planning to kill somebody? Petra's personal opinion was that he was always planning to kill someone, so there was no difference in his behavior to warn you if you were next. Go home and try to get some sleep, Virlomi. Even if Achilles has caught you trying to help me and has decided to have you killed, you won't be able to do anything about it, so you might as well sleep the sleep of a child.

Petra left the big barn of a room they all worked in and moved through the corridors as if in a trance. Had she been asleep when Achilles wrote to her? Who cared.

As far as Petra knew, she was the only one in Planning and Doctrine who even knew where Achilles' office was. She had been in it often, but was not impressed by the privilege. She had the freedom of a slave or a captive. Achilles let her intrude on his privacy because he didn't think of her as a person.

One wall of his office was a 2D computer display, now showing a detailed map of the India-Burma border region. As reports came in from troops in the field and from satellites, it was updated by clerks, so Achilles could glance at it any time and see the best available intelligence on placement. Apart from that, the room was spartan. Two chairs—not comfortable ones—a table, a bookcase, and a cot. Petra suspected that somewhere on the base there was a comfortable suite of rooms with a soft bed that was never used. Whatever else Achilles was, he wasn't a hedonist. He never cared much about personal comfort, not that she had seen, anyway.

He didn't take his eyes off the map when she came in— but she was used to that. When he made a point of ignoring her, she took it as his perverse way of paying attention to her. It was when he looked right at her without seeing her that she felt truly invisible.

"The campaign's going very well," said Achilles.

"It's a stupid plan, and the Thai are going to cut it to shreds."

"They had a sort of coup a few minutes ago," said Achilles. "The commander of the Thai military blew up young Suriyawong. Terrible case of professional jealousy, apparently."

Petra tried to keep from showing her sadness at Suriyawong's death and her disgust at Achilles. "You're not seriously expecting me to believe you had nothing to do with it?"

"Well, *they're* blaming it on Indian spies, of course. But there were no Indian spies involved."

"Not even the Chakri?"

"Definitely not spying for India," said Achilles.

"For whom, then?"

Achilles laughed. "You're so untrusting. My Briseis."

She had to work at staying relaxed, at not betraying anything when he called her that.

"Ah, Pet, you *are* my Briseis, don't you realize?"

"Not really," said Petra. "Briseis was in somebody else's tent."

"Oh, I have your *body* with me, and I get the product of your brain, but your heart still belongs to someone else."

"It belongs to me," said Petra.

"It belongs to Hector," said Achilles. "But . . . how can I bear to tell you this? Suriyawong was not alone in his office when the building was blown to bits. Another person contributed scraps of flesh and bone and a fine aerosol of blood to the general gore. Unfortunately, this means I can't drag his body around the walls of Troy."

Petra was sick inside. Had he heard her tell Virlomi, "I am Briseis"? And whom was he talking about, saying those things about Hector?

"Just tell me what you're talking about or don't," said Petra.

"Oh, don't tell me you haven't seen those little messages all over the forums," said Achilles. "About Briseis, and Guinevere, and every other tragic romantic heroine who got trapped with some overbearing bunduck."

"What about them?"

"You know who wrote them," said Achilles.

"Do I?"

"I forgot. You refuse to play guessing games. All right, it was Bean, and you knew that."

Petra felt unwanted emotions welling up—she suppressed them. If those messages were posted by Bean, then he *had* lived through the previous assassination attempt. But that would mean Bean was "HectorVictorious," and Achilles' little allegory meant that Bean was indeed in Bangkok, and Achilles had spotted him and tried again to kill him. He had died along with Suriyawong.

"I'm glad to have you to tell me what I know. It saves my having to actually use my own memory."

"I know it's tearing you up, my poor Pet. The funny thing is, dear Briseis, Bean was just a bonus. It was Suriyawong that we targeted from the start."

"Fine. Congratulations. You're a genius. Whatever it is you want me to say so you'll shut up and let me get some dinner."

Talking rudely to Achilles was the only illusion of freedom Petra was able to retain. She figured it amused him. And she wasn't dumb enough to talk to him that way in front of anyone else.

"You had your heart set on Bean saving you, didn't you?" said Achilles. "That's why when old Graff sent that stupid request for information, you tipped that Virlomi kid to try responding to Bean."

Petra tasted despair. Achilles really did monitor everything.

"Come on, the water fountain's the most obvious place to bug," said Achilles.

"I thought you had important things to do."

"Nothing's more important in my life than you, Pet," said Achilles. "If I could just get you to come into my tent."

"You've kidnapped me twice. You watch me wherever I go. I don't know how I could be farther in your tent than I am."

"In . . . my . . . tent," said Achilles. "You're still my enemy."

"Oh, I forgot, I'm supposed to be so eager to please my captor that I surrender my volition to you."

"If I wanted that, I'd have you tortured, Pet," said Achilles. "But I don't want you that way."

"How kind of you."

"No, if I can't have you freely with me, as my friend and ally, then I'll just kill you. I'm not into torture."

"After you've used my work."

"But I'm not using your work," said Achilles.

"Oh, that's right. Because Suriyawong is dead, so you don't need to worry now about having any real opposition."

Achilles laughed. "Sure. That's it."

Which meant, of course, that she hadn't understood at all.

"It's easy to fool a person you keep living in a box. I only know what you tell me."

"But I tell you everything," said Achilles, "if only you were bright enough to get it."

Petra closed her eyes. She kept thinking of poor Suriyawong. So serious all the time. He had done his best for his country, and then it was his own commander-in-chief who killed him. Did he know? I hope not.

If she kept thinking of poor Suriyawong, she wouldn't have to think of Bean at all.

"You're not listening," said Achilles.

"Oh, thanks for telling me that," said Petra. "I thought I was."

Achilles was about to say something else, but then he cocked his head. The hearing aid he wore was a radio receiver tied to his desk. Somebody had just started talking to him.

Achilles turned from her to his desk. He typed a few things, read a few things. His face showed no emotion—but that was a real change, since he had been smiling and pleasant until the voice came. Something had gone wrong. Indeed, Petra knew him well enough now that she thought she recognized the signs of anger. Or maybe—she wondered, she hoped—fear.

"They aren't dead," Petra said.

"I'm busy," he said.

She laughed. "That's the message, isn't it? Once again, your assassins have piffed it. If you want a job done right, Achilles, you've got to do it yourself."

He turned away from the desk display and looked her in the eye. "He sent out a message from the barracks of his strike force there in Thailand. Of course the Chakri saw it."

"Not dead," said Petra. "He just keeps beating you."

"Narrowly escaping with his life while my plans are never interfered with at all . . ."

"Come on, you know he got you booted out of Russia."

Achilles raised his eyebrows. "So you admit you sent a coded message."

"Bean doesn't need coded messages to beat you," she said.

Achilles rose from his chair and walked over to her. She braced herself for a slap. But he planted a hand in her chest and shoved the chair over backward.

Her head hit the floor. It left her dazed, lights flashing through her peripheral vision. And then a wave of pain and nausea.

"He sent for dear old Sister Carlotta," said Achilles. His voice betrayed no emotion. "She's flying around the world to help him. Isn't that nice of her?"

Petra could barely comprehend what he was saying. The only thought she could hold on to was: Don't let there be any permanent brain damage. That was her whole self. She'd rather die than lose the brilliance that made her who she was.

"But that gives me time to set up a little surprise," said Achilles. "I think I'll make Bean very sorry that he's alive."

Petra wanted to say something to that, but she couldn't remember what. Then she couldn't remember what he had said. "What?"

"Oh, is your poor little head swimming, my Pet? You should be more careful with the way you lean back on that chair."

Now she remembered what he had said. A surprise. For Sister Carlotta. To make Bean sorry he's alive.

"Sister Carlotta is the one who got you off the streets of Rotterdam," said Petra. "You owe her everything. Your leg operation. Going to Battle School."

"I owe her nothing," said Achilles. "You see, she chose Bean. She sent him. Me, she passed over. I'm the one who brought civilization to the streets. I'm the one who kept her precious little Bean alive. But him she sends up into space, and me she leaves in the dirt."

"Poor baby," said Petra.

He kicked her, hard, in the ribs. She gasped.

"And as for Virlomi," he said, "I think I can use her to teach you a lesson about disloyalty to me."

"That's the way to bring me into your tent," said Petra.

Again he kicked her. She tried not to groan, but it came out anyway. This passive resistance strategy was not working.

He acted as if he hadn't done it. "Come on, why are you lying there? Get up."

"Just kill me and have done with it," she said. "Virlomi was just trying to be a decent human being."

"Virlomi was warned what would happen."

"Virlomi is nothing to you but a way to hurt me."

"You're not that important. And if I want to hurt you, I know how." He made as if to kick her again. She stiffened, curled away from the blow. But it didn't come.

Instead he reached down a hand to her. "Get up, my Pet. The floor is no place to nap."

She reached up and took his hand. She let him bear most of her weight as she rose up, so he was pulling hard.

Fool, she thought. I was trained for personal combat. You weren't in Battle School long enough to get that training.

As soon as her legs were under her, she shoved upward. Since that was the direction he had been pulling, he lost his balance and went over backward, falling over the legs of her chair.

He did not hit his head. He immediately tried to scramble to his feet. But she knew how to respond to his movements, kicking sharply at him with her heavy army-issue shoes, shifting her weight so that her kicks never came at the place he was protecting. Every kick hurt him. He tried to scramble backward, but she pressed on, relentless, and because he was using his arms to help him scuttle across the floor, she was able to kick him in the head, a solid blow that rocked him back and laid him out.

Not unconscious, but a little dizzy. Well, see how you like it.

He tried to do some kind of street-fighting move, kicking out with his legs while his eyes were looking elsewhere, but it was pathetic. She easily jumped over his legs and landed a scuffing kick right up between his legs.

He cried out in pain.

"Come on, get up," she said. "You're going to kill Virlomi, so kill me first. Do it. You're the killer. Get your gun. Come on."

And then, without her quite seeing how he did it, there was indeed a gun in his hand.

"Kick me again," he said through gritted teeth. "Kick me faster than this bullet."

She didn't move.

"I thought you wanted to die," he said.

She could see it now. He wouldn't shoot her. Not till he had shot Virlomi in front of her.

She had missed her chance. While he was down, before he got the gun—from the back of his waistband? from under the furniture?—she should have snapped his neck. This wasn't a wrestling match, this was her chance to put an end to him. But her instinct had taken over, and her instinct was not to kill, only to disable her opponent, because that's what she had practiced in Battle School.

Of all the things I could have learned from Ender, the killer instinct, going for the final blow from the start, why was that the one I overlooked?

Something Bean had explained about Achilles. Something Graff had told him, after Bean had gotten him shipped back to Earth. That Achilles had to kill anyone who had ever seen him helpless. Even the doctor who had repaired his gimp leg, because she'd seen him laid out under anaesthetic and taken a knife to him.

Petra had just destroyed whatever feeling it was that had made him keep her alive. Whatever he had wanted from her, he wouldn't want it now. He wouldn't be able to bear having her around. She was dead.

Yet, no matter what else was going on, she was still a tactician. Thick headed as she was, her mind could still do this dance. The enemy saw things this way; so change it so he sees them another way.

Petra laughed. "I never thought you'd let me do that," she said.

He slowly, painfully, was getting to his feet, the gun trained on her.

She went on. "You always had to be el supremo, like the

bunducks in Battle School. I never thought you had the guts to be like Ender or Bean, till now."

Still he said nothing. But he was standing there. He was listening.

"Crazy, isn't it? But Bean and Ender, they were so little. And they didn't care. Everybody looking down at them, *me* towering over them, they were the only guys in Battle School who weren't terrified of having somebody see a girl be better than them, bigger than them." Keep it going, keep spinning it. "They put Ender in Bonzo's army too early, he hadn't been trained. Didn't know how to do anything. And Bonzo gave orders, nobody was to work with him. So here I had this little kid, helpless, didn't know anything. That's what I like, Achilles. Smarter than me, but smaller. So I taught him. Chisel Bonzo, I didn't care. He was like *you've* always been, constantly showing me who's boss. But Ender knew how to let me run it. I taught him everything. I would have died for him."

"You're sick," said Achilles.

"Oh, you're going to tell me you didn't know that? You had the gun the whole time, why did you let me do that, if it wasn't—if you weren't trying to . . ."

"Trying to what?" he said. He was keeping his voice steady, but the craziness was plainly visible, and his voice trembled just a little. She had pushed him past the borders of sanity, deep into his madness. It was Caligula she was seeing now. But he was listening. If she found the right story to put on what just happened, maybe he would settle for . . . something else. Making his horse consul. Making Petra . . .

"Weren't you trying to seduce me?" she said.

"You don't even have your tits yet," he said.

"I don't think it's tits you're looking for," she said. "Or you would never have dragged me around with you in the first place. What was all that talk about wanting me in your tent? Loyal? You wanted me to belong to you. And all the time you did that sabeek stuff, pushing me around—that just made me feel contempt for you. I was looking down on you the whole time. You were nothing, just another sack of testosterone, another chimp hooting and beating his chest. But then you let me—you *did* let me, didn't you? You don't expect me to believe I really could have done that?"

A faint smile touched the corners of his lips.

"Doesn't that spoil it, if you think I did it on purpose?" he said.

She strode to him, right to the barrel of the gun, and, letting it press into her abdomen, she reached up, grabbed him by the neck, and pulled his head down to where she could kiss him.

She had no idea how to do it, except what she'd seen in movies. But she was apparently doing it well enough. The gun stayed in her belly, but his other arm wrapped around her, pulled her closer.

In the back of her mind, she remembered what Bean told her—that the last thing he had seen Achilles do before killing Bean's friend Poke was kiss her. Bean had had nightmares about it. Achilles kissing her, and then in the middle of the kiss, strangling her. Not that Bean actually saw that part. Maybe it didn't happen that way at all.

But no matter how you cut it, Achilles was a dangerous boy to kiss. And there was that gun in her belly. Maybe this was the moment he longed for. Maybe his dreams were about this—kissing a girl, and blowing a hole in her body while he did.

Well, blow away, she thought. Before I watch you kill Virlomi for the crime of having compassion for me and courage enough to act, I'd rather be dead myself. I'd rather kiss you than watch you kill her, and there's nothing in the world that could disgust me more than having to pretend that you're the . . . thing . . . I love.

The kiss ended. But she did not let go of him. She would not step back, she would not break this embrace. He had to believe that she wanted him. That she was in his emossin' tent.

He was breathing lightly, quickly. His heartbeat was rapid. Prelude to a kill? Or just the aftermath of a kiss.

"I said I'd kill anyone who tried to answer Graff," he said. "I have to."

"She didn't answer Graff, did she?" said Petra. "I know you have to keep control of things, but you don't have to be a strutting yelda about it. She doesn't know you know what she did."

"She'll think she got away with it."

"But *I'll* know," said Petra, "that you weren't afraid to give me what I want."

"What, you think you've found some way to make me do what you want?" he said.

Now she could back away from him. "I thought I'd found a man who didn't have to prove he was big by pushing people around. I guess I was wrong. Do what you want. Men like you disgust me." She put as much contempt into her voice, onto her face, as she could. "Here, prove you're a man. Shoot me. Shoot everybody. I've known *real* men. I thought you were one of them."

He lowered the gun. She did not show her relief. Just kept her eyes looking into his.

"Don't ever think you've got me figured out," he said.

"I don't care whether I figure you out or not," she said. "All I care about is, you're the first man since Ender and Bean who had guts enough to let me stand over him."

"Is that what you're going to say?" he asked.

"Say? Who to? I don't have any friends out there. The only person worth talking to in this whole place is you."

He stood there, breathing heavily again, a bit of the craziness back in his eyes.

What am I saying wrong?

"You're going to bring this off," she said. "I don't know how you're going to do it, but I can taste it. You're going to run the whole show. They're all going to be under you, Achilles. Governments, universities, corporations, all eager to please you. But when we're alone, where nobody else can see, we'll both know that you're strong enough to keep a strong woman with you."

"You?" said Achilles. "A woman?"

"If I'm not a woman, what were you doing with me in here?"

"Take off your clothes," he said.

The craziness was still there. He was testing her somehow. Waiting for her to show . . .

To show that she was faking. That she was really afraid of him, after all. That her story was all a lie, designed to trick him.

"No," she said. "You take off yours."

And the craziness faded.

He smiled.

He tucked the gun into the back of his pants.

"Get out of here," he said. "I've got a war to run."

"It's night," she said. "Nobody's moving."

"There's a lot more to this war than the armies," said Achilles.

"When do I get to stay in your tent?" she asked. "What do I have to do?" She could hardly believe she was saying this, when all she wanted was to get out.

"You have to be the thing I need," he said. "And right now, you're not."

He walked to his desk, sat down.

"And pick up your chair on the way out."

He started typing. Orders? For what? To kill whom? She didn't ask. She picked up the chair. She walked out.

And kept walking, through the corridors to the room where she slept alone. Knowing, with every step, that she was monitored. There would be vids. He would check them, to see how she acted. To see if she meant what she'd said. So she couldn't stop and press her face against the wall and cry. She had to be . . . what? How would this play in a movie or a vid if she were a woman who was frustrated because she wanted to be with her man?

I don't know! she screamed inside. I'm not an actress!

And then, a much quieter voice in her head answered. Yes you are. And a pretty good one. Because for another few minutes, maybe another hour, maybe another night, you're alive.

No triumph, either. She couldn't seem to gloat, couldn't show relief. Frustration, annoyance—and some pain where he kicked her, where her head hit the floor—that's all she could show.

Even alone in her bed, the lights off, she lay there, pretending, lying. Hoping that whatever she did in her sleep would not provoke him. Would not bring that crazy frightened searching look into his eyes.

Not that it would be any guarantee, of course. There was no sign of craziness when he shot those men in the bread van back in Russia. Don't ever think you've got me figured out, he said.

You win, Achilles. I don't think I've got you figured out. But I've learned how to play one lousy string. That's something.

I also knocked you onto the floor, beat the goffno out of you, kicked you in your little kintamas, and made you think you liked it. Kill me tomorrow or whenever you want—my shoe going into your face, you can't take that away from me.

———

In the morning, Petra was pleased to find that she was still alive, considering what she had done the night before. Her head ached, her ribs were sore, but nothing was broken.

And she was starving. She had missed dinner the night before, and perhaps there was something about beating up her jailer that made her especially hungry. She didn't usually eat breakfast, so she had no accustomed place to sit. At other meals, she sat by herself, and others, respecting her solitude or fearing Achilles' displeasure, did not sit with her.

But today, on impulse, she took her tray to a table that had only a couple of empty spots. The conversation grew quiet when she first sat down, and a few people greeted her. She smiled back at them, but then concentrated on her food. Their conversation resumed.

"There's no way she got off the base."

"So she's still here."

"Unless someone *took* her."

"Maybe it's a special assignment or something."

"Sayagi says he thinks she's dead."

A chill ran through Petra's body.

"Who?" she asked.

The others glanced at her, but then glanced away. Finally one of them said, "Virlomi."

Virlomi was gone. And no one knew where she was.

He killed her. He said he would, and he did. The only thing I gained by what I did last night was that he didn't do it in front of me.

I can't stand this. I'm done. My life is not worth living. To be his captive, to have him kill anyone who tries to help me in any way . . .

No one was looking at her. Nor were they talking.

They know Virlomi tried to answer Graff, because she must have said something to Sayagi when she walked over to him yesterday. And now she's gone.

Petra knew she had to eat, no matter how sick at heart she felt, no matter how much she wanted to cry, to run screaming from the room, to fall on the floor and beg their forgiveness for . . . for what? For being alive when Virlomi was dead.

She finished all she could bear to eat, and left the mess hall.

But as she walked through the corridors to the room where they all worked, she realized: Achilles would not have killed her like this. There was no point in killing her if the others didn't get to see her arrested and taken away. It wouldn't do what he needed it to do, if she just disappeared in the night.

At the same time, if she had escaped, he couldn't announce it. That would be even worse. So he would simply remain silent, and leave the impression with everyone that she was probably dead.

Petra imagined Virlomi walking boldly out of the building, her sheer bravado carrying the day. Or perhaps, dressed as one of the women who cleaned floors and windows, she had slipped out unnoticed. Or had she climbed a wall, or run a minefield? Petra didn't even know what the perimeter looked like, or how closely guarded it might be. She had never been given a tour.

Wishful thinking, that's all this is, she told herself as she sat down to the day's work. Virlomi is dead, and Achilles is simply waiting to announce it, to make us all suffer from not knowing.

But as the day wore on, and Achilles did not appear, Petra began to believe that perhaps she had gotten away. Maybe Achilles was staying away because he didn't want anyone speculating about any visible bruises he might have. Or maybe he's having some scrotal problems and he's having some doctor check him out—though heaven help him if Achilles decided that having a doctor handle his injured testes was worthy of the death penalty.

Maybe he was staying away because Virlomi was gone and Achilles did not want them to see him frustrated and helpless. When he caught her and could drag her into the room and shoot her dead in front of them, *then* he could face them.

And as long as that didn't happen, there was a chance Virlomi was alive.

Stay that way, my friend. Run far and don't pause for anything. Cross some border, find some refuge, swim to Sri Lanka, fly to the moon. Find some miracle, Virlomi, and live.

15

MURDER

```
To:Graff%pilgrimage@colmin.gov
From:Carlotta%agape@vatican.net/
orders/sisters/ind
Re: Please forward
```

```
The attached file is encrypted.
Please wait twelve hours after the
time of sending and if you don't
hear from me, forward it to Bean.
He'll know the key.
```

It took less than four hours to secure and inspect the entire high command base in Bangkok. Computer experts would be probing to try to find out whom it was that Naresuan had been communicating with outside, and whether he was in fact involved with a foreign power or this gambit was a private venture. When Suriyawong's work with the Prime Minister was finished, he came alone to the barracks where Bean was waiting.

Most of Bean's soldiers had already returned, and Bean had sent most of them to bed. He still watched the news in a desultory fashion—nothing new was being said, so he was interested only in seeing how the talking heads were spinning it. In Thailand, everything was charged with patriotic fervor. Abroad, of course, it was a different story. All the Common broadcasts were taking a more skeptical view that Indian operatives had really made the assassination attempt.

"Why would India want to provoke Thai entry into the war?"

"They know Thailand will come in eventually whether Burma asks them or not. So they felt they had to deprive Thailand of its best Battle School graduate."

"Is one child so dangerous?"

"Maybe you should ask the Formics. If you can find any."

And on and on, everyone trying to appear smart—or at least smarter than the Indian and Thai governments, which was the game the media always played. What mattered to Bean was how this would affect Peter. Was there any mention of the possibility that Achilles was running the show in India? Not a breath. Anything yet about Pakistani troop movements near Iran? The "Bangkok bombing" had driven that slow-moving story off the air. Nobody was giving this any global implications. As long as the I.F. was there to keep the nukes from flying, it was still just politics as usual in south Asia.

Except it wasn't. Everybody was so busy trying to look wise and unsurprised that nobody was standing up and screaming that this whole set of events was completely different from anything that had gone before. The most populous nation in the world has dared to turn its back on a two-hundred-year-old enemy and invade the small, weak country to its east. Now India was attacking Thailand. What did that mean? What was India's goal? What possible benefit could there be?

Why weren't they talking about these things?

"Well," said Suriyawong, "I don't think I'm going to go to sleep very soon."

"Everything all cleaned up?"

"More like everybody who worked closely with the Chakri has been sent home and put under house arrest while the investigation continues."

"That means the entire high command."

"Not really," said Suriyawong. "The best field commanders are out in the field. Commanding. One of them will be brought in as acting Chakri."

"They should give it to you."

"They should, but they won't. Aren't you just a little hungry?"

"It's late."

"This is Bangkok."

"Well, not really," said Bean. "This is a military base."

"When is your friend's flight due in?"

"Morning. Just after dawn."

"Ouch. She's going to be out of sorts. You going to meet her at the airport?"

"I didn't think about it."

"Let's go get dinner," said Suriyawong. "Officers do it all the time. We can take a couple of strike force soldiers with us to make sure we don't get hassled for being children."

"Achilles isn't going to give up on killing me."

"Us. He aimed at *us* this time."

"He might have a backup."

"Bean, I'm hungry. Are you hungry?" Suriyawong turned to the members of the toon that had been with him. "Any of you hungry?"

"Not really," said one of them. "We ate at the regular time."

"Sleepy," said another.

"Anybody awake enough to go into the city with us?" Immediately all of them stepped forward.

"Don't ask perfect soldiers whether they want to protect their CO," said Bean.

"Designate a couple to go with us and let the others sleep," said Suriyawong.

"Yes sir," said Bean. He turned to the men. "Honest assessment. Which of you will be least impaired by failing to get enough sleep tonight?"

"Will we be allowed sleep tomorrow?" asked one.

"Yes," said Bean. "So it's a matter of how much it affects you to get off your rhythm."

"I'll be fine." Four others felt the same way. So Bean chose the two nearest. "Two of you keep watch for two more hours, then go back to the normal watch rotation."

Outside the building, with their two bodyguards walking five meters behind them, Bean and Suriyawong finally had a chance to talk candidly. First, though, Suriyawong had to know. "You really keep a regular watch rotation even here at the base?"

"Was I wrong?" asked Bean.

"Obviously not, but . . . you really are paranoid."

"I know I have an enemy who wants me dead. An enemy who happens to be hopping from one powerful position to another."

"More powerful each time," said Suriyawong. "In Russia, he didn't have the power to start a war."

"He might not in India, either," said Bean.

"There's a war," said Suriyawong. "You're saying it isn't his?"

"It's his," said Bean. "But he's probably still having to persuade adults to go along with him."

"Win a few, and they hand you your own army," said Suriyawong.

"Win a few more, and they hand you the country," said Bean. "As Napoleon and Washington showed."

"How many do you have to win to get the world?"

Bean let the question hang.

"Why did he go after us?" asked Suriyawong. "I think you're right, that this operation at least was entirely Achilles'. It's not the kind of thing the Indian government goes for. India is a democracy. Folding children doesn't play well. No way he got approval."

"It might not even be India," said Bean. "We don't really know anything."

"Except that it's Achilles," said Suriyawong. "Think about the stuff that doesn't make sense. A second-rate, obvious campaign strategy that we're probably going to be able to take apart. A nasty bit of business like this that can only soil India's reputation in the rest of the world."

"Obviously he's not acting in India's best interest," said Bean. "But they think he is, if he's really the one who brought off this deal with Pakistan. He's acting for himself. And I can see what he gains by kidnapping Ender's jeesh and by trying to kill you."

"Fewer rivals?"

"No," said Bean. "He makes Battle School grads look like the most important weapons in the war."

"But he's not a Battle School grad."

"He was *in* Battle School, and he's that age. He doesn't want to have to wait till he grows up to be king of the world. He wants everyone to believe that a child should lead them. If you're worth killing, if Ender's jeesh is worth stealing . . ." It also helps Peter Wiggin, Bean realized. He didn't go to Battle School, but if children are plausible world leaders, his own track record as Locke raises him above any other contenders. Military ability is one thing. Ending the League War was a much stronger qualification. It trumped "psychopathic Battle School expulsee" hands down.

"Do you think that's all?" asked Suriyawong.

"What's all?" asked Bean. He had lost the thread. "Oh, you mean is that enough to explain why Achilles would want you dead?" Bean thought about it. "I don't know. Maybe. But it doesn't tell us why he's setting up India for a much bloodier war than it has to fight."

"What about this," said Suriyawong. "Make everybody fear what war will bring, so they want to strengthen the Hegemony to keep the war from spreading."

"That's fine, except nobody's going to nominate Achilles as Hegemon."

"Good point. Are we ruling out the possibility that Achilles is just stupid?"

"Yes, that's not a possibility."

"What about Petra, could she have fooled him into sticking with this obvious but somewhat dumb and wasteful strategy?"

"That *is* possible, except that Achilles is very sharp at reading people. I don't know if Petra could lie to him. I never saw her lie to anybody. I don't know if she can."

"Never saw her lie to *anybody?*" asked Suriyawong.

Bean shrugged. "We became very good friends, at the end of the war. She speaks her mind. She may hold something back sometimes, but she tells you she's doing it. No smoke, no mirrors. The door's either open or it's shut."

"Lying takes practice," observed Suriyawong.

"Like the Chakri?"

"You don't get to that position by pure military ability. You have to make yourself look very good to a lot of people. And hide a lot of things you're doing."

"You're not suggesting Thailand's government is corrupt," said Bean.

"I'm suggesting Thailand's government is political. I hope this doesn't surprise you. Because I'd heard that you were bright."

They got a car to take them into town—Suriyawong had always had the authority to requisition a car and a driver, he just never used it till now.

"So where do we eat?" asked Bean. "It's not like I have a restaurant guide with me."

"I grew up in families with better chefs than any restaurant," said Suriyawong.

"So we go to your house?"

"My family lives near Chiang Mai."

"That's going to be a battle zone."

"Which is why I think they're actually in Vientiane, though security rules would keep them from telling me. My father is running a network of dispersed munitions factories." Suriyawong grinned. "I had to make sure I siphoned off some of these defense jobs for my family."

"In other words, he was best man for the task."

"My mother was best for the task, but this *is* Thailand. Our love affair with Western culture ended a century ago."

They ended up having to ask the soldiers, and they only knew the kind of place they could afford to eat. So they found themselves eating at a tiny all-night diner in a part of town that wasn't the worst, but wasn't the nicest, either. And the whole thing was so cheap it felt practically free.

Suriyawong and the soldiers went down on the food as if it were the best meal they'd ever had. "Isn't this *great*?" asked Suriyawong. "When my parents had company, and they were eating all the fancy stuff in the dining room with visitors, we kids would eat in the kitchen, the stuff the servants ate. *This* stuff. *Real* food."

No doubt that's why the Americans at Yum-Yum in Greensboro loved what they got there, too. Childhood memories. Food that tasted like safety and love and getting rewarded for good behavior. A treat—we're going out. Bean didn't have any such memories, of course. He had no nostalgia for picking up food wrappers and licking the sugar off the plastic and then trying to get at any of it that rubbed off on his nose.

What was he nostalgic for? Life in Achilles' "family"? Battle School? Not likely. And his time with his family in Greece had come too late to be part of his early childhood memories. He liked being in Crete, he loved his family, but no, the only good memories of his childhood were in Sister Carlotta's apartment when she took him off the street and fed him and kept him safe and helped him prepare to take the Battle School tests—his ticket off Earth, to where he'd be safe from Achilles.

It was the only time in his childhood when he felt safe. And even though he didn't believe it or understand it at the time, he felt loved, too. If he could sit down in some restaurant and eat a meal like the ones Sister Carlotta prepared there in Rotterdam, he'd probably feel the way those Americans felt about Yum-Yum, or these Thais felt about this place.

"Our friend Borommakot doesn't really like the food," said Suriyawong. He spoke in Thai, because Bean had picked up the language quite readily, and the soldiers weren't as comfortable in Common.

"He may not like it," said one soldier, "but it's making him grow."

"Soon he'll be as tall as you," said the other.

"How tall do Greeks get?" asked the first.

Bean froze.

So did Suriyawong.

The two soldiers looked at them with some alarm. "What, did you see something?"

"How did you know he was Greek?" asked Suriyawong.

The soldiers glanced at each other and then suppressed their smiles.

"I guess they're not stupid," said Bean.

"We saw all the vids on the Bugger War, we saw your face, you think you're not famous? Don't you know?"

"But you never said anything," said Bean.

"That would have been rude."

Bean wondered how many people made him in Araraquara and Greensboro, but were too polite to say anything.

It was three in the morning when they got to the airport. The plane was due in about six. Bean was too keyed up to sleep. He assigned himself to keep watch, and let the soldiers and Suriyawong doze.

So it was Bean who noticed when a flurry of activity began around the podium about forty-five minutes before the flight was supposed to arrive. He got up and went to ask what was going on.

"Please wait, we'll make an announcement," said the ticket agent. "Where are your parents? Are they here?"

Bean sighed. So much for fame. Suriyawong, at least, should have been recognized. Then again, everyone here had been on duty all night and probably hadn't heard any of the news about the assassination attempt, so they wouldn't have seen Suriyawong's face flashed in the vids again and again. He went back to waken one of the soldiers so he could find out, adult to adult, what was going on.

His uniform probably got him information that a civilian wouldn't have been told. He came back looking grim. "The plane went down," he said.

Bean felt his heart plummet. Achilles? Had he found a way to get to Sister Carlotta?

It couldn't be. How could he know? He couldn't be monitoring every airplane flight in the world.

The message Bean had sent via the computer in the barracks. The Chakri might have seen it. If he hadn't been arrested by then. He might have had time to relay the information to Achilles, or whatever intermediary they used. How else could Achilles have known that Carlotta would be coming?

"It's not him this time," said Suriyawong, when Bean told him what he was thinking. "There are plenty of reasons a plane can drop out of radar."

"She didn't say it disappeared," said the soldier. "She said it went down."

Suriyawong looked genuinely stricken. "Borommakot, I'm sorry." Then Suriyawong went to a telephone and contacted the Prime Minister's office. Being Thailand's pride and joy, who had just survived an assassination attempt, had its benefits. In a very few minutes they were escorted into the meeting room at the airport where officials from the government and the military were conferring, linked to aviation authorities and investigating agencies worldwide.

The plane had gone down over southern China. It was an Air Shanghai flight, and China was treating it as an internal matter, refusing to allow outside investigators to come to the crash site. But air traffic satellites had the story—there was an explosion, a big one, and the plane was in small fragments before any part of it reached the ground. No chance of survivors.

Only one faint hope remained. Maybe she hadn't made a connection somewhere. Maybe she wasn't on board.

But she was.

I could have stopped her, thought Bean. When I agreed to trust the Prime Minister without waiting for Carlotta to arrive, I could have sent word at once to have her go home. But instead he waited around and watched the vids and then went out for a night on the town. Because he wanted to see her. Because he had been frightened and he needed to have her with him.

Because he was too selfish even to think of the danger he was exposing her to. She flew under her own name—she had never done that when they were together. Was that his fault?

Yes. Because he had summoned her with such urgency that she didn't have time to do things covertly. She just had the Vatican arrange her flights, and that was it. The end of her life.

The end of her ministry, that's how she'd think about it. The jobs left undone. The work that someone else would have to do.

All he'd done, ever since she met him, was steal time from her, keep her from the things that really mattered in her life. Having to do her work on the run, in hiding, for his sake. Whenever he needed her, she dropped everything. What had he ever done to deserve it? What had he ever given her in return? And now he had interrupted her work permanently. She would be so annoyed. But even now, if he could talk to her, he knew what she'd say.

It was always my choice, she'd say. You're part of the work God gave me. Life ends, and I'm not afraid to return to God. I'm only afraid for you, because you keep yourself such a stranger to him.

If only he could believe that she was still alive somehow. That she was there with Poke, maybe, taking her in now the way she took Bean in so many years ago. And the two of them laughing and reminiscing about clumsy old Bean, who just had a way of getting people killed.

Someone touched his arm. "Bean," whispered Suriyawong. "Bean, let's get you out of here."

Bean focused and realized that there were tears running down his cheeks. "I'm staying," he said.

"No," said Suriyawong. "Nothing's going to happen here. I mean let's go to the official residence. That's where the diplomatic greeyaz is flying."

Bean wiped his eyes on his sleeves, feeling like a little kid as he did it. What a thing to be seen doing in front of his men. But that was just too bad—it would be a far worse sign of weakness to try to conceal it or pathetically ask them not to tell. He did what he did, they saw what they saw, so be it. If Sister Carlotta wasn't worth some tears from someone who owed her as much as Bean did, then what were tears for, and when should they be shed?

There was a police escort waiting for them. Suriyawong thanked their bodyguards and ordered them back to the barracks. "No need to get up till you feel like it," he said.

They saluted Suriyawong. Then they turned to Bean and saluted him. Sharply. In best military fashion. No pity. Just honor. He returned their salute the same way—no gratitude, just respect.

———

The morning in the official residence was infuriating and boring by turns. China was being intransigent. Even though most of the passengers were Thai businessmen and tourists, it was a Chinese plane over Chinese airspace, and because there were indications that it might have been a ground-to-air missile attack rather than a planted bomb, it was being kept under tight military security.

Definitely Achilles, Bean and Suriyawong agreed. But they had talked enough about Achilles that Bean agreed to let Suriyawong brief the Thai military and state department leaders who needed to have all the information that might make sense of this.

Why would India want to blow up a passenger plane flying over China? Could it really have been solely to kill a nun who was coming to visit a Greek boy in Bangkok? That was simply too far-fetched to believe. Yet, bit by bit, and with the help of the Minister of Colonization, who could take them through details about Achilles' psychopathology that hadn't even been in Locke's reporting on him, they began to understand that yes, indeed, this might well have been a kind of defiant message from Achilles to Bean, telling him that he might have gotten away this time, but Achilles could still kill whomever he wanted.

While Suriyawong was briefing them, however, Bean was taken upstairs to the private residence, where the Prime Minister's wife very kindly led him to a guest bedroom and asked him if he had a friend or family member she should send for, or if he wanted a minister or priest of some religion or other. He thanked her and said that all he really needed was some time alone.

She closed the door behind her, and Bean cried silently until he was exhausted, and then, curled up on a mat on the floor, he went to sleep.

When he awoke it was still bright daylight beyond the louvered shutters. His eyes were still sore from crying. He was still exhausted. He must have woken up because his bladder was full. And he was thirsty. That was life. Pump it in, pump it out. Sleep and wake, sleep and wake. Oh, and a little reproduction here and there. But he was too young, and Sister Carlotta had opted out of that side of life. So for them the cycle had been pretty much the same. Find some meaning in life. But what? Bean was famous. His name would live in history books forever. Probably just as part of a list in the chapter on Ender Wiggin, but that was fine, that was more than most people got. When he was dead he wouldn't care.

Carlotta wouldn't be in any history books. Not even a footnote. Well, no, that wasn't true. Achilles was going to be famous, and she was the one who found him. More than a footnote after all. Her name would be remembered, but always because it was linked with the koncho who killed her because she had seen how helpless he was and saved him from the life of the street.

Achilles killed her, but of course, he had my help.

Bean forced himself to think of something else. He could already feel that burning in his eyelids that meant tears were about to flow. That was done. He needed to keep his wits about him. Very important to keep thinking.

There was a courtesy computer in the room, with standard netlinks and some of Thailand's leading connection software. Soon Bean was signed on in one of his less-used identities. Graff would know things that the Thai government wasn't getting. So would Peter. And they would write to him.

Sure enough, there were messages from both of them encrypted on one of his dropsites. He pulled them both off.

They were the same. An email forwarded from Sister Carlotta herself.

Both of them said the same thing. The message had arrived at nine in the morning, Thailand time. They were supposed to wait twelve hours in case Sister Carlotta herself contacted them to retract the message. But when they learned with independent confirmation that there was no chance she was alive, they decided not to wait. Whatever the message was, Sister Carlotta had set it up so that if she didn't take an active step to block it, every day, it would automatically go to Graff and to Peter to send on to him.

Which meant that every day of her life, she had thought of him, had done something to keep him from seeing this, and yet had also made sure that he would see whatever it was that this message contained.

Her farewell. He didn't want to read it. He had cried himself out. There was nothing left.

And yet she wanted him to read it. And after all she had done for him, he could surely do this for her.

The file was double-encrypted. Once he had opened it with his own decoding, it remained encoded by her. He had no idea what the password would be, and therefore it had to be something that she would expect him to think of.

And because he would only be trying to find the key after she was dead, the choice was obvious. He entered the name *Poke* and the decryption proceeded at once.

It was, as he expected, a letter to him.

```
Dear    Julian,    Dear    Bean,    Dear
Friend,

Maybe Achilles killed me, maybe he
didn't. You know how I feel about
vengeance. Punishment belongs to
God, and besides, anger makes people
stupid, even people as bright as
you. Achilles must be stopped be-
cause of what he is, not because of
```

anything he did to me. My manner of death is meaningless to me. Only my manner of life mattered, and that is for my Redeemer to judge.

But you already know these things, and that is not why I wrote this letter. There is information about you that you have a right to know. It's not pleasant information, and I was going to wait to tell you until you already had some inkling. I was not about to let my death keep you in ignorance, however. That would be giving either Achilles or the random chances of life—whichever caused my sudden death—too much power over you.

You know that you were born as part of an illegal scientific experiment using embryos stolen from your parents. You have preternatural memories of your own astonishing escape from the slaughter of your siblings when the experiment was terminated. What you did at that age tells anyone who knows the story that you are extraordinarily intelligent. What you have not known, until now, is why you are so intelligent, and what it implies about your future.

The person who stole your frozen embryo was a scientist, of sorts. He was working on the genetic enhancement of human intelligence. He based his experiment on the theoretical work of a Russian scientist named Anton. Though Anton was under an order of intervention and could not tell me directly, he courageously found a way to circumvent the programming and tell me of the genetic change that was made in you. (Though Anton was under the impression that the change could only be made in an unfertilized egg, this was really only a technical problem, not a theoretical one.)

There is a double key in the human genome. One of the keys deals with human intelligence. If turned one way, it places a block on the ability of the brain to function at peak capacity. In you, Anton's key has been turned. Your brain was not frozen in its growth. It did not stop making new neurons at an early age. Your brain continues to grow and make new connections. Instead of having a limited capacity, with patterns formed during early development, your brain adds new capacities and new patterns as they are needed. You are mentally like a one-year-old, but with experience. The mental feats that infants routinely perform, which are far greater than anything that adults manage, will always remain within your reach. For your entire life, for instance, you will be able to master new languages like a native speaker. You will be able to make and maintain connections with your own memory that are unlike those of anyone else. You are, in other words, uncharted—or perhaps self-charted—territory.

But there is a price for that unfettering of your brain. You have probably already guessed it. If your brain keeps growing, what happens to your head? How does all that brain matter stay inside?

Your head continues to grow, of course. Your skull has never fully closed. I have had your skull measurements tracked, naturally. The growth is slow, and much of the growth of your brain has involved the creation of more but smaller neurons. Also, there has been some thinning of your skull, so you may or may not have noticed the growth in the circumferences of your head—but it is real.

You see, the other side of Anton's key involves human growth. If we did not stop growing, we would die very young. Yet to live long requires that we give up more and more of our intelligence, because our brains must lock down and stop growing earlier in our life cycle. Most human beings fluctuate within a fairly narrow range. You are not even on the charts.

Bean, Julian, my child, you will die very young. Your body will continue to grow, not the way puberty would do it, with one growth spurt and then an adult height. As one scientist put it, you will never reach adult height, because there is no adult height. There is only height at time of death. You will steadily grow taller and larger until your heart gives out or your spine collapses. I tell you this bluntly, because there is no way to soften this blow.

No one knows what course your growth will take. At first I took great encouragement from the fact that you seemed to be growing more slowly than originally estimated. I was told that by the age of puberty, you would have caught up with other children your age—but you did not. You remained far behind them. So I hoped that perhaps he was wrong, that you might live to age forty or fifty, or even thirty. But in the year you were with your family, and in the time we have been together, you have been measured and your growth rate is accelerating. All indications are that it will continue to accelerate. If you live to be twenty, you will have defied all rational expectations. If you die before the age of fifteen, it will be only a mild surprise. I shed tears as I write these words, because if ever there was a child who could serve humanity by having a long adult life, it is you. No, I will be honest, my tears are because I think of you as being, in so many ways, my own son, and the only thing that makes me glad about the fact that you are learning of your future through this letter is that it means I have died before you. The worst fear of every loving parent, you see, is that they will have to

bury a child. We nuns and priests
are spared that grief. Except when
we take it upon ourselves, as I so
foolishly and gladly have done with
you.

I have full documentation of all
the findings of the team that has
been studying you. They will continue to study you, if you allow
them. The netlink is at the end of
this letter. They can be trusted,
because they are decent people, and
because they also know that if the
existence of their project becomes
known, they will be in grave danger, for research into the genetic
enhancement of human intelligence
remains against the law. It is
entirely your choice whether you
cooperate. They already have valuable data. You may live your life
without reference to them, or you
may continue to provide them with
information. I am not terribly interested in the science of it. I
worked with them because I needed
to know what would happen to you.

Forgive me for keeping this information from you. I know that you
think you would have preferred to
know it all along. I can only say,

in my defense, that it is good for human beings to have a period of innocence and hope in their lives. I was afraid that if you knew this too soon, it would rob you of that hope. And yet to deprive you of this knowledge robbed you of the freedom to decide how to spend the years you have. I was going to tell you soon.

There are those who have said that because of this small genetic difference, you are not human. That because Anton's key requires two changes in the genome, not one, it could never have happened randomly, and therefore you represent a new species, created in the laboratory. But I tell you, you and Nikolai are twins, not separate species, and I, who have known you as well as any other person, have never seen anything from you but the best and purest of humanity. I know you will not accept my religious terminology, but you know what it means to me. You have a soul, my child. The Savior died for you as for every other human being ever born. Your life is of infinite worth to a loving God. And to me, my son.

```
You will find your own purpose for
the time you have left to live. Do
not be reckless with your life,
just because it will not be long.
But do not guard it overzealously,
either. Death is not a tragedy to
the one who dies. To have wasted the
life before that death, that is the
tragedy. Already you have used your
years better than most. You will
yet find many new purposes, and you
will accomplish them. And if anyone
in heaven heeds the voice of this
old nun, you will be well watched
over by angels and prayed for by
many saints.

With love, Carlotta
```

Bean erased the letter. He could pull it from his dropsite and decode it again, if he needed to refer back to it. But it was burned into his memory. And not just as text on a desk display. He had heard it in Carlotta's voice, even as his eyes moved across the words that the desk put up before him.

He turned off the desk. He walked to the window and opened it. He looked out over the garden of the official residence. In the distance he could see airplanes making their approach to the airport, as others, having just taken off, rose up into the sky. He tried to picture Sister Carlotta's soul rising up like one of those airplanes. But the picture kept changing to an Air Shanghai flight coming in to land, and Sister Carlotta walking off the plane and looking him up and down and saying, "You need to buy new pants."

He went back inside and lay down on his mat, but not to sleep. He did not close his eyes. He stared at the ceiling and thought about death and life and love and loss. And as he did, he thought he could feel his bones grow.

Part Four

DECISIONS

16

TREACHERY

To: Demosthenes%Tecumseh@freeamer
ica.org
From: Unready%cincinnatus@anon.set
Re: Air Shanghai

The pinheads running this show have
decided not to share satellite info
on Air Shanghai with anyone outside
the military, claiming that it involves vital interests of the
United States. The only other countries with satellites capable of
seeing what ours can see are China,
Japan, and Brazil, and of these
only China has a satellite in position to see it. So the Chinese
know. And when I'm done with this
letter, you'll know, and you'll
know how to use the information. I
don't like seeing big countries
beat up on little ones, except when
the big country is mine. So sue me.

The Air Shanghai flight was brought down by a ground-to-air missile, which was fired from INSIDE THAILAND. However, computer time-lapse tracking of movements in that area of Thailand show that the only serious candidate for how the ground-to-air missile got to its launch site is a utility truck whose movements originated in, get this, China.

Details: The truck (little white Vietnamese-made "Ho"-type vehicle) originated at a warehouse in Gejiu (which has already been tagged as a munitions clearinghouse) and crossed the Vietnamese border between Jinping, China, and Sinh Ho, Vietnam. It then crossed the Laotian border via the Ded Tay Chang pass. It traversed the widest part of Laos and entered Thailand near Tha Li, but at this point moved off the main roads. It passed near enough to the point from which the missile was launched for it to have been offloaded and transported manually to the site. And get this: All this movement happened MORE THAN A MONTH AGO.

I don't know about you, but to me

and everybody else here, that looks like China wants a "provocation" to go to war against Thailand. Bangkok-bound Air Shanghai jet, carrying mostly Thai passengers, is shot down, over China, by a g-to-a launched from Thailand. China can make it look as though the Thai Army was trying to create a fake provocation against them, when in fact the reverse is the case. Very complicated, but the Chinese know they can show satellite proof that the missile was launched from inside Thailand. They can also prove that it had to have radar assistance from sophisticated military tracking systems—which will imply, in the Chinese version, that the Thai military was behind it, though WE know it means the Chinese military was in control. And when the Chinese ask for independent corroboration, you can count on it: Our beloved government, since it loves business better than honor, will back up the Chinese story, never mentioning the movements of that little truck. Thus America will stay in the good graces of its trading partner. And Thailand gets chiseled.

Do your thing, Demosthenes. Get

```
this out into the public domain be-
fore our government can play toady.
Just try to find a way to do it
that doesn't point at me. This
isn't just job-losing territory. I
could go to jail.
```

When Suriyawong came to see if Bean wanted any dinner—a nine o'clock repast for the officers on duty, not an official meal with the P.M.—Bean almost followed him right down. He needed to eat, and now was as good a time as any. But he realized that he had not read any of his email after getting Sister Carlotta's last letter, so he told Suriyawong to start without him but save him a place.

He checked the dropsite that Peter had used to forward Carlotta's message, and found a more recent letter from Peter. This one included the text of a letter from one of Demosthenes' contacts inside the U.S. satellite intelligence service, and combined with Peter's own analysis of the situation, it made everything clear to Bean. He fired off a quick response, taking Peter's suspicions a step further, and then headed down to dinner.

Suriyawong and the adult officers—several of them field generals who had been summoned to Bangkok because of the crisis in the high command—were laughing. They fell silent when Bean entered the room. Ordinarily, he might have tried to put them at ease. Just because he was grieving did not change the fact that in the midst of crises, humor was needed to break the tension. But at this moment their silence was useful, and he used it.

"I just received information from one of my best sources of intelligence," Bean said. "You in this room are those who most need to hear it. But if the Prime Minister could also join us, it would save time."

One of the generals started to protest that a foreign child did not summon the Prime Minister of Thailand, but Suriyawong stood and bowed deeply to him. The man stopped talking. "Forgive me, sir," said Suriyawong, "but this foreign boy is Julian Delphiki, whose analysis of the final battle with the Formics led directly to Ender's victory."

Of course the general knew that already, but Suriyawong, by allowing him to pretend that he had not know, gave him a way to backpedal without losing face.

"I see," said the general. "Then perhaps the Prime Minister will not be offended at this summons."

Bean helped Suriyawong smooth things over as best he could. "Forgive me for having spoken with such rudeness. You were right to rebuke me. I can only hope you will excuse me for being forgetful of proper manners. The woman who raised me was on the Air Shanghai flight."

Again, the general certainly knew this; again, it allowed him to bow and murmur his commiseration. Proper respect had been shown to everyone. Now things could proceed.

The Prime Minister left his dinner with various high officials of the Chinese government, and stood against the wall, listening, as Bean relayed what he had learned from Peter about the source of the missile that brought down the jet.

"I have been in consultation off and on all day with the foreign minister of China," said the Prime Minister. "He has said nothing about the missile being launched from inside Thailand."

"When the Chinese government is ready to act on this provocation," said Bean, "they will pretend to have just discovered it."

The Prime Minister looked pained. "Could it not have been Indian operatives trying to make it seem that it was a Chinese venture?"

"It could have been anyone," said Bean. "But it was Chinese."

The prickly general spoke up. "How do you know this, if the satellite does not confirm it?"

"It would make little sense for it to be Indian," said Bean. "The only countries that could possibly detect the truck would be China and the U.S., which is well known to be in China's pocket. But China would know that they had not fired the missile, and they would know that Thailand had not fired it, so what would be the point?"

"It makes no sense for China to do it, either," said the Prime Minister.

"Sir," said Bean, "nothing makes sense in any of the things that have happened in the last few days. India has made a nonaggression pact with Pakistan and both nations have moved their troops away from their shared border. Pakistan is moving against Iran. India has invaded Burma, not because Burma is a prize, but because it stands between India and Thailand, which *is*. But India's attack makes no sense—right, Suriyawong?"

Suriyawong instantly understood that Bean was asking him to share in this, so that it would not all come from a European. "As Bean and I told the Chakri yesterday, the Indian attack on Burma is not just stupidly designed, it was *deliberately* stupidly designed. India has commanders wise enough and well-enough trained to know that sending masses of soldiers across the border, with the huge supply problem they represent, creates an easy target for our strategy of harassment. It also leaves them fully committed. And yet they have launched precisely such an attack."

"So much the better for us," said the prickly general.

"Sir," said Suriyawong, "it is important for you to understand that they have the services of Petra Arkanian, and both Bean and I know that Petra would never sign off on the strategy they're using. So that is obviously *not* their strategy."

"What does this have to do with the Air Shanghai flight?" asked the Prime Minister.

"Everything," said Bean. "And with the attempt on Suriyawong's and my life last night. The Chakri's little game was meant to provoke Thailand into an immediate entry into the war with India. And even though the ploy did not work, and the Chakri was exposed, we are still maintaining the fiction that it was an Indian provocation. Your meetings with the Chinese foreign minister are part of your effort to involve the Chinese in the war against India—no, don't tell me that you can't confirm or deny it, it's obvious that's what such meetings would have to be about. And I'll bet the Chinese are telling you that they are massing troops on the Burmese border in order to attack the Indians suddenly, when they are most exposed."

The Prime Minister, who had indeed been opening his mouth to speak, held his silence.

"Yes, of course they are telling you this. But the Indians also know that the Chinese are massing on the Burmese border, and yet they proceed with their attack on Burma, and their forces are almost fully committed, making no provision for defense against a Chinese attack from the north. Why? Are we going to pretend that the Indians are *that* stupid?"

It was Suriyawong who answered as it dawned on him. "The Indians also have a nonaggression pact with China. They think the Chinese troops are massing at the border in order to attack *us*. They and the Indians have divided up southeast Asia."

"So this missile that the Chinese launched from Thailand to shoot down their own airliner over their own territory," said the Prime Minister, "that will be their excuse to break off negotiations and attack us by surprise?"

"No one is surprised by Chinese treachery," said one of the generals.

"But that's not the whole picture," said Bean. "Because we have not yet accounted for Achilles."

"He's in India," said Suriyawong. "He planned the attempt to kill us last night."

"And we know he planned that attempt," said Bean, "because I was there. He wanted you dead as a provocation, but he gave approval for it to happen last night because we would both be killed in the same explosion. And we know that he is behind the downing of the Air Shanghai jet, because even though the missile was in place for a month, ready to be fired, this was not yet the right moment to create the provocation. The Chinese foreign minister is still in Bangkok. Thailand has not yet had several days to commit its troops to battle, depleting our supplies and sending most of our forces on missions far to the northwest. Chinese troops have not yet fully deployed to the north of us. That missile should not have been fired for several days, at least. But it was fired this morning because Achilles knew Sister Carlotta was on that airplane, and he could not pass up the opportunity to kill her."

"But you said the missile was a Chinese operation," said the Prime Minister. "Achilles is in India."

"Achilles is in India, but is Achilles working for India?"

"Are you saying he's working for China?" asked the Prime Minister.

"Achilles is working for Achilles," said Suriyawong. "But yes, now the picture is clear."

"Not to me," said the prickly general.

Suriyawong eagerly explained. "Achilles has been setting India up from the beginning. While Achilles was still in Russia, he doubtless used the Russian intelligence service to make contacts inside China. He promised he could hand them all of south and southeast Asia in a single blow. Then he goes to India and sets up a war in which India's army is fully committed in Burma. Until now, China has never been able to move against India, because the Indian Army was concentrated in the west and northwest, so that as Chinese troops came over the passes of the Himalayas, they were easily fought off by Indian troops. Now, though, the entire Indian Army is exposed, far from the heartland of India. If the Chinese can achieve a surprise attack and destroy that army, India will be defenseless. They will have no choice but to surrender. We're just a sideshow to them. They will attack us in order to lull the Indians into complacency."

"So they don't intend to invade Thailand?" asked the Prime Minister.

"Of course they do," said Bean. "They intend to rule from the Indus to the Mekong. But the Indian army is the main objective. Once that is destroyed, there is nothing in their way."

"And all this," said the prickly general, "we deduce from the fact that a certain Catholic nun was on the airplane?"

"We deduce this," said Bean, "from the fact that Achilles is controlling events in China, Thailand, and India. Achilles knew Sister Carlotta was on that plane because the Chakri intercepted my message to the Prime Minister. Achilles is running this show. He's betraying everybody to everybody else. And in the end, he stands at the top of a new empire that contains more than half the population of the world. China,

India, Burma, Thailand, Vietnam. Everyone will have to accommodate this new superpower."

"But Achilles does not run China," said the Prime Minister. "As far as we know, he has never been *in* China."

"The Chinese no doubt think they're using him," said Bean. "But I know Achilles, and my guess is that within a year, the Chinese leaders will find themselves either dead or taking their orders from him."

"Perhaps," said the Prime Minister, "I should go warn the Chinese foreign minister of the great danger he is in."

The prickly general stood up. "This is what comes of allowing children to play at world affairs. They think that real life is like a computer game, a few mouse clicks and nations rise and fall."

"This is precisely how nations rise and fall," said Bean. "France in 1940. Napoleon remaking the map of Europe in the early 1800s, creating kingdoms so his brothers would have someplace to rule. The victors in World War I, cutting up kingdoms and drawing insane lines on the map that would lead to war again and again. The Japanese conquest of most of the western Pacific in December of 1941. The collapse of the Soviet Empire in 1989. Events can be sudden indeed."

"But those were great forces at work," said the general.

"Napoleon's whims were not a great force. Nor was Alexander, toppling empires wherever he went. There was nothing inevitable about Greeks reaching the Indus."

"I don't need history lessons from you."

Bean was about to retort that yes, apparently he did—but Suriyawong shook his head. Bean got the message.

Suriyawong was right. The Prime Minister was not convinced, and the only generals who were speaking up were the ones who were downright hostile to Bean's and

Suriyawong's ideas. If Bean continued to push, he would merely find himself marginalized in the coming war. And he needed to be in the thick of things, if he was to be able to use the strike force he had so laboriously created.

"Sir," said Bean to the general, "I did not mean to teach you anything. You have nothing to learn from me. I have merely offered you the information I received, and the conclusions I drew from it. If these conclusions are incorrect, I apologize for wasting your time. And if we proceed with the war against India, I ask only for the chance to serve Thailand honorably, in order to repay your kindness to me."

Before the general could say anything—and it was plain he was going to make a haughty reply—the Prime Minister intervened. "Thank you for giving us your best—Thailand survives in this difficult place because our people and our friends offer everything they have in the service of our small but beautiful land. Of course we will want to use you in the coming war. I believe you have a small strike force of highly trained and versatile Thai soldiers. I will see to it that your force is assigned to a commander who will find good use for that force, and for you."

It was a deft announcement to the generals at that table that Bean and Suriyawong were under his protection. Any general who attempted to quash their participation would simply find that they were assigned to another command. Bean could not have hoped for more.

"And now," said the Prime Minister, "while I am happy to have spent this quarter hour in your company, gentlemen, I have the foreign minister of China no doubt wondering why I am so rude as to stay away for all this time."

The Prime Minister bowed and left.

At once the prickly general and the others who were most skeptical returned to the joking conversation that Bean's arrival had interrupted, as if nothing had happened.

But General Phet Noi, who was field commander of all Thai forces in the Malay Peninsula, beckoned to Suriyawong and Bean. Suriyawong picked up his plate and moved to a place beside Phet Noi, while Bean paused only to fill his own plate from the pots on serving table before joining them.

"So you have a strike force," said Phet Noi.

"Air, sea, and land," said Bean.

"The main Indian offensive," said Phet Noi, "is in the north. My army will be watching for Indian landings on the coast, but our role will be vigilance, not combat. Still, I think that if your strike force launched its missions from the south, you would be less likely to become tangled up in raids originating in the much more important northern commands."

Phet Noi obviously knew that his own command was the one least important to the conduct of the war—but he was as determined to get involved as Bean and Suriyawong were. They could help each other. For the rest of the meal, Bean and Suriyawong conversed earnestly with Phet Noi, discussing where in the Malay panhandle of Thailand the strike force might best be stationed. Finally, they were the last three at table.

"Sir," said Bean, "now that we're alone, the three of us, there is something I must tell you."

"Yes?"

"I will serve you loyally, and I will obey your orders. But if the opportunity comes, I will use my strike force to accomplish an objective that is not, strictly speaking, important to Thailand."

"And that is?"

"My friend Petra Arkanian is the hostage—no, I believe she is the virtual slave—of Achilles. Every day she lives in constant danger. When I have the information necessary to make success likely, I will use my strike force to bring her out of Hyderabad."

Phet Noi thought about this, his face showing nothing. "You know that Achilles may be holding on to her precisely because she is the bait that will lure you into a trap."

"That is possible," said Bean, "but I don't believe that it's what Achilles is doing. He believes he is able to kill anyone, anywhere. He doesn't need to set traps for me. To lie in wait is a sign of weakness. I believe he's holding on to Petra for his own reasons."

"You know him," said Phet Noi, "and I do not." He reflected for a moment. "As I listened to what you said about Achilles and his plans and treacheries, I believed that events might unfold exactly as you said. What I could not see was how Thailand could possibly turn this into victory. Even with advance warning, we can't prevail against China in the field of battle. China's supply lines into Thailand would be short. Almost a quarter of the population of Thailand is Chinese in origin, and while most of them are loyal Thai citizens, a large fraction of them still regard China as their homeland. China would not lack for saboteurs and collaborators within our country, while India has no such connection. How can we prevail?"

"There is only one way," said Bean. "Surrender at once."

"What?" said Suriyawong.

"Prime Minister Paribatra should go to the Chinese foreign minister, declare that Thailand wishes to be an ally of China. We will put most of our military temporarily under Chinese command to be used against the Indian aggressors as needed, and will supply not only our own armies, but the Chinese armies as well, to the limit of our abilities. Chinese merchants will have unrestricted access to Thai markets and manufacturing."

"But that would be shameful," said Suriyawong.

"It was shameful," said Bean, "when Thailand allied itself with Japan during World War II, but Thailand survived and Japanese troops did not occupy Thailand. It was shameful when Thailand bowed to the Europeans and surrendered Laos and Cambodia to France, but the heart of Thailand remained free. If Thailand doesn't preemptively ally itself to China and give China a free hand, then China will rule here anyway, but Thailand itself will utterly lose its freedom and its national existence, for many years at least, and perhaps forever."

"Am I listening to an oracle?" asked Phet Noi.

"You are listening to the fears of your own heart," said Bean. "Sometimes you have to feed the tiger so it won't devour you."

"Thailand will never do this," said Phet Noi.

"Then I suggest you make arrangements for your escape and life in exile," said Bean, "because when the Chinese take over, the ruling class is destroyed."

They all knew Bean was talking about the conquest of Taiwan. All government officials and their families, all professors, all journalists, all writers, all politicians and their families were taken from Taiwan to reeducation camps in the western desert, where they were set to work performing manual labor, they and their children, for the rest of their lives. None of them ever returned to Taiwan. None of their children ever received approval for education beyond the age of fourteen. The method had been so effective in pacifying Taiwan that there was no chance they would not use the same method in their conquests now.

"Would I be a traitor, to plan for defeat by creating my own escape route?" Phet Noi wondered aloud.

"Or would you be a patriot, keeping at least one Thai

general and his family out of the hands of the conquering enemy?" asked Bean.

"Is our defeat certain, then?" asked Suriyawong.

"You can read a map," said Bean. "But miracles happen."

Bean left them to their silent thoughts and returned to his room, to report to Peter on the likely Thai response.

17

ON A BRIDGE

To:Chamrajnagar%sacredriver@ifcom.
gov
From: Wiggin%resistance@haiti.gov
Re: For the sake of India, please
do not set foot on Earth

Esteemed Polemarch Chamrajnagar,

For reasons that will be made clear
by the attached essay, which I will
soon publish, I fully expect that
you will return to Earth just in
time to be caught up in India's
complete subjugation by China.

If your return to India had any
chance of preserving her independence, you would bear any risk and
return, regardless of any advice.
And if your establishing a government in exile could accomplish anything for your native land, who

would try to persuade you to do
otherwise?

But India's strategic position is
so exposed, and China's relentless-
ness in conquest is so well known,
that you must know both courses of
action are futile.

Your resignation as Polemarch does
not take effect until you reach
Earth. If you do not board the
shuttle, but instead return to
IFCom, you remain Polemarch. You
are the only possible Polemarch who
could secure the International
Fleet. A new commander could not
distinguish between Chinese who are
loyal to the Fleet and those whose
first allegiance is to their now-
dominant homeland. The I.F. must
not fall under the sway of
Achilles. You, as Polemarch, could
reassign suspect Chinese to innocu-
ous postings, preventing any Chinese grab for control. If you return
to Earth, and Achilles has influence
over your successor as Polemarch,
the I.F. will become a tool of conquest.

If you remain as Polemarch, you
will be accused, as an Indian, of

planning to pursue vengeance
against China. Therefore, to prove
your impartiality and avoid suspi-
cion, you will have to remain
utterly aloof from all Earthside
wars and struggles. You can trust
me and my allies to maintain the resistance to Achilles regardless of
the apparent odds, if for no other
reason than this: His ultimate triumph means our immediate death.

Stay in space and, by doing so,
allow the possibility of humanity
escaping the domination of a mad-
man. In return, I vow to do all in
my power to free India from Chinese
rule and return it to self-rule.

Sincerely, Peter Wiggin

The soldiers around her knew perfectly well who Virlomi was. They also knew the reward that had been offered for her capture—or her dead body. The charge was treason and espionage. But from the start, as she passed through the checkpoint at the entrance of the base at Hyderabad, the common soldiers had believed in her and befriended her.

"You will hear me accused of spying or worse," she said, "but it isn't true. A treacherous foreign monster rules in Hyderabad, and he wants me dead for personal reasons. Help me."

Without a word, the soldiers walked her away from where

the cameras might spot her, and waited. When an empty supply truck came up, they stopped it and while some of them talked to the driver, the others helped her get in. The truck drove through, and she was out.

Ever since, she had turned to the footsoldiers for help. Officers might or might not let compassion or righteousness interfere with obedience or ambition—the common soldiers had no such qualms. She was transported in the midst of a crush of soldiers on a crowded train, offered so much food smuggled out of mess halls that she could not eat it all, and given bunk space while weary men slept on the floor. No one laid a hand on her except to help her, and none betrayed her.

She moved across India to the east, toward the war zone, for she knew that her only hope, and the only hope for Petra Arkanian, was for her to find, or be found by, Bean.

Virlomi knew where Bean would be: making trouble for Achilles wherever and however he could. Since the Indian Army had chosen the dangerous and foolish strategy of committing all its manpower to battle, she knew that the effective counterstrategy would be harassment and disruption of supply lines. And Bean would come to whatever point on the supply line was most crucial and yet most difficult to disrupt.

So, as she neared the front, Virlomi went over in her mind the map she had memorized. To move large amounts of supplies and munitions quickly from India to the troops sweeping through the great plain where the Irrawaddy flowed, there were two general routes. The northern route was easier, but far more exposed to raids. The southern route was harder, but more protected. Bean would be working on disrupting the southern route.

Where? There were two roads over the mountains from Imphal in India to Kalemyo in Burma. They both passed through narrow canyons and crossed deep gorges. Where would it be hardest to rebuild a blown bridge or a collapsed highway? On both routes, there were candidate locations. But the hardest to rebuild was on the western route, a long stretch of road carved out of rock along the edge of a steep defile, leading to a bridge over a deep gorge. Bean would not just blow up this bridge, Virlomi thought, because it would not be that hard to span. He would also collapse the road in several places, so the engineers wouldn't be able to get to the place where the bridge must be anchored without first blasting and shaping a new road.

So that is where Virlomi went, and waited.

Water she found flowing cleanly through the side ravines. She was given food by passing soldiers, and soon learned that they were looking for her. Word had spread that the Woman-in-hiding needed food. And still no officer knew to look for her, and still no assassin from Achilles came to kill her. Poor as the soldiers were, apparently the reward did not tempt them. She was proud of her people even as she mourned for them, to have such a man as Achilles rule over them.

She heard of daring raids at easier spots on the eastern road, and traffic on the western road grew heavier, the roads trembling day and night as India burned up her fuel reserves supplying an army far larger than the war required. She asked the soldiers if they had heard of Thai raiders led by a child, and they laughed bitterly. "Two children," they said. "One white, one brown. They come in their helicopters, they destroy, they leave. Whomever they touch, they kill. Whatever they see, they destroy."

Now she began to worry. What if the one that came to take this bridge was not Bean, but the other one? No doubt another Battle School grad—Suriyawong came to mind— but would Bean have told him about her letter? Would he have any idea that she held within her head the plan of the base at Hyderabad? That she knew where Petra was?

Yet she had no choice. She would have to show herself, and hope.

So the days passed, waiting for the sound of the helicopters coming, bringing the strike force that would destroy this road.

———

Suriyawong had never been a commander in Battle School. They closed down the program before he rose to that position. But he had dreamed of command, studied it, planned it, and now, working with Bean in command of this or that configuration of their strike force, he finally understood the terror and exhilaration of having men listen to you, obey you, throw themselves into action and risk death because they trust you. Each time, because these men were so well-trained and resourceful and their tactics so effective, he brought back his whole complement. Injuries, but no deaths. Aborted missions, sometimes—but no deaths.

"It's the aborted missions," said Bean, "that earn you their trust. When you see that it's more dangerous than we anticipated, that it requires attrition to get the objective, then show the men you value their lives more than the objective of the moment. Later, when you have no choice but to commit them to grave risk, they'll know it's because this time it's worth dying. They know you won't spend them like a child, on candy and trash."

Bean was right, which hardly surprised Suriyawong. Bean was not just the smartest, he had also watched Ender close at hand, had been Ender's secret weapon in Dragon Army, had been his backup commander on Eros. Of course he knew what leadership was.

What surprised Suriyawong was Bean's generosity. Bean

had created this strike force, and trained these men, had earned their trust. Throughout that time, Suriyawong had been of little help, and had shown outright hostility at times. Yet Bean included Suriyawong, entrusted him with command, encouraged the men to help Suriyawong learn what they could do. Through it all, Bean had never treated Suriyawong as a subordinate or inferior, but rather had deferred to him as his superior officer.

In return, Suriyawong never commanded Bean to do anything. Rather they reached a consensus on most things, and when they could not agree, Suriyawong deferred to Bean's decision and supported him in it.

Bean has no ambition, Suriyawong realized. He has no wish to be better than anyone else, or to rule over anyone, or to have more honor.

Then, on the missions where they worked together, Suriyawong saw something else: Bean had no fear of death.

Bullets could be flying, explosives could be near detonation, and Bean would move without fear and with only token concealment. It was as if he dared the enemy to shoot him, dared their own explosives to defy him and go off before he was ready.

Was this courage? Or did he wish for death? Had Sister Carlotta's death taken away some of his will to live? To hear him talk, Suriyawong would not have supposed it. Bean was too grimly determined to rescue Petra for Suriyawong to believe that he wanted to die. He had something urgent to live for. And yet he showed no fear of battle.

It was as if he knew the day that he would die, and this was not that day.

He certainly hadn't stopped caring about anything. Indeed, the quiet, icy, controlled, arrogant Bean that Suriyawong had known before had become, since the day

Carlotta died, impatient and agitated. The calm he showed in battle, in front of the men, was certainly not there when he was alone with Suriyawong and Phet Noi. And the favorite object of his curses was not Achilles—he almost never spoke of Achilles—but Peter Wiggin.

"He's had everything for a month! And he does these little things—persuading Chamrajnagar not to return to Earth yet, persuading Ghaffar Wahabi not to invade Iran—and he tells me about them, but the big thing, publishing Achilles' whole treacherous strategy, he won't do that—and he tells *me* not to do it myself! Why not? If the Indian government could be forced to see how Achilles plans to betray them, they might be able to pull enough of their army out of Burma to make a stand against the Chinese. Russia might be able to intervene. The Japanese fleet might threaten Chinese trade. At the very least, the Chinese themselves might see Achilles for what he is, and jettison him even as they follow his plan! And all he says is, It's not the right moment, it's too soon, not yet, you have to trust me, I'm with you on this, right to the end."

He was scarcely kinder in his execrations of the Thai generals running the war—or ruining it, as he said. Suriyawong had to agree with him—the whole plan depended on keeping Thai forces dispersed, but now that the Thai Air Force had control of the air over Burma, they had concentrated their armies and airbases in forward positions. "I told them what the danger was," said Bean, "and they still gather their forces into one convenient place."

Phet Noi listened patiently; Suriyawong, too, gave up trying to argue with him. Bean was right. People were behaving foolishly, and not out of ignorance. Though of course they would say, later, "But we didn't *know* Bean was right."

To which Bean already had his answer: "You didn't know I was wrong! So you should have been prudent!"

The only thing different in Bean's diatribes was that he went hoarse for a week, and when his voice came back, it was lower. For a kid who had always been so tiny, even for his age, puberty—if that's what this was—certainly had struck him young. Or maybe he had just stretched out his vocal cords with all his ranting.

But now, on a mission, Bean was silent, the calm of battle already on him. Suriyawong and Bean boarded their choppers last, making sure all their men were aboard; one last salute to each other, and then they ducked inside and the door closed and the choppers rose into the air. They jetted along near the surface of the Indian Ocean, the chopper blades folded and enclosed until they got near Cheduba Island, today's staging area. Then the choppers dispersed, rose into the air, cut the jets, and opened their blades for vertical landing.

Now they would leave behind their reserves—the men and choppers that could bring out anyone stranded by a mechanical problem or unforeseen complication. Bean and Suriyawong never rode together—one chopper failure should not behead the mission. And each of them had redundant equipment, so that either could complete the whole mission. More than once, the redundancy had saved lives and missions—Phet Noi made sure they were always equipped because, as he said, "You give the matériel to the commanders who know how to use it."

Bean and Suriyawong were too busy to chat in the staging area, but they did come together for a few moments, as they watched the reserve team camouflage their choppers and scrim their solar collectors. "You know what I wish?" said Bean.

"You mean besides wanting to be an astronaut when you grow up?" said Suriyawong.

"That we could scrub this mission and take off for Hyderabad."

"And get ourselves killed without ever seeing a sign of Petra, who has probably already been moved to someplace in the Himalayas."

"That's the genius of my plan," said Bean. "I take a herd of cattle hostage and threaten to shoot a cow a day till they bring her back."

"Too risky. The cows always make a break for it." But Suriyawong knew that to Bean, the inability to do anything for Petra was a constant ache. "We'll do it. Peter's looking for someone who'll give him current information about Hyderabad."

"Like he's working on publishing Achilles' plans." The favorite diatribe. Only because they were on mission, Bean remained calm, ironic rather than furious.

"All done," said Suriyawong.

"See you in the mountains."

It was a dangerous mission. The enemy couldn't watch every kilometer of highway, but they had learned to converge quickly when the Thai choppers were spotted, and their strike force was having to finish their missions with less and less time to spare. And this spot was likely to be defended. That was why Bean's contingent—four of the five companies—would be deployed to clear away any defenders and protect Suriyawong's group while they laid the charges and blew up the road and the bridge.

All was going according to plan—indeed, better than expected, because the enemy seemed not to know they were there—when one of the men pointed out, "There's a woman on the bridge."

"A civilian?"

"You need to see," said the soldier.

Suriyawong left the spot where the explosives were being placed and climbed back up to the bridge. Sure enough, a young Indian woman was standing there, her arms stretched out toward either side of the ravine.

"Has anyone mentioned to her that the bridge is going to explode, and we don't actually care if anyone's on it?"

"Sir," said the soldier, "she's asking for Bean."

"By name?"

He nodded.

Suriyawong looked at the woman again. A very young woman. Her clothing was filthy, tattered. Had it once been a military uniform? It certainly wasn't the way local women dressed.

She looked at him. "Suriyawong," she called.

Behind him, he could hear several soldiers exhale or gasp in surprise or wonder. How did this Indian woman know? It worried Suriyawong a little. The soldiers were reliable in almost everything, but if they once got godstuff into their heads, it could complicate everything.

"I'm Suriyawong," he said.

"You were in Dragon Army," she said. "And you work with Bean."

"What do you want?" he demanded.

"I want to talk with you privately, here on the bridge."

"Sir, don't go," said the soldier. "Nobody's shooting, but we've spotted a half-dozen Indian soldiers. You're dead if you go out there."

What would Bean do?

Suriyawong stepped out onto the bridge, boldly but not in any hurry. He waited for the gunshot, wondering if he would feel the pain of impact before he heard the sound. Would the nerves of his ears report to his brain faster than the nerves of whatever body part the bullet tore into? Or would the sniper hit him in the head, mooting the point?

No bullet. He came near her, and stopped when she said, "This is as close as you should come, or they'll worry and shoot you."

"You control those soldiers?" asked Suriyawong.

"Don't you know me yet?" she said. "I'm Virlomi. I was ahead of you in Battle School."

He knew the name. He would never have recognized her face. "You left before I got there."

"Not many girls in Battle School. I thought the legend would live on."

"I heard of you."

"I'm a legend here, too. My people aren't firing because they think I know what I'm doing out here. And I thought you recognized me, because your soldiers on both sides of this ravine have refrained from shooting any of the Indian soldiers, even though I know they've spotted them."

"Maybe Bean recognized you," said Sirayawong. "In fact, I've heard your name more recently. You're the one who wrote back to him, aren't you? You were in Hyderabad."

"I know where Petra is."

"Unless they've moved her."

"Do you have any better sources? I tried to think of any way I could to get a message to Bean without getting caught. Finally I realized there was no computer solution. I had to bring the message in my head."

"So come with us."

"Not that simple," she said. "If they think I'm a captive, you'll never get out of here. Handheld g-to-a."

"Ouch," said Suriyawong. "Ambush. They knew we were coming?"

"No," said Virlomi. "They knew I was here. I didn't say anything, but they all knew that the Woman-in-hiding was at this bridge, so they figured that the gods were protecting this place."

"And the gods needed g-to-a missiles?"

"No, *I'm* the one they're protecting. The gods have the bridge, the men have me. So here's the deal. You pull your explosives off the bridge. Abort the mission. They see that I have the power to make the enemy go away without harming anything. And then they watch me call one of your departing choppers down to me, and I get on of my own free will. That's the only way you're getting out of here. Not really anything I designed, but I don't see any other way out."

"I always hate aborting missions," said Suriyawong. But before she could argue, he laughed and said, "No, don't worry, it's fine. It's a good plan. If Bean were down here on this bridge, he'd agree in a heartbeat."

Suriyawong walked back to his men. "No, it's not a god or a holy woman. She's Virlomi, a Battle School grad, and she has intelligence that's more valuable than this bridge. We're aborting the mission."

The soldier took this in, and Suriyawong could see him trying to factor the magical element in with the orders.

"Soldier," said Suriyawong, "I have not been bewitched. This woman knows the groundplan of the Indian Army high command base in Hyderabad."

"Why would an Indian give that to us?" the soldier asked.

"Because the bunduck who's running the Indian side of the war has a prisoner there who's vital to the war."

Now it was making sense to the soldier. The magic element receded. He pulled his satrad off his belt and punched in the abort code. All the other satrads immediately vibrated in the preset pattern.

At once the explosives teams began dismantling. If they were to evacuate without dismantling, a second code, for urgency, would be sent. Suriyawong did not want any part of their matériel to fall into Indian hands. And he thought a more leisurely pace might be better.

"Soldier, I need to *seem* to be hypnotized by this woman," he said. "I am *not* hypnotized, but I'm faking it so the Indian soldiers all around us will think she's controlling me. Got that?"

"Yes sir."

"So while I walk back toward her, you call Bean and tell him that I need all the choppers but mine to evacuate, so the Indians can see they're gone. Then say 'Petra.' Got that? Tell him *nothing* else, no matter what he asks. We may be monitored, if not here, then in Hyderabad." Or Beijing, but he didn't want to complicate things by saying that.

"Yes sir."

Suriyawong turned his back on the soldier, walked three paces closer to Virlomi, and then prostrated himself before her.

Behind him, he could hear the soldier saying exactly what he had been told to say.

And after a very little while, choppers began to rise into the air from both sides of the ravine. Bean's troops were on the way out.

Suriyawong got up and returned to his men. His company had come in two choppers. "All of you get in the chopper with the explosives," he said. "Only the pilot and co-pilot stay in the other chopper."

The men obeyed immediately, and within three minutes Suriyawong was alone at his end of the bridge. He turned and bowed once again to Virlomi, then walked calmly to his chopper and climbed aboard.

"Rise slowly," he told the pilot, "and then pass slowly near the woman in the middle of the bridge, doorside toward her. At no point is any weapon to be trained on her. Nothing remotely threatening."

Suriyawong watched through the window. Virlomi was not signaling.

"Rise higher, as if we were leaving," said Suriyawong.

The pilot obeyed.

Finally, Virlomi began waving her arms, beckoning with both of them, slowly, as if she were reeling them back in with each movement of her arms.

"Slow down and then begin to descend toward her. I want no chance of error. The last thing we need is some downdraft to get her caught in the blades."

The pilot laughed grimly and brought the chopper like a dancer down onto the bridge, far enough away that Virlomi wasn't actually under the blades, but close enough that it would be only a few steps for her to come aboard.

Suriyawong ran to the door and opened it.

Virlomi did not just walk to the chopper. She danced to it, making ritual-like circling movements with each step.

On impulse, he got out of the chopper and prostrated himself again. When she got near enough, he said—loud enough to be heard over the chopper blades—"Walk on me!"

She did, planting her bare feet on his shoulders and walking down his back. Suriyawong didn't know how they could have communicated more clearly to the Indian soldiers that not only had Virlomi saved their bridge, she had also taken control of this chopper.

She was inside.

He got up, turned slowly, and sauntered onto the chopper.

The sauntering ended the moment he was inside. He rammed the door lever up into place and shouted, "I want jets as fast as you can!"

The chopper rose dizzily. "Strap down," Suriyawong

ordered Virlomi. Then, seeing she wasn't familiar with the inside of this craft, he pushed her into place and put the ends of her harness into her hands. She got it at once and finished the job while he hurled himself into his place and got his straps in place just as the chopper cut the blades and plummeted for a moment before the jets kicked in. Then they rocketed down the ravine and out of range of the handheld g-to-a missiles.

"You just made my day," said Suriyawong.

"Took you long enough," said Virlomi. "I thought this bridge was one of the first places you'd hit."

"We figured that's what people would think, so we kept not coming here."

"Greeyaz," she said. "I should have remembered to think completely ass-backward in order to predict what Battle School brats would do."

———

Bean had known the moment he saw her on the bridge that she had to be Virlomi, the Indian Battle Schooler who had answered his Briseis posting. He could only trust that Suriyawong would realize what was happening before he found the need to shoot somebody. And Surly had not let him down.

When they got back to the staging area, Bean barely greeted Virlomi before he started giving orders. "I want the whole staging area dismantled. Everybody's coming with us." While the company commanders saw to that, Bean ordered one of the chopper communications team to set up a net connection for him.

"That's satellite," the soldier said. "We'll be located right away."

"We'll be gone before anyone can react," said Bean.

Only then did he start explaining to Suriyawong and Virlomi. "We're fully equipped, right?"

"But not fully fueled."

"I'll take care of that," he said. "We're going to Hyderabad right now."

"But I haven't even drawn up the plans."

"Time for that in the air," he said. "This time we ride together, Suriyawong. Can't be helped—we both have to know the whole plan."

"We've waited this long," said Suriyawong. "What's the hurry now?"

"Two things," said Bean. "How long do you think it'll be before word reaches Achilles that our strike force picked up an Indian woman who was waiting for us on a bridge? Second thing—I'm going to force Peter Wiggin's hand. All hell is going to break loose, and we're riding the wave."

"What's the objective?" asked Virlomi. "To save Petra? To kill Achilles?"

"To bring out every Battle School kid who'll come with us."

"They'll never leave India," she said. "I may decide to stay myself."

"Wrong on both counts," said Bean. "I give India less than a week before Chinese troops have control of New Delhi and Hyderabad and any other city they want."

"Chinese?" asked Virlomi. "But there's some kind of—"

"Nonaggression pact?" said Bean. "Arranged by Achilles?"

"He's been working for China all along," said Suriyawong. "The Indian Army is exposed, undersupplied, exhausted, demoralized."

"But . . . if China comes in on the side of the Thai, isn't that what you want?"

Suriyawong gave a sharp, bitter laugh. "China comes in on the side of China. We tried to warn our own people, but they're sure *they* have a deal with Beijing."

Virlomi understood at once. Battle School–trained, she knew how to think the way Bean and Suriyawong did. "So that's why Achilles didn't use Petra's plan."

Bean and Suriyawong laughed and gave short little bows to each other.

"You knew about Petra's plan?"

"We assumed there'd be a better plan than the one India's using."

"So you have a plan to stop China?" said Virlomi.

"Not a chance," said Bean. "China might have been stopped a month ago, but nobody listened." He thought of Peter and barely stanched the fury. "Achilles himself may still be stopped, or at least weakened. But our goal is to keep the Indian Battle School team from falling into Chinese hands. Our Thai friends already have escape routes planned. So when we get to Hyderabad, we not only need to find Petra, we need to offer escape to anyone who'll come. Will they listen to you?"

"We'll see, won't we?" said Virlomi.

"The connection's ready," said a soldier. "I didn't actually link yet, because that's when the clock starts ticking."

"Do it," said Bean. "I've got some things to say to Peter Wiggin."

I'm coming, Petra. I'm getting you out.

As for Achilles, if he happens to come within my reach, there'll be no mercy this time, no relying on someone else to keep him out of circulation. I'll kill him without discussion. And my men will have orders to do the same.

18

SATYAGRAHA

```
encrypt key ********
decrypt key *****
To: Locke%erasmus@polnet.gov
From:Borommakot@chakri.thai.gov/
scom
Re: Now, or I will
```

I'm in a battlefield situation and
I need two things from you, now.

First, I need permission from the
Sri Lankan government to land at
the base at Kilinochchi to refuel,
ETA less than an hour. This is a
nonmilitary rescue mission to re-
trieve Battle School graduates in
imminent danger of capture, torture, enslavement, or at the very
least imprisonment.

Second, to justify this and all
other actions I'm about to take; to

persuade those Battle Schoolers to come with me; and to create confusion in Hyderabad, I need you to publish now. Repeat, NOW. Or I will publish my own article, here attached, which specifically names you as a co-conspirator with the Chinese, as proven by your failure to publish what you know in a timely manner. Even though I don't have Locke's worldwide reach, I have a nice little email list of my own, and my article will get attention. Yours, however, would have far faster results, and I would prefer it to come from you.

Pardon my threat. I can't afford to play any more of your "wait for the right time" games. I'm getting Petra out.

encrypt key *****
decrypt key ********
To: Borommakot@chakri.thai.gov/scom
From: Locke%erasmus@polnet.gov
Re: Done

Confirmed: Sri Lanka grants landing permission/refueling privileges at Kilinochchi for aircraft on humanitarian mission. Thai markings?

Confirmed: my essay released as of now, worldwide push distribution. This includes urgent fyi push into the systems at Hyderabad and Bangkok.

Your threat was sweetly loyal to your friend, but not necessary. This was the time I was waiting for. Apparently you didn't realize that the moment I published, Achilles would have to move his operations, and would probably take Petra with him. How would you have found her, if I had published a month ago?

encrypt key ********
decrypt key *****
To: Locke%erasmus@polnet.gov
From: Borommakot@chakri.thai.gov/scom
Re: Done

Confirm: Thai markings

As to your excuse: Kuso. If that had been your reason for delay, you

would have told me a month ago. I
know the real reason, even if you
don't, and it makes me sick.

For two weeks after Virlomi disappeared, Achilles had not
once come into the planning room—which no one minded,
especially after the reward was issued for Virlomi's return.
No one dared speak of it openly, but all were glad she had
escaped Achilles' vengeance. They were all aware, of
course, of the heightened security around them—for their
"protection." But it didn't change their lives much. It wasn't
as if any of them had ever had time to go frolicking in down-
town Hyderabad, or fraternizing with officers twice or three
times their age on the base.

Petra was skeptical of the reward offer, though. She knew
Achilles well enough to know that he was perfectly capable
of offering a reward for the capture of someone he had
already killed. What safer cover could he have? Still, if that
were the case it would imply that he did not have carte
blanche from Tikal Chapekar—if he had to hide things from
the Indian government, it meant Achilles was not yet running
everything.

When he did return, there was no sign of a bruise on his
face. Either Petra's kick had not left a mark, or it took two
weeks for it to heal completely. Her own bruises were not yet
gone, but no one could see them, since they were under her
shirt. She wondered if he had any testicular pain. She wondered if he had had to see a urologist. She did not allow any
trace of her gloating to appear on her face.

Achilles was full of talk about how well the war was
going and what a good job they were doing in Planning. The
army was well supplied and despite the harassment of the

cowardly Thai military, the campaign was moving forward on schedule. The revised schedule, of course.

Which was such greeyaz. He was talking to the *planners*. They knew perfectly well that the army was bogged down, that they were still fighting the Burmese in the Irrawaddy plain because the Thai Army's harassment tactics made it impossible to mount the crushing offensive that would have driven the Burmese into the mountains and allowed the Indian Army to proceed into Thailand. Schedule? There was no schedule now.

What Achilles was telling them was: This is the party line. Make sure no memo or email from this room gives anyone even the slightest hint that events are not going according to plan.

It did not change the fact that everyone in Planning could smell defeat. Supplying a huge army on the move was taxing enough to India's limited resources. Supplying it when half the supplies were likely to disappear due to enemy action was chewing through India's resources faster than they could hope to replenish them.

At current rates of manufacture and consumption, the army would run out of munitions in seven weeks. But that would hardly matter—unless some miracle happened, they would run out of nonrenewable fuel in four.

Everyone knew that if Petra's plan had been followed, India would have been able to continue such an offensive indefinitely, and attrition would already have destroyed Burmese resistance. The war would already be on Thai soil, and the Indian Army would not be limping along with a relentless deadline looming up behind them.

They did not talk in the planning room, but at meals they carefully, obliquely, discussed things. Was it too late to revert to the other strategy? Not really—but it would require a strategic withdrawal of the bulk of India's army, which would be impossible to conceal from the people and the media. Politically, it would be a disaster. But then, running out of bullets or fuel would be even more disastrous.

"We have to draw up plans for withdrawal anyway," said Sayagi. "Unless some miracle happens in the field—some brilliance in a field commander that has hitherto been invisible, some political collapse in Burma or Thailand—we're going to need a plan to extricate our people."

"I don't think we'll get permission to spend time on that," someone answered.

Petra rarely said anything at meals, despite her new custom of sitting at table with one or another group from Planning. This time, though, she spoke up. "Do it in your heads," she said.

They paused for a moment, and then Sayagi nodded. "Good plan. No confrontation."

From then on, part of mealtime consisted of cryptic reports from each member of the team on the status of every portion of the withdrawal plan.

Another time that Petra spoke had nothing to do with military planning, per se. Someone had jokingly said that this would be a good time for Bose to return. Petra knew the story of Subhas Chandra Bose, the Netaji of the Japanese-backed anti-British-rule Indian National Army during World War II. When he died in a plane crash on the way to Japan at the end of the war, the legend among the Indian people was that he was not really dead, but lived on, planning to return someday to lead the people to freedom. In the centuries since then, invoking the return of Bose was both a joke and a serious comment—that the current leadership was as illegitimate as the British Raj had been.

From the mention of Bose, the conversation turned to a

discussion of Gandhi. Someone started talking about "peaceful resistance"—never implying that anyone in Planning might contemplate such a thing, of course—and someone else said, "No, that's *passive* resistance."

That was when Petra spoke up. "This is India, and you know the word. It's satyagraha, and it doesn't mean peaceful or passive resistance at all."

"Not everyone here speaks Hindi," said a Tamil planner.

"But everyone here should know Gandhi," said Petra.

Sayagi agreed with her. "Satyagraha is something else. The willingness to endure great personal suffering in order to do what's right."

"What's the difference, really?"

"Sometimes," said Petra, "what's right is not peaceful or passive. What matters is that you do not hide from the consequences. You bear what must be borne."

"That sounds more like courage than anything else," said the Tamil.

"Courage to do right," said Sayagi. "Courage even when you can't win."

"What happened to 'discretion is the better part of valor'?"

"A quotation from a cowardly character in Shakespeare," someone else pointed out.

"Not contradictory anyway," said Sayagi. "Completely different circumstances. If there's a chance of victory later through withdrawal now, you keep your forces intact. But personally, as an individual, if you know that the price of doing right is terrible loss or suffering or even death, satyagraha means that you are all the more determined to do right, for fear that fear might make you unrighteous."

"Oh, paradoxes within paradoxes."

But Petra turned it from superficial philosophy to something else entirely. "I am trying," she said, "to achieve satya-graha."

And in the silence that followed, she knew that some, at least, understood. She was alive right now because she had *not* achieved satyagraha, because she had *not* always done the right thing, but had done only what was necessary to survive. And she was preparing to change that. To do the right thing regardless of whether she lived through it or not. And for whatever reason—respect for her, uncomfortableness with the intensity of it, or serious contemplation—they remained silent until the meal ended and they spoke again of quotidian things.

Now the war had been going for a month, and Achilles was giving them daily pep talks about how victory was imminent even as they wrestled privately with the growing problems of extricating the army. There *had* been some victories, and at two points the Indian Army was now in Thai territory—but that only lengthened the supply lines and put the army into mountainous country again, where their large numbers could not be brought to bear against the enemy, yet still had to be supplied. And these offensives had chewed through fuel and munitions. In a few days, they would have to choose between fueling tanks and fueling supply trucks. They were about to become a very hungry all-infantry army.

As soon as Achilles left, Sayagi stood up. "It is time to write down our plan for withdrawal and submit it. We must declare victory and withdraw."

There was no dissent. Even though the vids and the nets were full of stories of the great Indian victories, the advance into Thailand, these plans had to be written down, the orders drawn up, while there was still time and fuel enough to carry them out.

So they spent that morning writing each component of the

plan. Sayagi, as their de facto leader, assembled them into a single, fairly coherent set of documents. In the meantime, Petra browsed the net and worked on the project she had been assigned by Achilles, taking no part in what they were doing. They didn't need her for this, and it was her desk that was most closely monitored by Achilles. As long as she was being obedient, Achilles might not notice that the others were not.

When they were almost done, she spoke up, even though she knew that Achilles would be notified quickly of what she said—that he might even be listening through that hearing aid in his ear. "Before you email it," she said, "post it."

At first they probably thought she meant the internal posting, where they could all read it. But then they saw that, using her fingernail on a piece of rough tan toilet paper, she had scratched a net address and was now holding it out.

It was Peter Wiggin's "Locke" forum.

They looked at her like she was crazy. To post military plans in a public place?

But then Sayagi began to nod. "They intercept all our emails," he said. "This is the only way it will get to Chapekar himself."

"To make military secrets public," someone said. He did not need to finish. They knew the penalty.

"Satyagraha," said Sayagi. He took the toilet paper with the address and sat down to go to that netsite. "I am the one doing this, and no one else," he said. "The rest of you warned me not to. There is no reason for more than one person to risk the consequences." Moments later, the data was flowing to Peter Wiggin's forum.

Only then did he send it as email to the general command—which would be routed through Achilles' computer.

"Sayagi," someone said. "Did you see what else is posted

here? On this netsite?"

Petra also moved to the Locke forum and discovered that the lead essay on Locke's site was headed, "Chinese treachery and the fall of India." The subhead said, "Will China, too, fall victim to a psychopath's twisted plans?"

Even as they were reading Locke's essay detailing how China had made promises to both Thailand and India, and would attack now that both armies were fully exposed and, in India's case, overextended, they received emails that contained the same essay, pushed into the system on an urgent basis. That meant it had already been cleared at the top— Chapekar knew what Locke was alleging.

Therefore, their emailed plans for immediate withdrawal of Indian troops from Burma had reached Chapekar at exactly the time when he knew they would be necessary.

"Toguro," breathed Sayagi. "We look like geniuses."

"We *are* geniuses," someone grumbled, and everyone laughed.

"Does anyone think," asked the Tamil, "we'll hear another pep talk from our Belgian friend about how well the war is going?"

Almost as an answer, they heard gunfire outside.

Petra felt a thrill of hope run through her: Achilles tried to make a run for it, and he was shot.

But then a more practical idea replaced her hope: Achilles foresaw this possibility, and has his own forces already in place to cover his escape.

And finally, despair: When he comes for me, will it be to kill me, or take me with him?

More gunfire.

"Maybe," said Sayagi, "we ought to disperse."

He was walking toward the door when it opened and Achilles came in, followed by six Sikhs carrying automatic weapons. "Have a seat, Sayagi," said Achilles. "I'm afraid we have a hostage situation here. Someone made some libelous assertions about me on the nets, and when I declined to be detained during the inquiry, shooting began. Fortunately, I have some friends, and while we're waiting for them to provide me with transportation to a neutral location, you are my guarantors of safety."

Immediately, the two Battle School grads who were Sikhs stood up and said, to Achilles' soldiers, "Are we under threat of death from you?"

"As long as you serve the oppressor," one of them answered.

"*He* is the oppressor!" one of the Sikh Battle Schoolers said, pointing to Achilles.

"Do you think the Chinese will be any kinder to our people than New Delhi has?" said the other.

"Remember how the Chinese treated Tibet and Taiwan! That is our future, because of *him*!"

The Sikh soldiers were obviously wavering.

Achilles drew a pistol from his back and shot the soldiers dead, one after another. The last two had time to try to rush at him, but every shot he fired struck home.

The pistol shots still rang in the room when Sayagi said, "Why didn't they shoot you?"

"I had them unload their weapons before entering the room," Achilles said. "I told them we didn't want any accidents. But don't think you can overpower me because I'm alone with a half-empty clip. This room has long been wired with explosives, and they go off when my heart stops beating or when I activate the controller implanted under the skin of my chest."

A pocket phone beeped and, without lowering his gun, Achilles answered it. "No, I'm afraid one of my soldiers went out of control, and in order to keep the children safe, I had to shoot some of my own men. The situation is unchanged. I am monitoring the perimeter. Keep back, and these children will be safe."

Petra wanted to laugh. Most of the Battle Schoolers here were older than Achilles himself.

Achilles clicked off the phone and pocketed it. "I'm afraid I told them that I had you as my hostages before it was actually true."

"Caught you with your pants down, né?" said Sayagi. "You had no way of knowing you'd need hostages, or that we'd all be here. There are no explosives in this room."

Achilles turned to him and calmly shot him in the head. Sayagi crumpled and fell. Several of the others cried out. Achilles calmly changed clips.

No one charged him while he was reloading.

Not even, thought Petra, me.

There's nothing like casual murder to turn the onlookers into vegetables.

"Satyagraha," said Petra.

Achilles whirled on her. "What was that? What language?"

"Hindi," she said. "It means, 'One bears what one must.' "

"No more Hindi," said Achilles. "From anyone. Or any other language but Common. And if you talk, it had better be to me, and it had better not be something stupid and defiant like the words that got Sayagi killed. If all goes well, my relief should be here in only a few hours. And then Petra and I will go away and leave you to your new government. A Chinese government."

Many of them looked at Petra then. She smiled at Achilles. "So your tent door is still open?"

He smiled back. Warmly. Lovingly. Like a kiss.

But she knew that he was taking her away solely in order to relish the time in which she would have false hopes, before he pushed her from a helicopter or strangled her on the tarmac or, if he grew too impatient, simply shot her as she prepared to follow him out of this room. His time with her was over. His triumph was near—the architect of China's conquest of India, returning to China as a hero. Already plotting how he would take control of the Chinese government and then set out to conquer the other half of the world's population.

For now, though, she was alive, and so were the other Battle Schoolers, except Sayagi. The reason Sayagi died, of course, was not what he said to Achilles. He died because he was the one who posted the withdrawal plans on Locke's forum. Being plans for a retreat under unpredictable fire, they were still usable even with Chinese troops pouring down into Burma, even with Chinese planes bombing the retreating soldiers. The Indian commanders would be able to make a stand. The Chinese would have to fight hard before they won.

But they would win. The Indian defense could last no more than a few days, no matter how bravely they fought. That was when the trucks would stop rolling and food and munitions would run out. The war was already lost. There was only a little time for the Indian elite to attempt to flee before the Chinese swept in, unresisted, with their behead-the-society method of controlling an occupied country.

While these events unfolded, the Battle School graduates who would have kept India out of this dangerous situation in the first place, and whose planning was the only thing keeping the Chinese temporarily at bay, sat in a large room with seven corpses, one gun, and the young man who had betrayed them all.

More than three hours later, gunfire began again, in the

distance. The booming sound of anti-aircraft guns.

Achilles was on the phone in an instant. "Don't fire at the incoming aircraft," he said, "or these geniuses start dying."

He clicked off before they could say anything in reply.

The shooting stopped.

They heard the rotors—choppers landing on the roof.

What a stupid place for them to land, thought Petra. Just because the roof is marked as a heliport doesn't mean they have to obey the signs. Up there, the Indian soldiers surrounding this place will have an easy target, and they'll see everything that happens. They'll know when Achilles is on the roof. They'll know which chopper to shoot down first, because he's in it. If this is the best plan the Chinese can come up with, Achilles is going to have a harder time using China as a base to take over the world than he thinks.

More choppers. Now that the roof was full, a few of them were landing on the grounds.

The door burst open, and a dozen Chinese soldiers fanned out through the room. A Chinese officer followed them in and saluted Achilles. "We came at once, sir."

"Good work," said Achilles. "Let's get them all up on the roof."

"You said you'd let us go!" said one of the Battle Schoolers.

"One way or another," said Achilles, "you're all going to end up in China anyway. Now get up and form into a line against that wall."

More choppers. And then the whoosh, whump of an explosion.

"Those stupid eemos," said the Tamil, "they're going to get us all killed."

"Such a shame," said Achilles, pointing his pistol at the Tamil's head.

The Chinese officer was already talking into his satrad. "Wait," he said. "It's not the Indians. They've got Thai markings."

Bean, thought Petra. You've come at last. Either that or death. Because if Bean wasn't running this Thai raid, the Thai could have no other objective than to kill everything that moved in Hyderabad.

Another whoosh-whump. Another. "They've taken out everything on the roof," the Chinese officer said. "The building's on fire, we've got to get out."

"Whose stupid idea was it to land up there anyway?" asked Achilles.

"It was the closest point to evacuate them from!" answered the officer angrily. "There aren't enough choppers left to take all these."

"They're coming," said Achilles, "even if we have to leave soldiers behind."

"We'll get them in a few days anyway. I don't leave my men behind!"

Not a bad commander, even if he's a little dim about tactics, thought Petra.

"They won't let us take off unless we've got their Indian geniuses with us."

"The Thai won't let us take off at all!"

"Of course they will," said Achilles. "They're here to kill me and rescue *her.*" He pointed at Petra.

So Achilles knew it was Bean that was coming.

Petra showed nothing on her face.

If Achilles decided to leave without the hostages, there was a good chance he would kill them all. Deprive the enemy of a resource. And, more important, take away their hope.

"Achilles," she said, walking toward him. "Let's leave these others and get out. We'll be taking off from the ground.

They won't know who's in what chopper. As long as we go *now.*"

As she approached him, he swung his pistol to point at her chest. She did not even pause, merely walked toward him, past him, to the door. She opened it. "Now, Achilles. You don't have to die in flames today, but that's where you're headed, the longer you wait."

"She's right," said the Chinese officer.

Achilles grinned and looked from Petra to the officer and back again. We've shamed you in front of the others, thought Petra. We've shown that we knew what to do, and you didn't. Now you have to kill us both. This officer doesn't know he's dead, but I do. Then again, I was dead anyway. So now let's get out of here without killing anybody else.

"Nothing in this room matters but you," said Petra. She grinned back at him. "Soak a noky, boy."

Achilles turned back to point the gun, first at one Battle Schooler, then another. They recoiled or flinched, but he did not fire. He dropped his gun hand to his side and walked from the room, grabbing Petra by the arm as he passed her. "Come on, Pet," he said. "The future is calling."

Bean is coming, thought Petra, and Achilles is not going to let me get even a meter away from him. He knows Bean is here for me, so I'm the one person he'll make sure Bean never rescues.

Maybe we'll all kill each other today.

She thought back to the airplane ride that brought her and Achilles to India. The two of them standing at the open door. Maybe there would be another chance today—to die, taking Achilles with her. She wondered if Bean would understand that it was more important for Achilles to die than for her to live. More important, would he know that *she* understood that? It was the right thing to do, and now that she really knew Achilles, the kind of man he was, she would gladly pay that price and call it cheap.

19

RESCUE

To:Wahabi%inshallah@Pakistan.gov
From:Chapekar%hope@India.gov
Re:For the Indian people

My Dear Friend Ghaffar,
I honor you because when I came to
you with an offer of peace between
our two families within the Indian
people, you accepted and kept your
word in every particular.

I honor you because you have lived
a life that places the good of your
people above your own ambition.

I honor you because in you rests
the hope for my people's future.

I make this letter public even as I
send it to you, not knowing what
your response will be, for my people must know now, while I can

still speak to them all, what I am
asking of you and giving to you.

As the treacherous Chinese violate
their promises and threaten to destroy our army, which has been
weakened by the treachery of the
one called Achilles, whom we
treated as a guest and a friend, it
is clear to me that without a miracle, the vast expanse of the nation
of India will be defenseless
against the invaders pouring into
our country from the north. Soon
the ruthless conqueror will work
his will from Bengal to Punjab. Of
all the Indian people, only those
in Pakistan, led by you, will be
free.

I ask you now to take upon yourself
all the hopes of the Indian people.
Our struggle over the next few days
will give you time, I hope, to
bring your armies back to our border, where you will be prepared to
stand against the Chinese enemy.

I now give you permission to cross
that border at any point where it
is necessary, so you can establish
stronger defensive positions. I
order all Indian soldiers remain-

ing at the Pakistani border to
offer no resistance whatsoever to
Pakistani forces entering our
country, and to cooperate by
providing full maps of all our
defenses, and all codes and code-
books. All our matériel at the
border is to be turned over to Pakistan as well.

I ask you that any citizens of
India who come under the rule of
the Pakistani government be treated
as generously as you would wish us,
were our situations reversed, to
treat your people. Whatever past offenses have been committed between
our families, let us forgive each
other and commit no new offenses,
but treat each other as brothers
and sisters who have been faithful
to different faces of the same God,
and who must now stand shoulder to
shoulder to defend India against
the invader whose only god is power
and whose worship is cruelty.

Many members of the Indian government, military, and educational
system will flee to Pakistan. I beg
you to open your borders to them,
for if they remain in India, only
death or captivity will be in their

future. All other Indians have no reason to fear individual persecution from the Chinese, and I beg you not to flee to Pakistan, but rather to remain inside India, where, God willing, you will soon be liberated.

I myself will remain in India, to bear whatever burden is placed upon my people by the conqueror. I would rather be Mandela than de Gaulle. There is to be no government-in-exile. Pakistan is the government of the Indian people now. I say this with the full authority of Congress.

May God bless all honorable people, and keep them free.

Your brother and friend,
Tikal Chapekar

Jetting over the dry southern reaches of India felt to Bean like a strange dream, where the landscape never changed. Or no, it was a vidgame, with a computer making up scenery on the fly, recycling the same algorithms to create the same type of scenery in general, but never quite the same in detail.

Like human beings. DNA that differed by only the tiniest amounts from person to person, and yet those differences giving rise to saints and monsters, fools and geniuses, builders and wreckers, lovers and takers. More people live in this one country, India, than lived in the whole world only three or four centuries ago. More people live here today than lived in the entire history of the world up to the time of Christ. All the history of the Bible and the Iliad and Herodotus and Gilgamesh and everything that had been pieced together by archaeologists and anthropologists, all of those human relationships, all those achievements, could all have been played out by the people we're flying over right now, with people left over to live through new stories that no one would ever hear.

In these few days, China would conquer enough people to make five thousand years of human history, and they would treat them like grass, to be mown till all were the same level, with anything that rose above that level discarded to be mere compost.

And what am I doing? Riding along on a machine that would have given that old prophet Ezekiel a heart attack before he could even write about seeing a shark in the sky. Sister Carlotta used to joke that Battle School was the wheel in the sky that Ezekiel saw in his vision. So here I am, like a figure out of some ancient vision, and what am I doing? That's right, out of the billions of people I might have saved, I'm choosing the one I happen to know and like the best, and risking the lives of a couple of hundred good soldiers in order to do it. And if we get out of this alive, what will I do then? Spend the few years of life remaining to me, helping Peter Wiggin defeat Achilles so he can do exactly what Achilles is already so close to doing—unite humanity under the rule of one sick, ambitious marubo?

Sister Carlotta liked to quote from another biblical git—vanity, vanity, all is vanity. There is nothing new under the sun. A time to scatter rocks and a time to gather rocks together.

Well, as long as God didn't tell anybody what the rocks were for, I might as well leave the rocks and go get my friend, if I can.

As they approached Hyderabad, they picked up a lot of radio chatter. Tactical stuff from satrads, not just the net traffic you'd expect because of the Chinese surprise attack in Burma that had been triggered by Peter's essay. As they got closer, the onboard computers were able to distinguish the radio signatures of Chinese troops as well as Indian.

"Looks like Achilles' retrieval crew got here ahead of us," said Suriyawong.

"But no shooting," said Bean. "Which means they've already got to the planning room and they're holding the Battle Schoolers as hostages."

"You got it," said Suriyawong. "Three choppers on the roof."

"There'll be more on the ground, but let's complicate their lives and take out those three."

Virlomi had misgivings. "What if they think it's the Indian Army attacking and they kill the hostages?"

"Achilles is not so stupid he won't make sure who's doing the shooting before he starts using up his ticket home."

It was like target practice, and three missiles took out three choppers, just like that.

"Now get us onto blades and show the Thai markings," said Suriyawong.

It was, as usual, a sickening climb and drop before the blades took over. But Bean was used to the sense of clawing nausea and was able to notice, out the windows, that the Indian troops were cheering and waving.

"Oh, suddenly now we're the good guys," said Bean.

"I think we're just the not-quite-so-evil guys," said Suriyawong.

"I think you're taking irresponsible risks with the lives of my friends," said Virlomi.

Bean sobered at once. "Virlomi, I know Achilles, and the only way to keep him from killing your friends, just for spite, is to keep him worried and off balance. To give him no time to display his malice."

"I meant that if one of those missiles had gone astray," she said, "it could have hit the room they're in and killed them all."

"Oh, is that all you're worried about?" Bean said. "Virlomi, I *trained* these men. There are situations in which they might miss, but this was not one of them."

Virlomi nodded. "I understand. The confidence of the field commander. It's been a long time since I had a toon of my own."

A few choppers stayed aloft, watching the perimeter; most set down in front of the building where the planning room was located. Suriyawong had already briefed the company commanders he was taking into the building by satrad as they flew. Now he jumped from the chopper as soon as the door opened and, with Virlomi running behind him, he got his group moving, executing the plan.

At once, Bean's chopper lifted back up and, with another chopper, hopped the building to come down on the other side. This was where they found the two remaining Chinese helicopters, blades spinning. Bean had his pilot set down so the chopper's weapons were pointed at the sides of the two Chinese machines. Then he and the thirty men with him went out both doors as Chinese troops across the open space between them did the same.

Bean's other chopper remained airborne, waiting to see whether its missiles or the troops inside would be needed first.

The Chinese had Bean's troops outnumbered, but that wasn't really the issue. Nobody was shooting, because the Chinese wanted to get away alive, and there was no hope of that if shooting broke out, because the airborne chopper would simply destroy both the remaining Chinese machines and then it wouldn't matter what happened on the ground, they'd never get home and their mission would be a failure.

So the two little armies formed up just like regiments in the Napoleonic wars, neat little lines. Bean wanted to shout something like "fix bayonets" or "load"—but nobody was using muskets and besides, what interested him would be coming out the door of the building. . . .

And there he was, rushing straight for the nearest chopper, gripping Petra by the arm and half-dragging her along. Achilles held a pistol down at his side. Bean wanted to have one of his sharpshooters take him out, but he knew that then the Chinese would open fire and Petra would certainly be killed. So he called out to Achilles.

Achilles ignored him. Bean knew what he was thinking—get inside the chopper while everybody's holding their fire, and then Bean would be helpless, unable to do anything to Achilles without also harming Petra.

So Bean spoke into his satrad and the hovering chopper did what the gunner was trained to do—fired a missile that blew up just beyond the nearer Chinese chopper. The machine itself blocked the blast so Petra and Achilles weren't hurt—but the chopper was rocked over onto its side and then, as the blades chewed to bits against the ground, it flipped over and over and smashed up against a barracks. A few soldiers slithered out, trying to drag out others with broken limbs or other injuries before the machine went up in flames.

Achilles and Petra now stood in the middle of the open space. The only remaining Chinese chopper was too far for him to run to. He did the only thing he could do, under the circumstances. He held Petra in front of him with a gun pointed to her head. It wasn't a move they taught you in Battle School. It was straight from the vids.

In the meantime, the Chinese officer in charge—a colonel, if Bean remembered correctly how to translate the rank insignia, which was a very high rank for a small-scale operation like this one—strode out with his men. Bean did not have to instruct him to stay far away from Achilles and Petra. The colonel would know that any move to get between Achilles and Bean's men would lead to shooting, since there was only a stalemate as long as Bean had the ability to kill Achilles the moment he harmed Petra.

Without looking at the soldiers near him, Bean said, "Who has a trank pistol?"

One was slapped into his open hand. Someone murmured, "Keep your hand on a real gun, too."

And someone else said, "I hope the Indian Army doesn't realize that Achilles doesn't have *any* Indian kids with him. They couldn't care less about an Armenian." Bean appreciated it when his men thought through the whole situation. No time for praise now, though.

He stepped away from his men and walked toward Achilles and Petra. As he did, he saw Suriyawong and Virlomi come out the door through which the Chinese colonel had just come. Suriyawong called out, "All secure. Loading. Achilles murdered only one of ours."

"One of 'ours'?" said Achilles. "When did Sayagi become one of *yours*? You mean that I can kill anybody else and you don't care, but touch a Battle School brat and I'm a murderer?"

"You're never taking off in that chopper with Petra," said Bean.

"I know I'm never taking off *without* her," said Achilles. "If I don't have her with me, you'll blow that chopper into bits so small they'd have to use a comb to gather them up."

"Then I guess I'll just have one of my sharpshooters kill you."

Petra smiled.

She was telling him yes, do it.

"Colonel Yuan-xi will then regard his mission as a failure, and he will kill as many of you as he can. Petra first."

Bean saw that the colonel had gotten his men on board the chopper—those who had come with him from the building and those who had deployed from the choppers when Bean first landed. Only he, Achilles, and Petra remained outside.

"Colonel," said Bean, "the only way this doesn't end in blood is if we can trust each other's word. I promise you that as long as Petra is alive, uninjured, and with me, you can take off safely with no interference from me or my strike force. Whether you have Achilles with you is of no importance to me."

Petra's smile vanished, replaced with a face that was an obvious mask of anger. She did not want Achilles to get away.

But she still hoped to live—that was why she was saying nothing, so Achilles wouldn't know that she was demanding his death, even at the cost of her own.

What she was ignoring was the fact that the Chinese commander had to meet the minimum conditions for mission success—he had to have Achilles with him when he left. If he didn't, a lot of people here would die, and for what? Achilles' worst deeds were already done. From here on, no one would ever trust his word on anything. Whatever power he got now would be by force and fear, not by deception.

Which meant that he would be making enemies every day, driving people into the arms of his opponents.

He might still win more battles and more wars and he might even seem to triumph completely, but, like Caligula, he would make assassins out of the people closest to him. And when he died, men just as evil but perhaps not as crazy would take his place. Killing him now would not make that much difference to the world.

Keeping Petra alive, however, would make all the difference in the world to Bean. He had made the mistakes that killed Poke and Sister Carlotta. But he was going to make no mistakes today. Petra would live because Bean couldn't bear any other outcome. She didn't even get a vote on the matter.

The colonel was weighing the situation.

Achilles was not. "I'm moving to the chopper now. My fingers are pretty tight on this trigger. Don't make me flinch, Bean."

Bean knew what Achilles was thinking: Can I kill Bean at the last moment and still get away, or should I leave that pleasure for another time?

And that was an advantage for Bean, because his thinking was not clouded by thoughts of personal vengeance.

Except, he realized, that it was. Because he, too, was trying to think of some way to save Petra and still kill Achilles.

The colonel walked up closer behind Achilles before calling out his answer to Bean. "Achilles is the architect of a great Chinese victory, and he must come to Beijing to be received in honor. My orders say nothing about the Armenian."

"They'll never let us take off without her, you fool," said Achilles.

"Sir, I give you my word, my parole. Even though

Achilles has already murdered a woman and a girl who did nothing but good for him, and deserves to die for his crimes, I will let him go and let you go."

"Then our missions do not conflict," said the colonel. "I agree to your terms, provided you also agree to care for any of my men who remain behind according to the rules of war."

"I agree," said Bean.

"I'm in charge of our mission," said Achilles, "and I don't agree."

"You are not in charge of our mission, sir," said the colonel.

Bean knew exactly what Achilles would do. He would take the gun away from Petra's head long enough to shoot the colonel. Achilles would expect this move to surprise people, but Bean was not surprised at all. His hand with the trank gun was already rising before Achilles even started to turn to the colonel.

But Bean was not the only one who knew what to expect from Achilles. The colonel had deliberately moved close enough to Achilles that as he swung the gun around, the colonel slapped the weapon out of Achilles' hand. At the same moment, with his other hand the colonel slapped Achilles' arm close to the elbow, and even though there seemed to be almost no force behind the blow, Achilles' arm bent sickeningly backward. Achilles cried out in pain and dropped to his knees, letting go of Petra. She immediately launched herself to the side, out of the way, and at that moment Bean fired the trank gun. He was able to adjust the aim at the last split second, and the tiny pellet struck Achilles' shirt with such force that even though the casing collapsed against the cloth, the tranquilizer blew right through the fabric and penetrated Achilles' skin. He collapsed immediately.

"It's only a tranquilizer," said Bean. "He'll be awake in six hours or so, with a headache."

The colonel stood there, not bending yet to even notice Achilles, his eyes still fixed on Bean. "Now there is no hostage. Your enemy is on the ground. How good is your word, sir, when the circumstance in which it was given goes away?"

"Men of honor," said Bean, "are brothers no matter what uniform they wear. You may put him aboard, and take off. I recommend that you fly in formation with us until we are south of the defenses around Hyderabad. Then you may fly your own course, and we'll fly ours."

"That is a wise plan," said the colonel.

He knelt and started to pick up Achilles' limp body. It was tricky work, and so Bean, small as he was, stepped forward to help by taking Achilles' legs.

Petra was on her feet by then, and when Bean glanced at her he could see that she was eyeing Achilles' pistol, which lay on the ground near her. Bean could almost read her mind. To kill Achilles with his own gun had to be tempting—and Petra had not given her word.

But before she could even move toward the pistol, Bean had his trank gun pointed at her. "You could also wake up in six hours with a headache," he said.

"No need," she said. "I know that I'm also bound by your word." And, without stooping for the gun, she came and helped Bean carry his end of Achilles' body.

They rolled Achilles through the wide door of the chopper. Soldiers inside the machine took him and carried him back, presumably to a place where he could be secured during flight maneuvers. The chopper was grossly over-crowded, but only with men—there were no supplies or heavy munitions, so it would fly as well as normal. It would simply be uncomfortable for the passengers.

"You don't want to ride home on that chopper," said Bean. "I invite you to ride with us."

"But you're not going where I'm going," said the colonel.

"I know this boy you have just taken aboard," said Bean. "Even if he doesn't remember what you did when he wakes up, someone will tell him someday, and once he knows, you'll be marked. He never forgets. He will certainly kill you."

"Then I will have died obeying my orders and fulfilling my mission," said the colonel.

"Full asylum," said Bean, "and a life spent helping liberate China and all other nations from the kind of evil he represents."

"I know that you mean to be kind," said the colonel, "but it hurts my soul to be offered such rewards for betraying my country."

"Your country is led by men without honor," said Bean. "And yet they are sustained in power by the honor of men like you. Who, then, betrays his country? No, we have no time for arguments. I only plant the idea so it will fester in your soul." Bean smiled.

The colonel smiled back. "Then you are a devil, sir, as we Chinese always knew you Europeans to be."

Bean saluted him. He returned the salute and got on board.

The chopper door closed.

Bean and Petra ran out of the downdraft as the Chinese machine rose up into the air. There it hovered as Bean ordered everyone into the one chopper that remained on the ground. Less than two minutes later, his chopper, too, rose up, and the Thai and Chinese machines flew together over the building, where they were joined by the other helijets of Bean's strike force as they rose up from the ground or converged from their watching points at the perimeter.

They flew together toward the south, slowly, on blades.

No Indian weapon was fired at them. For the Indian officers no doubt knew that their best young military minds were being taken to far more safety than they could possibly have in Hyderabad, or anywhere in India, once the Chinese came in force.

Then Bean gave the order, and all his choppers rose up, cut the blades, and dropped as the jets came on and the blades folded back for the quick ride back to Sri Lanka.

Inside the chopper, Petra sat glumly in her straps. Virlomi was beside her, but they did not speak to each other.

"Petra," said Bean.

She did not look up.

"Virlomi found us, we did not find her. Because of her, we were able to come for you."

Petra still did not look up, but she reached out a hand and laid it on Virlomi's hands, which were clasped in her lap. "You were brave and good," said Petra. "Thank you for having compassion for me."

Then she looked up to meet Bean's gaze. "But I don't thank *you,* Bean. I was ready to kill him. I would have done it. I would have found a way."

"He's going to kill himself in the end," said Bean. "He's going to overreach himself, like Robespierre, like Stalin. Others will see his pattern and when they realize he's finally about to put them to the guillotine, they'll decide they've had enough and he will, most certainly, die."

"But how many will he kill along the way? And now your hands are stained with all their blood, because you loaded him onto that chopper alive. Mine, too."

"You're wrong," said Bean. "He is the only one responsible for his killings. And you're wrong about what would have happened if we had let him take you along. You would not have lived through that ride."

"You don't know that."

"I know Achilles. When that chopper rose to about twenty stories up, you would have been pushed out the door. And do you know why?"

"So you could watch," she said.

"No, he would have waited till I was gone," said Bean. "He's not stupid. He regards his own survival as far more important than your death."

"Then why would he kill me now? Why are you so sure?"

"Because he had his arm around you like a lover," said Bean. "Standing there with the gun to your head, he held you with affection. I think he meant to kiss you before he took you on board. He'd want me to see that."

"She would never let him kiss her," said Virlomi with disgust.

But Petra met Bean's gaze, and the tears in her eyes were a truer answer than Virlomi's brave words. She had already let Achilles kiss her. Just like Poke.

"He marked you," said Bean. "He loved you. You had power over him. After he didn't need you anymore as the hostage to keep me from killing him, you could not go on living."

Suriyawong shuddered. "What made him that way?"

"Nothing *made* him that way," said Bean. "No matter what terrible things happened in his life, no matter what dreadful hungers rose up from his soul, he chose to act on those desires, he chose to do the things he did. *He's* responsible for his own actions, and no one else. Not even those who saved his life."

"Like you and me today," said Petra.

"Sister Carlotta saved his life today," said Bean. "The last thing she asked me was to leave vengeance up to God."

"Do you believe in God?" asked Suriyawong, surprised.

"More and more," said Bean. "And less and less."

Virlomi took Petra's hands between hers and said, "Enough of blame and enough of Achilles. You're free of him. You can have whole minutes and hours and days in which you don't have to think of what he'll do to you if he hears what you say, and how you have to act when he might be watching. The only way he can hurt you now is if you keep watching *him* in your own heart."

"Listen to her, Petra," said Suriyawong. "She's a goddess, you know."

Virlomi laughed. "I save bridges and summon choppers."

"And you blessed me," said Suriyawong.

"I never did," said Virlomi.

"When you walked on my back," said Suriyawong. "My whole body is now the path of a goddess."

"Only the back part," said Virlomi. "You'll have to find someone else to bless the front."

While they bantered, half-drunk with success and liberty and the overwhelming tragedy they were leaving behind them, Bean watched Petra, saw the tears drop from her eyes onto her lap, longed to be able to reach out and touch them away from her eyes. But what good would that do? Those tears had risen up from deep wells of pain, and his mere touch would do nothing to dry them at their source. It would take time to do that, and time was the one thing that he did not have. If Petra knew happiness in her life—happiness, that precious thing that Mrs. Wiggin talked about—it would come when she shared her life with someone else. Bean had saved her, had freed her, not so he could have her or be part of her life, but so that he did not have to bear the guilt of her death as he bore the deaths of Poke and Carlotta. It was a selfish thing he did, in a way. But in another way, there would be nothing for himself at all from this day's work.

Except that when his death came, sooner rather than later, he might well look back on this day's work with more pride than anything else in his life. Because today he won. In the midst of all this terrible defeat, he had found a victory. He had cheated Achilles out of one of his favorite murders. He had saved the life of his dearest friend, even though she wasn't quite grateful yet. His army had done what he needed it to do, and not one life had been lost out of the two hundred men he had first been given. Always before he had been part of someone else's victory. But today, today *he* won.

20

HEGEMON

To:Chamrajnagar%Jawaharlal@ifcom.
gov
From:PeterWiggin%freeworld@hemon.
gov
Re: Confirmation

Dear Polemarch Chamrajnagar,
Thank you for allowing me to reconfirm your appointment as Polemarch
as my first official act. We both
know that I was giving you only
what you already had, while you, by
accepting that reconfirmation as if
it actually meant something, re-
stored to the office of Hegemon
some of the luster that has been
torn from it by the events of recent months. There are many who
feel that it is an empty gesture to
appoint a Hegemon who leads only
about a third of the human race and
has no particular influence over

the third that officially supports him. Many nations are racing to find some accommodation with the Chinese and their allies, and I live under the constant threat of having my office abolished as one of the first gestures they can make to win the favor of the new super-power. I am, in short, a Hegemon without hegemony.

And it is all the more remarkable that you would make this generous gesture toward the very individual that you once regarded as the worst of all possible Hegemons. The weak-nesses in my character that you saw then have not magically vanished. It is only by comparison with Achilles, and only in a world where your homeland groans under the Chi-nese lash, that I begin to look like an attractive alternative or a source of hope instead of despair. But regardless of my weaknesses, I also have strengths, and I make you a promise:

Even though you are bound by your oath of office never to use the In-ternational Fleet to influence the course of events on Earth, except to intercept nuclear weapons or

punish those who use them, I know
that you are still a man of Earth,
a man of India, and you care deeply
what happens to all people, and
particularly to your people. Therefore I promise you that I will
devote the rest of my life to re-
shaping this world into one that
you would be glad of, for your people, and for all people. And I hope
that I succeed well enough, before
one or the other of us dies, that
you will be glad of the support you
gave to me today.

Sincerely,
Peter Wiggin, Hegemon

Over a million Indians made it out of India before the
Chinese sealed the borders. Out of a population of a billion
and a half, that was far too few. At least ten times that million
were transported over the next year, from India to the cold
lands of Manchuria and the high deserts of Sinkiang. Among
the transported ones was Tikal Chapekar. The Chinese gave
no report to outsiders about the fate of him or any of the
other "former oppressors of the Indian people." The same, on
a far smaller scale, happened to the governing elites of
Burma, Thailand, Vietnam, Cambodia, and Laos.

As if this vast redrawing of the world's map were not
enough, Russia announced that it had joined China as its
ally, and that it considered the nations of eastern Europe that
were not loyal members of the New Warsaw Pact to be

provinces in rebellion. Without firing a shot, Russia was able, simply by promising not to be as dreadful an overlord as China, to rewrite the Warsaw Pact until it was more or less the constitution of an empire that included all of Europe east of Germany, Austria, and Italy in the south, and east of Sweden and Norway in the north.

The weary nations of western Europe were quick to "welcome" the "discipline" that Russia would bring to Europe, and Russia was immediately given full membership in the European Community. Because Russia now controlled the votes of more than half the members of that community, it would require a constant tug of war to keep some semblance of independence, and rather than play that game, Great Britain, Ireland, Iceland, and Portugal left the European Community. But even they took great pains to assure the Russian bear that this was purely over economic issues and they really welcomed this renewed Russian interest in the West.

America, which had long since become the tail to China's dog in matters of trade, made a few grumpy noises about human rights and then went back to business as usual, using satellite cartography to redraw the map of the world to fit the new reality and then sell the atlases that resulted. In sub-Saharan Africa, where India had once been their greatest single trading partner and cultural influence, the loss of India was much more devastating, and they loyally denounced the Chinese conquest even as they scrambled to find new markets for their goods. Latin America was even louder in their condemnation of all the aggressors, but lacking serious military forces, their bluster could do no harm. In the Pacific, Japan, with its dominant fleet, could afford to stand firm; the other island nations that faced China across various not-so-wide bodies of water had no such luxury.

Indeed, the only force that stood firm against China and Russia while facing them across heavily defended borders were the Muslim nations. Iran generously forgot how threateningly Pakistani troops had loomed along their borders in the month before India's fall, and Arabs joined with Turks in Muslim solidarity against any Russian encroachment across the Caucasus or into the vast steppes of central Asia. No one seriously thought that Muslim military might could stand for long against a serious attack from China, and Russia was only scarcely less dangerous, but the Muslims laid aside their grievances, trusted in Allah, and kept their borders bristling with the warning that this nettle would be hard to grasp.

This was the world as it was the day that Peter "Locke" Wiggin was named as the new Hegemon. China let it be known that choosing any Hegemon at all was an affront, but Russia was a bit more tolerant, especially because many governments that cast their vote for Wiggin did so with the public declaration that the office was more ceremonial than practical, a gesture toward world unity and peace, and not at all an attempt to roll back the conquests that had brought "peace" to an unstable world.

But privately, many leaders of the very same governments assured Peter that they expected him to do all he could to bring about diplomatic "transformations" in the occupied countries. Peter listened to them politely and said reassuring things, but he felt nothing but scorn for them—for without military might, he had no way of negotiating with anyone about anything.

His first official act was to reconfirm the appointment of Polemarch Chamrajnagar—an action which China officially protested as illegal because the office of Hegemon no longer existed, and while they would do nothing to interfere with Chamrajnagar's continued leadership of the Fleet, they would no longer contribute financially either to the Hegemony or the Fleet. Peter then confirmed Graff as Hegemony Minister of Colonization—and, again, because his work was offworld, China could do nothing more than cut off its contribution of funds.

But the lack of money forced Peter's next decision. He moved the Hegemony capital out of the former Netherlands and returned the Low Countries to self-government, which immediately put a stop to unrestricted immigration into those nations. He closed down most Hegemony services world-wide except for medical and agricultural research and assistance programs. He moved the main Hegemony offices to Brazil, which had several important assets:

First, it was a large enough and powerful enough country that the enemies of the Hegemony would not be quick to provoke it by assassinating the Hegemon within its borders.

Second, it was in the southern hemisphere, with strong economic ties to Africa, the Americas, and the Pacific, so that being there kept Peter within the mainstream of international commerce and politics.

And third, Brazil invited Peter Wiggin to come there. No one else did.

Peter had no delusions about what the office of Hegemon had become. He did not expect anyone to come to him. He went to them.

Which is why he left Haiti and crossed the Pacific to Manila, where Bean and his Thai army and the Indians they rescued had found temporary refuge. Peter knew that Bean was still angry at him, so he was relieved that Bean not only agreed to see him, but treated him with open respect when he arrived. His two hundred soldiers were crisply turned out to greet him, and when Bean introduced him to Petra, Suriyawong, and Virlomi and the other Indian Battle Schoolers, he phrased everything as if he were presenting his friends to a man of higher rank.

In front of all of them, Bean then made a little speech. "To His Excellency the Hegemon, I offer the service of this band of soldiers—veterans of war, former opponents, and now, because of treachery, exiles from their homeland and broth-ers- and sisters-at-arms. This was not my decision, nor the decision of the majority. Each individual here was given the choice, and chose to make this offer of our service. We are few, but nations have found our service valuable before. We hope that we now can serve a cause that is higher than any nation, and whose end will be the establishment of a new and honorable order in the world."

Peter was surprised only by the formality of the offer, and the fact that it was made without any sort of negotiation beforehand. He also noticed that Bean had arranged to have cameras present. This would be news. So Peter made a brief, soundbite-oriented reply accepting their offer, praising their achievements, and expressing regret at the suffering of their people. It would play well—twenty seconds on the vids, and in full on the nets.

When the ceremonies were done, there was an inspection of their inventory—all the equipment they had been able to rescue from Thailand. Even their fighter-bomber pilots and patrol boat crews had managed to make their way from southern Thailand to the Philippines, so the Hegemon had an air force and a fleet. Peter nodded and commented gravely as he saw each item in the inventory—the cameras were still running.

Later, though, when they were alone, Peter finally allowed himself a rueful, self-mocking laugh. "If it weren't for you

I'd have nothing at all," he said. "But to compare this to the vast fleets and air forces and armies that the Hegemon once commanded . . ."

Bean looked at him coldly. "The office had to be greatly diminished," he said, "before they'd have given it to you."

The honeymoon, apparently, was over. "Yes," Peter said, "that's true, of course."

"And the world had to be in a desperate condition, with the existence of the office of Hegemon in doubt."

"That, too, is true," said Peter. "And for some reason you seem to be angry about this."

"That's because, apart from the not-trivial matter of Achilles' penchant for killing people now and then, I fail to see much difference between you and him. You're both content to let any number of people suffer needlessly in order to advance your personal ambitions."

Peter sighed. "If that's all the difference that you see, I don't understand how you could offer your service to me."

"I see other differences, of course," said Bean. "But they're matters of degree, not of kind. Achilles makes treaties he never intends to keep. You merely write essays that might have saved nations, but you delay publishing them so that those nations will fall, putting the world in a position desperate enough that they would make you Hegemon."

"Your statement is true," said Peter, "*only* if you believe that earlier publication would have saved India and Thailand."

"Early in the war," said Bean, "India still had the supplies and equipment to resist Chinese attack. Thailand's forces were still fully dispersed and hard to find."

"But if I had published early in the war," said Peter, "India and Thailand would not have seen their peril, and they wouldn't have believed me. After all, the Thai government didn't believe *you,* and you warned them of everything."

"You're Locke," said Bean.

"Ah yes. Because I had so much credibility and prestige, nations would tremble and believe my words. Aren't you forgetting something? At your insistence, I had declared myself to be a teenage college student. I was still recovering from that, trying to prove in Haiti that I could actually govern. I might have had the prestige left to be taken seriously in India and Thailand—but I might not. And if I published too soon, before China was ready to act, China would simply have denied everything to both sides, the war would have proceeded, and then there would have been no shock value at all to my publication. I wouldn't have been able to trigger the invasion at exactly the moment you needed me to."

"Don't pretend that this was your plan all along."

"It was my plan," said Peter, "to withhold publication until it could be an act of power instead of an act of futility. Yes, I was thinking of my prestige, because right now the only power I have is that prestige and the influence it gives me with the governments of the world. It's a coin that is minted very slowly, and if spent ineffectively, disappears. So yes, I protect that power very carefully, and use it sparingly, so that later, when I need to have it, it will still exist."

Bean was silent.

"You hate what happened in the war," said Peter. "So do I. It's possible—not likely, but possible—that if I had published earlier, India might have been able to mount a real resistance. They might still have been fighting now. Millions of soldiers might have been dying even as we speak. Instead, there was a clean, almost bloodless victory for China. And now the Chinese have to govern a population almost twice the size of their own, with a culture every bit as old and all-absorbing as their own. The snake has swallowed a crocodile, and the question is going to arise again and again—who is digesting whom? Thailand and Vietnam will be just as hard to govern, and even the Burmese have never managed to govern Burma. What I did saved lives. It left the world with a clear moral picture of who did the stabbing in the back, and who was stabbed. And it leaves China victorious and Russia triumphant—but with captive, angry populations to govern who will not stand with them when the final struggle comes. Why do you think China made a quick peace with Pakistan? Because they knew they could not fight a war against the Muslim world with Indian revolt and sabotage a constant threat. And that alliance between China and Russia—what a joke! Within a year they'll be quarreling, and they'll be back to weakening each other across that long Siberian border. To people who think superficially, China and Russia look triumphant. But I never thought you were a superficial thinker."

"I see all that," said Bean.

"But you don't care. You're still angry at me."

Bean said nothing.

"It's hard," said Peter, "to see how all of this seems to work to my advantage, and not blame me for profiteering from the suffering of others. But the real issue is, What am I going to be able to do, and what will I actually do, now that I'm nominally the leader of the world, and actually the administrator of a small tax base, a few international service agencies, and this military force you gave to me today? I did the few things that were in my power to shape events so that when I got this office, it would still be worth having."

"But above all, to get that office."

"Yes, Bean. I'm arrogant. I think I'm the only person who understands what to do and has what it takes to do it. I think the world needs me. In fact, I'm even more arrogant than you. Is that what this comes down to? I should have been humbler? Only you are allowed to assess your own abilities candidly and decide that you're the best man for a particular job?"

"I don't want the job."

"I don't want *this* job, either," said Peter. "What I want is the job where the Hegemon speaks, and wars stop, where the Hegemon can redraw borders and strike down bad laws and break up international cartels and bring all of humanity a chance for a decent life in peace and whatever freedom their culture will allow. And I'm going to get that job, by creating it step by step. Not only that, I'm going to do it with your help, because you want somebody to do that job, and you know, just as surely as I do, that I'm the only one who can do it."

Bean nodded, saying nothing.

"You know all that, and you're still angry with me."

"I'm angry with Achilles," said Bean. "I'm angry with the stupidity of those who refused to listen to me. But you're here, and they're not."

"It's more than that," said Peter. "If that's all it was, you would have talked yourself out of your wrath long before we had this conversation."

"I know," said Bean. "But you don't want to hear it."

"Because it will hurt my feelings? Let me make a stab at it, then. You're angry because every word from my mouth, every gesture, every expression on my face reminds you of Ender Wiggin. Only I'm not Ender, I'll never be Ender, you think Ender should be doing what I'm doing, and you hate me for being the one who made sure Ender got sent away."

"It's irrational," said Bean. "I know that. I know that by sending him away you saved his life. The people who helped

Achilles try to kill me would have worked day and night to kill Ender without any prompting from Achilles at all. They would have feared him far more than they feared you or me. I know that. But you look and talk so much like him. And I keep thinking, if Ender had been here, he wouldn't have botched things the way I did."

"The way I read it, it's the other way around. If *you* hadn't been there with Ender, *he* would have botched it at the end. No, don't argue, it doesn't matter. What *does* matter is, the world's the way it is right now, and we're in a position where, if we move carefully, if we think through and plan everything just right, we can fix this. We can make it better. No regrets. No wishing we could undo the past. We just look to the future and work our zhupas off."

"I'll look to the future," said Bean, "and I'll help you all I can. But I'll regret whatever I want to regret."

"Fair enough," said Peter. "Now that we've agreed on that, I think you should know. I've decided to revive the office of Strategos."

Bean gave one hoot of derision. "You're putting *that* title on the commander of a force of two hundred soldiers, a couple of planes, a couple of boats, and an overheated company of strategic planners?"

"Hey, if I can be called Hegemon, you can take on a title like that."

"I notice you didn't want any vids of me getting that title."

"No, I didn't," said Peter. "I don't want people to hear the news while looking at vids of a kid. I want them to learn of your appointment as Strategos while seeing stock footage of the victory over the Formics and hearing voice-overs about your rescue of the Indian Battle Schoolers."

"Well, fine," said Bean. "I accept. Do I get a fancy uniform?"

"No," said Peter. "At the rate you're growing lately, we'd have to pay for new ones too often, and you'd bankrupt us."

A thoughtful expression passed across Bean's face.

"What," said Peter, "did I offend again?"

"No," said Bean. "I was just wondering what your parents said, when you declared yourself to be Locke."

Peter laughed. "Oh, they pretended that they'd known it all along. Parents."

———

At Bean's suggestion, Peter located the headquarters of the Hegemony in a compound just outside the city of Ribeirão Preto in the state of São Paulo. There they would have excellent air connections anywhere in the world, while being surrounded by small towns and agricultural land. They'd be far from any government body. It was a pleasant place to live as they planned and trained to achieve the modest goal of freeing the captive nations while holding the line against any new aggressions.

The Delphiki family came out of hiding and joined Bean in the safety of the Hegemony compound. Greece was part of the Warsaw Pact now, and there was no going home for them. Peter's parents also came, because they understood that they would become targets for anyone wanting to get to Peter. He gave them both jobs in the Hegemony, and if they minded the disruption of their lives, they never gave a sign of it.

The Arkanians left their homeland, too, and came gladly to live in a place where their children would not be stolen from them. Suriyawong's parents had made it out of Thailand, and they moved the family fortune and the family business to Ribeirão Preto. Other Thai and Indian families with ties to Bean's army or the Battle School graduates came as well, and soon there were thriving neighborhoods where Portuguese was rarely heard.

As for Achilles, month after month they heard nothing about him. Presumably he got back to Beijing. Presumably, he was worming his way into power one way or another. But they allowed themselves, as the silence about him continued, to hope that perhaps the Chinese, having made use of him, now knew him well enough to keep him away from the reins of power.

———

On a cloudy winter afternoon in June, Petra walked through the cemetery in the town of Araraquara, only twenty minutes by train from Ribeirão Preto. She took care to make sure she approached Bean from a direction where he could see her coming. Soon she stood beside him, looking at a marker.

"Who is buried here?" she asked.

"No one," said Bean, who showed no surprise at seeing her. "It's a cenotaph."

Petra read the names that were on it.

Poke.

Carlotta.

There was nothing else.

"There's a marker for Sister Carlotta somewhere in Vatican City," said Bean. "But there was no body recovered that could actually be buried anywhere. And Poke was cremated by people who didn't even know who she was. I got the idea for this from Virlomi."

Virlomi had set up a cenotaph for Sayagi in the small Hindu cemetery that already existed in Ribeirão Preto. It was a bit more elaborate—it included the dates of his birth and death, and called him "a man of satyagraha."

"Bean," said Petra, "it's quite insane of you to come here.

No bodyguard. This marker standing here so that assassins can set their sights before you show up."

"I know," said Bean.

"At least you could have invited me along."

He turned to her, tears in his eyes. "This is my place of shame," he said. "I worked very hard to make sure your name would not be here."

"Is that what you tell yourself? There's no shame here, Bean. There's only love. And that's why I belong here—with the other lonely girls who gave their hearts to you."

Bean turned to her, put his arms around her, and wept into her shoulder. He had grown, to stand tall enough for that. "They saved my life," he said. "They *gave* me life."

"That's what good people do," said Petra. "And then they die, every one of them. It's a damned shame."

He gave one short laugh—whether at her small levity or at himself, for weeping, she did not know. "Nothing lasts long, does it," said Bean.

"They're still alive in you."

"Who am I alive in?" said Bean. "And don't say you."

"I will if I want. You saved *my* life."

"They never had children, either one of them," said Bean. "No one ever held either Poke or Carlotta the way a man does with a woman, or had a baby with them. They never got to see their children grow up and have children of their own."

"By Sister Carlotta's choice," said Petra.

"Not Poke's."

"They both had you."

"That's the futility of it," said Bean. "The only child they had was me."

"So . . . you owe it to them to carry on, to marry, to have more children who'll remember them both for your sake."

Bean stared off into space. "I have a better idea. Let me

tell *you* about them. And you tell *your* children. Will you do that? If you could promise me that, then I think that I could bear all this, because they wouldn't just disappear from memory when I die."

"Of course I'll do that, Bean, but you're talking as if your life were already over, and it's just beginning. Look at you, you're getting along, you'll have a man's height before long, you'll—"

He touched her lips, gently, to silence her. "I'll have no wife, Petra. No babies."

"Why not? If you tell me you've decided to become a priest I'll kidnap you myself and get you out of this Catholic country."

"I'm not human, Petra," Bean replied. "And my species dies with me."

She laughed at his joke.

But as she looked into his eyes, she saw that it wasn't a joke at all. Whatever he meant by that, he really thought that it was true. Not human. But how could he think that? Of all the people Petra knew, who was more human than Bean?

"Let's go back home," Bean finally said, "before somebody comes along and shoots us just for loitering."

"Home," said Petra.

Bean only halfway understood. "Sorry it's not Armenia."

"No, I don't think Armenia is home either," she said. "And Battle School sure wasn't, nor Eros. This *is* home, though. I mean, Ribeirão Preto. But here, too. Because . . . my family's here, of course, but . . ."

And then she realized what she was trying to say.

"It's because *you're* here. Because you're the one who went through it all with me. You're the one who knows what I'm talking about. What I'm remembering. Ender. That terrible day with Bonzo. And the day I fell asleep in the middle of a battle on Eros. You think *you* have shame." She laughed. "But it's OK to remember even *that* with you. Because you knew about that, and you still came to get me out."

"Took me long enough," said Bean.

They walked out of the cemetery toward the train station, holding hands because neither of them wanted to feel separate right now.

"I have an idea," said Petra.

"What?"

"If you ever change your mind—you know, about marrying and having babies—hang on to my address. Look me up."

Bean was silent for a long moment. "Ah," he finally said, "I get it. I rescued the princess, so now I can marry her if I want."

"That's the deal."

"Yeah, well, I notice you didn't mention it until after you heard my vow of celibacy."

"I suppose that was perverse of me."

"Besides, it's a cheat. Aren't I supposed to get half the kingdom, too?"

"I've got a better idea," she answered. "You can have it all."

AFTERWORD

Just as *Speaker for the Dead* was a different kind of novel from *Ender's Game,* so also is *Shadow of the Hegemon* a different kind of book from *Ender's Shadow.* No longer are we in the close confines of Battle School or the asteroid Eros, fighting a war against insectoid aliens. Now, with *Hegemon,* we are on Earth, playing what amounts to a huge game of *Risk*—only you have to play politics and diplomacy as well in order to get power, hold onto it, and give yourself a place to land if you lose it.

Indeed, the game that this novel most resembles is the computer classic *Romance of the Three Kingdoms,* which is itself based on a Chinese historical novel, thus affirming the ties between history, fiction, and gaming. While history responds to irresistible forces and conditions (*pace* the extraordinarily illuminating book *Guns, Germs, and Steel,* which should be required reading by everyone who writes history or historical fiction, just so they understand the ground rules), in the specifics, history happens as it happens for highly personal reasons. The reasons European civilization prevailed over indigenous civilizations of the Americas consist of the implacable laws of history; but the reason why it was Cortez and Pizarro who prevailed over the Aztec and Inca empires by winning particular battles on particular days, instead of being cut down and destroyed as they might have been, had everything to do with their own character and the character and recent history of the emperors opposing them. And it happens that it is the novelist, not the historian, who has the freer hand at imagining what causes individual human beings to do the things they do.

Which is hardly a surprise. Human motivation cannot be documented, at least not with any kind of finality. After all, we rarely understand our own motivations, and so, even when we write down what we honestly believe to be our reasons for making the choices we make, our explanation is likely to be wrong or partly wrong or at least incomplete. So even when a historian or biographer has a wealth of information at hand, in the end he still has to make that uncomfortable leap into the abyss of ignorance before he can declare why a person did the things he did. The French Revolution inexorably led to anarchy and then tyranny for comprehensible reasons, following predictable paths. But nothing could have predicted Napoleon himself, or even that a single dictator of such gifts would emerge.

Novelists who write about Great Leaders, however, too often fall into the opposite trap. Able to imagine personal motivations, the people who write novels rarely have the grounding in historical fact or the grasp of historical forces to set their plausible characters into an equally plausible society. Most such attempts are laughably wrong, even when written by people who have actually been involved in the society of movers and shakers, for even those caught up in the maelstrom of politics are rarely able to see through the trees well enough to comprehend the forest. (Besides, most political or military novels by political or military leaders tend to be self-serving and self-justifying, which makes them almost as unreliable as books written by the ignorant.) How likely is it that someone who took part in the Clinton administration's immoral decision to launch unprovoked attacks on Afghanistan and the Sudan in the late summer of 1998 would be able to write a novel in which the political exigencies that led to these criminal acts are accurately recounted? Anyone in a position to know or guess the real interplay of human desires among the major players will also be so culpable that it will be impossible for him to tell the truth, even if he is honest enough to attempt it, simply because the people involved were so busy lying to themselves and to each other throughout the process that everyone involved is bound to be snow-blind.

In *Shadow of the Hegemon,* I have the advantage of writing a history that hasn't happened, because it is in the future. Not thirty million years in the future, as with my Homecoming books, or even three thousand years in the future, as with the trilogy of *Speaker for the Dead, Xenocide,* and *Children of the Mind,* but rather only a couple of centuries in the future, after nearly a century of international stasis caused by the Formic War. In the future history posited by *Hegemon,* nations and peoples of today are still recognizable, though the relative balance among them has changed. And I have both the perilous freedom and the solemn obligation to attempt to tell my characters' highly personal stories as they move (or are moved) amid the highest circles of power in the governing and military classes of the world.

If there is anything that can be called my "life study," it is precisely this subject area: great leaders and great forces shaping the interplay of nations and peoples throughout history. As a child, I would put myself to sleep at night imagining a map of the world as it existed in the late fifties, just as the great colonial empires were beginning to grant independence, one by one, to the colonies that had once made up those great swathes of British pink and French blue across Africa and southern Asia. I imagined all those colonies as free countries, and, choosing one of them or some other relatively small nation, I would imagine alliance, unifications, invasions, conquests, until all the world was united under one magnanimous, democratic government. Cincinnatus and George Washington, not Caesar or Napoleon, were my models. I read Machiavelli's *The Prince* and Shirer's *Rise and Fall of the Third Reich,* but I also read Mormon scripture (most notably the Book of Mormon stories of the generals Gideon, Moroni, Helaman, and Gidgiddoni, and Doctrine and Covenants section 121) and the Old and New Testaments, all the while trying to imagine how one might govern well when law gives way to exigency, and the circumstances under which war becomes righteous.

I don't pretend that the imaginings and studies of my life have brought me to great answers, and you will find no such answers in *Shadow of the Hegemon.* But I do believe I understand something of the workings of the world of government, politics, and war, both at their best and at their worst. I have sought the borderline between strength and ruthlessness, between ruthlessness and cruelty, and at the other extreme, between goodness and weakness, between weakness and betrayal. I have pondered how it is that some societies are able to get young men to kill and die with fervor trumping fear, and yet others seem to lose their will to survive or at least their will to do the things that make survival possible. And *Shadow of the Hegemon* and the two remaining books in this long tale of Bean, Petra, and Peter are my best attempt to use what I have learned in a tale in which great forces, large populations, and individuals of heroic if not always virtuous character combine to give shape to an imaginary, but I hope believable, history.

I am crippled in this effort by the factor that real life is rarely plausible—we believe that people would or could do these things only because we have documentation. Fiction, lacking that documentation, dares not be half so implausible.

On the other hand, we can do what history never can—we can assign motive to human behavior, which cannot be refuted by any witness or evidence. So, despite doing my utmost to be truthful about how history happens, in the end I must depend on the novelist's tools. Do you care about this person, or that one? Do you believe such a person would do the things I say they do, for the reasons I assign?

History, when told as epic, often has the thrilling grandeur of Dvorak or Smetana, Borodin or Mussorgsky, but historical fiction must also find the intimacies and dissonances of the delicate little piano pieces of Satie and Debussy. For it is in the millions of small melodies that the truth of history is always found, for history only matters because of the effects we see or imagine in the lives of the ordinary people who are caught up in, or give shape to, the great events. Tchaikowsky can carry me away, but I tire quickly of the large effect, which feels so hollow and false on the second hearing. Of Satie I never tire, for his music is endlessly surprising and yet perfectly satisfying. If I can bring off this novel in Tchaikowsky's terms, that is well and good; but if I can also give you moments of Satie, I am far happier, for that is the harder and, ultimately, more rewarding task.

Besides my lifelong study of history in general, two books particularly influenced me during the writing of *Shadow of the Hegemon.* When I saw *Anna and the King,* I became impatient with my own ignorance of real Thai history, and so found David K. Wyatt's *Thailand: A Short History* (Yale, 1982, 1984). Wyatt writes clearly and convincingly, making the history of the Thai people both intelligible and fascinating. It is hard to imagine a nation that has been more lucky in the quality of its leaders as Thailand and its predecessor kingdoms, which managed to survive invasions from every direction and European and Japanese ambitions in Southeast

Asia, all the while maintaining its own national character and remaining, more than many kingdoms and oligarchies, responsive to the needs of the Thai people. (I followed Wyatt's lead in calling the pre-Siamese language and the people who spoke it, in lands from Laos to upper Burma and southern China, "Tai," reserving "Thai" for the modern language and kingdom that bear that name.)

My own country once had leaders comparable to Siam's Mongkut and Chulalongkorn, and public servants as gifted and selfless as many of Chulalongkorn's brothers and nephews, but unlike Thailand, America is now a nation in decline, and my people have little will to be well led. America's past and its resources make it a major player for the nonce, but nations of small resources but strong will can change the course of world history, as the Huns, the Mongols, and the Arabs have shown, sometimes to devastating effect, and as the people of the Ganges have shown far more pacifically.

Which brings me to the second book, Lawrence James's *Raj: The Making and Unmaking of British India* (Little, Brown, 1997). Modern Indian history reads like one long tragedy of good, or at least bold, intentions leading to disaster, and in *Shadow of the Hegemon* I consciously echoed some of the themes I found in James's book.

As always, I relied on others to help me with this book by reading the first draft of each chapter to give me some idea whether I had wrought what I intended. My wife, Kristine; my son Geoffrey; and Kathy H. Kidd and Erin and Phillip Absher were my most immediate readers, and I thank them for helping prevent many a moment of inclarity or ineffectiveness.

The person most influential in giving this book the shape it has, however, is the aforementioned Phillip Absher, for when he read the first version of a chapter in which Petra was rescued from Russian captivity and united with Bean, he commented that I had built up her kidnapping so much that it was rather disappointing how easily the problem turned out to be resolved. I had not realized how high I had raised expectations, but I could see that he was right—that her easy release was not only a breaking of an implied promise with the reader, but also implausible under the circumstances. So instead of her kidnapping being an early event in a very involved story, I realized that it could and should provide the overarching structure of the entire novel, thus splitting what was to be one novel into two. As the story of Han Qing-jao took over *Xenocide* and caused it to become two books, so also the story of Petra took over this, Bean's second book, and caused there to be a third, *Shadow of Death* (which I may extend to the longer phrase from the Twenty-third Psalm, *The Valley of the Shadow of Death;* it would never do to become tied to a title too early). The book originally planned to be third will now be the fourth, *Shadow of the Giant*. All because Phillip felt a bit disappointed and, just as importantly, said so, causing me to think again about the structure I had unconsciously created in subversion of my conscious plans.

I rarely write two novels at once, but I did this time, going back and forth between *Shadow of the Hegemon* and *Sarah,* my historical novel about the wife of Abraham (Shadow Mountain, 2000). The novels sustained each other in odd ways, each of them dealing with history during times of chaos and transformation—like the one the world is embarking upon at the time of this writing. In both stories, personal loyalties, ambitions, and passions sometimes shape the course of the history and sometimes surf upon history's wave, trying merely to stay just ahead of the breaking crest.

May all who read these books find their own ways to do the same. It is in the turmoil of chaos that we discover what, if anything, we are.

As always, I have relied upon Kathleen Bellamy and Scott Allen to help keep communications open between me and my readers, and many who visited and took part in my online communities at *http://www.hatrack.com, http://www.frescopix.com,* and *http://www.nauvoo.com*) helped me, often in ways they did not realize.

Many writers produce their art from a maelstrom of domestic chaos and tragedy. I am fortunate enough to write from within an island of peace and love, created by my wife, Kristine, my children, Geoffrey, Emily, Charlie Ben, and Zina, and good and dear friends and family who surround us and enrich our lives with their good will, kind help, and happy company. Perhaps I would write better were my life more miserable, but I have no interest in performing the experiment.

In particular, though, I write this book for my second son, Charlie Ben, who wordlessly has given great gifts to all who know him. Within the small community of his family, of school friends at Gateway Education Center, and of church friends in the Greensboro Summit Ward, Charlie Ben has given and received much friendship and love without uttering a word, as he patiently endures his pain and limitations, gladly receives the kindness of others, and generously shares his love and joy with all who care to receive it. Twisted by cerebral palsy, his body movements may look strange and disturbing to strangers, but to those willing to look more closely, a young man of beauty, humor, kindness, and joy can be found. May we all learn to see past such outward signs, and show our true selves through all barriers, however opaque they seem. And Charlie, who will never hold this book in his own hands or read it with his own eyes, will nevertheless hear it read to him by loving friends and family members. So to you, Charlie, I say: I am proud of all you do with your life, and glad to be your father; though you deserved a better one, you have been generous enough to love the one you have.

THE MEMORY OF EARTH

Book One of The Homecoming Saga

Orson Scott Card

Nearly forty million years have passed since
Harmony was colonised by humans. For all that time,
they have been protected by the Oversoul, an artificial
intelligence high in orbit around the planet. This master
computer has one overriding command:
guard the people of Harmony.

But now the Oversoul is in danger. Soon, within
a thousand years, catastrophic war will break out on
Harmony unless the Oversoul can be repaired. It has
determined itself that it must be taken back to Lost
Earth. For one family, about to be caught up in
an approaching civil war, life is going to
change for ever.

SEVENTH SON
Volume One of The Tales of Alvin Maker

Orson Scott Card

Amid the deep woods where the Red Man still
holds sway, a very special child is born. Young Alvin
is the seventh son of a seventh son, and such a boy is
destined to become great – perhaps even a man with the
enormous powers of a Maker. But even in the safety
of his home, dark forces reach out to destroy him.
Somewhere out there is a power that will do
anything to prevent him growing up.

Orbit titles available by post:

❑ The Memory of Earth	Orson Scott Card	£5.99
❑ The Call of Earth	Orson Scott Card	£5.99
❑ The Ships of Earth	Orson Scott Card	£5.99
❑ Earthfall	Orson Scott Card	£5.99
❑ Earthborn	Orson Scott Card	£6.99
❑ Seventh Son	Orson Scott Card	£6.99
❑ Red Prophet	Orson Scott Card	£6.99
❑ Prentice Alvin	Orson Scott Card	£6.99
❑ Alvin Journeyman	Orson Scott Card	£6.99
❑ Heartfire	Orson Scott Card	£6.99

The prices shown above are correct at time of going to press. However, the publishers reserve the right to increase prices on covers from those previously advertised, without further notice.

ORBIT BOOKS
Cash Sales Department, P.O. Box 11, Falmouth, Cornwall, TR10 9EN
Tel: +44 (0) 1326 569777, Fax: +44 (0) 1326 569555
Email: books@barni.avel.co.uk

POST AND PACKING:
Payments can be made as follows: cheque, postal order (payable to Orbit Books) or by credit cards. Do not send cash or currency.

U.K. Orders under £10	£1.50
U.K. Orders over £10	**FREE OF CHARGE**
E.C. & Overseas	25% of order value

Name (Block letters) . . . .

Address . . . .

. . . .

Post/zip code: . . . .

☐ Please keep me in touch with future Orbit publications

☐ I enclose my remittance £ . . . .

☐ I wish to pay by Visa/Access/Mastercard/Eurocard

Card Expiry Date